Women of Thunder

Women of Thunder

a novel by Jerry Craven

Fort Worth, Texas

Library of Congress Cataloging-in-Publication Data

Craven, Jerry, author.
Women of thunder / Jerry Craven.
pages cm
Women of thunder is a sequel to Jerry Craven's The wild part published by Angelina River Press, 2013--Author's website.
ISBN 978-0-87565-599-4 (pbk. : alk. paper)
1. Venezuela--Description and travel--Fiction. 2. Wild and scenic rivers--Venezuela--Fiction. I. Craven, Jerry. Wild part. Sequel to: II. Title.
PS3553.R275W66 2014
813'.54--dc23

2014011866

TCU Press
TCU Box 298300
Fort Worth, Texas 76129
www.prs.tcu.edu
To order books: 1.800.826.8911

For Sherry

1

In late afternoon sun I climbed a river palm, machete adangle at my waist, secured the rope to prevent a fall, and glanced down. That's when the *gringo* emerged from the river jungle, stood among savanna grass, and watched. He wore high-moon white from head to foot except for the belt snaking black among loops to a silver clasp and what appeared to be a leather bag attached beside the buckle. The Panama hat affected by *touristas* dropped a shadow over his eyes like a smudge of charcoal, and his beard twitched and gleamed blond-red in the sun. Perhaps he was smiling.

With a shrug, I loosened the machete and swung an awkward arc to cut the lowest frond. It fluttered groundward, and I cut another, then another until it became necessary to move around the tree. As I secured the machete, I glanced down again. The man below gathered fronds and stacked them in a proper way for carrying. He turned his shadowed eyes and gleaming beard toward me again and said something in a low tone. It sounded like "mosquito." I moved the safety rope while toeing around the trunk to cut more fronds, trying to ignore the tourista below. When the blade bit into the base of the final frond, the last the tree could give without being brought close to death, the man in high-moon white spoke again. This time the word came to me in a musical buzz, a drawing out of the syllables like a chant: "Roe-SEE-taaa."

Rosita. A child's name, a mythic name, a word that tumbled in similar tones from the lips of *Abuelita,* my grandmother, when she sang my name with affection. It was a name I had not responded to since I was fourteen years old. For a second I remained motionless, looking down with only a movement of eyes, then busied myself with the machete and the rope to begin the descent, imagining that the gringo saw my frozen moment, imagining him to know how the name reached inside me to touch old pain. And I wondered about stains on my blouse, perspiration beads on my forehead, the odor of my body unpleasant in heat from gathering roof thatching. I wondered if he would be offended by the tiny leather pouch on a necklace of rawhide, offended by the magic of it because he once scorned all magic. I wondered about the fullness of my skirt that, high in the palm, might have exposed more of me than should be exposed even to one who had once walked beside me in the jungles, both of us nude like innocent savages. That was before the time of cholera.

I shook off the memory with anger, soothing myself by remembering an earlier, happy time, eighteen years ago. We were children then, children doing something remarkable. Of course the gringo in high-moon white might not have within him the boy I remembered. He might be only another tourista, crude and self-serving.

When I reached the ground and turned toward him, he stepped back, uncertainty on his face, maybe fear, and I knew at that moment the boy stood before me in the sun, watching from behind those adult eyes. I fought the impulse to touch his face and take his hand, an impulse that came not from the moment there beside palm fronds he stacked at the threshold of savanna and jungle. The impulse came instead from a distant and dead past.

"Rosita," he said in a whisper. "Surely we both knew I would return." His Spanish seemed fluid, flawless. This was no tourista speaking.

"Rosa," I corrected. "Rosita died in a cholera epidemic fourteen years ago."

"No. Your face, your voice. You are Rosita."

"Once, perhaps. But you must not call me that."

"Rosa, then." He turned to the stack of fronds. "May I carry these for you?"

"Yes. That way." I indicated the direction with a pucker of lips.

"Pointing with lips. I had forgotten the custom. But I know the way to your home, of course." He glanced toward the evening sun and picked up the stack of palm fronds. "It took me most of the day to locate you. People around here don't easily tell the location of their *curandera.*"

"I am a nurse, Don. *Enfermera,* not *curandera.*"

"Tom. Please. Call me Tom. Or Tomás, as you prefer. It's my middle name and the one I use now."

"Tom? This is almost the same as Don."

"Yes, just as Rosita is almost the same as Rosa, yet you think the difference is important."

We walked a path through the tamed jungle, crossed a cement footbridge over the low waters of El Tigre River, and climbed the embankment toward my home. El Tigrito began beyond the canebrake that walled my yard from the village. The gringo kept his attention on the trees and undergrowth around the river as we walked, his eyes darting about, searching, his face tight and lined as if he feared something.

"This isn't the river jungle of our childhood." I stopped beside him and we turned to survey the tangled mass of green along the river.

"No. The trees seem smaller than I remember."

"They are shorter. The trees grow slender and new. Today only thatch palms and mangoes stand tall. Loggers had no use for palms and they respected the mangoes for their fruit. But others they cut not long after your family left the village, even young trees they chopped aside to get to the big ones. What do you call this jungle now? Secondary growth? It's *monte nuevo,* brush and weeds and sad little trees where even monkeys no longer make their homes." I urged him toward my house so he could drop the load of thatching, pointing to a place beside the door.

He set the fronds where I indicated, then smudged his forehead with a swipe of a hand. The white of his trousers and shirt bore dusty imprints of palm fronds, though he seemed not to notice. That lack of concern with grime, I told myself, is the boy in him, the one I knew and loved as only an innocent child can love: he might be grown to manhood, but the child is still there.

All of his attention focused on my home. "River mud and grasses."

He ran a finger over the wall beside the door. "Whitewashed. And thatching." He touched the roof just above his head. "And a doorway dropping inward to a floor of packed earth that you sprinkle and sweep. The river jungle might be all askew and wrong, but this house resembles houses along the river when we were children. This one reminds me of one from some dim memory. Was it the one in the gold country where we bought supplies, the one where a pig toppled my chair?"

"On the outside not much has changed. But inside you'll find electric lights, a telephone, and indoor plumbing. I don't keep pigs."

He looked at me, startled. "I meant no insult."

"I know. You've come back seeking the land of childhood and hope to find it the same. But it is not, Don. That land is gone forever, fled from us both." For a moment I considered speaking to him in English to show how changed I was from the Rosita he knew. But my accent in English wasn't good. I sang the language, my teacher had told me, in charming Latina notes. I had no desire to show off my poor pronunciation or to appear charming.

"Tom, not Don."

"Tom, then. The years have changed us both. Did you marry? Do you have children?"

He held up his hand to show he wore no rings. "I'm not married. My sister has children. Do you remember her? She has three children. I like reading to them. Poetry. Nonsense poetry." His voice grew faint and distant, then he looked at me and became present again. "Do you have children?"

"As you see," I gestured toward the tiny house, "I never married. You see how we have fallen. I am no longer Rosita, and the giant trees are gone from the river jungle, and the monkeys have fled, and parrots no longer fly in vast flocks, and my hands," I turned palms up for him to see, "are calloused with work, and your fine white clothes are smeared with dust. Why did you come?"

"You know why." His voice dropped low.

I thought such use of his voice was deliberate for effect, and I resented it, and yet a tingling spread across my back. "You returned to go to the wild part in the interior, to ride the river as we did years ago." It was the promise that brought him back, the promise I had come to believe he had forgotten, if he still lived, given how many young gringos had died in Vietnam. I touched the magic pouch suspended on a leather necklace. He remembered, though we were only children burying bones beneath a stand of banana trees when we made our promise.

"And you will go with me, won't you?"

"I don't know why I would."

"Look, Rosita—Rosa. Look." He fumbled with the leather bag at his belt, unsnapped the top. "I have the eye of the Irishman." When his hand came out of the bag it held a globe of glass that looked at me. "And I have the finger bone of the *Indio*." He dug into the pouch again to take out some old coins and a brown lump of bone.

"And I. I have a bone from the same ancient hand." My voice came in a whisper and I touched the pouch hanging about my neck.

"You will go with me."

"No. Perhaps. I don't know." Somehow tears threatened, and I blinked hard.

2

It occurred to me in a flash that Rosa looked too Asian, and while the dizziness came I tried to reason it through: maybe it was her downcast and shadowed eyes creating an illusion of epicanthic folds, or maybe I was annoyed by the way she clutched the amulet, or maybe it was her peasant's clothing and the thatching and the jungle and the unwashed smell of her and the heat—God I had forgotten the dry-season heat that could bake lice right out of your hair and dog the air with black odor. In such dizzy moments, anger like a snake rasping against itself could push inside to make my lungs shallow and play tricks with vision, so I closed my eyes, leaned against the mud hut, feeling the sun it had soaked up and knowing, if I looked, that Phung would be standing close, looking with an air of profound indifference at the rattan strip in his hand.

"Tom?" She touched my arm and the snake ceased its rasping, stopped making my lungs shallow, and the air wasn't dog anymore but sweet with fresh-cut palm fronds, and the image of Phung vanished, and I looked into the concerned face of a little girl whose hand was upon my arm.

"Rosita." I tried for a smile. "Rosa. Maybe going with me is a bad idea."

She moved back. "You kept the Irishman's eye and the bone from our cave."

Surprised to see my hand holding the glass eye and to feel the piece of bone in the other hand, I slipped the objects back into my bag while looking at the magic amulet around her neck and feeling more than a bit foolish. "I have a pickup truck to take us across the savanna. We could leave now, drive all night."

She looked alarmed. "But no. I must consider the decision. Even if I agreed to go, I would have to prepare."

"Did we prepare last time?"

"We were children."

"We will become children again."

"We will not. Stop it, Tom, and listen. I have people who depend on me, people who are ill. I cannot abandon them without medical help. Even if they found another enfermera, there would be much packing for a such a trip as you suggest."

"Pack what?"

"For one thing we would need *chinchorros* to keep us off the ground at night or we risk bites from the kissing bug that carries American encephalitis."

"But we took nothing before, not even chinchorros." I enjoyed the sound of the word chinchorros, enjoyed rolling it across my tongue and visualizing the webbed hammock the word named. I had forgotten the term until Rosa spoke it.

"Stop it. We were children."

"Pack little, then."

"You speak as if we will be going. But Tom, this is too sudden. I must become accustomed to the idea before even considering a decision. You've thought about it, planned it, traveled from your country, spent time selecting a pickup and looking for me. You're ready. I'm not ready even to consider a decision. My heart is not ready. My head is not prepared to think of the trip."

Rosita always had more sense than I, and this Rosa showed that some things don't change, so I nodded a curt acknowledgment that she was right. "Tomorrow you will tell me, then."

"Too soon. Not tomorrow."

"When?"

"I don't know. Three days. More. Be patient with me, Tom, as you often were not in the past."

"May I come back tomorrow?"

"Stay here, if you wish. I have an extra chinchorro, if you can remember how to sleep in one. Bring your pickup here, park in my yard."

"Your cousin would not approve."

"Cousin?"

"Manuél. I found him almost by accident. He's the one who directed me to this house, though I thought he did so with misgivings. He would disapprove of your allowing me to stay in your house."

"So let him." She shrugged. "My cousins know I do as I wish."

"And the people of the village? How will they respond to your having a man stay in your home, especially a foreigner?"

"What I do with my private life is my concern. They expect me to behave in odd ways because they see me as curandera."

"You said enfermera. A nurse. You told me you are a nurse."

"I am. It is they who think I'm a witch that cures with magic and herbs."

I pointed at her amulet. "It contains more than the finger bone of an ancient Indio. You have other items in there. Snake's knees, chicken teeth, tadpole toenails. Magic things. Isn't that so?"

"Keep talking like that and I'll be compelled to call you Don, your childhood name. I shall think of ways to ridicule your beliefs and make you sorry for regarding me as a simpleton. Bring your truck, then help me prepare dinner." She ducked into the doorway and vanished in shadows.

This Rosa is no Catrina, I told myself as I turned my back with reluctance to the honest jungle house with its whitewash and thatching to walk beyond the canebrake back to the village to get the pickup, but there stood Catrina waiting on the other side of the cane, her eyes intent with something, contempt maybe, perhaps anger. "What did you mean by that, what did you mean she is not me?" Catrina demanded.

"Go away." I walked past her with downcast eyes in an attempt not to look at the strawberry mark on her neck that she tried without success to cover with beads.

"Why are you here, Tom? What does it mean?"

"This is my life. You betrayed it, remember? Go away. Go away." I glanced over my shoulder, noting with relief that she had gone away. "And stay away. None of this concerns you."

"But it does concern me," she said without bothering to show herself again. Her voice faded and I knew she was gone, though of course she would come back.

My truck was across the highway and up a street that had a grotesque familiarity about it, as did the house I had parked beside, a house that had caught my attention with glass panes behind window bars, with a cement water tower in the backyard, with a corrugated zinc roof, a house that looked too tiny to be the home of my Venezuelan childhood, but the water tower was a dead giveaway. Had I found the house earlier in the day, it would have saved me much time in locating Rosa.

In my search for Rosa, I had knocked on the door. When a shy girl peered out at me, I found myself babbling about how I had lived in that house when I was a boy. She listened, wide-eyed, held up one finger and closed the door. It opened seconds later and out stepped a young man who had something familiar about him, though I was sure I had never seen such a pencil-thin moustache or such a strange scar bisecting an eyebrow.

"You lived in this house as a child?" he asked, his eyes round in astonishment. "You are Don Seal. Or perhaps you are Todd?"

"Are you Ramón?"

"I am his brother, Manuél." His hand shot out and I clasped it.

"When we were children, people called me Don. But now I use the name Tomás. I have returned to El Tigrito to find your cousin, Rosita Rojas."

He had dropped my hand and frowned, stretching the scar in his brow into an angry red line.

I looked back again at the cane fence where Catrina had waited to question me, the fence that gave privacy to Rosa's home and no doubt served superstitious neighbors as a comfort barrier between them and the witch nurse, the curandera Rosa Rojas with her magic amulet of bones and who knows what other souvenirs and trash she crammed into the leather pouch, for there was no doubt in my mind that she cooked up herbal teas simpled at night in the jungle along with weird roots, mushrooms, toads, lizards, and god knows what other exotic tropical life that yielded alkaloids to confuse and cure, to cause peasants to hallucinate and dream, to have amazing illusions, delusions, nightmares. I had seen a curandera at work, drunk the magic tea to become a fish and a parrot and to watch Rosita metamorphose into a Jesus frog that hopped on water. Sylvia. That was the name of the witch who had tricked us with the fake magic of drugs into experiencing the fantastic back when we were children lost in the wild part of Venezuela, back when we learned to love Sylvia even after the tricking, and perhaps in Rosita's case because of the faux magic, for she knew it to be real. When I told Catrina about Sylvia's fake magic, she said I was wrong, that I had become the fish and parrot, and if I took her sugar cube in the dim candles of her California flat I could again smell the green of the jungle and taste the blue sky of childhood and know with certainty Rosa had become a Jesus frog. But I wouldn't touch the cube and Catrina laughed without humor, laughed with derision and contempt before taking me in her arms.

I stopped walking long enough to shake off the memory of Catrina, to tell myself the time had come to move on, to think about Rosita become Rosa, now grown and herself a curandera, even if she tried to disguise her profession by proclaiming to be a nurse. She's still a little girl, I thought with satisfaction as I walked past a *chaparro* tree toward the highway: she's a child in a woman's body, a voluptuous woman's body, though her sexual beauty wasn't something I planned on dealing with since it was her innocence I treasured in memory and her innocence I hoped to find intact despite the ravages of growing up, her little girl wisdom and innocence.

What about the fear biting into me when I thought she looked Asian? I waved my hand in dismissal and disgust, hoping the moment came not from her but from my own confusion, my own demons, the ones that caused me to seek a childhood playmate and a jungle that hides no soldiers but instead offers gifts of fruit, the guava, cashew, papaya, and banana on shore and fish to catch in the river with bark string and wooden hooks, fish for skewering and roasting to serve on fronds from ground palms clean and green and waterproof for building shelter from rain in a jungle of climbing trees and flowers and parrots and comical monkeys.

Rosa said she might not go with me, but I couldn't believe her, didn't believe her, and knew she had to go for her own sake and the sake of the trip long ago that so changed us both forever. She would go. She had to, she had to. I turned back to survey again the line of trees, the monte nuevo that followed El Tigre River, and as the sun crashed toward a short tropic twilight I laughed, unsure of why, feeling a surge of energy course through me from the mere thought of again traveling the wild river with the purity of Rosita beside me in a garden jungle of giant trees and ferns, banana leaves sweet as apples, redwood, mango, and palm.

3

When I telephoned Manuél, he asked if the gringo had found me, and he demanded to know what the man wanted. Cousins, brothers, uncles, and other such male relatives have long sought to take over the running of my life in their certainty that since my father was dead I needed to be watched over. None have ever succeeded.

"He wanted advice on how to gather palm fronds for repairing a roof," I said.

I listened to his long silence, to a slow exhalation of breath. "You like stories," he said, then he told me about the capybara and the *caribe.*

It was one I had heard before, though never in Manuél's version. It seems a female capybara took the form of a beautiful woman, for she hoped to find a mate among the river people. As she walked through the jungle in naked purity, a caribe cannibal fish saw her and thought to make a meal of her. So he climbed out of the water and became a glimmering man, and he called to her. "You are so beautiful that I could, uh, I could—"

"Marry me?" the capybara asked.

"Yes," the cannibal fish said, though marrying was not exactly what he had in mind. He moved close thinking to take a nibble from her neck, and in his lust for the taste of blood and flesh almost allowed his interlocking teeth to show. But before he could bite her, he saw that she was a capybara and not one of the river people. "We will marry, if you wish," said the fish, "but first you must show me where your family lives."

"If you see my family, you will know what I am," said the capybara, "and you will run from me and never marry me."

The caribe swore he wanted her as no man ever before wanted a woman, that he would marry her the instant she introduced him to her family. So the capybara took him to her home among the rushes in a hidden inlet of the river and pointed to her family swimming in the sunshine. As soon as he saw them, he grabbed the capybara woman and ate all the flesh from her skeleton. Then he returned to the river where he again became a fish, and he took thousands of his relatives to the hidden inlet where they attacked and ate all the capybara, reducing them to gleaming white bones.

"So, Manuél," I said when he finished the story, "you're afraid Tomás will harm me, then come after you and your family. This is a foolish fear."

"I fear he might not be what he seems."

"And you also fear that I'm not what I seem? You fear I have the soul of a rodent in the body of a woman."

"No, Rosa, no. You don't understand. I fear Tomás and his kind. They are shimmering and white and say smooth, flattering things, but beneath the charm, they have the teeth of cannibal fish."

"Then you told the story in the wrong way."

"I told it the proper way. Rosa, forget the story and listen to me. This man has hired me to drive you and him into the dark interior of our country. He wants me to abandon him and you there, then go downriver to a village he showed me on a map and wait for you. He said it might take as much as two weeks for the two of you to travel the river to the fishing village where I wait with the truck. But since he left my home, I have been thinking."

"He hired you for that? Tomás has learned to plan better than he did when we were young."

"This is a good plan to you? Rosa, he'll put you in much danger. The rainy season will start any time now, and the river will grow to a torrent, and you will perish in the currents."

"He and I took such a trip when I was twelve years old and he only eleven. As children we traveled that river in April with the rains heavy and the river strong. If we did it as children, we can do it now."

"What of the jungle? Such dangers lurk there. The jaguar. Snakes that poison. In the river are anaconda who swallow women. There are *caimanes negros.* The black *caimán* grows longer than the gringo's truck, and it loves to eat people. There are bats that drink blood. I cannot allow you to go."

"You forgot to mention the ants that eat flesh and the poisonous toads that can kill you if you step upon them and the plants that hungry people might eat and be transformed into monkeys or tapirs. You forgot the poisonous darts of the jungle people and the spider that grows larger than your hand and can jump five meters to kill you with a single bite on the neck. You forgot the snakes that like to drop out of trees on you to wrap about your neck and choke you to death. You forgot the angry spirits that live underground and in hollow hills who can entrap the unwary and change them into stones or pigs. You forgot malaria and dysentery and microbes that poison food and leap into cuts to fester away fingers or legs."

Again I listened to his silence. Then he sighed. "You will go with him, then? There's nothing a cousin can do to show you the foolishness of such a trip with a gringo ignorant of jungle dangers?"

"Nothing. You could, I suppose, refuse the job of driving us to the wild part of the country. But we would simply hire another driver. I would prefer to find you waiting at the end of our river trip, Manuél." So I have decided to go without knowing I had decided, I thought. Amazing.

"What do you mean we would hire? Are you paying for this insane trip?"

"You know me. I will be in debt to no man so that none will think he has power over me."

"Ah." His voice was laden with disgust. "You are more man than woman."

"Thank you for the compliment. I called not to be lectured but to thank you for directing Tomás to my house."

"I should never have done it."

"It doesn't matter. He would have found me, for he's a man with much determination. I'll tell him that we must find another driver."

"No. I will take you. Better me than a stranger who might cut both of your throats for the gringo's money and the truck."

I chided my cousin for having such a black vision of the souls of men.

After hanging up the phone, I showered and put on jeans, a red shirt, and *alpargatas*. Tom had noticed my bare feet, and I noticed his noticing. Briefly I wished for better shoes than alpargatas, then dismissed the wanting, for my purpose was not to impress him.

What was my purpose? Did it have to do with childhood or with my bad behavior when the epidemic swept away my family? Not that, I told myself: this return of Don become Tom had nothing to do with the cholera, for he had been gone when the sickness struck.

I took the small four-burner stove to the table beside my house and connected it to the hose from bottled gas. Tomás would return, park his pickup beside the stand of cane to hide it from neighbors, and we would eat corn cakes with eggs. He would struggle to sleep in a chinchorro and grumble about it and talk of making a bed of banana leaves such as we made on the limestone hill above the wild river, and I would warn him of scorpions and ants that could crawl into his cars if he slept on such a mat. But what was my purpose in having him in my home?

We will breakfast on crumbling white cheese and tortillas, I told myself, and talk of the food an ancient jungle could offer, of papaya and fish, and he will drive his truck to another place for fear of disturbing my reputation with the villagers, though I'll tell him he need not do so. I will consult my records, take my medical bag, and go to the homes of the ones who are ill to give treatment where necessary and to tell them not to expect me for two weeks or more. But what is my purpose in going to the wild river?

In the evening Tomás and I will argue over when to go and what to take. He will want only a machete. But I will take a travel bag and a change of clothes and a knife strapped to my leg. I will take cassava flour and a pan for cooking cakes and fish. He will complain and say we took no such provisions before, and I'll remind him that we're no longer children who go on hope alone, that we're adults and can plan ways to avoid danger and discomfort. We'll agree to embrace some discomfort, and I'll argue to keep it within bounds. He will accept what I say though not without complaint.

But what is my purpose?

Children make promises to one another and forget them as they mature. We made a promise to return to the wild river. There's the past, then, the bond of the past, and it is strong. But what of the future? Perhaps I seek something new in the strange game this gringo and I play.

The jaguar and the anteater once played a strange game, according to an old story told by grandmothers and old men. The anteater challenged the jaguar to a juggling match, but being animals of the jungle, they had nothing to juggle, so they juggled their own eyes. This was risky business, they told each other, yet the anteater popped out his eyes and juggled them with great dexterity, tossing them high, and finally catching them in his eye sockets. "I can do better," the jaguar boasted, and she took out her eyes and began to juggle. Because she was faster than the anteater, she could throw her eyes higher and farther, then dash to them before they fell to the ground and catch them. With each successful toss and catch, the jaguar became bolder and threw her eyes higher until they stuck in a tree. Blinded and sad, the jaguar lay on the riverbank, and the anteater, distraught for his friend, scratched her ears and wondered what to do.

The solution came to anteater when he spotted a parrot on a tree branch that dipped into the water. The parrot leaned low, filled its great beak with water, then stood up to swallow. "Parrot, my friend," the anteater called out, "will you take water in your magic beak, shape it into a new set of eyes, and drop them into the empty sockets of the unfortunate jaguar?"

The parrot turned one way then another to eye the anteater and the blind jaguar. "I'll do it," he said, made the eyes, flew to the jaguar, perched on her head, and dropped them into the empty sockets. The eyes of water, according to the story, allow jaguar to see better in the dark than other animals, and when night falls, the new eyes reflect all light.

Perhaps I agree to play foolish games with Tomás in hopes of some strange gain, some water eyes whose nature I cannot even guess at the outset of play. There is, of course, my son and the guilt that washes over me at the mere thought of him. But no. I will not toy with such guilt.

4

M*anuél drove* the pickup, sullen and tight-lipped, his eyebrow unhinged by the scar, and Rosa stretched in luxuriousness beside him with arms across the top of the seat, brushing fingers against my collar if I leaned back and her unaware of the almost touch and unaware of how I sat forward to gaze at the unending savanna and to keep those fingers from my collar, though from time to time forgetting, relaxing back against the seat where the heat of her hand and arm reminded me to sit forward again.

Two days in El Tigrito with the length of three long nights wrestling with Rosa's spare chinchorro had fatigued me, though the nightmares didn't come, Phung didn't come but stayed in other jungles of tripwires and mouse deer, of durian and mud and the stink of rotting fruit. The shower in Rosa's home had been a surprise, though of course there was no hot water nor the need for it. I roamed the village during the day, buying ayakas and white corn cakes from street vendors, staying away from Rosa to allow her time for recommending other witches to her patients and to save her from gossip, and at night avoided watching her in the scant cotton of her nightgown. We said little. Neither of us asked anything of significance about the years since we had sneaked aboard the candyman's truck and become lost in the wild part of Venezuela; and though sometimes in the early light of morning she had given me long, appraising looks, analytical and curious, I volunteered nothing.

It was good to be on our way, to leave behind the wrestling with the chinchorro, that parody of a hammock made from netting, and to be heading across the high savanna plains toward the river of my childhood. We drove the same dirt road taken by the candyman. I was sure of that even if Rosa said there was no way to tell because we had been inside the windowless *casita* on the back of his truck and thus had no way to watch the route he took. "Even if we had announced ourselves and sat in the cab of the truck beside the candyman," Rosa said, "we would today be unsure of the road he took because we were children. Tom, that was eighteen years ago. Nobody remembers such details after eighteen years and growing into adulthood."

"I do." I heard much more certainty in my tone than I felt.

"You believe you do, but you don't."

"I remember what the one-eyed woman said. She said—"

"Carmen?" Rosa's voice had a touch of awe in it for the memory. "Do you mean Carmen who sang like an angel?"

"I had forgotten her name. Carmen. She said that believing it to be true was the only thing that made something true."

"She did not say that. She said that believing creates truth, and she was right."

"Then it's true I remember the route of the candyman since I believe I do. But of course I'm speaking nonsense. I think I remember the route, but I might be wrong."

Manuél coughed and cleared his throat. "Eighteen years ago I was only seven years old. I remember almost nothing about being seven years old."

"We forget most details of days gone by," Rosa said, "but the feelings we had about them sometimes stay with us forever."

Another pickup drove onto the road, coming from the left, from a smaller dirt road. His tires raised a cloud of dust, and Manuél slowed to avoid it. "Too much traffic," he said and chuckled. "That is the third driver we've seen on the road in the last hour."

"There was no traffic eighteen years ago," I said. "Or so I now believe."

The savanna rose and dipped in long, shallow valleys. Wind shifted, leaning the grasses a different direction and changing their color, and we saw a few chaparro trees, stumpy, short, sculpted by wind. In the afternoon we drove beside a canyon where the prairie fell away to sudden cliffs. Trees grew in the canyon, and brush, and birds flew among the trees. Close to the canyon's rim some fifty meters off the road stood two huts made from matted grass. "Blueskirts," Manuél said. "They make cheese." He pulled off the dirt road, drove across waist-high savanna grass that clinked against the grill and hood, and when he stopped, he left plenty of distance between us and the huts. "They will sell their white cheese. It might be better if you stayed in the truck." Manuél found a path to the houses of the Indios.

"The blue-skirted Indians tell wonderful stories," Rosa said.

"Stories?"

"Myths. They make sense of life with myths."

We watched Manuél negotiate with two women in front of one of the huts. All three did much talking and waving of arms while two blue-skirted men stood close by with their hunting bows and dogs to stare alternately at Manuél and at the pickup. He returned with a dripping package wrapped in broad leaves. "Dinner," he announced, handed the package to Rosa and backed the pickup to the road. While Manuél drove I took corn cakes from a plastic bag, and we ate them with crumbled goat cheese.

He drove most of the night, as I had hired him to do, though he grumbled about it and though Rosa tried to argue there was nothing magic in driving through the night just because the candyman had done so eighteen years before, that we would be better off making camp on the savanna and continuing in the morning. I leaned against the door and snoozed, and Rosa fell against me in her sleep, which was good because we had slept in a chaste tangle of one another's arms and legs while crossing the savanna in the candyman's truck. I liked the woman smell of her and a scent like fresh corn from her hair and the odor of chicory coffee Manuél poured into the plastic lid of his Thermos and the smell of rain sprinkling us when we caught the edge of a thundercloud zipping across the high plains as harbinger of the rainy season and the sweet smell of goat cheese and corn cakes that lingered along the edges of my moustache. All the odors combined with delicious anticipation of finding the ancient river where I would purchase a canoe for the first leg of our trip through primordial jungle. Images from that distant past came to me: El Loco with his wheelbarrow, Carmen singing "*ku-ku-rrrru-ku-ku paloma*," the *pistolero* marching us to the little river, the boat Rosita and I stole to escape, the jungle, the immense green of the jungle and lianas and parrots and flooded lands along the bank with swimming capybara.

When Manuél stopped in darkness, Rosa rubbed her eyes, pushed away from me while mumbling apologies, and I snapped awake. Manuél had said something and was repeating himself: "I don't believe it. Don't believe. But there it is."

"There is what?" Rosa said through a yawn.

"The cantina Tomás told me to watch for, though I knew it would be gone after all these years. It is gone, of course, but here are the remains of it. Can you read the sign in the headlights? It's old."

Old, yes, but readable. In bleached-out letters that might have once been red written on a board half collapsed with age were the words Cantina Moreno. *Cerveza y Comida*. Rosa read them aloud, her hands braced on the dash, her back straight and her voice strong, wide awake, excited.

Manuél switched off the headlights and darkness crowded in. I opened the door, resenting the dome light for I wanted my eyes to adjust, wanted to see using only the light of stars. Behind me Rosa made the noises of getting out of the truck while I scanned the darkness and tasted the air. "Perhaps my eyes are too old," I muttered.

"For what?" Rosa stood beside me with a light touching of my arm.

"For dilating fast to take in light from stars." I could make out nothing.

"Clouds hide all stars," she said. "The rains come. Listen."

It had been there all along, the chorus of whistle frogs, but I hadn't heard them until that moment. "The same frogs," I said.

"No. Not the same ones. That was eighteen years ago."

"The same, or close enough. Their eggs became tads to grow frogs to make eggs and frogs again and again until we have returned and stand once more in the same place to listen to the same frogs."

"Not the same place, exactly." She patted my arm.

"Close enough. But where is the cantina?"

Manuél spoke from in front of the pickup: "Burned. I saw it in the truck's lights. It's a heap of blackened walls, burned years ago. There." His flashlight illuminated burnt walls that once enclosed Moreno's cantina. Mamacita Moreno would be dead now, I told myself, dead or ancient with white hair and perhaps a cane, and her pig would be dead, eaten long ago so it could never again sleep indoors or be mistaken by such a boy as I for a sack of grain when his toes bumped it under the table.

"Thank you, Manuél," I said. "Please turn off the light. Sleep here for the remainder of the night, if you wish. Rosa and I will go from here on foot."

Manuél said, "We can camp in the bed of the pickup until light comes. I have my shotgun, if we need protection."

"Shotgun?" A chill gripped me. "Shotgun?"

"Behind the seat. I'll get it."

"No. Leave it there. Leave it, I tell you."

"There's no problem, Tomás." Rosa patted my arm. "He will leave the shotgun, if that's what you wish."

"Shotgun," I whispered. "God, Rosita, do you remember how Sylvia died?" I stumbled forward. "There must be no shotgun in our jungle." My voice became louder, unsteady, and the dizziness came upon me.

5

When I caught up with him, he had fallen into cactus.

Manuél caused most of my delay, for he had slipped into being Mr. Macho, and I had to persuade him, again, that he had no control over me, even if he thought he was trying to help. Also, I had to get the travel bag and put on my alpargatas, slipped off for the ride. I had to put Tom's hunting knife into the bag, for he left it on the floor of the pickup. I had to locate the machete. All that took time while Tom walked into darkness.

He sat on the ground and held up hands against my flashlight. I ran the light down his body, finding the prickly pear stuck to his trousers. "Manuél," he said. "The shotgun."

"There's no shotgun. Manuél will be waiting for us in the fishing village, as you instructed. Sit still and hold this light while I take care of those cactus spines."

He didn't flinch when I lifted the prickly pear. "Spines on this variety of cactus," I told him, "have a hollow place just behind the needle point. Do you know what that means?"

"The points will break off instead of coming out?"

"Exactly." I engaged him in focusing on the cactus because his breath came ragged and he trembled, and it was clear that what disturbed him had little to do with cactus. "The thorn points must await daylight for me to extract them, but the wounds they made need attention now. Pull up your trouser leg."

When he did so, I used a gauze pad to apply salve. He leaned close to watch. "What are you rubbing on me?"

"Antibacterial ointment." I held the tube into the light so he could see. "It will kill most microbes."

"What? No herbs? What kind of curandera are you?"

"Herbs would work, especially the root of the purple coneflower. But it takes time to find proper herbs and time to prepare them. If you wish, we can find herbs when daylight comes."

"I was joking."

"I was not. You could be much worse off. You could have fallen and had cactus spines stab your eyes."

Tom recoiled. "Eyes. In my eyes. I would be blinded like Allen. I might think of suicide."

"You would not. Do you have other thorns? In your hands perhaps? In the other leg?"

"No." His breathing had become more normal. "It wasn't smart, my walking so fast in the dark, especially with the dizziness. But I thought my eyes would adjust."

I took the flashlight from him and turned it off. "The clouds. They block all light from moon and stars. This isn't the same night that the candyman drove off without knowing he left us here."

"Don't lecture me."

"You need lecturing, Don."

"Tom. Call me Tom."

"Then you must not call me Rosita, as you did before you sprinted into the dark."

"I called you that?" He seemed amazed.

My nod was lost in darkness. I closed the travel bag, packed so full it bulged and weighed too much. "The frogs," I said.

"I had forgotten. A maniac with a shotgun and a few cactus thorns affect memory, I guess. Frogs attract snakes, and we need to find a chaparro tree." He stood but took no steps. "Do you have antivenom in that bag?"

"No."

"Good."

"You might change your opinion later," I said, then added: "The Irishman had a flashlight."

He chuckled. "You're a smart woman, Rosa. You speak in code: the Irishman had a flashlight that we used when we were in the jungle as children so it's okay to use a flashlight now. Remember, though, that his batteries died."

"And you think these will last two weeks?" I turned on the light, handed it to him. "Find us a tree with a good roost. What kind of nest did you call it?"

"A crow's nest. But I thought you brought chinchorros in the travel bag."

"I did. But we won't find trees close enough together for hanging them, not on the savanna, and we shouldn't go into a river jungle at night. Did you say crow's nest?"

He panned the area, then fixed on a direction. "It's what my brother called a place where a tree branched in many directions and made a good place to sit."

Off to our left we saw the flicker of Manuél's flashlight as he prepared to sleep in the truck and in front of us a breach in the wall of darkness from our own light. In our light we could see a fine mist beginning to fall. "We'll get wet." Tom's voice sounded cheerful.

"And cold," I said, "and muddy. A chaparro would be a welcome sight."

We walked through several shallow wash areas and picked our way among puddles from a previous rain. Drops in the mist became larger, hitting me like needles of ice. I fumbled with the bag, unzipped it enough to feel inside, took out a poncho. Setting the bag down for only seconds, I slipped the poncho on, then caught up with Tom. He stood on the edge of an arroyo. "The same gully," he said. "Our chaparro tree will be one direction or the other, on the edge."

"You believe that?"

"No. But I like the idea of it."

We turned right, walking several meters from the arroyo with the rain coming in a loud hiss on bushes and grass. "I have another poncho," I offered.

"I don't need it."

"It will keep you dry and warm."

"You're cold? I don't get cold."

"You never became cold on our entire trip as children. I forgot that your ancestors dived into fjords. Mine lived in sunny Spain and in tropical jungles and swam only in warm rivers."

"There." He pointed the light to the right, away from the arroyo. "Two chaparro trees. One big."

"Big for a chaparro, which isn't big." I waited under the tree while he climbed. Broad leaves took the raindrops like drums.

"An excellent crow's nest, better than the chaparro beside the gully of our childhood. Come on up." He turned the light to the trunk.

"Take the bag?" I lifted it over my head.

"Leave it. We don't need a bag."

"Leave the antibacterial ointment. Leave the machete. Do you mean that?"

"Yes." He took the bag. "But for you, the bag of magic will hang here, on this branch above our heads to help keep us dry."

I climbed the tree feeling the wet of my jeans cold against my legs. "The crow's nest is too small."

"It's perfect. Settle here, in front of me." He guided me to sit with my back against his chest.

"You're warm." It felt good to settle against him.

"Yes. Yes. Warm and wet and in a chaparro tree deep in the wild part of Venezuela again with you to await the dawn."

"We should sleep." I yawned.

"Sleep?" The idea seemed to astonish him. "Sleep. We should, though of course I'm too high to sleep. You get some rest and I'll hold you and listen to the rain on leaves, taste the thick wet air, feel the grace of chaparro bark, smell wet grasses below us, and watch for the first greening light of morning." He twitched about, shaking the small tree.

"You have the soul of a poet, while I—"

"You are the very soul of innocence and goodness."

"—while I have the body of a wet and tired woman. Go to sleep, please."

"Impossible."

"Then talk to me. Talk to me about why mentioning a shotgun

made you run into the night to find cactus thorns. Talk about why you felt dizzy."

He became still, rock still, as I had when high in the thatch palm I first realized the identity of the gringo watching from below. "I know few whys," he said.

"Why is a bad question."

"Asking how is easier. Why takes wisdom, and I have no wisdom. None at all, while you have always been wise, even when that crazy missionary killed our Sylvia with his shotgun, then put it into his mouth after I shouted at him."

"You feel guilt for what happened to Sylvia and for the missionary's suicide. That's part of the why?"

"I don't know. Yes. Perhaps. But I prefer not to talk about it."

"You must talk about it. Do you know the story of Mata-Mata?"

"No. Tell me."

The story I told Tom there in the wet chaparro tree came from Abuelita, who got it, she said, from her grandmother who was Indio and lived in ancient jungles. Mata-Mata returning to his jungle village from hunting found a stranger raping his wife. She had been digging cassava root when the man sprang upon her, and he had her pinned and helpless when Mata-Mata happened along. Enraged, Mata-Mata shot a poisoned arrow into the rapist's back, and the man died in minutes. Mata-Mata slashed the body to draw blood, then flung him into the river where cannibal fish in numbers large enough to make the water seem to boil stripped the man to a skeleton before he reached bottom.

Mata-Mata then turned his wrath on his wife. He beat her with the stick of his bow, took her home and tied her hands and feet with leather strips and beat her some more. When night came and Mata-Mata fell into a troubled sleep, he dreamed of the rape, and he awoke distraught. Terrible with anger, he choked his wife with his bowstring, then in stealth carried her body into the jungle and buried her, watched only by an armadillo hiding in the brush.

The next day, Niñato, the son of Mata-Mata, went searching for his mother. Armadillo, who heard Niñato crying out for his mother, told the boy where the woman was buried. While the two dug her up, Armadillo told about Mata-Mata's crime.

Because he had his father's temperament, Niñato's wrath was dreadful. He changed himself into a macaw, ate the seeds of a flowering thorn tree, and dropped his excrement on the shoulder of his father. From the shoulder of Mata-Mata sprung a huge tree, a burden that the macaw said he would carry forever. Groaning under the weight of the tree, Mata-Mata wandered far in the jungle. When he brooded in silence, the tree grew massive and heavy, making him stumble through the jungle at night, shrieking in pain from the burden, and where he walked rivers dried up and fruit trees shriveled. When he found people who would listen, he told his story of killing his wife, and the monstrous tree on his shoulder shrank in size, and banana trees and guava heavy with sweet fruit grew around him as he talked.

When I finished the tale, Tom said, "That's a weird story. Even the magic in it makes no sense. A boy changing into a macaw. A man with a thorn tree growing from his shoulder. It's a wild and nonsensical kind of fantasy."

"The story is a folk myth, and it has some useful truth in it, some that perhaps applies to you."

"Truth in a story about absurd magic? None of that applies to me."

"Tell me about Sylvia's death."

"You know about it. You were there, you saw the missionary kill her."

"Yes, and I felt it, and feel it still. But what do you feel, Tom? What do you feel about the death of Sylvia that makes you run from the idea of a shotgun and makes you dizzy?"

"I don't know. Is it guilt?"

"You tell me."

"I don't know. I don't know. I don't know." He drew trembling breaths and seemed about to cry.

I sought his hand, drew it around me. "Talk more about the thorn tree as a burden at a later time. For now we should enjoy the coming of the sun. Look, clouds are moving on. Against the horizon where light begins, can you see a river jungle rising above the savanna?"

6

Rosa and I watched clouds flame orange, lifting with the tropic sun that always came up fast to burn away a short twilight, and I didn't want to give up the chaparro tree yet, the comfort of it, the holding of Rosa in innocence. Phung Phuoc had stood in darkness beside the burnt walls of Cantina Moreno, and the dizziness came, and I had to go, to go somewhere fast—but how could I tell Rosa about him when I suspected he wasn't real even if he was standing there, suspected it but didn't know and thus couldn't stay still and wait for him to vanish from beside burnt walls that were real. So I walked into a night dark as any wet Asian jungle until finding cactus spines, and I had waited for Rosita to find me, coming as Rosa the curandera who used antibacterial ointment instead of herbs.

Pressed together in the crow's nest of the chaparro, her back to me and hips between my legs, she patted my arm, held it to her breast in such a way that part of me knew it would be easy to slip into wanting her as a man wants a woman while most of me knew what I needed, what she needed wasn't arousal but touching like the touching of children or like puppies I saw in a Fort Worth zoo, African puppies too cold from late autumn Texas air making them pile together, noses under one another's paws and ever shifting to get closer in part for warmth and in part for the comfort of touching in a cold land so far from home.

It was time to leave the chaparro, but I held to the green moment of dripping leaves. Rain clouds drifted away and savanna grass gleamed with diamonds of water. To the west the plains rose with hills not high enough to be called hills except by prairie dwellers, not high enough to obscure a distant line of trees following a river. "Are you better now?" Rosa asked.

"Yes. I hardly feel the cactus wound. Shall we find breakfast?"

"That isn't what I meant, but never mind. Breakfast hangs above our heads in the travel bag. But first I should take care of your leg."

Once on the ground she shook her poncho, misting a rainbow around her or maybe a sundog, though she seemed unaware of the mist or colors. I watched her hang the poncho on a low chaparro limb, watched her kneel beside me with her bag, produce a swab and alcohol, peer close with a magnifying glass to tweeze out what the prickly pear left, and when she applied the bandage I remembered an image until then lost from memory. Rosita had crushed medicinal leaves to cover a spot on my ankle where bats had bitten me in the night. That day long ago we had worn only grass shoes.

"Your travel bag is stuffed and huge," I said.

"Yes. Perhaps I brought too much. Here." She took out the machete and handed it to me. "That will lighten my load. And this canteen. Put it on your belt."

"Carry water? When we will be riding on a river?"

"I have tablets to purify what we drink. We were lucky as children when we drank from the river, and today the river is more polluted. We'll still drink from it, but we'll be more careful. Take the canteen. Take the hunting knife, also."

"I don't want either. My belt pouch is too much, small as it is. I should have left it in the pickup."

"Then take them for me, to keep me from worrying and so I won't have to carry such a heavy bag."

She was right about the water, I knew that from experience in Asia. She was right about the knife, too. And about the load in her bag, the bag itself with its arsenal of medications against microbes, even if I didn't want her to be right. I threaded the knife's scabbard and the canteen to my belt and tucked the handle of the machete beside them so it hung by my leg like a sword.

After eating cashews and molasses cookies we left the shade of the chaparro, which gave me a moment of sadness, for I liked the little man. Lurking in the word *chaparro* is the connotation of a squat, fat man. It seemed to me that such a man would have to be a loner and stubborn and perhaps a bit abrasive since the tree prefers to live almost isolated, dotting the savanna with its stumpy hard limbs and its fig-leaf shaped leaves that grow rough enough to use for scouring out pots.

"Toward the river jungle?" Rosa asked. "I think it must be the small river where we once borrowed a canoe."

"Yes, but we need not be in a hurry. I want to explore those low hills. Do you suppose El Loco Merzi is still around there?"

"No. He found enough gold to return to California with Carmen, his bride, where they built a lovely house on a wine plantation. She gave birth to two children, a boy and a girl, who are now almost grown. The children like to get their mother to tell them about how she inspired people in the gold country to rise up against the bandits who oppressed them. They like to have their father tell about how he pretended to be crazy so people wouldn't figure out where he dug his gold."

"How do you know all that?"

"I don't. I guess and hope in the making of the story. Carmen and El Loco deserve to have someone such as I to build that California house for them, though it is possible they did it for themselves. When I tell myself the story, when I tell it to you, it becomes true."

"But," I said, "that makes no sense."

"Stories must be beyond reason and logic. Who would want to live a life that always made sense? Not I, or I wouldn't be here with you on the high plains of Venezuela on some impossible and unreasonable quest for something we don't even understand. Shall we follow the arroyo again, as we did when we were unreasonable children?"

"Do you think it's the same arroyo?"

"Of course I think that, though it's not true." Her cheeks dimpled, and in that moment she was the lovely Rosita teasing me.

Rosa wore light blue denim, her blouse cut in tails designed to be tucked into pants, though she wore them untucked with the front tails tied into a knot above her navel, brown and lovely. A simple clasp at the back of her neck kept her hair behind her to show she had no strawberry on the side of her neck, her hair thick and as dark as her eyes and falling below her shoulders. Her brows arched above wide-set eyes just beginning with age to acquire worry lines at the corners but too light to notice unless I looked close which was hard to do because of the distraction of her full lips and cheeks that dimpled often when she talked. She stood a head shorter than I, though it was impossible to think of her as short when listening to her speak, and she had breasts such breasts above a tiny waist, and legs almost as long as mine. Her body wasn't that of Rosita, I told myself as we waded through grasses to darken our pants legs with moisture.

The sun had steamed away all but a few puddles when we came to the mine entrance. It wasn't much, just a hole made square with timbers, a black opening at the base of what might pass for a hill. A man with the broad face and leather skin of an Indio pushed a wheelbarrow of rocky dirt from the mine. He paused to offer us a worried smile. "The boss and his wife are waiting for you," he said. "You will find them in the rabbit burrow beyond that hill." He indicated the di rection with a jerk of his head, his lips puckered.

"Thank you," Rosa said and urged me with a nudge toward the hill. "El Loco," she said when we were some distance from the mine. "Do you suppose the boss is El Loco?"

"No. He's in California with his wife and children."

"Are you making fun of me?"

"Maybe," I said. "Just a little. But not in a mean way. Did the Indio say rabbit burrow? And that the boss is waiting for us?"

"He did, which is crazy and which is why I thought of El Loco."

"El Loco wouldn't wait for anyone, especially not us and not for eighteen years. He wasn't crazy; he merely acted crazy. How different from me—I don't act crazy, but often I am."

"You are not crazy," Rosa said, "but you are odd."

We walked over a rise and stopped to stare at a house painted on the rock hillside. It looked like something a third-grader might draw after seeing Rosa's home in El Tigrito, a kid with an eye for detail but no knowledge of dimension or chiaroscuro. The entrance was real, a screen door attached to a boarded-up mine shaft. The third-grader had applied paint to the boards and the timbers framing the shaft to suggest whitewashed walls under thatching. A real shed beside the painted house held a portable electric generator chained to a corner post beside several gas cans. "How strange," Rosa said, and she jumped a bit when the screen door opened.

A man stepped into the sun, blinking, a white man perhaps from Caracas or Europe or North America, a man stooping with age and wearing liver splotches on a bald scalp. "Hurry," he said in a voice deep and strong for one so old, a voice with the flavor of German behind his Spanish. "She might be dying."

"Someone is ill?" Rosa shifted the bag from her shoulder.

"My wife. My wife. Please." He stepped aside and held the door open as we approached.

"But we're not—"

"Hush, Tom," Rosa whispered. "Someone needs help." She led me into the dark, into the cool of the rabbit-burrow house, into air heavy with burning wax and baby powder.

"A stuccoed mine shaft," I said in astonishment. "Painted white."

"She's in the second room," the old man said, following us. "Forgive the candles. Norma hates electric lights, but I'll start the generator if you need more light. She thinks electric lights burn her like the sun. There are also kerosene lanterns."

I ran into Rosa when she stopped in a doorway, though it wasn't a door so much as the timbered entrance to a branch shaft, and the room she looked into was rounded like a cave with plastered walls and ceiling. A chinchorro swung from one wall to another, and in it lay a white woman with blond hair. Behind the chinchorro three tiny shelves jutted from the wall, each holding a burning candle. Beside the chinchorro stood an end table with an electric lamp on it, the cord running to a socket on the plastered wall, and beside the lamp a glass and a pitcher. Rosa set her bag beside the lamp and touched the woman's face. The woman moaned and turned her head, eyes remaining closed, and it was then I saw that she wasn't a woman at all but a girl, a pale girl, whiter than anyone ever, a girl with the facial features similar to the Indio we saw with the wheelbarrow.

"How long has she had a fever?" Rosa demanded.

"Two days," came the answer from behind me. I turned toward the old man, a question on my lips, one he answered without my speaking. "She is *Caquetio,* from the mouth of the Orinoco River. Albino. Her uncle brought her here away from the tribe. She is my wife."

"Wife," I marveled.

"She's older than she looks. Will she die?"

Rosa opened the bag, set aside her poncho and some other clothing, and took out a stethoscope. She gave me an impatient look for my astonishment over seeing the stethoscope. "No. She will not die. You men need to go on now and let me work. Go."

We waited in the hall, if you could call it that, where we sat on the floor opposite one another, leaning against stucco grit, I settling down with more deliberation than he for having to adjust the machete in my belt. He studied me. "So you're not a doctor," he said. "She is the doctor." He sighed, drew up his knees and rested his chin on them. "Such a strange world where a gentleman like you works as an aid to a mestiza woman—and she is the doctor. You are from a coastal city. European stock, and no doubt well connected in society."

"I'm from the north. The United States. And I'm hardly connected with any society."

He sat back amazed, then addressed me in English, also laced with a German accent: "An American, by god, out here in this forsaken place. The doctor is your woman."

"No. She is a friend. Her name is Rosa, and she's a nurse."

"Not a doctor?"

"A nurse. Perhaps a curandera."

"Of course. Just a native, then—a 'companion,' shall we say. What about you? You're here for gold, just as I am, though I haven't found enough to pay for an ounce of cassava flour. Did you come here to find happiness?"

The question startled me. "Happiness?" I shifted the machete around, scraping it on the floor of the mine. "Is happiness something someone can find?"

7

With *Tom* and the German out of the way, I could get to work properly. The girl's heartbeat sounded strong and young, and her lungs were clear. She watched me with fevered eyes, eyes that seemed bleached of color, like her hair, and when I explained about the tongue depressor and the flashlight, she cooperated, allowing me to see the ravages of a throat infection. "The cause of your illness," I told her, "is at the base of your tongue."

She nodded. "Someone has sent me an evil spell."

The sound of her voice caused the German to stop his chattering, and he appeared at my side. "She talked. Norma hasn't talked since yesterday."

"She will recover. Now get out and let me work. I'll explain to you later what you must do to get her well."

"Me?" He seemed surprised by the suggestion.

"Yes. Who else? Out with you." I took his arm and turned him around. He shook my hand away and went back into the other part of the cave house.

Norma's eyes looked worried, her brow knit. "Will you drive out the spirits of envy?"

"I'll show you and the German how to cure you. You have tiny *animales del monte* living inside your throat, and they don't belong there. You must kill them by swallowing pills." I held up a tablet of penicillin. "One with each meal and one before going to sleep. Also you must gargle with salt water."

"This will drive away the spirits?"

"Not spirits. Tiny animales del monte. Yes. You will become well with the help of the German. He is your husband?"

"I think not, even if he says it is so. We had no ceremony. Will I become dry?" She cupped a hand over one breast.

"That's possible. You have a child, then."

"My baby must drink the milk of another." She sighed and turned her head away.

I poured a glass of water. "Three pills," I told her. "Two will make you less hot, the other will begin killing the tiny animals in your throat."

She lifted her head, took the pills. "You must do the rituals of healing. I cannot become well only from swallowing shards of fish bone."

"You sleep. I shall perform the rituals when you sleep."

She nodded and relaxed as I touched her face and head. Then I reloaded the travel bag and sought the German.

He and Tom sat at a table in another cave room. A taller table held dishes and a glowing oil lamp. Shelves along the wall held pots, glasses, and cups. "Norma?" the German said.

"She will be fine. She needs rest and antibiotics. I gave her aspirin to bring down her fever. Do you not have aspirin here?" I could hear accusation in my tone.

"Aspirin? Yes. For headaches."

"It will bring down fever. Didn't you know that?"

"No. Maybe I did."

"Did you try other means to get her cool? Wetting her skin?"

"I'm no nurse."

"You are a husband. It's your duty to help her when she's ill."

Tom chuckled. "You must do as she says if you want your wife to get well. You must do as she says."

The German glared at me, then spoke to Tom in English. "I'm a man. Taking care of the sick is women's work."

"Shall I translate?" Tom asked in Spanish.

"No. Let him keep his poisoned words in one language only. I think he wants the child to die."

The German seemed to wilt. "Please. No. I will, of course, help if you will be kind enough to show me how. Would you care for a drink? I can offer coffee, tea, or water. All has been boiled and all is cool, unfortunately. Or I could send a servant to heat tea or coffee."

"Water. Thanks." I noticed only then that Tom and the German held cups.

The man poured me a drink from a pitcher on the taller table. "Please sit with us, if you will." He then addressed Tom in English. "I so tire of speaking Spanish. Is there a chance you speak German or French? Perhaps Portuguese?"

"No chance at all," Tom said in Spanish, glancing at me.

"Talk whatever language you want," I said.

"I intended to do just that," the German said to Tom in English. He turned to me, a startled look on his face, and asked in Spanish, "Do you understand English?"

"I have no desire to speak English," I said. It was true, too. I didn't want them to hear my bad accent. But that was not all. I didn't want to admit knowing any English because I wanted to find out what they would say when they thought I couldn't understand. A twinge of guilt hit me for the trick on Tom, and I resolved to set him straight if he started saying anything that might embarrass him for me to know.

"I thought not," the German said, again switching to English. "She's your woman, after all. Nurse, you say. Hah! I understand such nursing, but don't get me wrong. I don't condemn any man for being a man. But how rude of me. I haven't introduced myself or learned your name."

"I'm Tom." He glanced at me to see if his speaking English was acceptable. When I smiled and nodded, he looked relieved, then went on speaking to the German. "It's enough of a name for me in this country. I already told you her name is Rosa."

The man nodded. "Osterwitz, that's me. People call me Oz."

"Oz?" Tom seemed amused.

"Oz. Like the Wizard of Oz. It's a nickname people hung on me long ago, made from the first and last letters of my name. I do have a legitimate first name, but nobody uses it, even my wife back in Texas."

"Wife?" Tom looked bewildered. "She died, perhaps?"

"Not at all. She's alive and well in a little town named Sherman where our children are in college. Living in the tropics isn't something she likes, and she wants to be close to our kids, even if they're grown or nearly grown. They're college kids."

"Does she know about, uh, about—?"

"Norma? Of course not. I go back once a year, spend a month in the States, and do some business to keep our cash flow healthy."

"You sell gold?"

"Not yet. I sell stones." Oz and Tom sipped from their cups and eyed each other in the dim light. Cool air moved through the cave room, the plastered and painted room that might once have been a mine. "Stones from Brazil. Before I came here, I lived in Brazil with another woman I called my wife. She wasn't, of course, but I called her that for the sake of her family—not that they gave a damn. But what's a man to do? A real man with sand in him needs a woman, and mine was in Texas. Besides, she's old. Hah! I'm old, but what of that? You see what money can buy—new wives, young ones, willing ones with hot eyes. So what if they're younger than my children. I'm a man, and I still have plenty of sand. The wife in Brazil, she was a firecracker and made much of the right kinds of noise when we loved, so it shocked me when she tried to get me killed for my car and the money in my wallet, which wasn't much. I didn't even carry enough to keep her in clothes for six months, and she would have killed me for it. For pocket change." Oz made an impatient gesture. "Forget her, I said, and locked her out of my apartment. She came with young thugs and banged on the door and screamed that I was a goat, old and limp, which she knew to be a lie, and the thugs kicked in my door to find me waiting with a pistol. They backed out fast and the woman who had passed herself off as my wife said they would return."

"Three wives?" Tom said. "You know how to complicate your life, Oz."

"Always have I been foolish when it comes to pretty women." Oz cut his eyes toward me. "If she weren't your woman, I might be flattering this mestiza with the fine breasts, telling her she's beautiful, which she is, and telling her she is smart. You see, with beautiful women you must flatter them by talking about their brains. All women doubt they are smart enough—and they doubt it with just cause. Beautiful women respond to flattery about their brains and not their body or face. Tell them they are beautiful and they're unimpressed and take your words as what is due to them. But talk about their fine brains and you have them. This isn't so good, I know, this flattery to get them into bed. Not so good at all, not for a young man like you or for an old one like me. It destroys women and it gets you in trouble. I was in trouble with the firecracker of a woman in Brazil, in trouble with her and with her thugs and lovers who would come back in the night with knives or guns. Did you know you can hire a killer to remove a bothersome person for just a few dollars? I was a marked man."

"So you left Brazil?" Tom asked.

"Yes. And no. I have business in Brazil, a tourmaline mine and a factory that cuts gemstones. Amethyst. Citrine. Aquamarine. Even emeralds and a few diamonds. I found some gold and sank a shaft and began a producing mine, but the Eye of Envy watched. When gold began to come from the mine, they took it from me, the Brazilians, calling me a foreign devil. Gold makes men crazy. But it isn't so bad with gemstones, especially tourmaline and other colored stones, because few know how to turn them into cash. Any fool can turn gold into cash, so the fools left me alone with the stones. I sold the apartment through an agent and announced to all that I was leaving Brazil for good, which was a lie on account of the holdings in gems I mentioned. The girl I called my wife left for Rio with her thugs, I heard later, and they robbed the wrong man and the police caught them. They're dead now, killed for robbing the wrong man, and it's a shame because she was such a beautiful girl before I ruined her with money. She would have married some strong and stupid peasant to raise a family of strong and stupid children, and she would have had something of a happy life. But I came along to flatter her and bed her and ruin her with clothes and jewelry. So you might say I killed her."

"All the while you had a family in Texas. A wife and children in college."

"Yes. Yes. Yes." Oz shook his head. "But of course, my kids were not in college then. They were in private school in Houston. You see what money can do. Gold is worse, even the Indios around here know that. An old fellow from a village downriver told me the story of Orocón, a local man who discovered he could take lumps of gold to cities near the coast and trade them for guns and knives and even women—for almost anything. Orocón dug tiny bits of gold from a hillside, making the hole deeper and deeper, for he could hear the mother lode of gold calling him from within the hill, until he punched into the hollow heart of the hill where trickster spirits live. They came bounding out through Orocón's hole, turning themselves into tapirs and monkeys, into anacondas and jaguars. The jaguars ripped Orocón open and the monkeys stuffed his mouth and stomach with pure gold from the mother lode inside the hill. The tapirs trampled him flat and the anacondas dragged him to the river where the current swept him into the shallows. You can still hear Orocón, the old villager told me, weeping in his death agony when waters become shallow and rush over the bone of his head, now become a stone, and you can hear in the gurgle of the water over the gold scattered around him in the river, laughing at the foolishness of Orocón for following their call to his doom. Do you understand the meaning of this story?"

"You tell me the meaning."

"It's a warning against going after gold, for it will lure you to your destruction."

"Do you believe that? Do you believe gold will kill you?"

"Yes."

"And yet you're here in the gold country looking for it. That's your mine we saw, and this house. It's an abandoned mine."

"Yes. I'm here listening to the call of gold. It makes no sense. But there's something about gold, something that gets into the blood and fills men with a lust no woman can satisfy. It will destroy me, I'm certain, but the gold lust drives me on. Finding it is to win as I've never won with money or gemstones. So far I haven't won, but I will. I will. Then somehow the gold will destroy me, as it will destroy you and any other man who lusts for it. It will destroy me, and I have no doubt that I deserve being destroyed."

"This makes no sense," Tom said, "your living here, waiting to be destroyed by that which you seek."

"No." Oz smiled in a sad way. "It makes no sense. Yet here I am."

8

What a strange fellow this Oz Osterwitz, and what an eerie scene he conducted with me and Rosa sitting in the rabbit burrow of a house, once a mine and now plastered, painted, furnished as a home for him and his wife who wasn't his wife but just a native girl and not exactly that either, for her skin, hair, and eyes marked her as no ordinary Indio, and motherhood lifted her beyond childhood. Oz was a wizard of an engineer. He restructured the abandoned mine, rid it of bats and guano, remade the walls, used his engineering wizardry to create air shafts for ventilating the home necessary with its darkness to be easy on albino eyes. He told me she never left the house.

"But she could wear sunglasses," I said.

"She won't. Besides, it isn't only her own eyes that worry her. Others would see her and gape and nudge one another. She'll not endure it, she says, so she has learned to love the mine-home. She said she will live her life as if she were a trickster spirit locked within a hollow hill and will come out only when she can shift her shape into that of a tapir, like the women of thunder."

At Oz's command an Indio woman joined us from another room. She stood short and thick with heavy breasts and downcast eyes, and on her back she carried a child, Edward, the son of Oz and Norma, who looked over the woman's shoulder to regard us with dark eyes in an unflinching and steady way as if he saw more than one so young could be expected to see, as if he understood all we said and found it profound and profoundly wrong, for he never smiled and never relented in his gaze shifting from one of us to another. An old soul, that's what Catrina in her California way called Edward, explaining his steady gaze that seemed so wise in its shifting scrutiny. While Rosa cooed at the child and Oz watched them, Catrina leaned over the back of my chair to whisper her explanation: "That child first came into the world at least twelve thousand years ago and has lived many lifetimes and has accumulated wisdom so vast that he still remembers much of it though he is a child again." I glanced back at Catrina, seeing she wore bell-bottoms and a shirt made of fake buckskin and the beads, always the beads, almost hiding the strawberry on her neck. Oz didn't bother to introduce the Indio woman any more than he would have introduced a cow, and though Rosa spoke to her, the woman said little, giving one-word responses and looking only at the floor as if she feared eye contact. Catrina put her hand on my shoulder, but when I reached to knock it away, it was gone and Catrina was gone, leaving behind only the musk of her perfume to drift through Oz's rabbit-burrow home.

Rosa liked the child, but she seemed disturbed by its presence. "He's so vulnerable," she said. "Someone must watch a child at all times, especially a boy."

"What are you talking about?" I asked.

She shook her head to dismiss the question, then went to the room of the albino woman.

Edward reminded me of my sister's boy, of the way he once watched my lips with rounded eyes as I read Lewis Carroll to him and his sisters, rosy-cheeked girls who asked me again and again to read about the Jubjub bird and the Jabberwock, words that made no sense except for the beat, the rhythm, and they repeated some of the words: "slithy toves, slithy toves," loving the magic of them while Catrina had watched, had yearned, she said, to have children with me, though of course she lied. "It was no lie," Catrina said, and I looked around, expecting to see her standing close in buckskins and beads, but she had fled, leaving the mineshaft of a room redolent of her perfume.

Rosa tended Norma, returned to listen to Oz and me, tended Norma, and returned again. Her face showed little, so it seemed she sat with us as a child might, one with a young soul Catrina might say, listening but comprehending nothing, or it would seem that way if I didn't know her or at least the Rosita she once was and know to watch her eyes as they measured Oz Osterwitz. She might not understand English, but she seemed to understand plenty about Oz, and she didn't much like what she saw in him.

"The fever has broken," Rosa announced in the afternoon, or I thought it might be afternoon, for Oz had summoned the Indio wet nurse to bring us food and she had vanished and returned with fried plantains, cheese, and cassava cakes hard as plywood. In the rabbit-burrow house it was difficult to judge time of day. We ate and Oz talked of gold and Rosa excused herself from time to time to check on Norma, returning finally to announce the breaking of the fever.

Later, after more visits to the sick girl, Rosa came in to say, "I left the penicillin beside the dead lamp. Remember, one with each meal and one at night before she goes to sleep. Use all of the pills or she might become sick again. You will take care of her."

"It's women's work, I say." Even in the dim light Oz must have seen the storm building on Rosa's face. "But I'll do it," he added in haste.

Rosa turned to me. "We leave now."

"I took the liberty," Oz said to her, "to negotiate with Tom for your fee. He wanted only a canoe so he and you can boat out of gold country. That's so odd, you know, since I thought Tom had come here looking for gold."

"I don't hear the call of gold," I said.

"That's good, considering the wisdom in the story of Orocón. But of course things other than gold can destroy men when they seek them with vigor."

"A canoe?" Rosa brightened. "You have a canoe?"

"In the small river. Yes. It's now yours. Boating down the big river might not be as dangerous as finding gold, but it comes close."

When we stepped outside, late afternoon sunlight stabbed our eyes like cactus spines. Oz summoned Norma's uncle, explained to him about the canoe, and appointed him our guide to the small river while I looked again at the painting on the rock, the amateur painting of a jungle house around the entrance of what once was a mine. The Indio nodded and said a single word: "Norma?"

"She's better," Oz said. "This curandura worked her magic and your niece will be well within days. This is not the healer we sent for but another, a better one, who happened by. Have you seen the other healer?"

"No."

"If he comes, send him away."

"One more thing," Rosa said as Oz turned to go back into the rabbit burrow. "Have you ever heard of a white North American called El Loco Merzi?"

"No. I'm the only white man within hundreds of kilometers."

"He mined gold in odd ways, and he might have married a local woman with only one eye."

"Of course he mined gold—why else would he be known as El Loco? Perhaps people around here call me that, too, given the nature of my house, my wife, and the way I listen to the call of the gold from within the hills."

"What about bandits?" Rosa asked. "Have you heard of bandits that once killed a local landowner and terrified people of the region? The people rose up against the bandits and perhaps killed them."

"A crazy man, bandits, and a revolution. Such a colorful history this place seems to have." Oz shook his head. "I'm sorry, Rosa. I've never heard of such people or events."

On our way to the small river, Rosa said, "It's better this way."

"What way?"

"Following a guide to take a canoe I earned instead of being escorted by a pistolero to a place where we must steal a canoe."

"You called it borrowing, back then."

"Yes. Borrowing. Earning is better than borrowing."

We walked behind Norma's uncle, who wore khaki trousers with the cuffs worn into threads, whose bare feet, archless, left prints like bricks in the soft ground of a savanna trail at the edge of the jungle, where savanna grass gave in to leafy ground cover and some scattered trees like guava, thatch palm, and cashew. I stopped, intending to pick some cashew fruit with the great nut husks growing on the ends of them, but Rosa tugged on my sleeve. "It's getting dark."

"As it well should." I plucked a single cashew, bit into its waxy hide for the taste, the smell, remembering too late the kerosene flavor and green persimmon pucker waiting in cashew juice.

Rosa watched my facial contortions, her cheeks dimpled in amusement, and she tugged again on my sleeve. "We should not take the canoe on the small river after the sun sets," she said.

"Yes, we should."

"We cannot and should not become children again, not in a strange jungle at night."

She was right, of course, I told myself, not believing we could be doing anything wrong in shoving off after dark. We followed the Indio into real jungle so dense in its high canopy that little direct light made it through, allowing only scattered ground creepers to survive, plants with names like peperomia, plants that curanderas liked to gather for medicine and magic. The base of the huge trees looked like fins on moon rockets, and I saw some old friends among the giants: rosewoods and the fabulous silk-cotton trees, once cut by men who were after their fibers for stuffing them into life jackets. The canopy opened a crack for the river, sandbarred and dry-season shallow but on the rise with new rain, and ground palms, ferns, and other low plants reveled thick along the edge to take in all the light allowed by the canopy crack. In a machete-chopped clearing we found the canoe lying bottom up. We turned it over, slid it down an incline into the water while the night sounds of the jungle began dim and soft. As I eyed the trees and groundcover with growing uneasiness, the Indio produced two paddles and a rusting coffee can from a thicket of ground palms. He thumped the can. "This canoe leaks." He shook his head as in apology, handed me the dipper and paddles, and turned to Rosa. "We are pleased for Norma," he mumbled and left.

"A leaking canoe." Rosa's voice carried an edge of worry. She tossed the travel bag into the boat.

"All jungle canoes leak. At least it has seats to hold us above the bilge water. I'll take the back this time."

When we shoved off in the narrow river, Rosa busied herself with pushing vines and drooping branches out of the way so she could watch for logs in the water. "Darkness comes. Already it's difficult to see," she said.

"I like it." And that was the truth even if dizziness threatened.

"I know. The truth is that I like it, too. But liking the thrill of what we're doing doesn't remove any danger."

The river widened, narrowed again, twisted through green-black light to keep Rosa busy with vines. Nighttime jungle buzzing and chirping became insistent, loud, almost blocking out water sounds along the bank and from my paddle, and the realization came to me that jungles east or west sounded the same in darkness; that insects, birds, frogs increased their volume in similar ways the world over, as daylight fled. The flow made paddling easy, and paddling helped stave off the dizziness that crowded the corners of my vision and threatened to break through, making me want to snatch up my M-14 though I knew I didn't have it, not in this jungle.

"Talk to me, Rosa. Keep me here."

She turned a surprised face to me, then went back to pushing aside overhanging plants. "I keep thinking about Oz. Such a strange man and strange house."

"Oz. Yes." The dizziness at the edges of vision lessened. "Say more."

"He has the tree of Mata-Mata on his shoulder."

"What does that mean?"

"What does it mean, Tom?"

I watched the swirls made by the paddle, watched the front edges of the canoe to keep them from getting into either bank. A flick of the paddle on one side of the canoe or the other was enough to center us in the narrow stream, hardly a river. "This water reminds me of Village Creek in East Texas."

"What does it mean? You're avoiding my question." The river widened again, freeing Rosa from the task of shoving our way through overhangs. She turned to look at me. "What does it mean?"

9

Trees vanished from overhead, and the night sky opened to moon and stars as we emerged from the small river into the big one. I almost cried for the beauty of the water and sparkling lights and the singing of the night jungle.

"Like a lake." Tom's voice was thick with emotion.

"Yes." Eighteen years before, when our canoe drifted into the big river, there was no light because of rain clouds, and we thought we had entered a lake.

"We slept in the canoe."

"Yes," I repeated. "On the leaves of ground palms we had used as umbrellas."

"We slept holding each other in the purity of childhood." Tom's statement sounded like an invitation.

"We can't do that now. The canoe is too narrow for adults to lie side by side." I bit my lip and hesitated. *Talk to me, Rosa. Keep me here,* he had said, and I tried to keep him talking. Was Tom slipping somehow into another place and time? Or was he dreaming while awake as I dreamed of Mata-Mata speaking with my father's voice? Did he feel the need to sleep touching as we did when we were children in order to stay present?

"Back then, how far did we drift with the current while we slept, before the canoe stopped against the log?" Tom dipped the paddle, nosing the canoe toward the center of the river. The tone of his voice sounded better, calm.

"Perhaps far. Perhaps not so far. We must stay awake this time to make sure we don't crash into the bank and overturn. We cannot go ashore."

"I know. You told me the risks of a strange jungle at night." Tom clanked something in the shadows of the boat. "This canoe leaks less than the one we borrowed. There's hardly any water for me to bail out. Do you know what that means?"

"That we're lucky?"

"Yes. It means we can tie the canoe to a tree where current will keep us from the shore. It means we can wait out the night in the canoe, perhaps even sleep."

"Can you talk to me about what happened back in the small river? When you feared not being present?"

"Not now. Maybe not ever." Tom found a tree leaning into the current and I tied the bow to a branch while the current swung us around. The river sparkled with stars and moon.

"Don't hang over the side," I warned. "Settle completely inside the canoe and let the jungle sing you to sleep."

"A lullaby. I hear it. The jungle's voice is a lullaby. It feels safe here, Rosita."

"Rosa."

"Rosa. Safe."

Tom went to sleep like a child and I might have drifted off from fatigue and relief that Tom could sleep when the low rumble of a male voice awakened me. A tree moved close on the shore, and even in the dim light I could tell it was a thorn. It moved again as trees are not supposed to move, and I saw its roots sinking into the shoulder of a man. He glimmered in the moonlight, and he groaned from his load. "Rosa," he said in a voice that made my scalp prickle.

My father's voice.

"Go away," I said.

"Rosa. I killed my wife."

"You're not my father," I told him. "Quick, tell your story, Mata-Mata, and shrink your load and be on your way."

"I killed her with the bowstring of cholera. My wife. I killed her. And you, Rosa, what did you do with my mother, with your abuelita? Take my tree, Rosita. It belongs on your back. Take it."

"Go away," I said.

"You killed Donito."

"I forbid you to speak that name. Go away."

The glimmering figure moaned and sat on the bank, dangling his feet into the river, and watched me from eyes that flashed in the darkness like the water eyes of a jaguar. His thorn tree had become a bush. In the shadows of the bush, among the thorns, the face of Abuelita appeared, thin and drawn. "Do not go to Contaura. Do not go to the Sisters of Mercy," she said. "They can teach you nothing of the ways of the curandera."

The voice of a haughty child came from my mouth, the voice of Rosita. "They are enfermeras. They teach modern medicine, and I will become a nurse."

"They know nothing of herbs. They know nothing of magic. Stay, Rosita, finish learning the ancient ways, or the knowledge will die with me."

Mata-Mata stirred the water with his feet. "Where were you when cholera came to our home? Where was I? We were gone, both of us, and now I have the thorn on my shoulder. What do you have? The pale-skinned one? The wild river? The memory of Donito and El Lobo?"

A scraping sound and the rhythmic splash of water awakened me. It came gradually, the awakening; it came with a slow realization of pain in my shoulder and a slitting of eyes to see Tom dipping water from the canoe. The phantom of dawn was upon us. I sat up half expecting to find Mata-Mata's thorn tree sprouting from my shoulder, but the pain came from sleeping against my canoe paddle.

"You slept," Tom said. He stopped dipping and grinned at me.

"Maybe."

"Not maybe. Your jeans are soaked with bilge water. So is your blouse. We're both wet. We slept while the river seeped into the canoe and into our clothes. It was a perfect night." He resumed dipping water from the canoe.

"I'm cold."

"Cold?" Tom looked surprised. "Cold?"

"Yes. Wet and cold. You're not cold?"

"I'm cool, maybe. Comfortable. We need to get out of these wet clothes."

"Yes. I brought dry clothes. For both of us."

"I thought—" Tom chewed his lip. "I thought that we—"

"Don't rush things, Tom."

"Rush? Rush?"

"Because we walked nude in the jungle as children doesn't mean we should do so today."

Tom looked disappointed, then tapped my bag with the dipping can. "How did you know what size clothing I wear?"

"I measured your pants and shirt in my home while you slept in the chinchorro, then bought clothes for you at Mahadi's department store. Your dry clothes are rolled up in a tight bundle inside the travel bag. There are socks, also, and underwear." I dipped my canteen into the water, took a purification tablet from the bag.

"Mahadi. I had forgotten the name. I played chess with him once."

"The bag is waterproof. We need dry clothing to keep molds from growing on us."

"Molds? That didn't happen before."

"Perhaps not. But we live in a different world now." I began untying the rope from the tree. "We'll go ashore to change and to find a place to hang our wet clothes."

By the time Tom turned the canoe to point us downriver, daylight had come and the wet jungle steamed in morning sun. The loggers hadn't made it this far up the river yet, so the trees stood tall, and it took a while for the sun to climb above them and bathe the river in light. Dragonflies skimmed the water. Parrots flew over in squawking flocks, and butterflies gathered along the banks.

Tom nosed us into a sandbar, and I got out to pull the canoe from the water. Sand fleas hopped around my ankles, and a blue butterfly the size of my hand fluttered around me before vanishing into the trees.

After we changed, doing so apart from each other with the trunks of sweet beans and monkey-bed trees between us, we spread our clothes on bushes and agreed to look for breakfast where the jungle trailed off into savanna. "I'd settle for cashews or papaya," Tom said with the enthusiasm of a little boy. But we didn't make it to the savanna because of the dead anteater.

At first it looked like a seething blue mound. When we got closer, the butterflies that covered it flapped into the air, and the stench arose. We backed away, horrified at the sight of blue butterflies eating dead flesh. Without speaking, we returned to our wet clothes, took them from the bushes, and went back to the canoe. It wasn't until we were on the river that Tom spoke. "You saw it, too, didn't you?"

"Yes," I said.

"And yet they were beautiful. Beautiful."

"My grandmother told me about carrion-eating butterflies, but never until today had I seen any."

"We stopped in the wrong place," Tom said. "Our jungle doesn't have such beautiful creatures that do such disgusting things."

"Our jungle is gone, Tom."

"No. Eighteen years ago we floated far down the river while we slept, floated past such monstrous beauty. We'll find the right place to go ashore farther downriver."

We paddled on in silence, winding with the river around rocks and sandbars, around brush piles protruding from the current, and past logs where turtles sunned. The image of the blue butterflies stayed with me, the image of their writhing about like maggots on the anteater, fluttering above it, resettling to feed. Eating breakfast right then was out of the question, though I still had some food supplies in the travel bag. We didn't speak again until we came to the village.

Naked toddlers played on a sandbar below the village. Women wandered beneath the houses built upon poles and walled with bamboo and thatching. Their skirts were made from gray cloth, their breasts bare. Some wore necklaces, and when they saw us, most came to the river's edge, calling for us to come ashore, smiling, chattering among themselves.

"No men," Tom said.

"Just one." I pointed. A man wearing a red breechcloth and red armbands stood in the shade of one of the houses, watching us. He waved. "We should stop for a visit."

"A brief one." Tom turned the canoe toward the sandbar, and most of the women scampered up the bank to the houses.

They returned as we came to the shore, and up close I could see that those who had gone to the houses and come back were the younger women, now wearing sashes tied over their breasts. "They've hidden their *tetas* because of you," I said. "I'll bet the younger ones have been to villages up and down the river and know the way mestizo men and white ones such as you stare at bare breasts."

Tom shot me an annoyed look. "I would not stare."

As we got out of the canoe I hooked the strap of the canteen to my waist and grasped the travel bag. "Tie the machete to your belt," I whispered.

"Why?" His startled look asked if there were danger here.

"These people regard ownership in foreign ways. Tie it to your belt or lose it. The same with your canteen and the hunting knife."

"You've been here before?"

"No. Of course not. But I've read about the ways of jungle people." I turned to them and smiled. "Good morning."

Most of the women giggled, hands over their mouths, and the children stood behind them, staring at us with solemn eyes. Girls not yet developing breasts wore panties and boys about six and older wore either breechcloths or shorts, ragged and cut down from larger sizes. Only the toddlers were nude. The entire group of twelve or so looked with expectation at Tom.

He seemed to realize that he needed to speak. "You live on the most beautiful place of the river." He smiled, and they again giggled, louder than before. The group turned to one of the women who had covered her breasts. "Did they understand that?" Tom asked me.

"Some of us understand," the woman said. "But not all here speak Spanish."

"My name is Rosa," I said.

"And I am Tomás."

The woman nodded and said something in her language to the others, something that included our names; then she turned to us. "Here they call me Kaita. When the missionaries come, they call me Katrina. Kaita is better. Our shaman told me to greet you and invite you to stay for a festival." She gestured toward the houses, toward the man with red armbands. In a lower voice she asked Tom, "Do you have magic for making medicine?"

"Yes. But Rosa is the one who understands the way of curing."

"Are you ill?" I asked.

"It's my son, my tiny son. The shaman says he will cure the boy tonight, but he said he would cure him last night and the one before. He cures with smoke, and it has not worked with my son. Don't tell him that I asked." She glanced toward the shaman in a furtive way. "He would speak with you now."

"I cannot cure everything," I warned as we walked up the bank toward the shaman.

10

It took some paddling, tight-lipped silent paddling of the canoe through primeval jungle to recover from anger at the butterflies and anger at the anteater for becoming such a roiling and putrid mass. Its odor had been there all along, faint and lurking beneath the clean smells of the river, the ferns, the lianas and trees and ground palms, and yet I didn't identify the smell of death until we startled the butterflies and the image of the anteater bled into the image of the mouse deer that had tripped our wires.

Charlie drove them at night, the mouse deer, panicking Bambi after Bambi into cleaning their path of mines, drove them in the drizzle and mud beneath our bunkered hill until they hit the wires to set off globes of flame in the wet night. Allen poured fire down the hill into darkness and jungle and mouse deer, saying he wanted to kill Charlie, and I fired my piece again and again, fired blind into the dark as wind picked up and thunder came with monsoon rain. In the morning we slogged down the hill to find bits of mouse deer with staring eyes, large, brown, and bodies become meat already clouding moist air with that faint smell like the anteater before we disturbed the butterflies. Beyond chunks of Bambi lay the bodies of men ripped up from the fire we rained upon them in the night, bodies already steaming into the mud with the odor of the dead anteater, bodies with faces of boys. "They're just children," I told Allen, and he said "Ho Chi Minh's boys. Killers." And I said yes and he tried to light a cigarette but his hands shook too much and somehow those trembling fingers made the smell worse as did the butterflies flying from the corpse, and I had to paddle hard and angry, and Rosa paddled hard though I couldn't see her face, couldn't tell if the butterflies made her as angry as they did me.

The village came as a surprise, a welcomed surprise with its little girls and boys naked as tiny kids in such a jungle should be. The older women had triangular flaps of breasts hanging over distended bellies and the younger ones wrapped their breasts because of me, Rosa said, though when the heat of day slowed our movements, one took off her wrap, Kaita, the lovely one, the one who spoke Spanish and had asked me for medicine. She took it off and mopped her body, her forehead, and the others watched Kaita and watched me to see if I would stare before they bared their own breasts in the jungle heat. Rosa also watched me. "What do you think?" she asked.

"What am I supposed to be thinking about?"

"You're a man. You tell me." She dimpled.

I knew, and I knew better than to talk about it. Sylvia the witch had bared her large and magnificent breasts when Rosita and I were nude savages emerging from the jungle, bared them to show she was like us in innocence, and Rosita had become angry when I made the mistake of looking. "She has the body of a child," I said, hoping for the right words, for safe words.

The shaman squatted on the ground making a cigar. He glanced, one-eyed and sinister with a black-toothed smile. "Good women," he said. "Sweet women. Perhaps I live in this village for the women. The young ones have such tetas as men from the coast would die for."

Rosa and I sat on grass mats beneath the shaman's house. Behind it and the dozen or so other houses, where jungle had been burned, grew the crops of the village: maize, sugarcane, plantains, tobacco. The evidence of burning was almost gone, reduced to a scorched stump here and there by the greening of the garden and the jungle creeping back to reclaim its own.

"You have not always lived with the jungle people," I said, wanting to move the conversation to something besides tetas.

"No. But my father came from this jungle tribe, and perhaps his father. Who knows? I went with him to the coast as a boy when An-jang, the Spirit of the Dead, crept into the village at night to yell 'meh,

meh, meh,' and the rains didn't come, and evil spirits emerged from trees and from the hollow earth to bring sickness, and people died. My mother died."

"You learned Spanish on the coast," I said. "And went to the cinema."

"Yes. But I was born with the ear lobes of a shaman and this white eye that sees spirits."

When we had first approached him, the shaman introduced himself as Doctor Livingston which I decided to take as a welcome bit of foolery to help with humor in putting the blue butterflies, the mouse deer, the dead boys of Ho Chi Minh, and the stench of death behind me, though the shaman's demeanor seemed more hostile than comical. "I am Tomás," I said. "This is Rosa. How do you presume to be Doctor Livingston?"

I could tell that Rosa was alarmed by the shaman's eyes, one dark and the other white, something that was obvious even from a distance, especially the white eye. Up close it became clear that one eye was milky with blindness, such an eye as people in many parts of the world would cover with a patch, but not the shaman, who knew his white eye could see spirits.

He tilted his head in dog-like amazement, then set a sinister twist into his brows and lips. "It isn't my real name. You are to call me Columbus."

"That isn't your real name either." I spoke with conviction and challenge in response to the annoying arrogance of his command.

"No. I have tried for years to discover my real name. My parents thought it was Poí, and I accepted that until I went to live on the coast. There they called me Chico until I went to a cinema and saw the story of Columbus."

"Then you saw another cinema and saw the story of Doctor Livingston and changed your name again. What do the people here call you?"

"Poí. But you are to call me—"

"Then Poí," I said, "your real name remains a secret. I will reveal it to you before we leave this village." I chuckled.

Rosa got me aside later to warn me about the shaman. "Please don't joke about his magic. If you must be a clown, never laugh."

"Never laugh?"

"It's an insult, especially to the men. Among these jungle people, laughter is effeminate—even the women cover their mouths when they laugh."

During the day the women of the village fed us boiled plantains and dried fish, and the shaman made cigars, huge ones wrapped with tawari bark, "for tonight's magic," he explained, holding up for my inspection a cigar longer than my foot. He also told us about his struggle to achieve immortality.

"You're tall," Poí said, arranging thin tawari bark for making another cigar. "Tall men live longer. I'm short, but you will pull on my arms and legs to stretch me and give me longer life."

This is a joke, I thought, and he doesn't laugh because men here don't laugh, though he is amused and likes amusing me and Rosa. But I was wrong: he took height seriously and did ask me that night to stretch him.

He rolled another cigar and tied strips of tawari bark to keep it together. "I sometimes become immortal," he mused, tapping the cigar to shape it. "But my magic for it is weak, and I cannot become immortal for longer than three days at a time."

I slapped my hand over my mouth and Rosa elbowed me.

When evening came, after the men returned with their blowguns and poisoned darts carrying dead monkeys and rabbits and a basket of birds, after the women moved down the riverbank to do the skinning and plucking and cutting, the skewering and roasting, Ne'eng, the village chieftain in his broken Spanish invited Rosa and me into his home. We climbed a notched log to sit on mats beside Kaita, whose husband, she explained, was upriver in a quest for gold. She held her son, a lethargic child whom Rosa had already examined and treated with antibiotics. "He has intestinal worms," Rosa confided to me, "but his immediate problem is a throat infection."

The chief, a blocky little man whose smile revealed gaps in his teeth and who had a scar on the side of his face running all the way to his ear, cast furtive glances at the shaman busying himself with some final shaping of his gigantic cigars. "Sit here," Ne'eng said and gestured toward some grass mats on the floor. Several other men joined us, and behind them came their wives. Serving women gave each of us a cup of foul-looking brew, an act that elicited sounds of appreciation from the men. I swirled my drink around and asked Rosa, "What is this stuff?"

"Cassava beer. It has a high alcohol content, which kills bacteria and makes it safe to drink—safe except for what the alcohol can do to you."

It tasted like fermented sawdust but went down well. The serving women brought banana leaves to set on the floor before each of us, then put bowls of steaming rice on the leaves and beside the bowls they laid browned pieces of meat. The rice contained twigs and speckled things but looked edible enough, unlike the meat.

I stared at the meat, knowing it to be howler monkey, remembering the recurring nightmare of childhood: Uncle Ray lifting his rifle in anger because howler monkeys had begun screeching just as he was about to shoot a buck deer, and the deer bolted into the brush, and Uncle Ray hated the monkeys in that instant enough to snap a shot into the trees. When he reached the one that dropped to the ground, it sat muttering at the blood flowing from the hole in its side, and it picked up bits of leaves and sticks to poke into the hole in its attempt to staunch the flow of blood. I drank the entire cup of weird beer, hardly noticing the taste, my attention fixed on the meat. A woman filled my cup again.

Catrina leaned over my shoulder to get a better look at the roasted meat. "That might be the same monkey that your Uncle Ray shot," she said, her voice dripping with disgust.

"He wasn't my uncle," I said. "We just called him uncle."

"What?" Rosa touched my arm and looked alarmed.

"Your pet jungle savage wants some attention," Catrina said with a laugh.

"Go away, Catrina," I said.

"Catrina?" Rosa tightened her grip on my arm.

I looked back, expecting to see her in her fake buckskins and her beads that almost hid the strawberry on her neck, but she had gone. Her perfume, a wisp of odor I could almost see, floated through the hut toward the windows; it smelled like frangipani blossoms but weaker, and certainly much weaker than the rancid odor of roasted monkey and the sour smell of the people who sat staring at me. "I cannot eat monkey," I told Rosa.

She patted my arm, released it, and said in a reassuring tone, "It isn't required. Eat the rice?"

Ne'eng spoke in his language to Kaita, who replied, then turned to me.

"I explained," she said in Spanish, "how monkey meat causes your stomach to hurt."

One of the women replaced my monkey meat with a roasted bird. Nodding to Kaita in gratitude, I picked up the bird and took a bite, only to discover it to be tough as a piece of canvas. Everyone resumed eating while I struggled with the canvas bird until it came to me what kind of bird the men had killed and the women plucked and skewered for the fire.

Parrot. I set the bird aside and, pretending to rub my chin, removed the parrot flesh from my mouth. A parrot could live sixty years or more and in spite of its small brain had the intelligence of a chimpanzee. Parrots have the capacity to problem-solve, to play and amuse themselves like children, so eating one was similar to eating a monkey, and eating monkey struck me as tantamount to cannibalism.

"What did you expect when you came among these savages?" Catrina asked from somewhere in the shadows of the hut.

"I want to get back to the jungle," I told Rosa. A woman filled my cup again.

"We are in the jungle."

"Back to our jungle." I picked up the bowl of rice, hoping it would purge the taste of parrot, and Catrina, without showing herself, laughed at my distress.

11

Tom pretended to talk with spirits. Poí pretended not to notice Tom's leaning back to speak with no one. Kaita clutched her sick boy, watching everyone, and she seemed to take special delight in Tom's discourse with spirits.

After the meal, after the women cleared away banana leaf plates and bones and rice bowls, Poí announced it was time to sing spirit songs. He stood, cleared his throat several times, and began a chant. Women joined the singing, providing a background of four repeated notes, breaking their voices to click from low to high notes. The shaman moved his hands in a ritualized way to imitate the flight of a bird, closed his eyes, and sang his tuneless chant. When he finished, he sat again and looked satisfied with himself.

Ne'eng, looking pleased, said some words in his language to the shaman, then turned to Tom. "Now you sing for us and for your spirits."

I wanted to tell Tom not to do it, that such singing might be an affront to the shaman, but I could tell he was annoyed with Poí. Tom stood, impressing everyone with his height, and sang an English song, one I knew, about Mother Mary offering comfort: "Let it be," he sang, not getting all the words right but singing the tune with precision in a pleasant tenor.

"This is good," Ne'eng said and others nodded, pleased. Kaita looked at Tom with open adoration, and Poí drew a sour face.

"We will speak a spirit poem," Poí said. He stood and walked around Tom, leaning toward him in a challenging way, then began his poem. Tom snapped his fingers to the rhythm of the poetry and looked as if he could understand the words. When Poí completed the poem, he delivered the final stanzas with his face close to Tom's, his clouded spirit eye bulging and shining, his face set with hostility. "Now you," he said. "Now you tell us a poem." He started to return to his mat but Tom stopped him with a touch and walked around him in a parody of the way Poí had moved. This is not good, I thought, not good at all.

"My poem is in the true language of spirits." Tom turned to the women who had sung their four notes for Poí. "I will not sing, but it would be good if you would sing like this while I speak." He looked at Kaita, and she translated. Then he demonstrated with four notes, "Da-DOO-lee-duh, da-DOO-lee-duh, da-DOO-lee-duh," until the women joined in. Tom placed a finger to his lips to signal that they reduce their volume, then he began his English poem:

"'Twas brillig and the slithy toves
Did gyre and gimble in the wabe;
All mimsy were the borogoves,
And the mome raths outgrabe."

"Da-DOO-lee-duh, da-DOO-lee-duh," the women chanted, and some began to tap knuckles on the floor to help with the rhythm. Tom moved around the shaman as he delivered his poem, raising his brows and dropping them into a fierce frown, grimacing, and managing to look amused and superior at the same time.

"'Beware the Jabberwock, my son!
The jaws that bite, the claws that catch!
Beware the Jubjub bird, and shun
The frumious Bandersnatch!'"

Some of the men added their voices to the background, "Da-DOO-lee-duh," and the shaman looked increasingly alarmed.

"He took his vorpal sword in hand;
Long time the manxome foe he sought—
So rested he by the Tumtum tree
And stood awhile in thought."

Kaita, her eyes shining, turned to me. "He is a true shaman," she said loud enough for Poí to hear. "He will cure my child." She turned again to listen to Tom.

"And, as in uffhish thought he stood,

The Jabberwock, with eyes of flame,
Came whiffling through the tulgey wood,
And burbled as it came!"

Poí scowled. "This is no spirit poem," he declared, trying without success to speak over the chanting voices. Tom pretended to wield a machete, aiming invisible blows at the shaman as he recited.

"One, two! One, two! And through and through
The vorpal blade went snicker-snack.
He left it dead, and with its head
He went galumphing back."

Poí, seeming to understand the gestures, rubbed his neck.

"'And hast thou slain the Jabberwock?
Come to my arms, my beamish boy!
Oh frabjous day! Callooh! Callay!'
He chortled in his joy."

Tom bowed to show he was finished, and the chorus ceased chanting their four notes. Ne'eng knocked his beer cup on the floor in appreciation, then said, "Speak again, white man. Speak like rain splashing into the river."

"An encore?" Tom looked at Poí, and the chorus began chanting as he continued:

"'Twas brillig and the slithy toves
Did gyre and gimble in the wabe;
All mimsy were the borogoves,
And the mome raths outgrabe."

Tom sat on the grass mat beside me as his audience banged beer cups on the floor. I put my lips to his ear and whispered, "You put us in danger."

"I doubt that." He picked up his mug and a woman hurried over to refill it.

"It's now time," Poí said, "to cleanse the room of unfriendly spirits." Tom laughed, drank more cassava beer and looked around as if checking out his legion of spirits. Producing a match as from the air, Poí struck it with a thumbnail and lighted one of his over-sized cigars.

He pulled huge amounts of smoke into his lungs without coughing. I noticed he was careful not to clamp his lips around the cigar so that he drew in air along with the smoke. As he exhaled, he muttered some words, and I saw Kaita stiffen.

"What is it?" I asked her.

"He summons the spirit of tapé-tapen, the white scissor-tailed hawk. It's a spirit of sorcery and not of healing."

The room became unpleasant with smoke as Poí moved around, puffing, mumbling, and blowing smoke into each corner, spewing much smoke in the area behind Tom, whose attention seemed not to be upon the shaman. He dug into the leather pouch strapped to his belt.

"The foreign spirits have fled from my magic smoke, and tapé-tapen is upon me," Poí announced through a cloud of tobacco. "I can now cure anyone by taking the spirits of illness within me, raking them with the talons of the mighty tapé-tapen, and throwing them wounded to the hollow space beneath the earth where they belong." He knelt before Kaita and her child and blew smoke in her baby's face, then into his own fist. "You said the foreigners cured your baby's throat with white lumps of spirit medicine. But look," he put his fingers to the child's throat and withdrew a nasty lump of brown matter. It looked like a chewed piece of monkey meat. "This is the body of the spirit left behind when I pulled its essence into me and locked it beneath the earth. With the help of tapé-tapen and my spirit eye, I see into all things, something he cannot do." Poí pursed his lips with contempt toward Tom.

"I know you now," Tom said, pitching his voice low and sinister. He leaned toward the shaman, who still squatted before Kaita and her child. "I see you and into you and see that it is not the spirit of the white scissor-tailed hawk behind your milky eye. I see within you the spirit of the blue butterfly that eats the flesh of the dead." In slow drama he lifted the eye of the Irishman to hold its glassy stare focused on Poí.

"Please, Tom," I said.

A loud gasp came from the chief and others, and the shaman fell from his squatting position as if slapped down. Tom scanned them all with the eye, just as he had done to frighten the villagers so long ago in our childhood jungle. "This eye hurts no one," Tom said. "It sees into the truth. It sees the real name of this man who has within him the essence of the dirty blue butterfly that he mistakes for a hawk. It sees his real name and it tells me what it sees.

"My real name?" Poí stammered. "My real name?" He sat up.

"Yes. You are Humpty Dumpty. Say it."

"Hoom-tí Doom-tí," Poí said in awe. "Hoom-tí Doom-tí. This is a powerful spirit name, and I thank you for it. Please cast the spirit of the trickster butterfly out of my body." The shaman pushed himself up into a squat and duck-walked to Tom.

If Tom was surprised by the suddenness and totality of his victory over the shaman, he didn't show it. Instead he pulled a Bolívar coin from Poí's ear, held it up for everyone to inspect, and flipped it into the air for Poí to catch. "You hold the body of the butterfly," Tom said, "locked within that coin."

"Did you see how it fluttered to my hand?" Poí said in amazement. "Hoom-tí Doom-tí. Such magic." He held the coin between thumb and finger and turned toward Ne'eng. "Silver. A male coin. This is an ancient silver coin that traps the butterfly."

"Cure my baby," Kaita said, her voice quivering. She held her boy toward Tom. "Cure my baby."

"Rosa has already done that with her medicine, though the cure will take more than one day."

"It is an evil spirit that causes him to be ill. Look at it with your magic eye and lock the spirit of sickness away in the earth."

"Very well." Tom scanned the child with the Irishman's glass eye, then pulled a loche from the baby's ear. "Here, take this coin," he offered the loche to the shaman. "It contains the spirit of the sore throat."

Poí took the coin, examined it, then blew cigar smoke on it. "Old," he announced. "And copper. The coin is female, so now we know the spirits of hurt throats are female. I will bury this female copper so deep in the earth that the spirit will never emerge to plague the people of the river."

After the rituals concluded, after Poí asked Tom to pull on his arms and legs to make him taller so he might live longer, after people drifted off to their own huts, the shaman invited us to stay in his home for the night.

"Thanks," Tom said. "But we need to move on down the river."

I noticed in his voice a slight slur from too much cassava beer. "Tom," I said, "I don't want to sleep in the canoe again, and it's too late to find a proper camping ground. I think we should put up our chinchorros in the shaman's home and sleep where it's safe."

"Then we'll hang our hammocks right here in the witch doctor's house." He grinned in a silly way.

"But this isn't the shaman's house," I said. "It's Ne'eng's house, remember? The head man of this village?"

We climbed down the notched log that served as stairs, Tom a bit unsteady in doing so, and followed the shaman to his hut. I stood, holding the travel bag while Poí and Tom went up the log to the entrance. "Take this, Tom." I handed him the bag. "I'll go to the river to retrieve our chinchorros. The mosquito netting is rolled up inside the bag. Get them out for when I return."

But when I reached the canoe, it was empty: someone had taken the paddles and the hammocks. I returned and told Poí. He shrugged. "River people take what they need from the jungle, and they take whatever they need from each other. It's the proper way here, though mestizos on the coast would call it stealing."

"But we need our chinchorros," I protested.

"Perhaps I can get them back." He climbed down the notched pole and headed toward a small group of people.

"We don't need hammocks," Tom said.

"You're drunk. You already forgot what I told you about the kissing bug that crawls on your face at night."

"We're in the wrong jungle." Tom sighed and spoke over his shoulder to the air behind him: "Go away, Catrina."

"Someday, Tom," I said, "when you feel safe with me, I'll ask why this Catrina haunts you."

Poí returned carrying two hammocks. He began hanging them from poles in his house. "But," I said, "those hammocks are not ours."

"I couldn't find the ones from your canoe. Kaita sent these for you."

"These are good," I said, feeling the texture of one. "Better than the ones I brought."

"Yes. Kaita likes Tomás." Poí seemed amused, and Tom looked dumbfounded. I was not surprised or amused.

12

Catrina followed us from the head man's house across a bare stretch of ground to the shaman's smaller hut, and she shinnied up the entry log like a monkey, her fake buckskins rasping like paper and her beads clicking together and sliding apart to show the strawberry on her neck. She winked when I told her to go away, so it was a surprise when she followed Humpty Dumpty out of the hut to vanish into the darkening jungle.

I wanted to sleep on the floor so I could hold Rosa, but that desire came as much from the sawdust beer as it did from wanting her to be Rosita again. Maybe it also came from having to sit close to the musky warmth of Kaita and her bare tetas and from the hot puffs of Rosa's breath when she put her lips to my ear to warn me about the shaman. Desire of any sort didn't come from the surroundings. Poí's hut had monkey skulls and feathers dangling from the thatched roof. Blowguns carved from dark wood leaned against each wall of the hut, quivers of poisoned darts hung on pegs from the support poles, and the place smelled of urine.

While Poí and Rosa hung Kaita's hammocks, I stood at the window to watch the final light of day wash over trees across the river and over river boulders with their speckling of flat moss, to listen to Piha birds piping their last calls for the day, pee-PEE-o, and locusts begin their nighttime buzzing. Sun bitterns had vanished into the trees and parrots ceased flying for the night. By the time I got into a hammock, night jars and frogs had added their voices to the chorus of jungle sounds to sing me to sleep, but I wasn't so sound asleep that I didn't hear the creak of the floor and see through the mosquito netting the shaman's shadow creep to the spot beside my hammock where I had dropped my clothes. "If you try to take my magic eye," I said, "I'll shrink you so much that you'll die in three days." The shadow became still, then drifted back to Poí's hammock. I put the leather bag containing the Irishman's eye into the hammock with me.

In the gray light of morning I awakened to the sound of the shaman peeing. Poí stood at the back window aiming his water at the jungle, spattering leaves far below like he was hitting a photograph or like a rattle similar to the rasp of Catrina's fake buckskins. Crude bastard, I thought, fouling the air of his own home with the odor of urine.

Rain came early, making it necessary to stay in Humpty Dumpty's hut until the entire village was awake, and by the time Rosa and I emerged and sun came out to steam away the rain, half of the morning was gone. "Your knife and scabbard," she said.

"Gone. Vanished while we slept, and good riddance, I say. No doubt our host took them in the night."

"At least he left you the machete. Keep it tied to your belt."

Kaita and other women brought boiled plantains to where we sat on mats beneath Ne'eng's home, and villagers came to grin and watch us eat. "I know where the spirits emerge from the ground to bring illness," Kaita said. She handed her child to another woman. "Come. Look at the hole with your magic eye and stop the spirits from coming out to plague us."

"Your baby seems better this morning," Rosa said.

"Yes." Kaita kept her gaze on me. "Tomás has strong magic. Come." She took my hand to pull me to my feet. I looked at Rosa with my brows raised.

"Go with her." Rosa's cheeks dimpled in amusement. "But beware."

"What are you telling me?"

"The jungle is full of dangers."

"There are no dangers near our village," Kaita said.

"You take dangers with you, and some might follow. Should I go with you to see the spirit hole, Kaita?" Rosa gave me a tiny smile that said she already knew the answer.

"No. If he is to work his magic, he alone must come with me."

"Take care which magic you use." Rosa put her hand over her mouth, her eyes showing amusement.

As I followed Kaita into the woods, I glanced sidelong at the jiggle of her tetas and knew the dangers Rosa warned me about, or I thought I knew. We walked past reddish-barked sweet bean trees and parkias, into the canopied forest where little vegetation grew on the ground; we walked past trees whose trunks were clumped with termites and beneath the huge rosewoods and silk-cotton trees, their trunks flaring into braces, and as we walked, she told me a story about the armadillo and the water bugs.

During the time when animals could talk with each other and with people, Armadillo wandered to the river for a drink, and there he saw the dizzying dance of water bugs scooting and spinning together on the surface of the water. He was so delighted with their dance that he forgot the work of his burrowing in the forest and sat the entire day watching the dance on the water. As twilight came, the bugs transformed themselves into beautiful people, both men and women, and they continued their dance, nude, on the shore of the river, stopping now and then to bow to Armadillo who squeaked in delight. "You are the best audience we have ever had," a female dancer told Armadillo. "Follow us into the forest where we will dance by whatever moonlight comes through the high leaves."

Armadillo followed the dancers and watched them do their fantastic dance with spins and short runs so quick like water bugs that Armadillo could hardly see the motion of their feet for the speed of them. As moonlight ebbed, the nude dancer-woman who had spoken to him sat beside Armadillo and wept while she stroked his tough hide and tiny ears. "Why do you cry?" he asked.

"Because," she said, "we must now return to our home underground, and a tiny door it is that we must go through, so we must become bugs again to fit in the tunnel. If the hole were bigger, we could go underground as people and emerge as humans to dance when light returns to the forest." She showed Armadillo a hole so small that only bugfolk could creep into it.

"I can dig that hole bigger with my magic claws," Armadillo said.

All of the dancers stopped dancing and turned to him with looks of joy, and the woman who stroked his ears kissed him. "It would please me if you helped us with your digging," she told him.

So Armadillo dug, dragging and flinging the dirt, until he had a hole so wide the dancers could fit into it and so deep that he came to a floor of rock. "Dig through the rock," the bug-woman urged, and Armadillo scratched and clawed until he dug through to the underworld. As soon as he rolled the last rock out of the burrow, evil spirits began springing from the hole, and Armadillo knew he had done a wicked thing, for though the spirits took many forms, Armadillo could see through their shimmering skin the foulness of their intent. "You tricked me," Armadillo said to the bug-woman, whose skin began to shimmer with her own kind of corruption.

"Yes," she said. "You've dug into the pit of sickness and released us so we can come out in our true form. Our job is to bring illness of a thousand thousand kinds to animals and people alike."

From that day on, Kaita assured me, the creatures of the earth were afflicted with sores and fevers, with coughs and body pains, with all the illnesses of the world, and it became necessary for some people to become shamans so they could pull evil spirits from the bodies of the sick, contain them with their magic, and cast them back underground.

"You've told me the story of Pandora's box," I said.

"Box? I don't understand." Kaita stopped beneath a silk-cotton tree and pointed. "There. From that hole came the spirit that made my son ill. Seal it with your magic eye." She stepped close to me as if afraid, her nude tetas warm against my side.

"Move back. Move back so I can seal the hole."

She ran her fingers down my back to send a thrill through me with rippling skin, and she smiled to watch my response. "Use your magic. Then join me there." She pointed at a woven mat between two fins of the silk tree's trunk where it braced itself to the forest floor.

As she pushed away from me, I took out the glass eye and mumbled in English, "This isn't about the armadillo's hole and it isn't about spirits of illness; it's about the dangers we brought with us from the village." I bent down to scan the hole with the Irishman's eye just as Catrina's perfume cut into the moist air to make me almost faint from the sweetness of it, and I knew if I stood she would be in front of me wearing only her beads, the beads she hoped would cover the strawberry on her neck but didn't, and she would take my hand to lead me to her bed, and in my foolishness I would go thinking maybe this time she meant something more than to amuse herself, and in spite of my anger I felt the arousal Catrina's musk and soft voice and lips always engendered in me. "I won't do it, Catrina," I said, not looking up. "Not now, not ever again. Have one of your many other lovers suck strawberries onto your neck. I'm done with you. Done with you. Done with you."

"Are you now?" Catrina's voice mocked. "Then go to your jungle bunny who awaits in a savage stench beneath the lifesaver tree."

Her voice faded as I stood, and Catrina shimmered like one of the water-bug dancers turning into an illness, shimmered fine and clear until she vanished altogether and I looked up into the canopy of the silk-cotton tree thinking it would make thousands of lifesavers, if people still used the pulp of the tree to stuff life jackets—which no one has done for years. I turned around with some dread to deal with the tetas and insistence of Kaita's temptation.

She lay on the mat, her skirt beside her, her dark triangle shimmering in the jungle canopy light, her tetas more magnificent than ever; she lay in stale musk, jungle musk unwashed and unperfumed, though the lack of perfume didn't keep Kaita's face from becoming Catrina's face or stop the two names from swimming before me: Kaita Catrina Kaita Catrina Kaita in similar sounds pounding in my ears though Catrina's body was tall, white, alabaster, cream, and this Kaita was short, brown, nut-brown, glorious. The words of Robert Burns came to me: "A standing cock hath no conscience"; with the words came a quickening of breath, fingers—my own fingers—going to the buttons of my shirt, hesitating, dropping away. "But you have a husband," my voice said, my ears scarcely hearing, my fingers returning to the buttons.

"Come to me." She reached a brown hand toward me in sign language speaking a universal sensuality where perfume didn't matter, where stale jungle musk unwashed became equal to soaped and powdered and perfumed female flesh. "The way of the jungle people is not the same as the way of the white missionaries. Come to me."

I took a step, loosened a button. "The way of the jungle people or your way?"

"My way. Come to me. My husband goes often upriver. I become lonely. Lonely. Come to me."

"You have done this before." My fingers, loosening another button, became still.

"Yes."

The button slid back into its slot. "With Poí."

"Yes. The shaman. What does it matter? What does it matter if I take lovers? Come to me."

A glance at my shirt told me all buttons were buttoned, secure, safe. Robert Burns was wrong, then, and I could look at her as I looked at Catrina when her beads clicked apart to reveal the strawberry of her infidelity, the spot she would hide from me and yet not hide and laugh at my discomfort and say love was love and I had no business judging how she loved, and she would reach for me from the nebula of her musk and desire. I could say no. I could say it.

Kaita caught up with me just after I saw Poí salute me with his blowgun and make a show of dropping the dart, blackened, toxic, deadly, into a quiver, then move like a shadow to vanish among the tree trunks of the forest; she caught up with me as she tied the skirt to her waist, leaving her tetas bare to remind me of what I refused. I stopped and looked at her in a slow and sensual raking of eyes from her head to her feet and back again to her wonderful tetas so that, watching my eyes, she caught her breath. "The mat," she began.

"No. But Kaita, you are so beautiful.

13

Just as I finished loading chinchorros and mosquito netting and travel bag into the canoe, Poí emerged from the forest, coming from the direction Kaita had taken Tom. A chill came over me when I saw the shaman carrying one of his blowguns and a quiver of darts. I bent to the scabbard of the hunting knife strapped to an ankle, unsnapped it, and went over the motions in my mind: if Poí had put one of his lethal darts into Tom, I would kneel close to the shaman, then stand with a sudden thrust to slam the knife beneath his ribs and up into his heart. Breathing became labored and shallow as I approached the shaman, and I wondered *can I do it? Can I do it?* knowing all the while that I could and would though it went against all the training of the Sisters of Mercy. "Have you seen Tomás?" I asked and wiped the perspiration from my palm.

"Such a strange man." Poí grinned. "He used his magic eye to examine the burrow of an armadillo and muttered magic words while Kaita dropped her dress upon the mat she had left in the woods for their meeting. I know that mat. She thought any man would come to her if she called, but she was wrong. I like this Tomás, though I thought for a moment he would rip the clothes from his body and take her. Ha! The look on Kaita's face when he turned away. She needs a man to take a stick to her."

"Someone took the paddles from our canoe." I turned so he wouldn't see the relief on my face. Relief for what? I asked myself. For Tom being still alive, certainly, but what else? For not having to feel the quiver of the shaman's heart as it died on the point of my knife? For Tomás turning away from the nude jungle woman?

"There, on the bank downriver, see the canoes of the village? Take any paddles you want from those canoes. It isn't stealing, not here, and the people expect it of you."

When I returned with the paddles, Tom was pushing our canoe into the river, and Kaita, her face burning, helped him. Villagers came to say farewell. Tom pressed some Bolívars into Ne'eng's hand. "For salt," he said.

Ne'eng started to protest, then shrugged. "I'll have the salt when you return."

Kaita looked at Tom with a shy smile. "Thank you for using your magic to cure my baby and to seal the hole in the forest."

Tom's beard shone red in the sun and his Panama hat dropped a shadow over his eyes. He glanced at her with a curt nod and climbed into the canoe. The village women, hands over their mouths, giggled perhaps at Tom, perhaps at Kaita's burning face.

Beyond a single bend of the river the banks took on the look of undisturbed jungle, and it was as if the village didn't exist, as if people had never come to that part of the river. Tom paddled hard, too hard. I looked back at him, at his fixed jaw and determined eyes. "You can slow down now," I said. But he didn't break the rhythm of stroking the water. "So you used your magic to seal the hole in the forest, did you?"

"You know I don't believe in magic."

"I know nothing of the sort. You did a wonderful job with magic yesterday evening. What magic did you use on Kaita in the forest?"

"Maybe I did use a kind of magic. I didn't make her pregnant."

Perhaps I deserved that, I thought, turning my back to him and dipping the paddle into the river. So the shaman had been wrong. Somehow Poí watched Kaita and Tom long enough to conclude they would not lie together on the mat, and he left them, left chuckling to himself and thinking his mistress needed a man to take a stick to her. Probably he would be that man, perhaps he would be beating her as we paddled down the river. The idea of it offended me and yet I found no sympathy for Kaita even if she didn't deserve to be beaten. She also didn't deserve to have Tom lie with her.

As I paddled I became more bothered by images of Tom rutting over the body of the jungle woman and I kept thinking of how he sat behind me in the crow's nest of the chaparro tree. His legs wrapped my thighs, his arms held me, and he did all that in innocent sensuality. Then on a woven grass mat with a stranger—

Stop it, I told myself. What does it matter? He came close to death—that mattered. If Poí had seen Tom sexing with Kaita, a poisoned dart would no doubt have gotten him. But Poí had not seen them, and Tom was alive here in the canoe, and I was here with him. It had not been necessary for me to puncture the shaman's heart with my knife. That mattered. I glanced at Tom working hard with the paddle, and I struggled to feel relief, struggled to push down anger.

His beard glistened red. I set the paddle aside and turned around to face him. A parrot flew across the river to a low branch dragging water, and the bird dipped its great curved beak into the river. I thought of the juggling myth and imagined the parrot to be using its magic beak for fashioning water eyes to set into the head of the eyeless jaguar, the unwise jaguar who risked her eyes in a foolish game but would have new eyes, better ones that saw in the dark. Anger ebbed and with it came worry for Tom. "Is this a good time to ask you about the name you spoke, to ask about Catrina?"

He set the paddle across the canoe, took off his hat, and wiped his face on a sleeve. "She had the mark of a strawberry on her neck." He shook his head as if shaking away a fly. "I don't need to be paddling so hard, do I? I don't need to be wound so tight that I miss seeing the jungle and the river. Orchids grow in that tree, and look. Parrots eat the orchids. What a salad, what a magnificent and beautiful salad." He put his hat on and smiled. "Perhaps we're entering our jungle at last."

"So it's not a good time to ask, is it?"

"No. Yes. I don't know." He stroked his beard, watched the parrots.

I waited. "Maybe we should float downriver in the shade as much as possible." I reached for the paddle.

"Sit back, please." He took his paddle and used it as a rudder to guide us into the strip of shade close to the edge but not so close as to get us into the shallows where rocks like bones, like the skull of Orocón in Oz's story, protruded to make the river speak its warning. Tom dragged the paddle to keep us in the channel and we watched the greenery, listened to the river and the birds, especially the three-note call of the piha bird, and the heat of day increased. We eyed each other, and it seemed to me we both let go of the hostility engendered by our stay in the jungle village. Neither of us spoke until Tom spotted the jaguar.

"Look." He pointed, and I turned toward the far bank to see the cat drinking. It looked at us, water dripping from its chin, its water eyes glistening like sun striking the river. "Magnificent. Like a house cat, but more beautiful, far more beautiful."

His voice was so full of awe that I almost saw the jaguar as he did. It stood upright and held one paw up, crooked, watching us. "Not like a house cat. It looks at us with measuring eyes. The jaguar would eat us if it could. Look at its size, so huge. I've heard that only the Bengal tiger is bigger, that this jaguar is as fierce in its ripping into the human body with teeth and claws as any tiger in the orient." I glanced at Tom and regretted my words.

The sense of wonder dropped away from his face and he seemed to sag. "I see it," he whispered. "I see it. Maybe we haven't reached our jungle yet."

"Can I ask you now about the woman who haunts you?" I could see as soon as I asked the question that the timing was right. He nodded a slow nod and we watched the jaguar resume drinking, though it still observed us, and Tom began talking.

So Rosa wanted to hear about Catrina, did she? I stared at the big cat and thought about Joey, about the tiger that nearly got him, about the heat and stink of another jungle, about the laminated photograph I used to carry before Phung Phuoc pissed on it; I stared at the jaguar's predatory eyes knowing they weren't those of a house cat after all but like those I imagined the tiger to have as it stalked the starburst of sleeping soldiers, and I began telling Rosa about Catrina though it wasn't so much about her as a jumble of other details that included

Catrina, or at least her photograph. In another jungle, I told Rosa, not so long ago, after I found the strawberry beneath Catrina's beads, after I filed divorce papers, after I joined up and went through basic training and crossed the Pacific and bunkered into a hill where we rained nighttime death on the boys of Ho Chi Minh when they drove mouse deer to clear the path of mines; after rain fell over the jungle enough times to wash holes in my heart, the lieutenant told us to bed down in star formation, which were his words for circling with our heads together and feet out like a starburst so if any hostiles appeared from any direction we could sit up and open fire without hitting our own men. Allen spread his poncho on my right, Joey on my left. We slept in our clothes, boots and all, which was fortunate for Joey because in the night the big cat grabbed him by a boot.

"The latrine is under that durian tree," the lieutenant said. "Bury your shit and don't smoke tonight. Charlie has a nose like a bloodhound and will find us if we hang any spoor on the wind."

"Snakes can find us," Allen said, glancing about, "spoor or no spoor. Cobras. Maybe king cobras."

Nobody in that jungle owned a chinchorro. I told Rosa we slept on the ground, told her what the lieutenant said, what Allen said about Catrina fucking all of my buddies, and I struggled with the words because in brushing up on Spanish before going to Venezuela to find Rosita I used books that didn't contain such words as fucking, and the nasty ones I learned as a child struck me as children's words, lacking the raw power and nastiness of a word like fuck. I told Rosa we bedded down damp with fungus working away between my toes and all of us reeking like a locker room so it didn't matter if we didn't bury our shit or if we smoked since there was plenty of spoor leaking from each of us for the wind to catch if any came up, plenty to grab the bloodhound nose of Charlie and lead him right to our star formation on the jungle floor, not that we made much of a starburst with there being only six of us left after the firefight that morning.

Allen watched me take a laminated photograph from my billfold. "You stare at that bitch every night," he said.

"Yeah." I held Catrina, who looked at me from behind the plastic lamination, and she was a knockout in her fake buckskins and with her beads and her million-kilowatt smile.

"And yet she fucked all your buddies and you had to get rid of her. That's goddam weird."

"Yeah. Only it was mainly women she was after, it turns out."

"A lesbo. Goddam. You didn't tell me that." Allen propped himself up on an elbow and reached for the photograph. "Lemme see her."

"She told me love is love and it wasn't my business to judge how she loved." I handed him the picture. "It was a man, though, that put the strawberry on her neck. Todd. My brother."

"No shit? She diddled your brother and her married to you? No shit. She swings both ways, and your own brother put a hickey on her neck—that must have been a real downer. She is fucking gorgeous, though. Fucking gorgeous." He passed the photo back to me. "How come you look at her every night?"

"I don't know. I just do it, and seeing her makes this frigging war a little easier to take." I didn't tell Allen that I sometimes talked to her and I imagined how she would answer. Later, she started talking to me without my having to imagine it or look at her photograph, which I didn't have anyway, not after Phung Phuoc pissed on her; she started talking to me after he took to wielding the rattan, after the long marches at night with my hands tied, after I got loose and Allen handed me the sharpened bamboo stick with its black point glistening from moisture and dirt and I went after Phung Phuoc and the dizziness hit me for the first time but not the last to be sure. Not the last.

I looked at Catrina's photograph again, not with anger but wishing she had been able to commit herself as I had committed to her. I might as well have been angry at the insects for making the jungle so loud at night. Or angry at the fungus growing between my toes or the clouds for dumping on us or the durian tree for befouling the air.

"Goddam stinking tree," Joey muttered.

"If you'd just eat a durian," Allen said, "you'd appreciate the smell."

"Only a goddam gook could eat something that smells more like dog shit than dog shit." Joey's voice went up an octave, and he sounded like a pimple-faced and burger-uniformed kid you would expect to find at a McDonald's counter, which is just what he was except that he wore damp combat fatigues and lay on the floor of a jungle in starburst formation, his piece beside him ready to deal death. "One sumbitching durian tree stinks up the whole jungle, the whole fucked-up country to make you want to puke, and dumb shits like you come along to talk about eating one."

"Elephants like them," Allen said.

"That makes elephants shit-eaters, same as the gooks."

"No, listen, goddamit. Vietnamese think the ripe pulp of the durian fruit is an aphrodisiac. When they fall out of the tree, they're damn near ripe, and folk gather the big spiky bastards, hack them open, and eat them. You know what they say? They say when the durians come down, the sarongs go up."

"Nasty," Joey said.

"No, listen. Like I said, elephants eat the fruit and a lot of times they swallow them whole, and the fruit goes through the elephant to get dropped out when it shits. Vietnamese poke through elephant shit for the durians because the elephant guts ripen the fruit to perfection. You eat an elephant-ripened durian and you can diddle away for hours. Days, maybe."

"What a bullshit country," Joey said. "Whole goddam country ought to be on a leash."

"The fruit is sweet, damn sweet. Eating a durian is like sitting over the honey bucket in the latrine and eating raspberries. They're good to eat even if they smell like shit."

"Eat raspberries in the latrine? Allen, you're one sick mother fucker." Joey snorted.

"There's wild elephants around here. I aim to find a pile of elephant shit and fish out a durian for you, Joey, and if you got any balls, you'll eat the gut-cured durian. What do you say, Don? Think we ought to get Joey to eat an elephant-shit durian? If he starts stalking the mouse deer and humping water buffalo, we'll know the gooks ain't lying about durian being an aphrodisiac."

"You guys hold it down," the lieutenant said. "Knock off the gab and get some sleep."

We did it: we scrunched around on the ground to smooth out lumps, and we went to sleep like tired animals, or at least I did in spite of the buzzing of cicadas, the croaks and bleeps from jungle creatures, the boinging cry of a bird that Allen called a night jar, a big goofy-looking bird that made electronic boings loud enough to be heard over the insects and frogs, though none of them kept me from drifting off and dreaming about Catrina, which is what I was doing when Joey started screaming.

It was shaping up to be a wet dream, a holy dream, with Catrina wearing only dangly earrings and working me over with her lips and tongue, and the ecstasy of our touching blended us into one, into a union so profound only a dream could do justice to it because words never would, though I knew even as I dreamed and knew it to be a dream that what we had, Catrina and I, was mystic in its beauty, holy, divine, sacred; and I wept, lying on the jungle floor in a starburst formation with five guys who smelled worse than the durian tree—I wept while watching and feeling the dream of blending through sex with Catrina; I watched my past self that didn't weep, didn't think, didn't know anything but the moment, the ecstasy, and sure didn't know she used her body to stir others, plenty of others, my own brother even, and women, into heights I thought accessible only to us in our blending love. It was from such a dream that Joey's screaming jerked me back into the nasty jungle.

I snatched up my piece when Joey opened fire even while he screamed, and the staccato light from his barrel showed me a tiger holding Joey's foot in its mouth to drag him from our starburst, the eyes of the tiger surprised by the light and noise, surprised enough for the tiger to drop the booted foot, and Joey kept firing, aiming high. The lieutenant got a flashlight beam on the tiger as it vanished among the trees and Joey stopped firing. "A fucking tiger, a fucking tiger," Joey said in his high-pitched voice.

We were all on our feet except for Joey who lay prone, babbling in a shaking voice, "a fucking tiger," seeming unaware of the lieutenant's flashlight right in his face so we could see drool starting to foam around his lips.

"Stand up, goddamit," the lieutenant told him, and Allen grabbed Joey like he was a child and stood him on his feet.

We went back to sleep, five of us, with the sixth sitting up like a spike in the starburst to watch for the tiger or for Charlie in case he heard Joey's firing. The lieutenant said he should have posted a watch but didn't believe Charlie would find us in the dark or sniff us out with his bloodhound nose on account of the stink from the durian tree giving cover for our locker-room smell, and he hadn't even thought that a tiger might want to make a snack of one of us. Who would think of a tiger, anyway? the lieutenant demanded of us and we all shrugged because none of us ever heard of a tiger trying to eat an American grunt, and Allen said he always figured if a dangerous animal came around it would be a snake. The next morning in the green light coming through high leaves Joey looked at his boot, at the tooth marks, looked at the ground where his body left a scraped place from being dragged by the tiger, and he laughed shrill and high with a crazy edge to the laughter, an edge that set my backbone to tingling and made Allen pound on Joey's back like he was choking, and I wanted to take Catrina's photo out and talk to her but I didn't because of the other guys standing around looking embarrassed for Joey. I didn't tell Rosa about wanting to look at the photo, didn't look at Rosa much while I talked but looked mainly at the edge of the canoe and the skull rocks protruding from the shallows at the edge of the channel, at my hands turning the paddle to keep us in out of the dangerous shallows.

When I stopped talking and looked at Rosa, it startled me to find her cheeks wet with tears.

14

"I *warned you* that I was crazy," Tom said. "But you said I was only weird."

"Maybe it's the world that's crazy." I wiped my cheeks and suddenly became aware of the heat. There was more he needed to talk about, more that I wanted to know, especially about Catrina and the mystery man Phung Phuoc he kept mentioning. But the moment shifted, driven away partly by heat, and it wasn't the right time to ask. Our canoe slipped in and out of the shade as the sun neared noon. "We need to put ashore now and wait out the hot part of the day under some tree. We could nap in our hammocks, if you want."

A squirrel chattered, a tall bird at the edge of the water used its orange beak to spear a frog, and from somewhere among the trees came the flapping sound of doves flying. Such sights and jungle noises appeared to soothe Tom. "Maybe we've finally reached our jungle. Maybe we've finally gone past the areas we missed in our sleep that first night when you were still Rosita and we thought this was a lake. I want to go ashore—and don't tell me again that our childhood jungle is gone. It isn't."

We put ashore behind a finger of a sandbar that reached into the river where it turned. Ground palms, ferns, lianas, and other plants crowded the water's edge. Tom stepped into the vegetation, machete swinging, and in minutes had a path cleared into the shade of taller trees. He grinned at me. "We could walk through the woods to the savanna, leaving a trail of twigs to mark the way back. You don't know how many times I've relived that memory. The papaya we found. How you stood on my shoulders to pick it from the tree. The berries you plucked to dye my hair brown so the locals wouldn't mistake me again for the son of El Don; how the dye didn't work as you planned, and you gave me purple hair, and I tried to see it in the fracturing mirror of the river. I loved that purple hair, though it alarmed my parents when I made it back home. You can dye my hair purple again, if you want."

I stepped from the canoe, alpargatas in hand, liking the cool of the water, the clarity of it in the calm place behind the sandbar. "We'll bathe here before going on. I brought soap."

"Of course you brought soap. You brought everything in that magic bag. Medicine. Food."

I waded ashore. "The food is gone. We'll have to find something here. Nuts, maybe, or bananas."

"Or papaya." There was such enthusiasm in his voice that I began to feel excited by the prospect of foraging. "Mangoes, maybe," he added.

"Mangoes. Yes. Or we could catch some fish."

"Fish! I had forgotten. Fish." He stood on the trail he had hacked, machete in hand and steaming with sweat, his beard shining and his eyes those of a little boy looking at me in adoration. It was not adoration of me but of the moment, of the jungle, of the notion of catching fish, of recapturing something we shared eighteen years ago, and I felt it, too, with a quickening of my heart.

"I'll strip some bark for twine," I said, and though I had brought a ball of fishing string and hooks, the time wasn't right to get them out. The moment demanded bark twine and wooden hooks.

Tom reached into his leather bag, clinked around among the glass eye and bone and coins, and he pulled out a pocketknife. "A Barlow. Look. It took me most of one day back in the States to find a Barlow like this. It looks exactly like the one I carried into the jungle before, except for being stainless steel. I'll use it to carve hooks, if I can find some hardwood." He turned to poke through the brush.

"Didn't we carve a fishhook with the machete?" I meant my comment as teasing, but he turned a serious face to me.

"Machete? Not with the Barlow?"

"I think the Barlow got washed away with our clothes at the waterfall. We used a machete."

"Yes." He folded the Barlow, dropped it into the leather pouch. "And we were nude because of falling in the bat shit cave and having to wash our clothes." He began unbuttoning his shirt.

"We were children, Tom. Stop that."

"Yeah." His voice sounded vague, the tone distant. "Children." He rebuttoned his shirt with one hand while the other used the machete to move aside brush in his quest for hardwood.

Under the high canopy I found the bark that made string, stripped enough for fishing, and returned to the canoe. Tom sat on a boulder, carving his fishhook with the machete. I dropped the bark string beside him and waded to the side of the canoe. "Only one chinchorro," I said. "While I was getting paddles someone took one of our chinchorros. This is bad."

"Oh yeah? Snitched a hammock, did they." He made a dismissive gesture. "We don't need it."

"I still have the mosquito netting. But only one hammock."

"So we sleep on the ground. I know, I know. You say the kissing bug will nibble on our cheeks and leave us with encephalitis. We'll climb a tree, then. Or double up in the hammock."

A quick check of the twine Kaita had used to make the chinchorro reassured me. "We can sleep two in this one. It's strong enough. I'll show you how it works—your head at one end, mine at the other to divide the hammock into two that are almost like separate ones. There will be a wall of mesh between us."

"We don't need that," Tom said.

While he continued with his carving, I hung the chinchorro between two trees where thick shade made the air cool. I sat on the hammock and watched Tom push the machete into moist earth close to the water and find a grub. "Bait," he said, holding it up. "I'll catch some lunch."

"Rest first," I suggested, patting the hammock. "Let the heat of day pass, then we'll catch a meal and cook it."

"You rest." He walked on the sandbar and looked at the deeper part of the river. After securing a river stone close to the hook, he dropped the bait into the water and settled on the sandbar to wait. I dropped my sandals, dusted my feet, and stretched out in the hammock, glad mosquito netting wasn't necessary right then. The heat, oppressive in the sun, was less bad beneath the trees, and the hum of insects blended with the gurgle of the river and with the dizzying heat to weigh heavy on my eyelids.

A tree in the forest moved, a close one, and I wondered how that could be when there was no breeze. It moved again, coming closer, leaning left then right as it approached, and I recognized it as a thorn just as Mata-Mata pushed close to the hammock and leaned to look me in the eye. "I did a terrible thing," he said. "I killed my grandmother."

The message puzzled me until I realized that the voice, the face was not that of Mata-Mata but mine. "Abuelita," I whispered. "Did I kill you?"

She lay in the hammock, Abuelita, tiny and emaciated from the cholera. "You murdered Poí," she accused, her voice strong in spite of the frail body, the yellow eyes with lids half-closed and the eyes within sliding toward death, sliding dry and yellow and creaking in their slide, creaking like a door on a rusty hinge.

"No," I said, and the tree on my shoulder grew, staggering me. "But it isn't fair. I didn't kill anyone."

"You unsnapped your knife," Abuelita's voice came out in a shriek. "You planned to plunge it under his ribs and up into his heart. That's the same as killing him, the same to your soul even if he still lives."

"But I didn't do it," I said and sat up in the hammock.

"That's all right," Tom said. "I did it for us."

"Did what?" My hand went to my shoulder, and I expected to feel the trunk of the thorn protruding from it. Abuelita's voice shrieked again. I looked at Tom in bewilderment.

"Caught a catfish. A big one. It's tied through the gills to the canoe. Perhaps it's time to siesta. You can show me how to sleep two to the hammock now."

"But that noise." Even as I spoke, the meaning of the sound came to me. "A monkey. Tom, there is a monkey, and look! Another!"

"Yeah." He chuckled. "It's been whooping and yelling at me, just one, and I could hear others off in the distance answering. I guess the others are arriving. They're kind of comical for all the noise they produce."

"No." I sprang to my feet, the visions of Mata-Mata and my grandmother fading into the heat. "No. Not comical. Take down that side of the chinchorro. Do it fast."

"But why?" He caught the urgency in my voice and began working on the rope. The knot on my side resisted, remained tight, and I broke a fingernail just as the first monkey threw its foul missile. It whizzed past me and splattered against a tree. The jungle filled with the shouts of the monkeys.

"Howler monkeys," I said.

"Ay-yi-yi," Tom said as two black spots appeared with successive thumps on the front of his shirt. "They're throwing their own shit."

"Yes. Hurry." Some caught me in the hair, some on the cheek, odious, stinking. An entire tribe of howlers had gathered, shrieking, baring teeth, leaping from tree to tree and throwing.

"Leave the hammock." Tom fled as more excrement hit him.

I bent, grabbed my alpargatas with one hand and took the hunting knife from its scabbard in the other, and I stood in a parody of the way I had planned to do in killing Poí. With a couple of quick hacks on the rope, I freed the end of the chinchorro, then stepped to the other tree for the other end as the monkeys bombarded me. The howlers turned up their volume and hit me again and again as I gathered the chinchorro and ran down the trail.

Tom had untied the canoe. "Hurry!" He climbed into the boat as the howlers reached the bank, scrambling through the thicket of undergrowth, shouting and filling the air with filth.

I threw the hammock, sandals, and knife into the boat and got in fast. But not fast enough. More excrement hit me on the arms, the back. The canoe tipped, settled as I grabbed the paddle and Tom pushed us into the river's flow.

The hoots and screams of the howlers faded behind us as we plunged paddles into the water. "Shit-slinging monkeys," Tom said in wonder.

I stopped paddling, turned around. "It's in your hair, on your cheek."

"They got you worse," Tom said. "You're covered in shit. We both are."

"Let's find a place to bathe. Fast."

"Not so fast. The monkeys will catch up with us and do it all over again, though I can't figure out how they can shit so much." Tom tried for a laugh but it came out more like a snarl.

Breathing through my mouth and hoping the monkey shit wouldn't run down my face to my lips, I resumed paddling with great vigor. The stench was nearly unbearable, and the heat from the sun and from my body made the smell worse. Our canoe went with such speed that the catfish Tom had caught and tied to the side surfaced and struggled to dive. When we spotted rocks and sand catching a calm place in the river, we angled toward it without speaking, and without speaking we plunged overboard in the shallow water, splashing, stripping, throwing our clothing on boulders. Tom sat on the bottom, bending forward to thrust his head under and came up sputtering, rubbing his scalp. I took the rope and secured the canoe to a rock, then reached into the travel bag for a bar of soap.

Tom took it from me and began soaping my hair. I took it back and lathered his head, and we peered at each other through slit eyes with him bending forward so I could better reach the top of his head. His beard resisted lathering and felt like wire, but I persisted until his whole head was white like that of a cockatoo, his eyes closed, his hands still on my head. "Sit," I said, and we both sat on the sandy bottom. He leaned forward and held the soap while I rinsed his head.

"Now you." He rubbed the lather from my hair as I dipped again and again into the water.

I flipped my hair forward, twisted the water from it, flung it back, and said, “Stand.” Tom stood and I moved around him, soaping his chest and back. He dived flat with a huge splash, then returned.

"Now you," he said, and I held my arms out and turned as he rubbed me with soap.

15

It arrived, I thought with a thrill that ran from the top of my head to my feet and the excitement of it clutched my stomach, brought tears not just from soap burn but something more profound in the shade of banded palms leaning toward the river where I washed the brown body of Rosita become Rosa, Rosita with breasts high and wonderful and eyes closed in pleasure with such eyelashes curling upward as I'd never seen, the corners of her eyes tipping up from Indio heritage that ultimately came from Asia, a good Asia of the distant past and not the one where a tiger had dragged Joey from the starburst, not the Asia of Phung Phuoc but a clean Asia like the clean soap I rubbed on Rosa's back: the moment has arrived at last, the magic moment of being nude to the river and jungle and sun and one another in intense innocence. It finally arrived.

She dove shallow as I had done, dove and turned, stood to splash herself where foam floated, drifted, the river carrying away lather, her body sparkling with beads of water like diamonds when sun made it to her in specks through high fronds of the banded palm. For a long moment we stood, dripping, looking at each other, stood in crystal water and air perfumed from orchids, pure air warm and rich and filtered through a jungle garden perfect in the perfect moment of Rosa wading to me, around me, to run a finger the length of a scar and press her lips to it. "What wounded you here?"

"Rattan. A springy piece fresh stripped of bark. I heard it whistle in the air, and it ripped my shirt when it hit. Don't ask me about that right now."

"We'll wash our clothes, then. And the chinchorro. Those monkeys are so disgusting. And yet there's something else about their presence. I'm glad that the monkeys came."

"Glad? Glad to be covered with monkey shit? Amazing."

"Yes. If it had not been for their horrid roaring and flinging of filth, we would still be dressed and formal. From excrement and corruption came our trusting bath together. It was a gift to be so attacked, though when they were messing into their hands and throwing at us it wasn't possible to think of their action as a gift."

"It seems I'm not the only one present who is weird. Glad." I shook my head, amazed at the connection between the arrival of our magic moment, the moment I knew would come without knowing the exact form it might take, the connection between such intimacy as adults seldom feel and the shit-slinging monkeys. Rosa made the connection, so it would be, I decided, enough to be glad that she found some explanation, however odd and far-fetched. I could be glad right then even for monkey shit.

The sun crept over us as we soaped and pounded our clothes, working like the women I remembered from childhood who gathered under a highway bridge to dunk clothes in the waters of El Tigre River, dunk them and twist them into lumps and lay them on a boulder to pound with stones. A uniformed policeman watched the women, and my mother turned to my father with a question: "What is he guarding them from?" But this was the wrong question my father said, the wrong question because it was based on a foreign notion of the presence of police, a belief that someone in uniform had the duty to protect citizens, a notion that I had to unlearn in the jungles and rice paddies of Asia. The policeman stood beside the river, my father explained, to collect tax, to charge the women for washing clothes in the government waters of El Tigre, though the only part of the government to profit from such tax was the policeman himself and his boss, the chief of police for the village. Women would sneak past the government if they could, so the uniformed policeman watched, counted, kept track of who entered the waters with baskets of clothes.

I wasn't so good at clothes washing the native way, though of course the native women in the El Tigre River even back in the time of my childhood weren't nude nor the river water so pristine nor the jungle behind them like the primordial garden Rosa and I finally found beyond flesh-eating butterflies, beyond the shaman who pissed on leaves with the sound of urine hitting a photograph, beyond Kaita's calculated infidelity, Kaita unaware of her shaman lover watching, waiting to put a dart tipped with poison into my back, poison that could kill in seconds if I did as my brother had done when Catrina tempted him, though I wasn't present when she did it, when Todd succumbed to Catrina's temptation, wasn't watching like the shaman who wanted to put a dart in my back in the way of Mata-Mata killing the man who raped his wife even if Kaita weren't the shaman's wife and I no rapist; I wasn't so good at pounding rolled-up cloth with a river stone and yet the black filth that I was supposed to be glad about lifted away to leave only brown stains, and we hung the clothes and the hammock on bushes as we had hung our clothing to dry on the bank of the same river eighteen years before. "We'll sunburn," Rosa said; I knew she was about to say it before the words came out, knew how it would sound in the richer voice of Rosa instead of the higher and thinner voice of Rosita when she worried about the sun.

"I don't care." And I didn't. Let me roast, I thought. Crisp. Die, even, if dying were the price of bathing nude and washing one another and monkey-shit clothes in the wild river with Rosa.

"I wish. I wish." Rosa's voice trailed off. We sat on a warm rock, a clean rock in a small bit of shade sprinkled with sun and the sweet smell of orchids, dangling our feet in the water.

"Wish what?" I prompted.

"That you hadn't made love with Kaita."

I stared in astonishment. "But I didn't. Not that she wasn't tempting. I didn't. If I had, Humpty Dumpty would have shot one of his poisoned darts into me, and I'd be dead instead of sitting here with you, more alive than I've been in eighteen years."

"You exaggerate. Catrina must have made you feel alive."

"Yes. Once." Confusion washed over me in brown, unclean waves.

"And you turned down Kaita because you feared the shaman's dart?"

"No. I saw him later. No." Somehow the moment fled. "We'll sunburn." I stood in the shallows, waded toward the canoe. "Didn't you say you brought extra clothes for us both?"

Wearing khaki trousers and tee shirts, we cleared a path through a tangle of plants to the shade of the canopy, the high canopy that was as much jungle to me as the plants I hacked through at the water's edge, plants like those Ramar of the Jungle fought with his jungle knife, plants that in the movies looked impenetrable, which is what *jangala* meant in Sanskrit before the word wore away to the English jungle, though of course the jungle attacked by Hollywood men in British white and pith helmets was no more impenetrable than were the plants at the river's edge. On the silver screen Ramar of the Jungle never sweated as I did in clearing a path, as Rosa did. By the time we reached the shade, our tee shirts were wet and clinging, Rosa's doing so in a way to remind me her *tetas* were far better shaped than those of Kaita, a thought that annoyed me not because of Rosa's beauty but because I didn't want to see her as a beautiful woman, not right then in our jungle—if we had reached our jungle and weren't walking in a South American version of an Asian jungle, a place that could produce such people as Phung Phuoc or Dumb Fuck as Allen called him though not to his face at least not more than once but under his breath for only me to hear and make me laugh in spite of rope cutting my wrists and thirst and the pain Dumb Fuck's rattan left on my back in bloody lines to grab with scabs what was left of my shirt.

I pulled my tee shirt off, slung its wetness over my shoulder. "Keep yours on, if you wish, though it doesn't cover much when it's wet." I worked not to look at her.

"It'll dry when I become still."

"We should eat, though I dread building a fire in this heat."

"I would build a fire out there, on the sandbar." She pointed with her knife. "Perhaps you have learned to clean a catfish since we were children?"

"Yes. Skin it, gut it, wash it in the river. I'll do that."

"Take care when blood gets in the water. It'll attract caribe. Blood could attract other creatures as well."

Caribe. It named a tribe of native people along the Orinoco River, though as a child I didn't know that; I knew only that it named cannibal fish, called by people elsewhere piranha. We returned to the river, to the open sun, and I slipped the wet tee shirt back on. "Other creatures such as what?"

"Do you remember any of them from our last trip on this river?"

"No."

"Tom. Stop being dense. Remember how the anaconda took the deer?"

"I doubt an anaconda would find blood interesting. It likes to eat its meals whole and not bleeding. Crushed, maybe, and drowned. But not bleeding."

"Maybe. What about the black caimán? The one that came for me when I jumped into the river to wash off the ants. That one was longer than our canoe."

"Not quite that long."

"We argue over silly matters, and it's my fault. Just be careful, please?" She began gathering wood for the fire.

Smoke drifted down the river until Rosa cupped her hands to splash water on the fire. We retreated to the cool canopy to eat catfish from broad leaves, and the meat tasted as sweet and delicious as I remembered from childhood, though the raw fishy odor on my hands annoyed me as did a place on one thumb where a catfish fin got me; and I wasn't entirely pleased with the chemical taste of water in our canteen. Rosa had made a mat of broad leaves for our picnic, and we sat leaning against the fin-like brace of a silk-cotton tree while we ate. "Rain will come," Rosa said, "before the day is over."

"Our clothes." I started to get up.

She took my arm. "Not yet. Finish eating, then we'll find a way to keep our clothes from becoming more wet. Perhaps here, where this tree curves, we can be out of the rain or out of most of it. Drops will get us from the high leaves."

When rain came, we had our laundry, still damp, on a rack made of branches and covered with broad leaves. The canopy stirred to the sound of water as if a river washed over us in the high green, and it took long minutes for water to drip from leaf to leaf before any fell around us. Light fled into a twilight from the clouds and the canopy, and the air cooled with the great drops hitting us now and then in spite of the way we sheltered against the trunk of the vast silk-cotton tree, cooled enough for Rosa to shiver and draw closer to me, though I found the cool a welcome change. "I didn't think to build a fire," she said with a note of apology.

"Neither did I." My comment was supposed to be irony for humor, but she glanced at me with a serious look.

"Men never have thought about fire in the ways women do," she said, then told me a story she had learned from her grandmother, an unpromising story at first, though it became wonderful before taking a dark turn.

Long ago before people had fire, they cooked their cassava cakes in the sun or by holding the dough in their armpits. "That's gross," I said, and reminded her of Mamacita Moreno's husband bringing us *pan de mano* clutched under his arm while he carried bowls of beans in his hands, reminded her that neither of us would eat the bread after it rode from the kitchen to the table among the arm hair and foul smells of his unwashed body.

"I remember. I agree. But Abuelita told me the story with that detail in it: people cooked their bread by holding it in their armpits. Probably only men ate the bread." Her cheeks dimpled.

Wind stirred high overhead to ripple leaves and sift mist upon us, and Rosa shivered against me. Her hair smelled like fresh corn.

A woman and her daughter, back when men ate armpit bread, erected a ladder against a cliff, and the mother held the ladder for her daughter to climb to a macaw's nest for the eggs, which they would eat raw because people didn't know about fire and because the woman and daughter had no desire to eat body-heated cassava mush. The girl's father watched, knowing he would be the first to eat though he refused to take part in the building of the ladder or holding it for the safety of his daughter; he stood at the cliff's talus looking up so he saw the angry Macaw when it rushed into the face of the girl, startling her so much she dropped the eggs, which turned into stones in the air and bloodied the nose of the father. He became so angry that he removed the ladder, leaving his daughter stranded on a tiny ledge, and he forced his wife to accompany him back to the village, striking her with a stick when she whimpered about the fate of their daughter.

The girl stayed for days high on the cliff, starving and becoming thinner until a jaguar happened by, a mother jaguar who recognized the girl as a cub in need of help, and it was no ordinary jaguar back in the days when people had no fire and animals could talk, for this jaguar carried something people had not invented. It carried a bow, a quiver of arrows, and a length of rope. She tied the rope to an arrow, told the girl to be still, and fired her arrow into the cliff beside the stranded girl. "Slide down the rope," the jaguar said, but the girl was too frightened by the gleam of the jaguar's teeth, by the sudden flight of the arrow and the rope like a snake striking the cliff, by the idea of sliding down a thin-looking rope, but the jaguar coaxed her until she took the rope and slid down, burning her hands to make her cry out in spite of her joy to be down from the cliff. "Ride on my back," the jaguar said. "I'll take you to my den."

"You'll cut me into pieces with your great claws and eat me with your gleaming teeth," the girl said, trembling.

"I'll love you as a daughter. I'll feed you and play with you and never abandon you as your human parents did." The voice of the jaguar purred and soothed; climb on my back, she said, and ride through the garden jungle of frangipani blossoms sweeter than banana leaves, of orchids and parrots and piha birds to my den where you will never be hungry, and the girl, her fear slipping away, climbed on the animal's back where fur softer than feathers soothed her thin legs, and powerful muscles beneath the fur rippled with movement smooth and quick, hypnotic in the female jaguar's loping rhythm beneath perfumed trees.

16

A*t first Tom* loved the story of the jaguar carrying her adopted daughter through the jungle. We settled on the ground, on a mat of leaves, and leaned against the tree and each other. Rain fell noisy like a windy surf above us, and huge drops gathered in the trees before falling around us.

The female jaguar, I told Tom, carried the starving girl to its den where it fed her cooked meat, for the jaguar knew the magic of fire. The girl had never tasted meat so good because people didn't know about fire. She liked to watch the yellow light dance above the crackling wood, and she wanted to touch it. Jaguar kept her fire in the end of a hollow log beside her den, and the girl played around the log.

Mother jaguar watched in amused indulgence, but the jaguar's mate was less amused. He became jealous of the attention his wife gave to the human cub. The female jaguar taught her new daughter the use of bow and arrow and taught her to roast meat. The male jaguar waited until his mate went on a hunting trip, then scratched the girl's face. She took up the bow and arrow and killed the male jaguar. Then she put some cooked meat into a leather pouch and fled with it and with the bow and a quiver of arrows.

Back in her own village, she shared the meat with her parents. Her father took the weapons and the meat to neighbors, and he claimed he had discovered them. Never had people eaten such good meat, and they wanted more, so the father forced his daughter to take him to the jaguar's den so he could steal fire. But the log was too heavy for people to carry, so they sought help from animals. Many gathered to watch and many offered help, but none had the strength to lift the log until the tapirs came along. They lifted the log and carried the fire away from the jaguar's den. Bits of fire sputtered out of the log, and the father asked the toad to put it out because he didn't want the jaguar to keep any of the fire. So the toad hopped along behind the tapirs, spitting on all the bits of fire that fell out, extinguishing them.

When the mother jaguar returned from her hunt, she was furious at the murder of her mate and the theft of her fire. She vowed to be an enemy of people from then on. She vowed never again to use bow and arrow but to rely on her teeth and claws. She vowed never to use fire again except in her angry eyes at night.

Tom had become brooding and quiet as I finished the story. "The middle part was good," he said.

"And you disliked the last part?"

"Yes."

"Why?"

"I don't know. I just didn't like it."

"Good." I patted his arm. "What part did you dislike?"

"I don't know. The girl killed the male jaguar."

"He scratched her."

"Yes. There's that. But to kill for a scratch? And she stole from her adopted mother, who loved her."

"You didn't like the betrayal."

"No. And her father. I didn't like him, either."

"Why?"

"I don't know. I just didn't."

"You understand the story well, Tom. I like you for that. Abuelita told me some people regard the father as a hero for bringing fire to humans. It seems to me that the story would have to be told in a different way for the father to be a hero."

"I liked the jungle garden that the mother jaguar walked through, carrying her new daughter."

"Yes. That's the best part of the story, the part where there is nothing in the future but hope and promise. Or it seems that way when you don't know about the fire and the male jaguar and the thieving girl."

We waited out the rain in silence, huddling close though closeness was an illusion. Tom had not been close since he announced it was time to put clothes on, and I grieved the loss of our magic moments of bathing and washing clothes. It was my fault, that loss, though I told myself more magic would come when the time was right for it.

Sitting on the leafy mat to await the end of the rain I knew part of the reason why I had come with Tom to the wild river and the wild jungle. It was for the magic that could come only in moments, moments neither he nor I could force and could not keep—except in memory, of course, like the memories of the magic moments we shared as children. I came for other reasons, ones that had to do with Mata-Mata and his wearing my father's face, reasons I didn't want to explore right then and perhaps not ever.

Ants had already gathered on the remains of our catfish meal when the sound of rain overhead ceased, though the high leaves kept dripping. As we emerged at the river's edge, we heard the roar of a one-engine airplane and caught a glimpse of it. "That doesn't belong here," Tom said.

He seemed angry. I took his arm and we waited, listening to the hum of the plane fade beneath jungle sounds, beneath the river's speaking its warning to gold hunters as it washed over stone skulls in the shallows, beneath the three-note cry of the piha, beneath squawks of a flock of parakeets. "Two rains came in one day," I said. "That might mean rainy season will bring more water than usual. The river could rise fast, and we could be in trouble. We should move on."

"Or it could mean our canoe highway will be bigger and better." He surveyed the trees. "We could make camp here, swing our chinchorro in that tree, stay for a day or two. Remember the Jesus frogs? Maybe we could find one in the heart water of a bromeliad. I had to do some research to find that word, *bromeliad*, since we didn't know it when we were children."

"Jesus frog," I whispered. "Of course I remember. The witch Sylvia turned me into one and I hopped for kilometers on the surface of the river. You saw me."

"That was an illusion created by the witch's hallucinogenic tea, not magic. I became a parrot."

"A beautiful parrot with white plumes."

"Green. I was green."

"Green, then. And it was not magic? But don't answer that. We were much farther down the river when we found the swampy area where the bromeliads grew. I doubt we'll find such plants around here. We should move on."

"One night then. Let's stay one night here." His voice became soft and he looked at the shallows where we had bathed.

"Yes. But don't count on a return of the magic of our bath."

"Magic. When you use the word in that way, I believe in it."

Later, after we shook rainwater from a bush and spread our damp clothes and chinchorro in the sun, after we laid poles and thatched a roof for the night, after we found and peeled guava for dinner, I confessed a fear. "I'm glad you will sleep in the same chinchorro with me because of what might come out of the jungle in the dark."

"What could come? A jaguar?"

"No." We sat on a speckled rock above the water with the sun rushing toward the trees. "You must promise not to laugh."

"Have I ever laughed at you?"

"Yes."

"In a mean way?"

"No. And you better not start now."

"So what could come out of the jungle in the night? Our hammock will be two meters from the ground, so high we'll have to get into it from up in the tree. What could come that could reach that high?"

"I saw him that first night while you slept in the canoe. He wore my father's face."

"Who?"

"Mata-Mata. You remember. The man who had a thorn tree growing from his shoulder."

"You're talking about a dream? Then nothing came from the jungle. Mata-Mata isn't real."

"No? What about Catrina? You said she comes to you and even talks to you. Is she real?"

"Yes. No. I don't want to talk about her. She hasn't bothered me since, since—"

"It's all right, Tom. I'm sorry I mentioned her. To me Mata-Mata was real, and he spoke with my father's voice. He was real, Tom, even if he was not. But I know I make no sense."

"Maybe not. I don't know."

"Thanks for not laughing. If Mata-Mata comes in the night from wherever he comes from, he'll frighten me, and I'll be glad you're there beside me."

"Catrina doesn't frighten me when she comes. She annoys me, and I always tell her to go away."

"Does she?"

"Sometimes. And sometimes I know she isn't really there, though knowing it doesn't make her not be there. Now I'm not making sense."

"But you are."

"She wears buckskins. Fake ones. And beads to cover up the strawberry on her neck, though it always shows, and I know it's there and I know my own brother put it there."

"Have you talked with Todd about your anger with him?"

Tom looked startled. "Anger? With my brother? I'm not angry with Todd. He's a man. Catrina went to him, tempted him, and he did what men do when a beautiful woman presents herself no matter if she's married or not married."

"You sound angry."

"I'm not. Not at Todd. At Catrina, maybe."

"Maybe. Kaita was beautiful."

"Yes."

"And she was married."

Tom looked at me, his lips a thin line, and his beard trembled in the sun. "And I'm a man," he whispered. "I said no, didn't I? But Todd didn't."

"He betrayed you in a moment of weakness. My guess is that he regretted it. Did he tell you about his regret?"

"We never talked about what he and Catrina did."

"Never talked?" The enormity of the matter staggered me. "Never talked?"

"There was no need. I saw his guilt in his eyes, and he saw in mine that I knew."

"You assume too much. You need to talk to your brother."

"We do talk."

"About Catrina?"

"What he and Catrina did happened three years ago. It doesn't matter now."

"It matters. Catrina still haunts you. Her name means *gato,* right? She is a cat?"

"Yes. How did you know that?"

"Everyone knows some English, even in Venezuela. My grandmother would say the spirit of a cat comes to you in the guise of your wife."

"Ex-wife."

"Ex-wife." I bit my lip, for the idea of his having been married and divorced disturbed me, even if it should not. What business did I have to regard this strange man as a possible mate, even if he once was Don, the love of my childhood? Still, the idea that he was divorced bothered me. "My grandmother would say it would help if you explored the nature of the cat spirit that comes to you."

"That's nonsense."

"Be patient with me. There are characteristics of the wild cat, perhaps the jaguar, that would be useful to examine."

"Not to me. I don't deal in such wild speculations. Let other people worry about spirits and ghosts and black magic and other stupid nonsense."

I wanted to tell him not to be so literal. I wanted to tell him the myth of the avenging jaguar, but something about him looked black, and I knew the moment was wrong for telling such a story. Perhaps there would be a proper moment later. "Did you like the guava?"

Tom seemed relieved by the change of subject. "It was the best guava I've ever had. Street vendors in Saigon sell guava, or they used to. They would peel them, cut out the pith in the center, slice them up to remind me of green apples, green all the way through, and drop them into jars of water to keep them crisp for customers like me, though the official word from the army was to avoid eating anything from street vendors, a bit of advice that never stopped me from eating guava from those jars, pulpy and sour and hard and not at all sweet. It wasn't so much that the guava of the street vendors was tasty as it was fun to eat, like chewing on flavored wood. But the guava we just had was sweet. For guava."

"The canoe," I said, "is like a signal that someone is here. We should pull it ashore among bushes."

"Who would travel the river at night?"

"I don't know. Poí might decide to steal more from us. He wants your glass eye, and if he came, words might not stop him this time. He could come with poisoned darts."

17

C*limbing into* the chinchorro from a tree branch proved impossible for me, though Rosa did it with a minimum of trouble. I rehung the hammock lower to the ground, chest-high for me, and I threaded my fingers into a step for Rosa. She stretched the netting, dividing it, and told me to lie in my half, my head at the opposite end from hers, something I resisted at first even knowing her to be right in claiming we would balance better, be more comfortable than with heads together. Our hips touched through the wall of chinchorro that sprang up between us, and we hung together like twins in a cocoon. Mosquito netting flowed around us, gossamer and white in the short twilight, and giant mosquitoes bumped and buzzed against it like slow drones, though Rosa said they weren't the kind that bite, that they were attracted by our warmth, that biting mosquitoes were tiny and fast and some would get to us in spite of the netting, if there were any in the neighborhood.

Rosa wore jeans, still damp, and a white tee shirt, and she smelled fresh, clean, while I had a more sour smell from the shirt and pants I kept on at Rosa's insistence. "They'll provide some protection from insects," she said, "and if you have to get up in the night for any reason, it would be better not to be undressed. Clothes will also keep you warm."

"Warm? I need to keep warm in the jungle?"

"Maybe not. But I do. This is a high jungle following a river on the high plains, after all. To me it gets cool at night."

As we settled into the hammock and the night creatures of the jungle began their chorus, we heard the voices, two of them, indistinct beneath the jungle's singing. "Kaita," I whispered.

"Yes. And Poí in a canoe, and looking for us. Keep quiet."

I glanced at the gleam of the machete hanging on a branch within easy reach, reassured by its presence though it would be no protection if Poí came for us with his blowgun, which he didn't; the splash of paddles and the voices went past us, following the river, and the jungle ratcheted up its volume as final light of day slipped into darkness. "They won't be back tonight," I whispered.

"No."

"You were right to hide the canoe."

"Yes. Go to sleep."

Impossible, I thought, and went to sleep.

"Abuelita," Rosa said, her voice parting the noises of the jungle night. "Abuelita."

I glanced around half expecting to see a person, a bent and tiny woman perhaps, a wrinkled woman who would fit the term abuelita, little grandmother, but I saw only trees glimmering in bits of the moon floating through high leaves.

"Mata-Mata," Rosa said, "take your tree and go away."

"But I must tell my story," a voice said from nowhere, from everywhere. Story. Tell. My. The words seemed jumbled and I wondered if I got them right.

"You're not my father. Go away. Speak no more of Abuelita."

Mata-Mata spoke again and I reached for the words, took some of them, thought them wrong and replaced them with others, none of which made sense, a slow process that told me in a slow way that I was dreaming even if the thorn tree moved and at its base a gnome of a man struggled with its weight. "You're just a dream," I said in words that slurred from a fat and inarticulate tongue.

"It is not a dream." Rosa's voice was clear though the words she spoke were not. I remade them. "Magic cats are not dreams." That wasn't quite right, I thought: try again. "Magic is truth." Was that what she said? "Magic is real. Jaguar. Cat. Spirit."

The gnome with his tree gave me a nasty look over his shoulder, around the thorn's trunk, and Cat laughed, Catrina jiggling her beads and her breasts, her hard nipples crinkled and alive, Catrina laughed soft and not mean but breathy, her earrings dangling silver in the moon leaning over me, her hand taking me, and Catrina humming words of union and love as beads clicked apart to show the strawberry, Todd's strawberry and not mine for I never sucked a strawberry onto anyone's neck, certainly not Catrina's, Catrina who didn't belong here with me, not in the jungle moon, not with Rosa beside me where the two of us hung like a cocoon in Kaita's ample chinchorro now ours. "Go away," I said in thick, difficult, dream-trance words, and she said it's not a dream, the gnome is not a dream, and she laughed mean this time with intent to hurt and it did, it did, and I put a pen to the paper in the lawyer's office while blinking hard against stinging eyes and signed the papers, my fingers moving through the image of the beads and the strawberry leaving ink black and final to banish her laughter beneath the street sounds beyond the window of the lawyer's office, street sounds that slipped into the choral voice of frogs, birds, insects, deadfalls in the jungle night, and Rosa's voice:

"Abuelita, I'm sorry. Don't die, Abuelita. I'll be good. I'll be good."

Not Rosa's voice, I realized, coming awake, fully awake. Rosita's voice. And yet it came from Rosa beside me in the cocoon of a hammock with mosquito netting enfolding the two of us into one tiny world. Rosita's voice crying.

I wanted to kiss her forehead, to touch her cheeks, to take away her tears, but that wasn't possible, not in that cocoon and not with her tears coming from a world that had nothing to do with me, a past I was no part of any more than Rosa was a part of the soggy jungle where Allen and I found bits of mouse deer blown apart by our mines, where the boys of Ho Chi Minh steamed into leafmold, where the tiger tried to take Joey, where Phung Phuoc tied my hands in front of me before stripping a length of rattan from the thicket beside a brown river. I listened to Rosita cry, and I remained still in the howling jungle night.

Sleep came in bits and pieces, without dreams, and earth whirled us into dawn at a thousand miles an hour to remind me of Kipling's line about the sun coming up like thunder, a line that made no sense to me as a child because the dawn came in silence, made no sense until

Todd explained it was the speed of thunder and not the sound that Kipling's Burmese and tropical sun imitated in the bringing of light with a morning twilight so short, quick, thunder-like, and as soon as light fell in patterns through the leaves Rosa came awake to tell me she had slept as I had, in bits and pieces and with disturbing events beside our chinchorro: "Mata-Mata came again, and he was real."

"I saw him," I said.

She sat up, rearranging the way our cocoon hung, her head lifting the mosquito netting to look ghost-like through the white mesh with eyes set and a storm building on her face. "You're laughing at me."

"No. I saw Mata-Mata. He was a little gnome of a man carrying a huge tree, and he left when you told him to. You asked your abuelita not to die."

She pulled the netting from her face, from mine, winding it into a white ball, and the storm had abated leaving her with moist eyes, soft eyes mouse-deer brown and large to look at me with what? Pain? Joy? Both? "You saw. You saw. Don, you cannot know how much that moves me."

"Tom, not Don."

"Tom. You saw Mata-Mata come to us in the jungle night with his tree, and you saw Abuelita dying from cholera. How can it be that you slipped into my dream?"

"You said he was real. Now you say it was all just a dream."

She made an impatient gesture, swung her legs from the hammock, dropped to the ground with the grace of an acrobat and put her face close to mine, the web of the hammock between us. "Are you telling me dreams are not real?" Her face remained soft, her eyes large, dark with their wounds. "You came into my dream. I saw you watching while I spoke to Abuelita, felt you watching. I remember that now. You will not deny what happened." She stepped back, holding eye contact, took her sandals from a branch, dropped them and stepped into them and vanished down the path we had cut from the river. As I struggled from the hammock, her voice came wrapped in the sound of the river: "I'll bathe now. You will join me."

This time with the slanting morning light beaming through trees there was no rubbing each other with soap, no touching of scars, but we did pass the soap bar back and forth and glance at one another and splash to add drops to the mist and insects suspended like stars in shafts of light slanting across us. Her skin rippled from the cool. When we sat on a river rock to dry, she asked me to share my warmth, to hold her, and we sat in a tangle of arms and legs with a quickening of my pulse. For the first time since Rosita became Rosa I was ready to make love with her, ready in innocence and intensity until I saw the water on her cheek came from her eyes, until she said, "I killed my grandmother," and the readiness vanished.

"No. Cholera killed her."

"I know. Cholera was the instrument, I the cause. She could have lived, but for what I did."

I put my cheek against hers. "Rosita did not kill her grandmother." We sat in silence, cheek to cheek, the river water running off of us, evaporating. "You smell like fresh corn."

She patted my arm, a signal of dismissal, and we drew apart. As we dressed, as she pulled a tee shirt over her head, she said, "Ask me again at a better time and I will."

"I didn't ask."

Her cheeks dimpled and she cut her eyes toward me, eyes no longer sad. "Not in words. But you asked."

After taking down the hammock, after loading the canoe with the few items we had, after putting the canteen on my belt and slipping the machete in place like a sword, after we pushed off from the sandbar and I began with the paddle to guide our journey in the deep part of the river, she turned to me. "You asked. And you heard my wordless reply. You're a good man, Tom. When the right moment comes, perhaps I will do the asking. Without words." She turned around, took her paddle, and helped move the canoe.

In the intoxication of the morning, I had forgotten Poí and Kaita until that moment, as had Rosa. She turned back to me, her eyes wide, and I nodded. "We could come upon them at any time."

"Ashore. We must go ashore and wait." She scanned the banks on both sides.

"We could hide the canoe and find fruit for breakfast." I started to say more but saw the smoke, too much to come from a campfire. It lifted through trees, above them, white and with a faint crackle. "Someone just now set that fire."

"Another village?" Rosa stopped paddling. "Likely it's people practicing slash-and-burn farming."

The river turned and we saw the bamboo walls, the longboats made from machined lumber with outboard motors sinister in red and black and tilting their propellers out of the water, three boats tied to a platform set too low to the water to survive when wet-season rain swelled the river. Even the bamboo wall might be washed away, though the houses rising behind it sat high enough on the bank to survive. "Corrugated fiberglass roofs," I said. "The sun will destroy those roofs within two years." We drifted closer, and I heard voices coming from the direction of the smoke. There was another sound, a humming as of a gas-driven engine.

A door in the bamboo wall opened and a man in white stepped into the sun, a man whose trousers were fresh ironed, razor-creased, with a stylish flare over white boots, whose starched and creased shirt and white captain's hat seemed out of place in the jungle, my jungle, as did the pistol he had snapped into a leather case on his hip, black leather, deadly and impossible because of Venezuelan laws but there it was, riding on his hip. He lifted his hand and called out, "Howdy, strangers. Can you stop for a minute?"

18

"No," *I whispered,* but Tom seemed not to hear. He angled toward the dock, bringing us beside it so we could step out of the canoe. The man with the captain's hat made no move to help, a signal for us not to come ashore. He kept his eyes on Tom.

"I suppose there's not a chance that you're a doctor, is there?" The man's English had an odd accent. I had heard it before, that accent, and it had been identified to me as southern.

"Rosa is a nurse." Tom nodded toward me.

This is too abrupt, I thought. The man wanted to find out if we could be useful to him before asking us ashore. I started to speak up, to tell him that we were in a hurry to get down river, but I held my tongue. Tom would be shocked, I thought, if I let him know in such a moment that I knew English. I resolved to tell him soon, when we were alone.

The man looked at me with a quick flicker of green eyes, looked at my breasts, at the contents of our canoe. "I have a sick man in there. He's our medic, but he doesn't know what disease he has. Can you look at him?"

My tee shirt felt inadequate, so I covered my breasts with one arm. "We need to go, Tom," I said in Spanish.

"What did she say?"

"She said we need to move along." Tom pushed his paddle against the dock.

"Please. Wait. My friend is dying. Perhaps she could take a quick look at him?"

Tom translated. "Dying," I said with a shake of my head. "Dying. Tom, I have to try to help, though there is something about that man I don't like, and it's not just his pistol." I reached into the bag, took out a blouse. "You stay right beside me and bring the machete."

"She will do what she can." Again he brought the canoe against the dock and again the man in the captain's hat made no move to help.

Once on the platform, Tom secured the machete to his belt and offered a handshake. "Tom Seal. This is Rosa Rojas."

"Brother Maybre." He clasped Tom's hand and nodded to me with a brief and forced smile. His eyes seemed too deep-set, his nose too thin, too red. A gold tooth flashed in the brief smile. He is either cold and distant by nature, I thought, or insincere to the bone. He caught me looking at the holster on his belt. "For snakes." He tapped the pistol. "We're new here and are still struggling to tame the small bit of jungle around our compound. That smoke comes from some of the boys burning a place for planting corn. But I forgot. You don't understand English."

Tom translated as we followed Brother Maybre through the bamboo fence and up the riverbank on a cement sidewalk. The river will wash it away, I thought, when rains make the water rise. "This man is no monk," I said.

"True. Some North Americans use the word *brother* in loose ways."

"And I don't trust him. That sound, like a motor running—I don't like it, either. Motors should not be in our jungle."

My statement seemed to startle Tom. He took my arm. "*Our* jungle. Yes."

The smell of frying onions came to us from one of the smaller houses. An adolesçent girl with mere buds of breasts knelt among pansies and begonias beside the walk, raking the soil with a gardener's trowel. Behind her grew oleander bushes with red and white flowers, and ground orchids held blue flowers on long stems. She smiled at me, glanced at Maybre and lost the smile. Her face seemed to become drawn and thin. Brother Maybre paused beside her. "Rochelle, tell your, ah, mother that we will have two guests for breakfast." He patted her head in a condescending and inappropriate way; I felt my distrust for the man deepen.

"We start our day here early," he said, addressing Tom and ignoring me. "The men are clearing some jungle to enlarge our garden and the women are preparing food. We eat," he glanced at his watch, "in ten minutes. You will join us, of course."

"We've been invited for breakfast," Tom told me.

"There are papayas and bananas in the jungle," I said. Tom raised his brows and tilted his head with a shrug I took as agreement: he didn't want to stay here either, even for the hour or so it would take to eat.

At the top of the riverbank, houses sat on cement slabs, houses such as I had seen in movies and pictures of North American suburban homes, though these buildings had green roofs, fiberglass, Tom had said. This is crazy, I thought. Jungle houses should be on stilts above vermin and floods. Didn't these people bother to learn anything from the locals? Brother Maybre led us toward the large house, too large for a single family. The other five buildings were no doubt single-family dwellings. Behind one, under a huge canvas canopy, stood two rows of tables and chairs, and I caught a glimpse of women setting flatware on the tables. "That's the commons," Brother Maybre said, waving toward the women. "We eat there, and we gather there for meetings." Beyond the tables stood a huge block of cement with a bell hanging above it. A covered walkway led to the bell. Covered walkways connected all the buildings. At least, I thought, the builders had the sense to leave trees for shading their ridiculous homes.

The interior of the big house reminded me of Oz Osterwitz's cave house. "Where are the windows?" Tom whispered, and I knew he also must be thinking how strange the building seemed. Electric lights hung from the ceilings, and I realized the motorized hum had to come from an electric generator.

"These people are rich," I said. "They brought a machine for generating electricity out here. How?"

"They must have a runway nearby. Remember the airplane we saw yesterday? My guess is that they airlifted everything into this place. But why?"

Brother Maybre turned to us, his eyes shadowed and his face looking ghostly in the artificial lights. "The sick man is through this door. We call him 'the poet.'"

Tom didn't bother to translate. Inside the room, the poet, a bald man with heavy brows, lay sleeping on a cot, and it took some effort for Brother Maybre to rouse him. He looked at me with yellow eyes, watched me place the stethoscope to his chest. The man was large like a bear, and like a bear his abdomen was covered with hair so thick that I wondered if it might muffle the sound of his heartbeat. "You're young," I said, and his brows knit. Tom started to translate, but I waved him into silence. "Such a strong heart, and yet I believe you are dangerously ill."

"Speak again, sweet angel," the poet said in English.

"She's no angel," Brother Maybre said. "She's a native girl who happens to know a little about medicine, but no angel. We must guard against blasphemy."

I turned to Brother Maybre. "You will keep quiet or leave the room."

Tom translated, and the poet convulsed with laughter turning into coughs.

Speaking English would be better, but for me to do so now felt inappropriate. "Translate for me, Tom, and please ignore that pig with the pistol."

"She has the voice of an angel," the poet said.

I asked my questions and waited for the unnecessary translations. The poet suffered from an unrelenting headache, and he had fever at times. He could eat little and had problems with vomiting. He slept too much. I turned to Maybre for confirmation, and he said what I feared: the poet has slipped in and out of a coma, and he had been ill for almost three weeks, "in spite of prayer vigils," Brother Maybre said.

"Encephalitis, perhaps," the poet said.

"You have had medical training?" I asked.

"Some. I didn't finish medical school, though."

I listened to Tom's translation, then said, "Encephalitis, yes, but what form? The symptom is inflammation of the brain. The cause might be viral—whooping cough or mumps, though you seem to have had neither. Pneumonia can cause it, or a toxic reaction that caused prolonged high fever."

"Impressive," Brother Maybre said when he listened to Tom's translation.

"She knows more medicine than I do," the poet said. "I'd like to talk more, but I'm so tired. You will come back, sweet angel?"

"I have a few more questions." I turned to Tom.

The poet listened to Tom, then looked at me with half-shut eyes. "Tomorrow, tomorrow, and tomorrow." His voice faded and he fell asleep.

Brother Maybre approached the bed. "I'll wake him."

"No." I caught his arm.

"But you said you must leave."

"We'll stay until this afternoon."

Tom seemed surprised and perhaps pleased, though what could please him was a mystery to me. He made the translation, and Brother Maybre nodded, his shadowed eyes and pale face looking more sinister than ever.

"There are too many people in here," I told Tom. "We tire him. I should come back in an hour or so. Perhaps you can occupy this false monk so he won't be in here with me?"

"But you'll need an interpreter."

"I won't. Believe me in this."

"She'll examine him again later, without us," Tom said in English.

It was a relief to leave the dim house with its unnatural lights. Brother Maybre led us to the area he called the commons, sat us at one of the tables under the canopy. Perhaps, I thought, the cement block and the brass bell served for signaling time for meals. On the cement beneath the bell lay a meter-long iron rod that construction workers put into cement—for ringing the bell, I conjectured, though no one approached it to signal breakfast. Men drifted in from the jungle, six of them. They smelled of wood smoke and had ashes on their shirts. Ten women, two of them pregnant, served the tables, setting out plates heaped with sausage, eggs, and hashed potatoes, and in minutes all were seated. The women wore long black skirts and white blouses. Each had her hair pulled back and pinned into a bun, and none wore makeup, not even lipstick. Black skirts, I thought, shaking my head. Such clothing wasn't wise in a country where the sun turns black cloth into a solar heater. The men dressed more sensibly, though not by much. They wore jeans of light denim and long-sleeved khaki shirts dark enough to catch more of the sun's heat than they needed to contend with, shirts with dark stains around the armpits and along their backs. What struck me as most strange was the silence. No one spoke, not even Rochelle, who sat close to the end of the table beside Brother Maybre, though she seemed to be leaning away from him.

He stood, and the people bowed their heads. "Lord," Brother Maybre said, his eyes seeming closed though it was hard to tell with the simian shadow over them, "we pray for the poet. We pray that this native woman is an agent of God and has brought the knowledge to heal him. We pray, Lord, for patience in this hard land. We pray the rains will hold off a few more days while we clear the land. We pray for Thy bounty and Thy guidance and we hope Thy coming will be soon to deliver us from the difficulties of this flesh, amen."

Only after the chorus of *amens* did conversations begin around the two tables. People glanced at us with curious faces, their curiosity polite and gentle. "Good morning," Rochelle said to me in a shy way. I said hello to her in Spanish.

"This is my mother," Rochelle nodded toward the woman across the table from her. "Her name is Louise."

"Hello," Louise said. "I'm sorry that I speak no Spanish."

Tom translated, and I told him not to worry about me. "You need not repeat what they say. Small talk is universal, and I'll get by well enough." I turned to Louise. *"Me llamo Rosa."*

"Rosa." Louise looked much like her daughter when she smiled. "A beautiful name."

To my surprise the eggs and potatoes were heavily spiced with pepper. "Delicious," I told Tom. "I thought your people didn't like hot food." *Comida piquente.*

When he translated my observation, the people at our table laughed, even the sour Brother Maybre. "Most of us are from South Texas," he said. "And we like chili peppers and jalapeños."

Tom said Spanish never used the same word for hot when speaking of pepper and speaking of fire. "English has the word *piquant,*" Tom said. "We just don't use it."

"I never thought of that," Louise said.

"We grow our own peppers," Brother Maybre said. "There's a native pepper that only a few of us can eat because it's so hot." He turned to me. "Ask her if there are jungle plants we should never eat, no matter what—if there are plants that are poisonous."

When Tom finished his translation, I said, "Eat nothing growing in the jungle unless you are positive you know what it is. Many plants will make you sick."

"Will any of them kill you?" he asked.

"Some. But you bring plenty of poison into the jungle yourselves. The leaves of potato plants can be lethal. Oleander leaves are the most deadly."

Brother Maybre listened to Tom's interpretation and rubbed his chin. "Oleander plants?"

"Yes. The sap is deadly. Three leaves are enough to kill a full-grown horse. Some people have died from eating meat roasted on green oleander sticks. Even the flowers produce toxin. Sometimes honey bees gather from oleanders when nothing else is blooming, and the honey they make from it can kill." Having to wait for Tom's interpretation became tiresome, but there was nothing to do about it. And telling him when we found some time alone would not help. How could I confess to knowing English without looking deceptive or foolish to Louise and Rochelle? I didn't care what Brother Maybre thought of me. He seemed like such an oily and insincere man that I wanted as little to do with him as possible.

"Poisoned honey?" Louise looked alarmed. "But honey is a natural product."

"So is oleander," Brother Maybre said. "It's a gift from God."

19

Rosa disliked Brother Maybre, she had said so, and her body language confirmed it in ways I hoped were too subtle to insult anyone at breakfast. The man led the strange group, misfit and misplaced in a foreign jungle and in need of him as leader, maybe father of Rochelle if Rochelle's unspoken affection for him meant anything and maybe husband of Louise if placement in seating meant anything. I liked Brother Maybre from the first, found his steady way of looking at me and into me similar to Uncle Ray's way of looking, even the deep-set eyes like Uncle Ray's; I found the concern for his friend the poet touching in a way to make me wonder about Rosa's harsh words, a pig she called him with such an attitude that made me glad she knew no English so I could protect Brother Maybre from the worst edge of her scorn though not all of it.

After breakfast when it became clear the women expected Rosa to help clear away the dishes, and the men expected it, I could see fire building in Rosa's eyes to surprise me not for her responding to the unfairness but for her being Venezuelan and a woman and yet chaffing about being expected to be a servant, as if she were somehow ignorant of the Venezuelan conviction that cooking and cleanup are women's work. I half expected to hear Catrina laugh and see her in her fake buckskins looking with contempt upon what she would call fem-slaves at their domestic chores and looking with hostility at the men who kept their women in black skirts even in the heat and kept them with no makeup and their hair in buns to be uniformed and unattractive and stripped of sexuality, to keep them in line, she would say. But Catrina didn't appear.

Brother Maybre excused himself saying he had much to do to supervise the compound and advising us to go where we wished though Rosa should stay away from two of the buildings, "men's dorms," he called them, where women were allowed only in threes and only to clean the rooms when the men were away. "Check on the poet often, please." He looked at her with eyes that conveyed appreciation.

Rosa's refusal to help with the dishes drew surprised looks from the women, Rochelle especially. "I don't like this place," Rosa told me after Brother Maybre wandered off to check on how the men were coming in their task of clearing ground for a larger garden.

"Breakfast was wonderful."

"Yes. Did we come to the wild part of Venezuela to eat such breakfast?"

"We'll leave. Now, if you want."

She chewed her lower lip; her brows knit. "The poet. He's very ill. If he has American encephalitis there's nothing to be done. But if it's something else, perhaps I can help. To leave him might be a death sentence, and I would be at fault."

"But you gave him no medicine."

"I wanted to think about what to do, to check him again. Maybe a broad-spectrum antibiotic." She started toward the large building, and I followed. "You need not go with me."

"But you told me to stay close to you."

"That was earlier." She seemed distracted. "I need to tell you something, but not now. Now I check on the poet."

I wandered around the compound, found it surrounded by bamboo fencing, tall, well braced with only three gates, one leading to the river, one to a garden, and the third padlocked, no doubt opening to undeveloped jungle. With one of the women watching me while she seemed not to watch, I stood in the gate that opened to the garden and inspected corn and beans, the bean vines snaking through the corn stalks, climbing them, potatoes on hills for draining, Swiss chard, carrots, okra, and other plants I couldn't identify. Beyond the garden lay the airstrip.

I walked toward it noting along the way a group of papaya trees, knee-high, planted in a row, several of them male plants that would produce no fruit, and the sight of them triggered an odd memory of my father following the advice of a Venezuelan neighbor who claimed that if you clipped the top of the male papaya and set a rock on it like a hat, the plant would turn into a female and bear fruit. That's absurd, I wanted to tell him since even as a child I had scorn for magical thinking; that's absurd like the children's tale of kissing your elbow, and it won't work, but I said nothing, especially after Dad said it was worth testing the belief and cheap enough to do, for all it cost was the stunting of a papaya tree that wasn't going to give us any fruit, rock or no rock. A gift from the papaya trees was the hummingbirds that gathered to drink from the cone-shaped flowers, gathering in a buzz and blur of wings with such enthusiasm that I wanted to taste the flowers myself, and my brother Todd said there was no way I could get my tongue into them for the nectar.

Brother Maybre joined me before I reached the airstrip, took my arm in the same way Uncle Ray once did when I was a boy and knew Uncle Ray to be the nicest and the most brilliant man ever. "Walk with me into the devil's domain," Brother Maybre said, pointing toward the trees close to the locked compound gate, and I nodded, liking the easy affection of his touch.

"I walk there often, though always by myself and always armed," he tapped the leather holster on his hip, "since the devil has ways of harming as well as tempting. Is she your woman?"

"What?" I stopped in the edge of shade from smaller trees and looked at him in confusion.

"Rosa. Your wife? Your concubine?"

"A friend from my childhood. A good friend, though I'll confess to not knowing her very well these days."

"I have devised an entertainment for her. May I offer it to her without offending you?"

"Offer her what you wish." We resumed walking. "She'll be frank in her feelings about you, I'm sure of that." I started to add that he wouldn't like her frankness but did not. Let him discover her hostility for himself.

"I'll send you a gift so you'll get something from the deal. But here, look. Here is where the devil monkeys came when we were new to this hot country. They defecated into their hands and flung their filth upon us."

"I met that tribe of monkeys up the river. Disgusting."

"We shot some of them, and that discouraged them enough to stay away, though I was sorry to see the suffering of the wounded."

Like Uncle Ray, I thought, when he shot the howler monkey, Uncle Ray who learned not to kill anything larger than a bird when he saw the howler trying to staunch the flow of blood with sticks and twigs. It was a lesson he passed on to me just from the telling of it, though I forgot the lesson in another jungle after I fell into adulthood and fled from Catrina and her strawberry. I fled into that other jungle where the memory of Uncle Ray's description came back but not before the exploding of the mouse deer and my firing into darkness to kill Charlie who turned out to look like mere boys lying twisted in monsoon mud. I shook my head to dismiss the memory. "Not all jungle is the domain of the devil."

"No?" Brother Maybre's intonation said I was wrong, wrong in spades. "Look around you. This might look like the Garden of Eden, but if it is, it has fallen as far as the serpent could drop it. I seldom walk farther than we are now. There—that tree. That's where I always stop. It isn't wise to tempt deeper into the jungle."

"The howlers never returned?"

"Never. I'm working on forgiving them and on forgiving myself for shooting them. They're just beasts, after all, and easy prey to the Master of Darkness."

Some things about Brother Maybre bothered me. Seeing Satan as a literal person was a kind of magical thinking. He must have read my response, for he added: "Has nothing or no one ever offended you deeply?"

"Catrina," I blurted out. "Todd, my own brother," and I found myself sketching the tale of the strawberry under the beads, of my retreating to the lawyer's office and to Asia. The tale seemed to fall out of me, and Brother Maybre put his hand on my shoulder.

"So you haven't spoken to your brother since?"

"No."

"Or to the woman who was your wife?"

"To her, yes, plenty of times, though I never returned to California to do it."

"The anger will destroy you."

"Anger keeps me focused, or it did in the jungles of war." I went to the tree that marked the limit of Brother Maybre's meditative walks into the devil's domain. Its bark was riddled with tiny holes, perfectly round and so many of them that I wondered how the tree could survive such an onslaught of insects. He joined me.

"Learn to speak to your brother. The first step in forgiveness is the hardest. It requires you to give up the hope of ever having a better past."

"That's a silly thought."

"Yes." He looked at his watch. "So early, and yet I'm anxious for siesta time, if you know what I mean." He nudged me with an elbow.

I didn't know, but I welcomed the change in conversation. On the way back to the compound I tried to explain about the jungle as a place of innocence and beauty, a concept he swept aside with a wave of a hand. "Our airplane returns this afternoon with vital supplies and perhaps with medicine for the poet, should we need it. I'm still waiting for the sign."

"The sign?"

"God speaks in signs, if we can only learn to read them."

"That, Brother Maybre, is unmitigated bullshit."

"Perhaps you're the sign, though I doubt it. You're in deep darkness."

I wanted to slug him for being so superstitious, to shake him, to tell him how like Uncle Ray he could be if he dropped all the god-sign stuff and darkness shit.

Back at the compound, he showed me a room in the large building, a tiny cubical containing only a cot, a chair, a chest of drawers, and a shower stall. "This is your room for siesta time today and for tonight, if you will agree to stay. The small bed is all we have, unfortunately, but it's plenty wide if you use your imagination. The walls are thick and absorb sound, so you ought to enjoy the, ah, siesta without disturbance."

When siesta time came, after the landing of the small plane, after Brother Maybre stood on the landing strip talking to the pilot in ways that seemed to upset him, after he ordered the chopping down of the oleander bushes and their leaves and branches stacked on the cement block under the bell, after a light lunch in the commons with little conversation and Rosa worrying about the poet and excusing herself to check on him again, I saw others retiring for siesta, and I returned to the room, anxious to use the shower. I assumed Brother Maybre would assign a similar room to Rosa, perhaps in the women's dorm, an assumption based on my own misjudgment and naivete.

When I emerged from the shower stall, Rochelle sat in the chair. I clutched the towel to me, and she stood to greet me with a forced smile. "I showered before I came, and I put on a clean dress." Her voice was flat; she looked at the floor.

"You must leave." I glanced at my pants lying on the bed, at my shirt, wishing I had them on, and I felt vulnerable, afraid.

"No. I would be in trouble." She began unbuttoning the front of her dress.

"Stop that. Stop it. And leave right now." My words came out shrill.

She made eye contact, a desperate look on her face, her child's face framed with braided hair and tears glittering in her eyes and her head shaking a slow and steady no to make my stomach lurch from the sick wrong of her presence, of my standing before her with only a towel, of her continuing with unsteady fingers to unbutton. "I can't leave. There would be such trouble from Brother Maybre and God and Louise—"

"Keep your dress on. Turn your back to me. Please?"

Her eyes widened, perhaps at my pleading and frightened tone. She turned around, faced the door, and I grabbed my pants to pull them on with difficulty because of being wet, my shirt also clinging as I struggled into it.

20

The *he poet* opened his yellow eyes. "Brother Maybre is wrong. You are an angel. Only an angel would sit beside a dying man, and you've been there, looking at me for hours, it seems."

I raised my brows and shook my head to indicate I didn't understand. He seemed to find my response amusing. "You would be the perfect mate. You don't talk and you have the skills of a nurse. But of course you won't be my mate except in death. Maybre will find his sign any day now, and the sooner the better I say. I have American encephalitis, don't I? But of course you don't understand me, and I hate myself for not learning Spanish in school. He uses my money, but I don't mind since we seek the same thing even if he doesn't know it. He wants to join his God, he thinks, but he's in love with death. So am I."

Brother Maybre came in as I sponged the poet's forehead with a damp cloth. "He's awake," Brother Maybre said.

"Awake and barely alive," the poet said. "I've been telling this angel of mercy about our little group."

"Don't tell her much. She understands English. And don't look so surprised, Rosa. I watched you at breakfast. You knew exactly what was being said, even if Tom never caught on to that fact."

"English?" The poet pulled me close and whispered in my ear, "Come back alone, sweet angel, and I'll tell you the truth about this compound."

"What did you say?" Brother Maybre demanded.

"I told her I love her and that I wanted to take her away from all this." The poet waved his hand. "I said it in blank verse."

"We should call you the clown instead of the poet. Get some more rest, old friend, while I show Rosa to her siesta quarters."

Brother Maybre led me to a room not far from where the poet lay in his sickness, and as we entered, I asked, "Where is Tom?"

He followed me into the room. "Probably showering."

The room was enormous and dominated by a canopied bed. The realization of his intent came to me in a slow way, bringing the taste of something yellow from the back of my throat. I turned to face him.

"We can shower together." His smile looked hideous, his eyes more sunk in than ever, so I could see only a faint and predatory glitter of them as his hand went to the buttons of his shirt.

"Tom will not be pleased."

"He is being pleased right now, I'm certain of it. This was his idea. He has a lusty eye for one of our females, and he offered me a trade—a temporary trade, of course. So I showed him to his siesta room and sent the girl."

"If you undress in front of me, I'll make you sorry."

"You have the fire of the Latina woman. I like that. Your breasts are like twin doves." Maybre took off his shirt and began tugging on his belt.

With a quick dip of one knee I thumbed the snap over the handle of the hunting knife by my ankle and took the knife. "Take those pants off and I'll remove your *topocho* and both of your eggs."

He stepped back in surprise. "It's God's will. He sent you to me, He—"

"God has nothing to do with what you want. Step aside."

"Wait." He moved closer to the door, blocking it. "Tom said he hasn't known you and doesn't want to know you, but that he felt certain you would be full of heat and love."

"He said nothing of the sort. Get out of my way."

"He pines for Catrina."

"Catrina?" I whispered. "He told you of Catrina?" It took him so long to feel safe enough with me to tell about his wife, and yet to this vile stranger he opened his heart.

"But of course. He's filled with anger and yet he still yearns for her touch, and he said he dreads having sex with you, that your brown skin and dark eyes are wrong for him. I'm afraid your Tom is a racist. But I find you beautiful, so beautiful. Stay with me for one hour, my sweet Rosa, and you'll know how right it is for us to love."

I stepped toward him with the knife.

"Put that down and listen to me. Do you know why Tom so loved Catrina? Did he tell you? She was tiny, like a child. She stood only this tall," Maybre ran a finger across his chest, "and Tom found that attractive because Tom likes little girls. Do you know which of the females he asked for?"

Rochelle, I thought, hating myself for listening to this terrible man. Surely Tom would never touch a child such as Rochelle. He was attracted to Kaita, and she was tiny, and he called her a child. The ground seemed to be moving under me with the realization that I didn't know this man Tom who once was my Don. Could he trade me like a toy in order to do unspeakable things to a little girl?

"I see it in your eyes. You know, don't you? You know he asked me to send Rochelle to him. Give me the knife. He promised not to mark her neck with a strawberry."

Stunned, unresisting, I shook my head in denial as Maybre took the knife from me and dropped it on a bedside table, as he slipped an arm around me to draw me to him. He smelled of ashes and sweat. Without conviction or energy I pushed at him. "Your own daughter," I said. "Your own daughter."

"Rochelle? No. Not even Louise's daughter. Rochelle is a stray brought to me by a woman who killed herself with drugs. A needle woman." He pressed his lips against mine and sought to part them with his tongue.

I offered no help, nor did I resist his dragging me to the bed and pushing me upon it. He unbuttoned my blouse, his breathing becoming heavy. "Syphilis," I said. "A rare form and resistant to antibiotics."

His hand ran inside my tee shirt, then became still. "What? What was that?"

"To me it's mild and hardly worth bothering about. But I know it would rot away the organ of a man like Tom. That's the real reason he and I have not made love."

"This is a bad joke." He withdrew his hand, the passion gone from him, his breathing no longer heavy.

"Some women are carriers. I have a duty to tell you."

"You would give it to me. You would give me syphilis." He stood over me, stepped back, his eyes sunken into the shadows of his brow.

"No. You would take it from me." I spoke without energy. "You would spread it among all the women here. Then the rot would start with dripping pus. Penicillin would not touch it, and the disease would go to your brain. You would die like a tree, from the top down."

He rubbed his lips on his arm. "Can I get it from kissing?"

"It has happened, but it isn't likely."

"Is this the sign? Is this the sign, Lord?" It seemed clear enough that he was through with me. He stumbled against the door, paused long enough to straighten his pistol and notch his belt, and left.

I took a deep breath, stood, and kicked his shirt across the room, then put the knife back into my ankle scabbard. As I stepped out, I caught a glimpse of Maybre going through the gate. He left it open, and I watched him make his way among trees to vanish into the jungle.

No one else was around. I wandered toward the flowers where we first saw Rochelle, toward the stubble from cut oleander bushes, feeling disgust growing within me, rubbing my lips on the back of my hand to banish the feel of Maybre's tongue. The air smelled of ashes—or maybe it was my blouse, still unbuttoned, that carried the ashy smell from Maybre pressing himself against me.

Tom and Rochelle emerged from one of the houses, Tom still stomping to get his shoes on. He wore no socks, and his hair was disheveled and wet. From sweating over the girl, I thought, noting the top of her dress was unbuttoned. Tom carried the machete. "Have you seen Brother Maybre," he called out to me. Without waiting for an answer, he took Rochelle's hand and almost dragged her to me. "She's scared of Brother Maybre. She's scared of her mother. Stay with her."

"Why are you so angry?" I found it difficult to talk, and my voice sounded flat.

"I'll find him." Tom brandished the machete. "And look at you, just look at you." He started toward the garden gate.

"No. That way." I pointed.

Tom glanced at me, at the open gate leading to the jungle. "What has he done to you? To us?"

The look of disgust on his face pierced me like a knife. "The pistol," I warned, but Tom strode toward the jungle. I turned to Rochelle. "Did he hurt you?"

"No." Her eyes widened. "You know English."

21

Rosa stood among peonies, among gladiolus, poppies, pansies, among hibiscus, called by Malays *bunga raya* or the king of flowers, the irrelevant memory of the term coming to me through a mist of anger; she stood in the still air moist from the river and from the arrival of wet season and heavy with the nectar of flowers Rochelle liked to tend, heavy with perfume from jungle flowers, especially the frangipani blossoms in a tree towering over the bamboo wall, odors cloying with too much sweetness in the wet air. I glanced at Rosa's unbuttoned blouse and her tee shirt untucked in the front and remembered what Brother Maybre had said about offering her an entertainment and about sending me a gift so I would get something out of the deal. The unbuttoning and untucking had to be part of his notion of entertainment.

For an instant Rosa had a strawberry on her neck; she wore fake buckskins and beads, and her face slipped into Catrina's, but the instant came fast and went fast leaving no strawberry, only the worried face of Rosa who might or might not have enjoyed Brother Maybre's notion of entertainment. Certainly I hated what I got from his deal, hated finding in my room a child who thought she had to submit to adult abuse, hated Brother Maybre for sending her, hated him enough to go after him with a machete as I once went after Phung Phuoc with a sharpened bit of bamboo, enough to thrust Rochelle into Rosa's care, Rosa's unbuttoned blouse making my head light with anger to multiply hatred enough to look for him beyond the garden gate until Rosa called out to show me the unlocked jungle gate where Brother Maybre fled after his entertainment, fled to seek his God in a jungle he figured was the devil's dominion, though of course he knew nothing about the jungle as a truly evil place where a tiger could come for you in the night and the likes of Phung Phuoc cut rattan beside a brown river; I hated with the same cold fury that drove me to kneel beside the sleeping Phuoc and raise the stake, double-handed, its point black from the black earth.

"The pistol," Rosa called in warning, and I saw it black against his white pants his white shirt, saw it as I first did when he came to the boat dock—when? that morning? God was it just hours ago that I first saw him? Now I planned his death, if you can call cold fury planning. I saw the pistol or a bit of it under the leather covering and shook my head to fling away the vision. I went through the open gate, beneath frangipani blossoms, in a run to make the canteen bounce against my hip, heading toward the tree riddled with insect holes where I knew I'd find the man who sent a child—his own daughter—into my bedroom in exchange for Rosa, and I heard his words, "I have devised an entertainment for her," too pompous and absurd for me to consider any seriousness of intent on his part, heard my own voice in compliance without suspecting his dark design.

I heard him in the woods ahead and ducked, circled to watch for an opening so I could rush him before he unsnapped the pistol, heard his cry of alarm, heard him struggle. I moved faster, arm crooked and machete up, ready to strike and aware in a faint way of sweat sticky between my fingers. Then I saw him.

It must have dropped on him from a tree, and it pinned his arms to his sides. The snake's mouth clung to Brother Maybre's face, the top teeth holding just above one ear and the bottom gripping his jaw, and Brother Maybre struggled to get a hand to his pistol, had unsnapped the covering of the holster but could do no more because of the coils pinning his arms. The flare of its jaws, the size of it, the terrifying power of it stopped me for an instant, and I saw another snake in another jungle flare its neck, arch back and launch venom to glisten in a shaft of light, its spray aimed at Allen's eyes as he turned toward it, not knowing of its presence beside him where he sat, waiting for me, and I might have shot the snake before it spat its poison, but I didn't, I didn't.

The memory of my failure unfroze my legs, and I ran to Brother

Maybre, slipped the machete over his shoulder, beneath the python and drew the blade toward me with outward pressure to slice into the snake below its open mouth. The snake writhed and I felt water hitting me and thought it must be rain gathering in the canopy to fall in such large drops, and I sliced again and the snake writhed with the slicing, then became still and Brother Maybre had the pistol out but with the wrong hand and not gripped for firing so it was easy to take it from him to drop it to the ground and begin prying the snake's head from Brother Maybre's face. He fell to his knees. I kicked the pistol away, fearful he would pick it up and put it to his head, a fear that didn't make any sense, not there in the terrible jungle outside the compound on the river. I knelt beside him, ignoring his muttering, finding it necessary to lift the jaws, finding the snake's teeth curved inward for the lock on the head it had tried to swallow. When the snake gave up its grip on Brother Maybre's face and hit the ground, it moved as if to crawl away though I had thought it dead; it turned as if to escape into the jungle again and I snatched up the machete and chopped at its head, at the bloody place where the machete had bit into it, chopped again and again yelling "Die you goddam cobra, die, die," until the head lay apart from the huge body that continued to quiver while Brother Maybre staggered to his pistol, then stood over the severed head to point and make the pistol pop and put a hole near the python's nose.

"That was no cobra." His voice carried scorn for me perhaps or perhaps for the dead snake that wasn't a cobra, and he fell to his knees to mutter more words.

Only then could I stand still, could I realize the water I felt was snake blood that spurted my arms and chest, my pants and shoes—even on my hands, sticky and familiar on my hands in a way that sent a shiver of horror through me; but Brother Maybre had more on him, crimson, thick and darker than human blood, though some of that also trickled down his face from the stitching of teeth punctures. Snake blood covered his shoulder, his back and chest in fluid almost too thick to drip.

The cold fury had abated to leave me trembling and on the edge of being dizzy with the same spinning that got me after using the bamboo stake on Phung Phuoc. It wasn't until I had put the machete handle under my belt that I realized Brother Maybre wore no shirt, that he was still partly dressed for the entertainment he devised for Rosa, and the realization brought again a wave of fury, a small wave that came and went while I fumbled with the lid to the canteen to splash water on my hands for wiping the sticky off on the back of my pants. I commanded myself to listen to his words.

". . . for the snake and for deliverance from the snake, Lord, I thank Thee, and for this unholy baptism to show me thy covenant and let me know Thy time is at hand. I thank Thee for Tom and his righteous blade, for—"

"Can the bullshit, Maybre," I said. "I didn't come here to save you from a python. I came to kill you for, for . . ." I faltered. For what? Getting into Rosa's pants? Prostituting his daughter? I wiped my hands again.

"No, my friend. You came here to do what you did." He dropped the pistol into his holster and picked up the snake's head. "Satan, I fear thee no longer."

"It's only a snake, goddammit. A python. It felt your motion and figured you were a rabbit or an armadillo, and it released its grip on the tree hoping to fall on its lunch. If it had known how large an animal you are, it would have stayed in the tree."

"Thanks for the scientific explanation. You are, of course, wrong. But no matter. Believe what you want. I thought you might be the sign, then believed it to be Rosa with her dark eyes and beauty to disguise corruption. She had to be it, and I came into this fallen garden not knowing her to be a mere catalyst, that I would find the Prince of Darkness here as the sign, the final sign. You and I and Rosa are now bound by this blood. You are part of the covenant." He stood, cast down the python's head and stepped on it.

I followed him toward the compound. It took all my energy to hold back the dizziness, to keep from seeing the cobra lifting itself in front of Allen, and I knew I was stunned by the fury that had dragged me into the jungle to kill Brother Maybre, stunned by the killing of the python and the way my fury had vanished, stunned by the feeling of blood making my hands sticky. I wondered if I could take the machete and hack into Brother Maybre right there beneath the canopy of trees not unlike those Phuoc slept under when I got him with the sharpened bamboo, and I imagined doing it. I could grip the machete, take three quick steps, and sink it at an angle into his neck. His own blood, a lighter red, would gush over the thicker, darker snake blood and he would stagger and I would feel the quiver of his death throes through my grip on the machete as if it were a spear of bamboo, and he would half turn to look at me with eyes so similar to Uncle Ray's, eyes whose light faded even as he buckled to his knees. Could I do that?

The amazing thing to me wasn't that such an act seemed impossible but that it had been possible before the python fell on him, that only moments before I could have killed in hot blood. Then what? Then he would come to me in odd moments as Phouc came to me, as Catrina came to me though I didn't kill her, wouldn't under any circumstances kill her and yet I was a killer of men and worse, much worse than Uncle Ray when he shot the howler monkey or even afterward since he learned something from the act, while I didn't learn from what I did to Charlie or what I did to Phuoc with the sharpened bamboo; I didn't learn a thing or it would have been impossible to thrust Rochelle into Rosa's care and go after Brother Maybre, to stalk him, to watch for an opening so I could rush in to chop the machete into him before he could draw the pistol. Killer, killer, killer, they said to me when I came back to the States, the landlady said that when she asked if I was a vet and I said yes and she said to go away, that she didn't rent to killers so I had to learn not to confess to being a vet or else listen to their abuse and feel their anger, making what I had done in those evil jungles even worse than it had been before listening to their taunts, worse because I believed them and hated myself for being a killer, killer, killer. But that was in war, I argued again and again and perhaps came to believe the excuse though here in this jungle there was no war and yet I had the machete in hand with the same intent that I once gripped my rifle, the same intent that drove me to kneel over a sleeping man and raise the sharpened bamboo above his neck.

We reached the compound. Brother Maybre went to the commons, to the bell suspended above a cement block now covered with branches and leaves from the oleander bushes that he ordered cut after learning that they are poisonous, though why he kept the cuttings in the Commons was a mystery to me. He picked up a piece of rebar iron to ring the bell and I wandered toward the flowers hoping to find Rosa, needing the comfort of her presence even if she was no longer Rosita but a woman who might succumb to the charms of a man with eyes like Uncle Ray's, a man she disliked at first sight and yet unbuttoned for when he took her to his siesta room. No matter, I told myself. No matter. She didn't go after Brother Maybre with a machete. She is better than I, far better.

22

I wanted to go after Tom, to help him, and at the same time I wanted nothing to do with Tom. "He took you in his bed," I said to Rochelle. She nodded, and I wanted to go after Tom with my knife.

Rochelle watched me, alarm on her face; she glanced several times at one of the buildings, likely the one where Louise had gone for siesta. I asked some questions but she wouldn't speak. "Help me check on the poet." I remembered he had promised to tell me the truth about the compound. The girl followed me.

The poet was awake when we entered his room. "You're still here, are you?" He tried without much success for a smile.

"You said you would tell the truth about this compound."

"To you. But not to the child. Send her away."

Rochelle whimpered and moved toward the door. I caught her arm. "No. There's danger out there for her. She stays with me."

"The entire world is a dangerous place."

"What are you talking about?"

The poet closed his eyes, and for a moment I thought he had slipped into sleep. "I've never been safe," he said. "Not even my father's money could buy me safety, my money after he died. Brother Maybre seemed to offer safety and the promise of home. We'll all go home soon, he promised, and maybe I believed. No matter. You deserve better, but you won't get it. Not here. Perhaps not anywhere in this rotten world."

I waited, watching him breathe to make sure he was awake. He looked at me. "What? Still here?"

"The truth. You promised to tell me the truth."

"I have." He waved his hand, a languid motion that seemed to take all of his strength. "You should go. Flee into the jungle. Brother Maybre is plotting your death, though you shouldn't take it personally."

"What are you saying? Brother Maybre is a killer?"

"That's exactly what I'm saying. He thinks it's his God acting through him. He thinks he is an agent of God in the age of the apocalypse. He told me you are one of his minions, that you brought the knowledge he needed. That plane that arrived this morning? The pilot was supposed to bring a supply of arsenic, but he failed in his mission, something about the local authorities forbidding the sale."

"Arsenic? For what?"

"As an agent of death. Go. Into the jungle. Go soon. Tomorrow. Or even this afternoon. But don't tell Brother Maybre or he would stop you." The poet closed his eyes and drifted into sleep.

I turned to Rochelle. "Do you know about any of this?"

She shook her head, then nodded. "Please, find Tom and take me with you."

"Tom? But you said he took you to his bed."

"No. Not Tom. Brother Maybre. You asked me about Brother Maybre."

"Tom didn't hurt you?"

"No. Take me with you."

I put the stethoscope into my bag, picked up a bottle of antibiotics, hesitated, and set it back on the bedside table. That's when the bell started ringing in three beats followed by a pause, then three beats again. The poet's eyes opened. "Listen!" The bell continued its three-beat ringing. "Brother Maybre has found his sign. He'll come for me soon. Good. I'm ready. If you want to live, you'd better go now."

"I'll leave you some antibiotics." I showed him the bottle.

"Take them. I'm a dead man. Take them and go. Go now."

The urgency in his voice and the panic on Rochelle's face convinced me. I picked up the bag and shoved the antibiotics into it. Rochelle took my arm and pulled me toward the door.

When we got outside we saw people emerging from the other buildings. Brother Maybre stood in the commons, the rebar in his hand, hitting the bell. His body was painted red. Tom stood on the brick walk among Rochelle's flowers. He also was speckled with red paint. As we ran toward him, I realized the paint was blood, though he didn't seem wounded. "Tom," I said, breathing hard from the run. "The boats. The boats."

Rochelle started down the bank. I held out my hand. Tom took it and we ran after Rochelle. She opened the gate in the bamboo wall, and we paused to look back. Brother Maybre saw us and reached for his pistol. "Hurry," Tom said.

We ran to the platform. Our canoe was gone. "This one," Tom began untying the rope to one of the compound's canoes.

"You start the engine," I said. "I'll cast off." Tom scrambled into the long canoe, went to the back, and Rochelle followed. "Sit in the middle," I told her, threw my bag into the boat, and picked up the rope. Brother Maybre stopped in the doorway of the bamboo fence and pointed his pistol as I pushed us into the river's current. He fired a single shot, and I saw the splash from the bullet. Tom pulled on the starter rope, pulled again, then adjusted something and pulled again. The engine coughed. He pulled again. With a paddle I tried to turn us so we weren't broadside to the platform.

Maybre hurried to the dock and fired the pistol to knock some wood from the boat near Rochelle. I couldn't turn the boat, couldn't turn it. "Rochelle," Maybre said. She jerked her head up and started to stand.

"No," I said, but the word was drowned by the roar of the engine coming to life. Maybre fired in rapid succession and Rochelle jerked and fell into the water.

"Sylvia!" Tom lunged for her, almost tipping the boat, but he missed, and we went by where she fell, and she was gone under the dark waters. The name Sylvia caused my scalp to prickle. Maybre fired again and hit the boat. He began reloading the pistol.

"Sylvia," Tom cried in anguish. "Not again."

"Gone." I had to shout above the sound of the motor. "She's gone, Tom. Rochelle is gone. The motor, turn us." We headed straight toward the bank. I tried to turn us with the paddle, but it was no use. Just as

I thought we would smash into the rocks, Tom turned the boat, set us with the current, and sped up the engine. Maybre fired at us twice more before we went around a turn in the river.

We followed twists in the river, the sun moving from one side of the boat to the other, and we passed an inlet, one of the creeks that fed the river. Then the engine died. Tom unscrewed a cap on the motor and peered inside. "No gas," he announced with a sigh. "But we're far from the compound."

"Maybe. Maybe not."

"What do you mean?"

"We're far from it only on water. But I think the river twisted around so that we're still close, if you walk through the jungle."

"The people in the compound don't walk far in the jungle. They think it's an evil place." He looked at me with sudden intensity. "You spoke to Rochelle in English. You told her to sit in the middle of the boat. In English."

"Yes."

"You didn't tell me you knew English." He sounded offended.

"You didn't ask."

"But, but," he sputtered. "But it's my language."

"You'll have to share."

"What I mean is you pretended not to know and I translated for you and you listened to Oz and to Louise and to Brother Maybre and you said nothing. You were dishonest."

The words stung. "Yes. Listen to me." I switched to English. "I sing instead of talking, my English teacher told me. He said I sound like an ignorant street *mestizo* begging from gringo tourists. I was embarrassed to let you hear me." I reverted to Spanish. "After people thought I couldn't speak English, I was embarrassed to admit that I could. It felt bad, lying to you. Remember I said I had something to tell you? I wanted to tell you about my lying. I wanted to apologize."

Tom picked up a paddle. "Let's find a place to dock. I need to wash the snake blood from me."

"Snake blood?"

"I'll explain later." He closed his eyes and took a deep breath. "We did it again, didn't we?"

"Yes. But we didn't shoot Sylvia. It was that terrible man."

"She fell into the river, just as Rochelle did. She fell out of the canoe we were using to escape. It was Sylvia the witch I saw when the bullets ripped into Rochelle."

"I know. When Maybre's bullets knocked Rochelle overboard, you called out to Sylvia, and you reached into the water for Sylvia as much as for the child Rochelle."

We went past one of the small tributaries, and Tom turned us around.

"What is it?" I asked.

"Back there, in that inlet. I thought I saw a canoe."

"We should let it be."

"I think it was ours. I want it."

We paddled hard to maneuver the heavy canoe against the current, and not far into the creek we saw two canoes pulled out of the water. One was the canoe we bought from Oz Osterwitz. Tom brought us to the bank and I stepped out, rope in hand. The inlet was too narrow to turn the boat, though it could drift off and vanish into the current of the river if not tied. Ferns grew on the lower bank beside the water, small ones that would wash away as soon as rainy season brought the water higher. I secured the rope to a rock and we climbed the bank beside the two canoes someone had dragged over the ferns and left at an angle on the steep side of the creek. At the top, Kaita met us.

She held a hand over her cheek and one eye, and she had tied a cloth over her breasts. At that moment she looked more like a child than ever, and Maybre's words came to me about Tom liking little girls, so it distressed me when he took Kaita's hand away from her face. Her cheek was purple and her eye swollen almost shut. "I heard gunfire," she said. "Did the gringos kill Poí?"

"No." Tom seemed to caress her hand. "We haven't seen Poí. The gunfire had nothing to do with him. Who beat you? Poí?"

"No. My husband. He thought—"

"Where is Poí?" I asked.

Tom dropped her hand, took the machete from his belt, and looked around.

"Gone to see the gringos behind the bamboo wall. You're hurt?" Kaita reached a tentative hand toward Tom.

"This isn't my blood. Did you and Poí come looking for me?"

"Where is your baby?" I asked.

Kaita looked from Tom to me. "Baby," she said and burst into tears, wincing when she touched her face.

I went down the bank for the travel bag, for the ointment I had used on Tom when he walked in darkness and into the spines of cactus. Now I would use the ointment on Kaita whose body looked like that of a child. She sobbed and became quiet; I could hear Tom comforting her, sounds that annoyed me. When I returned, Kaita sat on the trunk of a fallen tree and Tom knelt beside her, a look of concern on his face. I pushed him aside.

As I put ointment on Kaita's face, I asked Tom, "You must tell me if Catrina was tall or short."

"Catrina?" He sounded astonished. "You're asking me about Catrina at a time like this?"

"Just that one question. I need to know."

"Tall. She was just under two meters—almost as tall as I. This is no time to talk about her. Kaita, did you and Poí come looking for me?"

"No. We fled for fear of what the villagers would do to Poí. He killed the man who was beating me."

"Killed? Poí killed your husband?" I capped the ointment. There was too much here to think about at once: Catrina stood tall like an adult and not a child. Maybre lied as part of his nature, lied as men will in order to bend women to their will. Poí would have killed Tom for having sex with Kaita, but Tom was not drawn to children as Maybre was, and Tom didn't tell me lies. He was gentle with Kaita, but then so was I. Her cheek and swollen eye glimmered from the medication.

"With a hunting dart. When it hit him in the back, he knew he was dead, and he cried out in fear. I pulled the dart from him, but it was too late."

"And your baby? You left your baby?" There was a note of angry disapproval in Tom's question.

"Yes. But not my baby. My sister's. The dead man had fathered him on my own sister, and he demanded that I take the baby as mine."

"Your husband made your sister pregnant?" Tom recoiled in disgust.

"Yes. Yes." Kaita began crying again.

23

There are lessons in humility here, I told myself: Poí had not come for me and my glass eye, nor did his paddling down the river have anything to do with me or with Rosa but with his own dark deeds, his killing of a man who offended him and someone he loved, though it hadn't occurred to me until then that Poí loved Kaita, or that I loved Rosa, who now dropped the ointment tube into her travel bag and glanced at me, caught my eye and smiled with dimples that came from childhood, an unqualified smile that vanished as soon as she turned to the weeping Kaita.

The sky rumbled and a cool wind announced the coming of rain. Kaita stifled her sobs. "This way," she said and led us to a tree notched for climbing, to a shelter in the tree thatched with ground palm fronds, a shelter made for only two so the three of us would have to crowd close in the branching of the crow's nest, but I declined the climb. "I found *grandua* nuts," Kaita said. "We can break them open after the rain."

"I need to wash the snake's blood from me," I said.

Rosa took a bar of soap from the bag, handed it to me, and checked among the rolled and tightly-packed clothing. "You have dry clothes. Wash what you have on. It might not be easy to get the snake blood out."

"Snake?" Kaita asked. She began the climb to the low crow's nest where thatching would keep off rain.

"He hasn't told me about the snake," Rosa said, following Kaita up the tree.

By the time I reached the edge of the creek, its water rippled from rain. I considered what might be in that water. Perhaps piranha, called caribe, or an electric eel waited for me, though neither seemed likely. The water was too shallow to suit caribe and moved too fast for electric eel, who liked to live in reedy, still water. Anaconda, I hoped, lived in deeper water. I might pick up a leech, unsavory but not dangerous.

Allen got leeches when we crossed a wet, grassy area, an opening in the jungle where Phung Phuoc thought Americans might have planted mines, so he drove us before him and his three men who looked like boys and who wanted to kill us but Phuoc said no. The four of them were singing their tonal language so Allen and I couldn't understand, but their body language was clear enough; Phung drove us across the grassy place as Charlie did the mouse deer that rainy night when Allen chopped up the jungle with rapid fire, and there in the grassy place Allen had three leeches, black and wormy, creeping up his pants, but I didn't, though one got on my boot, a tiny one and easy to rake off in the grass.

I got leeches later when we waded across a stream that reminded me of Phuoc for its color like his brown skin and for being cold and sudden and strong enough to be dangerous because it nearly washed me into the big river just meters away when I fell and slammed against the bank, my hands tied in front of me making it hard to grasp the root that held me long enough for Allen to fish me out of the water, to drag me up the bank where we lay gasping, he from the effort and me from almost drowning, and the four enemy soldiers laughed their soprano laughter until Phuoc swatted me and Allen with the rattan whip. "Get up, long nose," he said. "You no dead yet." When we camped for the night, when Phuoc had his boys tie our hands behind us and tie them to bamboo stakes, I found the leeches. They dropped away from my stomach to wriggle out of the tears in my shirt, fat from blood and leaving behind thin streams from their wounds to weep and weep and not to coagulate for hours because of the saliva they injected in the skin to keep blood from congealing, and there was nothing, absolutely nothing I could do because of being staked to the ground, hands behind me. Allen said it was when I slammed against the bank that the leeches got on me, and Phuoc told us to shut up.

I stood nearly knee deep in the water that would have been clear enough if it weren't for how fast it flowed and for the rain denting its surface, clear for being fresh rain and running over sandy gravel in its draining of a jungle more dangerous than I figured before discovering Brother Maybre's compound and Brother Maybre who could shoot his own daughter right out of the canoe like the missionary shot Sylvia, bloody and loud with his shotgun to open up her chest and put red spots on her face and neck, spots I saw only for an instant as she spun around in her fall to the river and the waiting caribe, spots I would never forget. This isn't good, I told myself, this memory coming so vivid and crowding into me with the other images from a distant and darker jungle. As I pulled off my shirt, half expecting to find it torn from Phuoc's rattan whip, Rosa spoke my name.

She stood in the edge of the water, her clothes, set aside and wet from rain, bent several small ferns almost to the ground. "May I help wash your shirt?" She spoke English in a singing way so unlike the tonal singing of Phuoc, and though Rosita's skin might be Asian in color and the slant of her eyes, the mouse-deer darkness of them, the jet black of her hair might suggest Vietnam and another jungle, I knew she came toward me in clean innocence, knew it in the catch under my ribs and the sting in my eyes, and all it took was for her to touch me, to pull me against her for me to cry like a child.

Lightning splitting the sky directly overhead and the rain's increasing intensity, in needles of cold water, brought me back, and I found myself holding Rosa, her skin rippling from the cool, the two of us standing in the middle of the creek, its clear waters gurgling around our legs. "You're cold," I said, and she said no, no, she had never been so warm. "The goose bumps on your skin say otherwise," I told her, and she leaned back, her arms still around me, and looked at me in dimpled amusement.

"Goose?"

That's when I realized we were speaking English. "An idiom," I said in Spanish. "A silly one. Kaita is watching us." We looked up the bank at Kaita holding a ground palm frond like an umbrella, staring with rounded eyes.

"I don't care. Let her look." Rosa turned her attention to me. "I found my old friend Don again, and again as in childhood you wept for Sylvia. But not just for her. You wept for Rochelle, and you wept for me, and most of all for yourself."

"Your old friend Don," I whispered and pulled her to me. While rain washed over us and creek water dragged at our legs I told her about the snake blood, about my mad jealousy, about my intent to sink the machete into Brother Maybre but didn't because of the snake. But I didn't tell her why the snake offended me even more than the terrible Brother Maybre.

"I lied to Maybre," she said. "I told him I had syphilis, and he backed away, but not before he unbuttoned me and groped around on me."

Relief swept over me as rain poured upon us in white waves, striking the jungle with the roar of a waterfall. I rubbed the soap bar along her back and she released me, held up her arms for me to bathe her and said, "I am unclean."

"No," I said. "If there's anyone in this jungle, this world, who is pure and good it is you."

"But you don't know me. You don't know what I've done in the past."

"I know who you are and what you are and were. I'll rub you with soap because it allows me to touch you like a beggar touching Buddha in Thailand. I watched him rub gold leaf on a statue of the Buddha, a few tiny strips of gold leaf pressed on the icon with the tenderness of lovers touching and with the awe of devotion."

She turned, her eyelids swept down like the Buddha's to allow my bathing her just as she had done when? The day before, I realized with astonishment, though this time there was more to the bath, much more to the way she turned in the clean rain, the way she stood on the clean gravel and sand of the creek's clean water, and more to the way I touched her, all of her down to her knees at the edge of the water, the rain falling hard enough to wash away soap almost as fast as I applied it while Kaita watched from the bank. Rosa took my shirt and began splashing it in the creek. "Bathe quickly," she said. "I'm becoming cold."

I glanced at Kaita, shrugged, and took off my pants and underwear. Rosa dunked them and twisted them while I soaped myself and used my nails to scratch at stubborn spots of snake blood, and we left the water clean and without leeches, the cool feeling good to me though getting on the edge of cold, and Rosa beginning to shiver.

After the rain, I chopped ferns and bushes, and the three of us dragged them to the canoes in case Maybre decided to come looking for us. Rosa and I built another shelter similar to the one we used the previous night, and Kaita set about improving her tree nest. She said Poí had taken our canoe because the one they took from the village leaked so fast they spent much time bailing out water, and he feared it would become worse and perhaps sink, so he crossed the jungle back to the bamboo fence with the intent of taking one of the large canoes and was surprised to find ours tied to the dock. He took it, she said, because it was smaller and faster, and he feared being caught if he took the time to take one of the bigger, more sluggish canoes, feared the wrath of gringos who didn't understand the ways of jungle people, gringos who carried pistols and might kill. So it wasn't theft, I told myself, not theft as I understood the term, not that Poí's taking the canoe seemed significant compared to other matters, not after the trauma of my going for Maybre with the intent to kill or after he shot Rochelle. Still, the theft annoyed me, even if it wasn't theft. Poí had lived on the coast, had gone to movies even, so it wasn't like he was a jungle innocent. Rosa said it didn't matter, that what mattered was we retrieved the canoe and with it our hammock and mosquito netting. The hammock, she pointed out as we hung it in a new shelter, was the handiwork of Kaita. Toward evening we heard the roar of an outboard motor.

"They'll go right by us," Rosa said.

I agreed, but we nevertheless prepared for a flight through the jungle. It seemed wise for me to hide among the brush at the entry to the creek so I could make sure Maybre went on down the river. Rosa argued that I needed to stay with her, but I pushed through underbrush and waited. When the motorized canoe appeared, it held only one man.

Poí slowed, guided the canoe into the creek, cut the engine, and leaned it forward to keep the propeller from striking bottom. He picked up a paddle as Kaita waded into the water to help with docking. I hurried through wet undergrowth, hoping not to pick up a leech, and I gripped the machete. Poí didn't seem surprised to see me and Rosa. We helped pull the canoe up the bank, and I took Poí's quiver of poisoned darts from it, hung it from one shoulder, and took his blowpipe.

For a jungle person, for a man who had in normal times such a ready and black-toothed smile, Poí looked grim, his milky eye sunken and his brow furrowed. We sat on mats Kaita had laid out after we pulled the stolen canoe from the water, after I slung the quiver of poisoned darts over my shoulder lest Poí decide to put a dart into my back, though he seemed happy enough to see me, happy in his grim and worried way. "They're dead." He shook his head as in wonder. "All of them are dead."

"Who?" Kaita asked.

"The gringos who built the crazy houses and the bamboo fence that will wash away soon. Dead."

"Someone killed them?" Kaita asked.

"Yes. I watched first through chinks in the fence, then as they began to eat the leaves, I climbed a frangipani tree for a better view."

"Oleander leaves," Rosa whispered.

"Oleander, yes. I thought at first they were ignorant of what they did, but they ate with purpose. The man who killed the girl with his pistol—"

"You saw that? You saw him shooting at us?" I asked.

"From the trees beside the fence, yes, I heard the bell and watched you run to the canoes, and I was sorry I had borrowed your canoe when I saw your distress. Kaita, the man I spoke of before, the one with white clothes and a pistol on his side, the one who seemed to have shadows instead of eyes—that man tried to shoot our friends. First he shot a little girl."

"His own daughter," I said.

"No," Rosa said. "He called her a stray."

"Tom used his magic to keep the bullets from striking him and Rosa, and he made clever use of the eyeless man's own motor to escape."

"I used no magic."

"That nasty man forced his people to eat oleander leaves," Rosa said.

"He talked to them, and they brought a sick man from the big house."

"The poet. He told me he was about to die. But I didn't understand. I didn't understand."

"The eyeless one talked to the people and they bowed their heads and he talked to the sky and a rain cloud moved over them and they ate the leaves as rain began to fall. I wanted to stop them, to warn them until my white eye told me they knew, and still they ate the leaves. That's when I climbed the frangipani tree."

"You sat among flowers to watch them die," I said.

"I didn't stay to watch them sicken and die. The women chopped up leaves, mashed them into fruit paste of some kind that they took from jars, and everyone came to the table beneath the bell to eat, and everyone ate enough of the poison to kill three people. Rain fell on them and some shivered and some shed tears, but all ate, and most ate without being forced. The last to eat was the man with the pistol. He didn't have to use the weapon to make all of them eat. Only four refused, one of them a man, and the others held them while the eyeless one pointed his pistol at them. Two of them vomited, and he made them eat again. I became ill and dizzy watching. There are evil spirits there, and I feared them, so I slipped down the tree, circled the fence, and took a canoe. I also took gasoline cans from other canoes, and I considered returning later after death came for the gringos, because they have many things worth having. But it would be taking from the dead, and that's always dangerous."

24

We sat in silence on the mats. Tom seemed to be watching something along the creek, and I wondered if Catrina the Cat had returned to haunt him. Poí stared at the mat, and Kaita rubbed her cheek. The poet had saved our lives with his warning, then he waited for death. Guilt hit me like a stab beneath my navel, an old and familiar and painful feeling. "The sick man," I said to Poí, "the one brought from the big house. Did he seem upset by the preparations for death?"

"No. He was the first to eat. I thought he was hungry and ignorant of what the leaves could do, but that wasn't true. He wanted to die, and he wanted to be the first."

"He warned me even before Maybre started ringing the bell. And he warned me again when the bell sounded. That is why I ran and urged you to run, Tom. The poet saved us. But I abandoned him. Perhaps I killed him."

"He took his own life," Tom said.

"I killed my grandmother. Abuelita."

Tom looked at me with raised brows. "Cholera killed her. But I'm familiar with guilt. It's strange how hearing about death makes you think of others you know who have died."

"I told Maybre about oleanders, remember? You left the compound with only snake blood on you. I left with the blood of all the women in the compound, and the men. The poet. Even the horrible Maybre."

"No. I gave him the sign, he told me, and he went to ring the bell to call people to death."

"So we both feel guilty," I said, "just as we both felt guilt over the deaths of Sylvia and the missionary."

"We were children. We knew so little."

"And we know more now? Poí, can you tell us the story of how the spirits of tapirs became imprisoned within the stone hill?"

"No."

"I know," Kaita said. "It's one of the stories of the women of thunder."

"Tell us," I said.

Kaita rubbed her face and we waited. When I had given up and thought I would have to be the one to tell the story, she began.

A tapir named Dolora had a dream that came to her each night for three nights. She dreamed a man floated on spider webs from the moon. The man had beautiful skin that shimmered with the gold of a full moon and eyes like still pools on dark nights. "Take me to the other women of thunder, Dolora," the moon man said to the tapir woman. "Let me ride on your back and I will bring gifts to all of them."

Dolora fell in love with the soft voice and the shimmering beauty of moon man and allowed him to ride upon her back. She took him deep into the jungle where her family lived. As she approached, the man leaned close to her ears and whispered that he came to lock all the women of thunder within stone hills so they could serve as beasts of burden for spirits of the night. Dolora tried to throw him from her back, but he wrapped his spider webs around her and there was nothing she could do. She had to watch as he killed all of her family and captured their spirits to take to a hollow hill beside a great river. While he was inside the hill, Dolora broke the webs that held her and hid among bamboo. Moon man returned and searched and called to her until the sky became light from the sun, which caused him to shimmer and vanish in the morning air.

Each night for three nights she had the same dream, and each morning she told the dream to her family as they walked beside a river to seek food. The first morning Dolora's sister told her the dream meant she would die. The second morning Dolora's mother told her the dream meant her family would die if they had anything to do with the men who lived in the forest. The third morning Dolora's grandmother told her the dream meant she must be loyal to her family and stay with them or they would all perish. Dolora thought they were all wrong, and she wandered far down the river to seek among the animals the meaning of her dream.

Armadillo told her she must learn to dig in the earth to discover the meaning of the dream. Anaconda told her she must learn to swim under the river if she wanted to discover the meaning of the dream. Parrot told her she must give up searching for the meaning of the dream if she wanted to learn the meaning of the dream.

Dolora dug in the earth but found only worms. She swam under the river but found only leeches. At last, she returned home to find the forest people had killed her sister and mother and grandmother and made a shelter from their hides. Inside the shelter was a young girl whose first moon had come upon her. Dolora found the girl did not know about the killing of the tapirs and did not know the walls of her shelter were made from hides of Dolora's family.

Dolora left with her sadness and wandered beside the river until she came to a stone hill with someone inside, knocking on the stone. She remembered the words of the armadillo and dug at the base of the hill until she found a cave that took her inside the hill. Within she found the spirits of her sister and mother and grandmother, along with the spirits of many other tapirs who had been killed by forest people to use the hides for shelters where they kept girls whose moon had come upon them. The spirits yearned to escape the stone hill and wander again in the forest. Dolora found a river that ran through the bottom of the hollow hill. She remembered the words of the Anaconda and dove deep into the river, swam under the rock hill, and emerged at night where the river flowed out of the hill. All of the tapir spirits followed her, and when they climbed to the shore, they shook themselves and stomped to get the water from them.

"Their shaking and stomping sounded like thunder," Kaita said. "When the forest people saw them in the moonlight and heard them, they named them the *women of thunder.*"

I waited for the rest of the story, but Kaita's silence said she was finished. "I heard the story differently," I said.

"The story is evidence that spirits live in the hills and under the earth," Poí said.

"The way I told the story is the true and proper way to tell it," Kaita said.

"The parrot was wrong," Tom said. "She never found the meaning of her dream because she stopped searching."

"But she did find the meaning," I said. "She found the meaning only when she stopped trying to find it. The parrot was right. We could learn from the parrot."

"It's just a story," Kaita said. "There's nothing to learn from it. Parents tell it to children to entertain them. I told it to you, and for a short time we forgot about my husband beating me and Poí stopping him with a poisoned dart. We forgot about the gringos murdering themselves and one another."

"Night will come soon," Poí said. "We haven't eaten."

"There is a guava tree with ripe fruit." Kaita pointed. "I have grandua nuts." She took three of them from a cloth pouch she had suspended in a tree. They were the size of coconuts.

"What are those?" Tom asked.

"Some gringos call them giant Brazil nuts," I said. "They're heavy with oil but will suffice for a meal. Eat with moderation, and eat more guava than nuts."

Poí borrowed Tom's machete, though Tom relinquished it with some hesitation. He kept Poí's quiver of darts close to him, and Poí seemed to understand. With the machete, Poí cut and sharpened two pieces of bamboo. He then opened the Brazil nuts and showed us the use of the bamboo for prying nut meat from the shell. Tom recoiled from the bamboo when Poí offered it, so I took it and began separating nut from shell.

"When you're ready," Poí said, handing the machete to Tom, "you might allow me to have the darts for my blowgun. I might get lucky and kill us some meat."

"I cannot eat monkey."

"I know. Perhaps bird, though not parrot. I saw you couldn't eat parrot, either."

"Right now I don't much like the thought of killing any creature."

"I understand," I said, and Poí gave us a puzzled look.

After our meal of oily nut flesh, after Poí cast some stones into the river and mumbled magic words to satisfy himself that we had a good chance of living for another ten days, Tom and I retired to the crude shelter we had built. Kaita and Poí climbed to their shelter, though how they planned to be comfortable sleeping in the small space was a mystery to me.

As the sun dropped into the trees, Tom and I arranged our mosquito netting and got into the hammock. Darkness came fast, and with it the nighttime sounds of the jungle. Especially abundant were the sharp notes of whistle frogs. "Where are Poí's poisoned darts?" I asked.

"Hidden close by. Perhaps I'm being too careful."

"Is it possible to be too careful in this jungle?"

We nudged each other through the web of the hammock, our hands touching, and our hips. "I wish," Tom said, "that we could sleep with our heads at the same end."

"Not possible. The hammock would—"

"I know. But it would be nice. Even better would be for us to sleep on a palm-frond mat, as we did above the bat caves when we were children."

"It was a mat made from banana leaves."

"It was? Banana leaves, then. I would give anything to lie beside you on a mat of banana leaves."

"Maybe it wasn't even banana leaves. I forget. But no matter. We would be in danger of getting the disease that afflicted the poet. The kissing beetle would—"

"I know. It would bite us on the face and leave its shit and we would scratch in the dark and open up places for the bacteria from the bug shit to get into us, and we would get the poet's nasty variety of sleeping sickness. You told me. But I still wish I could sleep beside you on whatever leaves would make a mat."

We listened to the whistle frogs, the night birds and buzzing insects, to the wet sound of the creek below us, to the crash of an occasional deadfall in the jungle. I thought perhaps Tom had drifted into sleep by the time Catrina appeared. She resembled Kaita in being short and dark and looking like a child, though of course parts of her were much the developed woman. She had the mark of a plum on her neck, and I wondered how Tom thought it looked like a strawberry. Perhaps I dreamed her, for she faded as Mata-Mata appeared with his thorn tree huge on one shoulder. He gleamed in the patchy moonlight, his skin patterned with leaves. "Tell your story and leave," I whispered under the buzzing and whistles so Tom wouldn't hear.

Mata-Mata groaned under his weight and drew closer. Again he had assumed the face of my father. "You killed Donito," he whispered.

"That's not your story. You may not talk of my Donito." The words were hard to say, and I feared Mata-Mata would hear the anguish in my voice when I said *Donito*.

"You killed the poet."

"Yes." I didn't want to hear those words, but almost any were better than more talk of Donito.

"And your own parents."

"Yes."

"And your grandmother."

"Yes." I began crying. "Tell your story and leave. Please."

"Not my story, Rosita. I must tell your story, for you have forgotten it. You killed Sylvia the witch, do you remember?"

"The sharpened bamboo sticks were a surprise," Tom said, and I realized he had not gone to sleep at all and that he had not seen Mata-Mata.

"Tell the gringo to shut up," Mata-Mata said.

"Were you asleep?" Tom asked.

"No. Look, beside us. Mata-Mata stands in the moonlight."

"Who?" Tom's movement tossed the hammock about, and Mata-Mata faded back into the taller trees, his white body glimmering then vanishing in the jungle.

"Nobody." I started to tell him again about the oleander leaves and about my part in the killing of the gringos, but he began talking about bamboo.

25

It was nothing more than a tool Poí made to get meat from the shell of the giant Brazil nut, but there was more to it, much more, though what that was exactly eluded me when Poí first offered me the stick, when I refused to touch it, when Rosa took the bamboo stake because she saw my distress and understood it better than I in that moment. Though it was clean and fresh-cut from new bamboo, I saw it with a blackened point, a dirty point from being driven into the jungle soil so Phuoc's boys could tie my hands behind me, jerk me to the ground, and tie my hands to the stake like hunters who found it necessary to stake their dogs but more cruel and with no concern for how tight the rope was and how it cut into my wrists to swell my fingers and make them throb while I watched the boys do the same to Allen so we sat side-by-side pinned to the ground in silence lest our talking annoy Phuoc enough to pick up his piece of rattan. Lying hip-to-hip with Rosa in our chinchorro, I tried to tell her about the sharpened bamboo, but words seemed inadequate to convey the magnitude of what Phuoc's boys did with it and the magnitude of what I did with it.

"They got sloppy," Allen whispered. He leaned toward me then away from me, doing something with his hands. With the short tropic twilight came the electronic sounds of a night jar to prime the insects and frogs and get them started into the screaming of a jungle night. Phuoc prepared a mat for sleeping, and his boys did the same farther away, all of them working like monkeys with branches and leaves except that no monkey I'd ever seen would make a nest on the ground. We were all dead tired from long days of marching through jungle, and two of Phuoc's monkeys fell asleep before they had much of a nest made; the third sat up as guard, trying to look awake, but I could tell he would go to sleep sitting up as soon as Phuoc began to snore, which didn't take long, not long at all, so there was still some light from the sun dropping toward darkness when Allen pulled his stake out of the ground. He scooted closer to me. "My wrists," he whispered. "Loose. Pick at the ropes."

Not a chance, I thought, moving my fingers. But it seemed easy, and somehow we had him untied. He took the rope from my wrists. "The monkeys are asleep," I whispered.

He put his lips close to my ear. "Quiet. Here." He put the bamboo stake into my hands. Even in the dim light I could see its dark point, glistening and moist. "Get Dumb Fuck with this if he wakes up. I'll grab his piece and off the other shits."

I knelt above Phung Phuoc's head, held the stake in both hands, measured the distance and arc for implanting the bamboo point in his neck, and thought of his use of the rattan and the ripping of my shirt and the look of profound indifference on Phuoc's face as he swung; I shifted around to feel the pull of my shirt sticking to the dried blood on the back and sides from where Phuoc's rattan got me. In the fading light all I could see was the spot on his neck moving with a heartbeat though I heard in a dim way the hushed noise of Allen picking up a rifle. My arms and hands seemed to do it independent of thought: they moved in a slow arc then in sudden and great speed with me watching as I might watch a truck out of control speeding into a car at a stoplight maybe, as I might stand on a sidewalk feeling helpless and horrified and absolutely unable to stop the truck or warn the driver of the car until the sharpened bamboo, black with jungle dirt, struck the spot moving with a heartbeat.

"Damn!" Allen whispered and was on his feet moving toward the monkeys, and the noise of the firing almost covered surprised cries and cries of pain and cries of death while Phuoc spasmed with hands rushing to his throat and his eyes yellow and black looking at me, looking at me, and the blood gushing into a sudden silence as night fell at that very moment to find the jungle silent because even the insects and frogs, even the night jars fell quiet for once, stunned by my violence and Allen's, and the stillness echoed with horror, my hands sticky, the short twilight gone so I could see nothing and hear nothing and feel only a desire wild, crazy to get the sticky off my hands with rubbing in the dirt, jungle dirt moist and unclean but better than the sticky sickness in my stomach and on my hands against leaves and bark. "Water," I said. "Water," and the insects began again, just a few at first, almost experimental to see if it were safe to buzz in the violent night, then the boinging of the night jar and then frogs and all other creatures bent upon adding their voices to the screaming night of an evil jungle.

I tried to tell Rosa about the sounds and the sticky on my hands and the way Allen's words make a knot in my stomach, words about Phuoc and his monkeys being dead meat and he repeated the phrase, *dead meat*, and laughed with a wildness to his voice like Joey's over the tiger grabbing his boot; I tried to tell Rosa about the terrible phrase dead meat with its human smell and about the sudden darkness of a Vietnamese night, raising my voice for Rosa above the chorus of a better jungle though not better by much, above whistle frogs that didn't live in Asia and above the insects that did live there to sing the same shrill notes; I tried to tell her about the restless night spent close to the bodies in utter darkness and the smell and the determination to stay there so we could wait for light and get their supplies, their arms and balls of rice, tried to tell about the way my fingers still stuck together in spite of spitting on them and rubbing, rubbing until they felt raw and still sticky, but the words didn't say it, only the facts of the night and not the horror and relief and joy to be free of Phuoc and darkness and horror, the unspeakable horror that wouldn't and couldn't be shaped into words. In the telling of it, in raising my voice above the sounds of the Venezuelan nighttime jungle, I felt a catching between my fingers and wanted to wash my hands, but I didn't tell her that, didn't tell her most of what I wanted to tell with words inadequate to say and heart beating wild from the memory and from feeling dumb to tell the vast significance of that distant night in Vietnam.

Allen worried about snakes. Pit vipers, he said, could kill you, though where they came from was beyond me for the jungle had no pits that I knew of except for the tunnels Charlie liked to dig, and they didn't count because pit vipers were there long before Charlie; and green tree snakes that seemed to have no fangs, Allen said, and the locals thought they weren't poisonous because of the lack of fangs, but in the backs of their mouths, folded and invisible until they needed them lay the fangs, he said, and a green tree snake could kill you. Even in the goddam ocean, Allen said, there were snakes, the most poisonous of all, sea snakes with venom that worked on your nervous system unlike the venom of Texas rattlesnakes that attacked soft flesh, and not in large amounts because sea snakes were small, but that didn't matter because one little bite could kill you. Green mambas were all over the friggin' jungle he said, with poison like that of the sea snake so the grunts he knew from near the coast called the green mamba a "two-step" because after one bit you, you could take only two steps before you died, and there was nothing, absolutely nothing you could do if you got bitten, and there wasn't much you could do in the dark of night if a two-step took a notion to bite you and kill you. There were plenty of black cobras, he said, with venom like that of the sea snake to work on your nervous system, plenty of them in the jungle and even in the palm oil plantations, though they moved in slow motion, too slow to survive in a fight with a mongoose who had no poison but moved fast enough to avoid being bitten and fast enough to snap its jaws on the black cobra's neck and kill it as sure as I had killed Phuoc when I plunged the bamboo stake into his neck, but the black cobra could get you unawares and even with its slow attack could inject you with its venom and kill you. "And the king cobra," Allen said, "is big as a Georgia alligator, and when you least expect it can be waiting in its deadly silence to kill you."

He told about having honey-bucket duty one morning, a job that involved emptying the barrels used at the latrines where guys sat on wooden benches with outhouse holes, the benches built on the side of a hill so the barrels sat under the holes, and soldiers called those barrels honey buckets, maybe so the words would make them seem less nasty and maybe for the grim humor of the term; and when he and his buddy went to empty the honey buckets they found a king cobra wrapped around one of them, spiraled all around it from bottom to top for the warmth and its gigantic head within inches of the outhouse hole where the guys sat to do their business. His buddy, Allen said, wouldn't go to the latrine after that, not to sit down, and he ended up going to the medic for constipation. "The goddam king cobra is the worst and scariest of the lot," Allen said, sitting beside me in the darkness with the smell of Phuoc and his dead monkeys drifting over to us and my fingers sticking together, "and when you least expect it, one of them big sumbitches can get you with fangs like hypodermics for horses, and it will sure as hell kill you."

I did manage to tell Rosa about the dizziness that came in the night, a spinning, sick feeling in my head and stomach that came from watching my hands plunge the bamboo into Phuoc's neck and from the steaming night making what was left of Phuoc and his three bullet-ripped monkeys turn ripe like durian so if they happened to be upriver from our chinchorro the carrion-eating blue butterflies would swarm to them, but they lay on the leafmold turf of an Asian jungle that had none of the shimmery blue butterflies to flock to the smell; I managed to tell about the sticky on my hands back in that nightmare night and again when I cut the snake from Maybre's face and again as I spoke beside her in the chinchorro, a sticky feeling between each finger to make me want to go to the creek and wash even if I knew it wasn't blood, not then, not suspended above the jungle floor with our hips pressed together by the hammock, with mosquito netting over us; we hung there safe enough from insects and most jungle animals except perhaps for Poí if he decided to come after me to get the Irishman's glass eye from my pouch, though that seemed unlikely since what drove him and Kaita to follow us wasn't a lust for the eye or even a lust to follow us but a desire to escape village justice for the blood he had on his hands even if he never touched Kaita's husband and no more had literal blood on his hands than I did to cause my fingers to feel sticky in the moist night.

26

The storm of Tom's guilt hit me hard. Mata-Mata shifted among the shadows, the thorn tree on his shoulder pushing against branches of rosewood and guava. He grinned a hideous and toothy grin, and that's all I could see of him, the grin, ghostly white among dark shapes of trees. I knew Tom's silence would draw Mata-Mata closer.

The smells of Tom's Asian jungle had drifted across us while he struggled to contain the horror he felt in the telling. But the horror was vivid and heavy even if he tried to be clinical in offering only forensic details of events. Part of the horror was the smell. I thought it might dissipate in the clean night air when he was done with the telling, but it did not.

The smell became worse, and with a tingling along the back of my neck I realized the smell had become the stink of cholera, of the death house where I came too late to see my parents alive and where I watched Abuelita slip into death.

The Sisters of Mercy forbade me to leave Cantaura, forbade me to go to El Tigrito, claimed there was nothing I could do in the epidemic except die. But I went. It took only a change of clothing and a walk to the highway where I waved down a truck coming over the mountains from Puerto La Cruz on the coast. The trucker dropped me off at a gas station close to the government tent set up to house the dying. Even from the station we could smell the diarrhea, the decimated bodies, the death.

"No," I said aloud, pushing away the memory, the smell, reaching for Abuelita as she had been before I went to study nursing with the Sisters of Mercy, before cholera came. Perhaps I slept.

"This," my grandmother said, holding a flower she had plucked in the edge of the savanna, "will help with many illnesses. This is the purple coneflower. We'll dig up its roots and dry them, then grind them into powder for sprinkling over rice or into soup. It's powerful medicine with powerful spirits."

I helped her dig with garden spades and a rake, helped her pull up and shake dirt from the roots and did so out of love for her but with contempt for her superstition about spirits living in roots. Later, in studying pharmaceutical uses of plants, I learned about the purple coneflower, called echinacea. It stimulates the immune system and does aid in healing. In the days before antibiotics it was a common drug in medicine cabinets of Europe and the Americas. When I became a nurse, I carried powdered echinacea in my medical bag, giving me the reputation of being a curandera, a witch who worked with weeds and spirits. Abuelita and I also gathered wild garlic.

The early light of morning awakened me, and I was surprised. Mata-Mata had stayed away. I managed to avoid going into the tent where my grandmother lay dying. Tom slept through the night after reliving the horror of Phung Phuoc. Night sounds gave way to the cries of birds who preferred to move about and feed during the day. Caciques and parakeets had begun singing, though they still waited for more light before taking flight. The air smelled clean and moist, and I liked the cool of it.

Poí had cut a spear and speared us a catfish, a big one, and Kaita skinned it, cut it into steaks, skewered and roasted them. Tom complained about the lack of salt, but he was pleased with the smoky meat. We sat on Kaita's grass mats to eat catfish and guava. "We're lucky," Poí said. "Food can be scarce in the jungle. Starvation took my mother and many others of my village. Starvation drove me to the coast to live among such strange people with strange notions of how to behave. But hardly anyone starves these days. People come in boats with motors, and they bring us rice when we are in need of it, and beans. They bring cassava."

"Who comes with such gifts of food?" Tom asked.

Poí shrugged. "People. I don't know. The government? Some are missionaries, but I don't like them coming around with their bleeding god. Of course, no one will be bringing us food while we float down the river. So we're lucky to have guava and catfish. We're lucky Kaita found the grandua nuts yesterday to go with the guava. Tomorrow we might not be so lucky."

"Not we," Tom said. "You and Kaita will leave in your motorized longboat. With it you can go upriver or down, as you choose, but you will go without me and Rosa."

This felt too clipped, too rejecting and rude, even if I agreed with it, so I spoke fast to keep Poí and Kaita from having to respond out of embarrassment: "Where will you go?"

"There's a village down the river where I might earn a living with my magic, though it seems unlikely. I must try hard, for Kaita is now my wife."

"I'm pleased for you both," Tom said.

"Do you understand the use of the blowgun and darts?" Poí asked Tom.

"No."

"Perhaps you will leave them where I might find them? I could use them to hunt food for me and my wife. I will never again use a poisoned dart on a human being."

"I understand." Tom nodded. "You're saying you will not kill me or Rosa. This is good."

"My magic is weak, and my milk eye tells me little of any use anymore. Perhaps you could use your magic eye to find me a better name so my magic will become strong again?"

Tom opened the leather pouch on his belt and took out the glass eye. "I kept this for eighteen years," he mused. "It didn't fit the Irishman. He won it when gambling with a wild man in Borneo, he said, and it was too large, causing headaches, and his other glass eye was too small. I don't even know why I kept the eye."

"Perhaps," I suggested, "it's time to give it up?"

Tom looked at me with a slow nod. He held up the eye to scan Poí. "Merlin. Your new spirit name is Merlin."

"Merlín." Poí's voice dropped to an awed whisper.

"Take this." Tom offered the eye. Poí cupped his hands to receive it and stared round-eyed as Tom dropped the eye into his hands. "The eye is now yours."

"My own eye. I now have three eyes, one for seeing this world and two for seeing other worlds. Tom, you're my brother. You have given me a way to be a powerful seer, and I can now make a living for my wife. Look, wife, look at this magic eye that is mine."

Kaita scrambled back when Poí turned to her with the eye. "Make it stop staring at me. Please."

"I've known that eye for as long as Tom has, Kaita. It cannot harm you, I promise."

"I don't like it looking at me."

"You need something to carry it in," Tom said. He removed the pouch from his belt, took out some coins, his Barlow pocket knife, and the ancient finger bone, which he hid in his palm. "This pocket trash can go into a regular pocket." He put the items into the pocket of his pants and handed the pouch to Poí.

"A leather eye socket," Poí said, pleased. "I'm now Merlín, the most powerful seer in South America."

It took Poí much fussing and muttering to decide which of the compound canoes to take. He consolidated the booty—gasoline cans, spare motor, paddles—into one canoe while Kaita broke camp.

"When I was a child," Tom told Kaita, "I went down this same river with Rosa. We found a waterfall not far beyond some limestone hills that had no trees on them. I think the higher hills protruded from the jungle on the left side of the river."

"It's possible the river has shifted its course in the last eighteen years," I said. "The hills might now be on the right side."

"The rock hills of the women of thunder," Kaita said. "We must not stop among them."

"Beware of the waterfall beyond the hill. Rosa and I saw a black caimán, and we hid in the canoe, so we didn't see the waterfall until it was too late. We lost our canoe and almost drowned."

"There are ways to slide a canoe downhill to avoid a waterfall," Kaita said. "The hard part is having to pull it uphill. We're lucky not to be going upriver."

We helped them float the canoe into the creek and watched them move into the river. As the current grabbed them and Kaita worked the paddle, Poí pulled on the starter rope and called to us, "May you know blessings from the women of thunder." The engine sputtered then came alive to cover bird calls and river sounds with the ugly grumbling of an outboard.

Tom and I stood in the creek where we had launched them. He took my hand and we listened to the fading of the motor and to the jungle sounds reasserting themselves. "I should have let the snake kill Maybre." Tom released my hand. "Or helped the boa. It seems certain that I used my machete on the wrong creature."

We waded ashore. I put on my alpargatos and Tom sat on the bank, propped up his feet to dry before putting on his boots. "Are you making yourself responsible for what Maybre did?" I asked.

"I could have saved Rochelle and all the other people in the compound by killing that terrible man."

"Is it right to preserve life by taking it?"

"Soldiers ask that question." Tom sighed. "Why did Brother Maybre kill his followers? Why did they allow it?"

"Do we ever find answers to such why questions?"

We took our time preparing our canoe for the trip so there would be little chance of overtaking Poí and Kaita. The sun had become brutal by the time we pushed into the main current of the river, so we worked to stay in the shade of the trees. "When we were children, we built a canopy over the first canoe we stole," Tom said.

"We stole no canoes."

"We stole them. The canoes belonged to mestizos who wouldn't understand stealing as the jungle people do."

"One we took from gold miners who threatened to kill us. The next we took from Sylvia's people, who were jungle people. It was the second canoe that had the canopy against the sun."

"I forget such details," Tom said. "They don't matter, now. Should we make a shade for this canoe?"

"Yes. But we won't. We'll go ashore when the heat becomes too much and wait until the sun slants enough to give more shade on the water."

"Good plan," Tom said.

Was this consensus, I wondered, or had Tom and I assigned me the job as leader, as we did the last time we traveled the river? I watched the shores and dipped the paddle infrequently, as did Tom, allowing the river to take us at its own pace. Lianas hung like ropes from trees along the edge, orchids in blue and yellow grew in clumps of threads on many trees, and some of the trees had begun to bloom. It was easy to slip into believing we traveled through a primordial garden, a paradise, an Eden before the fall. Perhaps, I thought, it was for such an illusion that I agreed to undertake a difficult and dangerous trip with this strange gringo who once was my childhood friend. And perhaps it was in hope that he would become more than a friend. I shook that idea away, reminding myself that he was married and that divorce was not an option for people such as I. To me, Tom was still married. Besides, I came not for Tom but for myself. The appearance of Mata-Mata confirmed it: I would have to face the reality of my having killed my family, of my guilt about the death of Sylvia the witch. Was that what Mata-Mata said? That I killed Sylvia?

And now. Now. Now I had to acknowledge my part in the death of the poet, of Rochelle. It's too much, I thought, forcing my attention back to the jungle, to watching a tree sloth, still as a statue and high in a tree, to listening to the squawk of parrots, to smelling the raw green of the forest, to feeling the cool wetness of the canoe paddle. But the copper taste of guilt remained on the back of my tongue.

27

We watched a sloth hooking its fingers to a high branch and looking back while the river murmured around us, murmuring loudest close to the shady shore where it washed over stones that looked more like skulls than some skulls I'd seen, a place on the river that reminded me of Oz and his story of Oracón while the deeper part of the river reminded me of years ago when Rosita and I saw a black caimán floating dead in the water, though why I would think of the big crocodilian right then was beyond me since the creature liked to live in swampy inlets, and there was no sign of swamp anywhere around; we watched the sloth as the waters swept us around a bend, so we didn't notice the rock hills until we were nearly upon them. Rosa uttered a little cry of pleasure. "They are in that hill," she pointed.

"What are?"

"The women of thunder. Look, a perfect place to take the canoe ashore, there among those bushes."

She was right. We brushed leaves as we approached, and I looked with some concern at the overhanging branches to make sure we weren't going to be swarmed by ants that liked to live in a particular kind of tree—what was it called? I struggled to remember, then shrugged, for the canoe quenched its speed in the slushy sand of shore, and Rosa hopped out to tie us to a rock. Then she was gone through the brush, and I could hear her scrambling up the incline to reappear on an outcropping of rock. "This is the place," she said.

"You think Dolora the tapir dug here to find her dead relatives?" I asked.

"Maybe. But what I had in mind was that this is the place where you and I camped and you saw a snake, or at least you said you did even though it was just a vine, and we found the bone caves, and I used a stone to get a rabbit for breakfast."

I looked at the rock hill rising from the jungle, a hill that seemed to pop out of the greenery like a blister, and I nodded. "This is the same place. I'm sure of it."

"We'll camp up there." She pointed. "Come on."

The note of excitement in her voice kindled a wild enthusiasm in my breast, a hunger to see the hill and the cave and the overhang at the top where we once slept on a bed of banana leaves. When I caught up with her, she stood on the rim of a rock bowl, a gigantic one that had soil in it and undergrowth and some trees, an area dominated by a tree taken directly out of my childhood memories. "The breadfruit tree," I whispered.

"Yes. Yes. Yes. The same one?"

"Either the same or one that grew from seeds produced by the one that fed us when we were naked little savages. You were nut-brown, nubile, fantastic in your beauty and I had hair the color of a grape."

"Purple hair, yes. I tried to dye it and got the dye wrong and gave you purple hair." Rosa took my hand but kept her attention on the tree. "We can eat breadfruit, but not yet. My memory is that we were not nude when we found the breadfruit tree. I was afraid you would sunburn. We didn't strip until we fell in the guano—something that we won't do this time."

"No," I agreed, though I planned to go into the cave again, even if she didn't.

A vague path still wound up the side of the hill and took us to the cave, though we didn't see it at first because of the brush and because we followed the path beyond it until Rosa pointed. "The bat cave. The bone cave." Her voice quivered with excitement, and I started back down the path. She caught my arm. "Not now. Now we climb to the overhang near the top where we once camped."

"Where the rabbit visited us. Where we slept on banana leaves." I followed her, the two of us almost running in spite of the heat and the effort it took to climb uphill.

Beside the end of the faint trail, where it vanished on a flat place, a small thorn tree stood, its roots winding into a crack in the rock, and I knew those roots tapped into a pocket of water inside the rock else the thorn couldn't survive a single dry season, unlike the cliff trees of Malaysia—trees that grew from a seed blown into a crack in a building, an old building like those in the Chinatown district of Kuala Lumpur, the tree growing because there was no dry season, because rain fell often enough to wash over the roots and give the plant life even if there was no soil, only the fake cliff of the British-era building where the tree would leaf and branch and grip the wall's cracks and send more roots down the side of the building to hang there in the air and pick up moisture from almost daily rains. But this tree, this small thorn beside the place where Rosita and I once camped, had to have its roots sunk into a rock cistern for survival. The stone overhang seemed smaller than I remembered, not as deep or as high, the way my elementary school seemed when I returned as an adult to find the chairs shrunken and the blackboards dingy, small, wrong, and yet the same ones. Rosa moved against me, her eyes brimming with tears, and I wondered about the tears, wondered about me that nothing stirred me enough to feel anything more than excitement about being again in the vicinity of the bone caves. She fingered the leather pouch hanging around her neck and whispered, "I'll return the finger bone."

"I planned to do that with my piece of the ancient Indio, though I didn't know you would do it."

"Yes, you knew it." Her tone was so solemn that I dared not contradict her. "You knew. One of the reasons for this trip for us both was to return the bones we took eighteen years ago."

"The Indios are dead. They won't care if we keep the bones or throw them into the river."

"No? Believe that if you wish. It's important to us to return the bones, whether the Indios notice or not. It'll be a most important ceremony, and you knew that or you would not have kept the bone, would not have brought it with you."

"I don't much go in for ceremonies. I thought I'd just go into the outer chamber and fling the bone into the darkness of the burial cave."

"Yes. I thought the same. We're much alike, you and I." She turned to me, her lashes still misty, and I felt my throat tighten. "We must say some words."

"To the Indios?" The notion of talking to long-dead bones astounded me.

"To them, yes. But mostly to us."

"We'll talk to ourselves?" This was a bit better, I thought, but still silly. "Why don't we just talk to each other like usual?"

"We will. And we'll talk to ourselves. That is the nature of a ceremony. It'll help clarify to us why we are here. It'll help heal us."

"Heal? We are in need of being healed?"

"We're wounded, both of us, so much so that we can hardly touch each other without pain. That's why you've kept your distance all this time, and why I've done the same. The bath we took in the river after the monkeys covered us with filth was a ceremony."

"It was a bath. We were filthy."

"At first it was a bath. Then it became a baptism."

"That makes no sense."

"You're right. Such ceremonies make no sense, not to our heads. To our hearts, though, they change us and soothe us and heal us, and when we're whole again, they keep us well. Ceremonies do that. Please be thinking about what words you will say when we return the bones."

Something about her intonations made my scalp prickle with a shiver that ran down my back, and I wondered if there were something right about her words even while knowing them to be absurd. Talking to the dead—this wasn't something I could be comfortable with any more than I would find it meaningful to talk to the stone hill or to the river.

Then I remembered Catrina's photograph, remembered talking to it, remembered Phuoc taking it from my billfold and tossing it to the ground, remembered his unzipping and urinating on it, then ordering me to do the same and I would not and he put a pistol to my head and Allen said, "For godsake, Don, piss on the picture. It's just a piece of paper with plastic on it. Piss on it and save your life," and I shook my head and Phuoc cocked his pistol and I told him to shoot me but he didn't. Instead he cut a piece of rattan, the first one he cut but not the last, and made it whistle through the air to hit my back again and again, each time pausing long enough to tell me to piss on her and I wouldn't and the rattan whistled again until Allen stepped over to the photograph and pissed on it and I wanted to hit Allen for doing that even when I knew he did it for me and not against me, and a part of me knew the photograph wasn't Catrina, and a part of me knew if it were Catrina, Allen would believe she needed to be pissed on for the strawberry on her neck that wasn't mine but my brother's, my own brother's, a memory that came and went and this time caused me to take a step and stumble with Rosa to catch my arm, to look at me with alarm and concern, to lean into me and press my cheek with an innocent kiss, to kiss me and rub a hand on my back across the ripples of the scars from Phuoc's rattan, an act that moved me to tell her about Phuoc and Allen and the photograph.

"It was like a rock, wasn't it?" I said. "Or a hill or a river. Like ancient bones of the long dead, finger bones. And yet I kept that photograph and even talked to it. Was that a ceremony, talking to the photograph?"

"You know the answer to that. And you still feel the wounds of that rattan."

"No. Scar tissue is insensitive."

Rosa looked at me and shook her head, her eyes telling me that I didn't understand, but she was wrong. I understood all too well. Allen should not have urinated on Catrina, even if he meant well.

"Will you sleep on a banana-leaf bed here with me?" I'd had enough of Phuoc and Allen and Catrina for the moment.

"Scorpions might crawl into our ears." She held up her hands to quiet my protest. "I know, none did so eighteen years ago. We were lucky. This time could be different, and the kissing bug—"

"Then I'll build tripods of bamboo to hold our chinchorro." I took the machete from my belt. "There, where the overhang will keep the rain off, if it rains in the night."

"It will rain. Bamboo grows not far from our breadfruit tree, and I have nylon string for tying it together. I brought it as fishing line, but it seemed better for us to fish with fiber from a tree." She gave me a tiny grin that played along the corners of her mouth but not her eyes. "Another time, perhaps, you will tell me more about what happened to you in Asia? Not now. I know the time is wrong now." She turned without waiting for an answer and took the trail where it appeared faint beside the small thorn tree that wasn't there eighteen years ago.

I followed her to the bamboo, admonished myself to beware of snakes, and began chopping; Rosa went toward the canoe. The cane I cut was no bigger around than my thumb, so I had to harvest enough to bind together for beefing up the legs of the tripods. I lopped the poles, cut away leaves that looked like grass but were sharp enough to slice skin, and dragged the cane up the hill with Rosa walking ahead of me carrying the travel bag, and we both made an effort not to look for the bone cave on our way up, a cave where we would soon hold the ceremony of dead fingers and she would talk to the spirits of the dead within the cave, even if there were nothing in there but bats, and she would turn to me expecting some ceremonial words, hard words to find, ones I would resist uttering, though I could of course quote from "Jabberwocky" again since much of what I had said to Poí was nonsense even when Dodson wrote it—a dangerous thing for me to do because she spoke English and might well recognize what I was up to, and she would be disappointed in me, which was something I wanted to avoid at all costs in that moment walking behind her as we climbed the hill of our childhood with me dragging bamboo enough to hold our chinchorro above possible scorpions and kissing beetles.

Beyond the thorn sapling with its roots in the crack of a cistern, beside the overhang where we would sleep, she turned and said, "Some ceremonies are not healing. Some are damaging."

"Then we won't say any words to the old bones?" I began sorting the bamboo into piles for binding together to make tripod legs.

"That's not what I meant. What Phuoc did to the photograph of la gata, and what he tried to get you to do was a ceremony. His use of the rattan was a ceremony. Your refusal to do as he said, and Allen's peeing on the photograph—"

"Please. Please."

"But of course. The moment is wrong." She took a spool of monofilament nylon line from the bag and handed it to me.

28

We ate the pulp of breadfruit for lunch. When the afternoon rain came, Tom stripped for a bath. "Join me," he said.

"Rain water falls like needles of ice in this high jungle. How do you stand it?"

"You said accurately that my ancestors dived into fjords. But this rain is warm."

"Warm?"

"Not so cold, at least."

I sat on the chinchorro, feeling only a mist reaching me because of the protection of the overhang while Tom, just meters away, soaped himself in the abundance of the rain. The triangular legs of bamboo held the hammock well, especially after Tom jammed the tops of his structures against the overhang of rock. He ignored me, though of course he knew I watched his bath. He needed it, for he sweated like *norte americanos* sweat from exertion, and he complained that it wasn't fair that I found the temperature and humidity comfortable.

After the rain passed, after Tom flipped away much of the water from his skin and dried in the drying air, after he dressed to cover himself from the sun and to cover his rattan scars from my eyes, he said, "I think I could say some words for the ceremony of dead fingers."

"You're making fun of me."

"I'm not. I'm trying to do what you want. Will we need to make torches?"

"Not this time. We have the flashlight, remember? Also, we'll go only into the outer chamber." I took the flashlight from my bag.

"Good. Everything is too wet to burn."

We took the path to the cave's mouth, and Tom hacked at the brush covering the lower part of the entry. I dragged aside what he cut. When the entry stood open and black against the hill, Tom started inside, and I stopped him with a touch. "I'm nervous," I said. "Please. Take a moment to talk about what we're about to do."

"Nervous? About what? Spirits?"

"No. I don't know. I feel unsettled. Do you?"

"No." The answer came too fast, and he almost seemed to know it, for he gave his head a tiny shake and added, "Rosita, I've dreamed about this cave for years and often returned to it with you."

"Shall I call you Don?"

"Why?"

"Because you just called me Rosita?"

"I did?" Tom stepped back from the entrance and turned to me. "I did. Then I am nervous, aren't I? But why?"

"That's what I wanted to talk about. Maybe there is danger in going in there?"

"From spirits?" His voice had an edge of contempt.

"Stop it, Tom. If there is danger from spirits, it comes from inside us, not from them. But what I had in mind was more tangible. This could be the lair of jungle animals, big ones as well as tiny creatures that bite and sting."

"What kind of big animals?"

"The jaguar, maybe. Perhaps a bear."

"Bears? In the jungle?"

"Yes."

Tom looked around with an elaborate show of caution. "We found no evidence of larger animals moving aside brush to get in."

"What about snakes? The jungle is full of snakes, many of them deadly—and yes, we saw few of them when we were children, but that doesn't mean there were none here. It means we were lucky."

"Do you want to stay out of the cave?"

"I didn't say that, Tom. I said I wanted to stop a minute and talk. When I ask to talk about a problem, it doesn't mean I want you to solve it for me. It means only that I want to talk."

He waited for a few seconds, looking perplexed. "Is there anything else you want to say? Do I need to say anything else?"

"Maybe not." I snapped on the flashlight and offered it to him. "Thank you for being willing to discuss all this."

The temperature dropped in the darkness. I held the back of Tom's shirt as we entered, and I watched the beam of light as he checked to the right. There was nothing there, as I remembered, since the entry to the bone chamber was to the left. It was a small shaft perhaps a meter from the floor, a tunnel into an area now occupied by bats. Tom turned left and became rigid in his stillness.

She lay on the floor with one leg against the back wall, her face turned away from us, her blond hair gleaming in the light, and I knew at a glance she was dead. The light went from head to foot, showing what I had missed at first. All that remained of her was hair and bones and clothing—pants and shirt that perhaps were once khaki, rotten now, and fouled with bat droppings left as the bats entered and left the chamber deeper in the cave.

Tom knelt beside her and nudged the skull with the flashlight. It rattled loose, and I jumped at the sound. He picked up something. "The front of the head is broken on top. Someone killed her with a hard blow to the forehead." Tom held the light so I could see the skull. It had rolled against the side of the cave and lay, jawless, in a mat of hair, and seemed to look at me from hollow eyes.

"We should leave now." I shivered.

"But what of the ceremony of dead fingers?" Tom picked at the clothing, breaking it like brittle glass, and he picked up a dark object. "I think this is a billfold."

"Stop it, Tom. Let's return the finger bones and leave. Now." I opened the drawstring on the leather pouch and took out the bone of the Indio.

Tom stood, ran the beam again over the remains of the murdered woman, then shined the light into the small shaft leading to the burial chamber. "Hold this," he said. I took the light while he dug in a pocket.

"I'm putting it back now," I said, holding the brown lump in the beam of light so I could see it for the last time. "Ancient woman, I thank you for loaning me your finger. It amazed me when I was a child, and it gave me comfort when my friend Don left for his home in the north, for it reminded me of him. It brought me good fortune, for your finger drew this man Tom, who once was my Don, again to Venezuela, and it brought us again to your burial chamber. Thank you for your presence and help." I tossed the bone into the darkness where it vanished without a sound. In my imagination I saw it clear the ledge of the small entry and fall on the deep mat of guano inside the burial chamber where Don and Rosita once slipped on the wet surface and fell close to the rock shelves along the walls where the ancients laid their dead.

"Steadfast and enduring bone," Tom said, "I give you back to darkness." He threw the other piece of the ancient finger into the chamber.

As I turned to leave the light swept across something beside the small entry.

"Wait," Tom said, taking the flashlight from my hand.

"I saw it, too. Writing."

Tom illuminated the wall. Someone had drawn on the stone a single eye, complete with eyebrow and lashes, a large eye with a malevolent slant to the brow. Beside it were the words, "We are watching. Leave before we kill you."

"The words are a lie," Tom said.

"Written by the one who killed this woman."

"Yes. Over ten years ago, I would guess. Perhaps up to eighteen."

"Maybe shortly after we were here?" I shuddered and took his arm. "Come. I need a bath."

"I'll bring you soap from the bag," Tom offered.

"Thanks, no. River water will be fine. Come."

Tom followed me out of the cave into light that stabbed our eyes, down the hill and to the canoe. I stepped out of my alpargatas and pulled off my clothes while Tom sat on a rock to look through the billfold he took from the murdered woman.

Kneeling at the edge of the river, I splashed water on my face, on my body, for the river was too deep and flowed too fast for wading.

"You're distractingly beautiful," Tom said.

"Don't talk like that. Not now." I sat beside him on the rock.

"Olivia. Her name was Olivia Radcliffe, and she came from England." He showed me a card with writing on it. "Her driver's license with an address in Brighton down on the southern coast of England. She carried photographs, all black-and-white."

One showed three women in black dresses and pointed hats. They stood behind a huge pot into which they were dropping small items. Behind them, painted on a wall, a stylized lightning bolt crackled from a tiny, puffy cloud. The three women all had light-colored, long hair, and their mouths were open as if speaking with intensity. "It's a ritual," I said. "I recognize them."

"Of course. These are the three witches from *Macbeth*."

"Perhaps they were once. But here, in this jungle, they are the women of thunder."

"Just looking at the photo is enough to conjure the words they speak: 'When will we three meet again in thunder, lightning, or in rain? When the hurly-burly's done, when the battle's lost and won.' They say other things, words that make no sense. These witches don't come from stories told by jungle people."

"Don't be so condescending. You're not the only one who can recognize Shakespeare. Still, to see them as English witches, you must remove them from the cave of the dead, from this jungle, perhaps from South America. Here, those three blonde women dressed in black with the lightning bolt behind them are tapir-women, thunder women, women from the hollow hill."

"Perception creates what they are?"

"Yes."

"Your perception, then."

"Yes."

"The other photographs show the same women." Tom spread the pictures on the rock between us, taking care not to get them wet. Water from my bath still dripped from me. "They're wearing clothing from the early 1950s. Are they women of thunder in these other pictures?"

"No. They are lovely young European or North American women. In these there is no context to make them tapir women."

"But there is. Look at the jungle around us."

"Do you see them as women of thunder?"

"No. That's what I'm saying."

"Neither do I. So they are not."

Tom looked at me with raised brows and the shadow of a smile. "You're playing with me. You're repeating what the one-eyed whore told us long ago, that believing something makes it true."

"Carmen was right in some ways. Did you know that I saw Mata-Mata again last night?"

"I didn't see him."

"But you did before. You might again. Did you know that I fear the coming of night because I think he'll come again?"

Tom picked up the photographs. "I have my own demons."

"I've learned their names. Catrina. Phung Phuoc. Allen. I can help you cast them out, if you want."

We sat in silence, both of us unmoving, then Tom turned to me and I became uncomfortable about being nude, or I did until he said, "Perhaps that's why I came here—to cast out some old demons. Perhaps that's part of the reason I searched for you. Because I believed you could help me."

"You want my help?"

"Yes."

"And I want yours. We can create rituals to help us both."

"Rituals? Like the ceremony of dead fingers?"

"You make it seem absurd."

"It wasn't absurd. Your words moved me, and when you spoke them, I saw you as Rosita at first, then as Rosa. But there's something else. Something disturbing."

"About what I said?"

"No. About this river, about this jungle. The blue butterflies. That strange shaman and Kaita and Rochelle and the terrible Brother Maybre and the oleanders of death. Even the filthy monkeys. The jungle seems full of horrors. They distract us and refocus us and befoul us in terrible ways. Even in our cave there are the bones of Olivia Radcliffe."

"There have been bones in that cave for hundreds of years, maybe for thousands. But I know what you mean."

"We must do something about her, just as we must do something about the mass murders and suicides led by Brother Maybre. Even if we could choose to do nothing, these people distract us. Even dead they distract us."

"Especially dead they distract us, but of course, it's more than that. They have become part of us, or a part of our past, which is the same thing." I stood, rubbed some drops from my arms, and went to my clothes.

"Amazing," Tom said. "Amazing. I had for a short while forgotten you were nude."

"Then I was not nude, was I?"

"But you were. You are."

I slipped my clothes on. "No. I was dressed. I am dressed again. What are we going to do about Olivia? She's now a part of our past. And our present."

29

*R*osa confounded me. The past was the strawberry on my wife's neck and her beads clicking together over it and my brother's guilt; the past was Vietnam and Dumb Fuck with his rattan and Allen and the bamboo stake with a black point glistening moist from the jungle soil and Phuoc pissing on Catrina and Joey firing his piece into the night while the tiger dragged him by his boot and the pieces of mouse deer and the bodies of Charlie steaming into smells like the dead anteater under a carpet of butterflies. The past wasn't yesterday or the day before; it wasn't twenty minutes ago in the cave of childhood where the bones of a Brighton woman intruded, unwelcomed, out of place, a woman whose oversized locket I had stashed away in a pocket, perhaps as a surprise gift for Rosa. Having Olivia's necklace in my pocket was the present, and picking it up, picking up the billfold with the photos, looking at them with Rosa (nude and wet with river water) happened just minutes ago, and minutes ago wasn't the past. Or so I thought until Rosa pointed out that the past runs up to now.

"So we aren't making a very good past," I said. We walked around the rim of the rock bowl that held enough soil to give life to a breadfruit tree.

"We do the best we know how. Some of what you and I now put into our past is wonderful."

What she said brought to mind some words from Brother Maybre, and I repeated them: "Forgiveness begins only when we give up the hope of ever having a better past."

Rosa stopped at the foot of the hill and turned to me, her face intent with surprise. "Say that again."

"Why? It's nonsense."

"No. It's wisdom that I need and that you need. Say it again."

"Brother Maybre spoke those words before I knew him to be so foul. Immediately afterward he asked me if he could devise an entertainment for you. Can you imagine? That's what he said: devise an entertainment. He meant have sex with you, but I didn't understand. Forgiveness begins only when we give up the hope of ever having a better past. That's what he said, Brother Maybre, the child molester, the murderer. We should never take words from such a man as being wise."

"The words are wise, the man was not." She started up the shadow of a path that zigzagged on the rock hill. "Or he was wise once, then became something else. Or he was patchy and full of holes, full of dark and empty places. Maybre was an evil man. Yet he said something that I needed to hear. He said it to you, and you remembered it for me. For you."

I followed her up the hill, beyond the cave of our childhood that was no longer just a bat cave containing bones of ancient Indios but a place where Olivia Radcliffe had been murdered; we climbed in silence toward the thorn sapling drinking its life from a crack in the rock hill that held water enough for a small tree, and I walked behind Rosa, close enough to know she smelled like fresh corn, and I gave all of my attention to her black hair and brown arms and the clean smell of her so I didn't see the snake until she stopped and pointed, and even then I looked at her finger, her nut-brown hand until she became impatient and spoke a single word: "Snake."

It crawled under our chinchorro in slow, worm-like movements, and it wore rings of red, yellow, and black. "A coral snake," I said. "It's beautiful."

"And deadly. Its poison works on your nervous system. One bite from that tiny snake will kill you as surely as a dart from Poí's blowgun. Need I point out where it is right now?"

"We slept there, once, on the ground. But its timing is wrong if it wants to kill us. It came eighteen years too late." I took the machete from my belt.

"Please don't kill it."

"It's a snake, a poisonous snake."

"For my sake, then."

"This doesn't seem right." The snake didn't object to my scooping it onto the flat blade and carrying it to the edge of the cliff where the hill dropped away to a strip of jungle and to the river. I tossed the snake into the greenery below.

Allen and I once walked under similar greenery. We carried foreign weapons and foreign food, rice balls looking dirty in a dirty bag and smelling rancid, and I walked behind Allen, who did not smell like ripe corn; I kept him in sight most of the time while fingering the foreign rifle and aware of the pistol slung around Allen's hip in a holster not unlike the one Brother Maybre wore, the same pistol Phuoc cocked when he wanted to scare me into pissing on Catrina but I wouldn't do it, Allen's pistol at that moment and mine not much later, mine until I turned it in along with the report on my dead comrades, the firefight that killed them, being captured and Allen pulling the bamboo stake from the ground and my putting it into the neck of a sleeping man and the way the jungle killed Allen when Charlie could not. "Come sit for awhile," Allen called to me, and I tried to quicken my pace but didn't succeed. I smelled worse than the rancid rice, smelled of sweat and dried blood, smelled bad enough to attract buzzing insects that could do what they wanted because I was stumbling tired, too fatigued to wave a hand to shoo them away even if some of them might be laying eggs where Phuoc opened the skin with his rattan, eggs that could hatch into white worms like the ones that once hatched in my scalp when I was a kid living in El Tigrito, maggots my mother called them even if Dr. Bresaño called them jungle worms, *gusanos del monte*, and the kids over in San Tomé took to calling me maggoty head when I made the mistake of telling that little blonde girl about what the doctor pushed out of the soft spot on my scalp. That's what I was thinking about as I stumbled toward Allen, and I made up a rhyme about it to keep me going: Don, Don the foreigner's son, maggoty-headed and on the run, the words repeating themselves and building to a dirty tune until I saw the black shape lift beside Allen and flare its neck, saw the shaft of sunlight playing upon them from the high canopy, saw that Allen did not see the cobra until he turned toward it, perhaps not even focusing his vision on it, saw the sparkle of fluid fly from the cobra's mouth into Allen's face. He screamed and roiled on the ground, hands on his face.

By the time I got there, the cobra had slithered away. I poured a canteen of water into Allen's face, fighting him to do it, pushing his hands out of the way and yelling for him to open his eyes.

His words came out indistinct, moaning, mere growls in the back of his throat, and I could make out some of them: "Spitting cobra, spitting cobra," he said, his legs in motion, hands on his eyes like he was punching them out, clawing them out, "blind, blind, blind," and other words I couldn't make out. I managed to get the canteen from his belt, a foreign canteen, Chinese-made perhaps or Russian like the one that I carried but not empty, canteens we took from corpses that morning as soon as there was light, corpses already ripe like the anteater with my breathing shallow and through parted lips and having no idea that soon I'd be pouring the water into Allen's face hoping some of it would get into his eyes, hoping he would stop the growling words and the kicking, the twisting around on the jungle floor, hoping to save him some pain, but it was no use, no use at all even when one hand dropped away from his face and I had a better chance to slosh water into the burning eyes, those bleeding eyes like Oedipus coming from his wife's chamber and blood on Allen's fingers still clawing away while I shook the final drops of water from the canteen, watching them fall and not seeing the pistol until an attempt to slap it away was too late, the sharp crack of it and the splatter on both sides of his head causing me to leap backward, to gag, convulse, and lose the rancid rice beside a still body, eyeless and dead to amaze me for Allen's being so still when he had been in such constant motion just seconds before.

The nausea hit me again, not so bad this time, and I wished I had chopped the coral snake into red-and-yellow twigs, wished I had lifted the foreign rifle and fired a bullet through the flared neck of the cobra before it flung its venom into Allen's eyes, wished with a fervor, a trembling fervor that took me away from the edge of the cliff, turned me around to discover Rosa tugging my sleeve and not a ripped one, pulling at my shirt, a whole one I noticed with a surprised glance and not torn from Phuoc's rattan and not open to insects to lay eggs on my wounds for hatching into gusanos del monte; and I let her lead me to the chinchorro while I muttered, "Don, Don, the foreigner's son, maggoty-headed and on the run. I could have killed the goddam cobra, could have lifted the rifle with an easy motion to snap a single shot that would save Allen's eyes, could have chopped the coral snake into twigs," and she leaned me against the chinchorro, pushed me into it as the tight spot in my stomach loosened and I looked at Rosa, saw her hair tumbling forward with a clean odor of fresh corn, her face smooth and young with eyes dark, almost Asian, lovely, her lips full and parted and moving in saying something to soothe, to bring me back from the cobra's venom sparkling in a shaft of light, back to our childhood jungle with Rosa standing over me to touch my face with a touch that ran through what was left of the tight spot, down to my feet, a touch that made me still and quiet until I became aware of my breathing, until I could make an attempt to tell her about the way Allen died.

The story came out in short sentences, in few words to amaze me with how little time it took in the telling and how flat it sounded, those bare facts, compared to the storm of feelings that had come with the memory there at the edge of the cliff where I dropped the coral snake from the flat blade of my machete.

"I doubt you could have saved Allen," Rosa said, her hand still on my cheek.

"But I should have tried harder and in better ways."

"You still cannot save Allen. What happened is what happened."

"It isn't fair. It isn't fair."

"No," she said. "It is not at all fair."

30

*M**ata-Mata* came at night as I feared he would. He came not long after the bats left.

We ate breadfruit, pulpy and sweet though not so sweet as mangoes. I opened the breadfruit with my hunting knife and tossed the peeling from the ledge where Tom had thrown the coral snake, and we sat side-by-side on the chinchorro for the meal. As we finished, twilight came and with it the bats emerged like a thick rope. They flared into a wide band and broke into clumps of black clouds to spread over the jungle across the river. At the sight of the first bats Tom uttered a cry of delight and jumped from the chinchorro. I joined him on the edge of the cliff and we stood only a few meters from where the rope of bats spread into black clouds. Their wing beats were loud enough to fill the air with a hum and wild enough to fan us with bat-air.

"Astounding," Tom said. "Astounding."

"Yes." I moved against him and we stood in the twilight, breathing cave air sucked out by bats, watching what we had seen as children, the same bats becoming the same black clouds, more of them than I remembered.

When the bats had dispersed and the air again became jungle-sweet and the wing beats turned into the night cries of the jungle below us, we returned to the chinchorro to lie hip-to-hip in the webbing, heads at opposite ends. Tom fell asleep like a baby, and I had begun to drift off when I heard the sounds of Mata-Mata struggling up the hill. His groaning gave him away, so I knew his thorn tree would appear first and that it would be enormous from not telling his story in many days. I expected him to be wearing my father's face, but what staggered toward us moaning from guilt and the weight of the great tree was not my father. It was Maybre.

"Tom," I whispered, nudging him through the webbing, "Mata-Mata has returned."

He came awake with a start and shifted for a better view. "Go away," Tom said.

"No," I said. "I need you to stay until I learn what you have to teach me. Tell me your story, Maybre."

"He isn't Brother Maybre. He's Mata-Mata."

"I killed the child Rochelle," Maybre said, and the thorn tree on his shoulder rustled, perhaps shrinking. "I took her to my bed, and I killed her when she tried to get away from me."

"You should not have abandoned your wife," Tom said.

"I had no wife. I had many wives. They ate poisoned plants because I forced them. I killed everyone in the compound." The thorn shrank and Mata-Mata shifted around.

"You whipped her with your bow," Tom said, "when she needed your support. You signed the papers and joined up and abandoned her."

"Be quiet, Tom," I said, then spoke to Mata-Mata. "Finish your story, then I can tell mine."

"The crow that planted the thorn on my shoulder wasn't a crow at all, nor was it my son. I am the crow and the boy and man with the burden."

"Women also carry burdens," I said. "Mine comes from another river, a quiet river, and a place for swimming. But I cannot think about that. I would have killed Poí."

"Poí?" Tom looked at me in astonishment, then seemed to listen to Mata-Mata, though the glimmering figure stared at us in silence. "You're lying, Mata-Mata," Tom said. "Olivia Radcliffe is not Catrina's mother."

"I would have killed Poí," I said. "I planned to stand in a sudden way to pull the hunting knife with a single murderous motion from its scabbard on my ankle and thrust it into his heart because I thought he had killed Tom. And I would have done it."

"Poí is still alive," Tom said.

"She's talking about intent," Mata-Mata said. "Intent is nearly as important as doing."

"That's absurd," Tom said. "Olivia is now only bones, so there's no way to know if she has a strawberry on her neck."

"Please, Tom," I said, "stop changing the subject. Let us tell what we must tell."

"I'm not changing the subject." Tom sounded querulous.

"Then be quiet for a while, please," I said. "I killed the people in the compound. They died because I told Maybre about oleanders. Doing so was like handing a loaded pistol to a man who has no conscience."

"If you don't finish your story," Tom said, "the tree will weigh you down. Speak."

Perhaps he was talking to Mata-Mata, but I took his words to refer to me, so I spoke. "When I thrust aside the stink of cholera and death, I entered the tent and found Abuelita on a cot. She looked dead but was not, for her eyes opened at my approach and I could tell she wanted to reach for me but lacked the strength. When she spoke, I had to put an ear to her lips because her spirit was too weak for more than whispering. They're dead, she told me, both of my parents, dead, and she could have helped them with magic and herbs except that she was too weak to do the simpling, the gathering and preparing, 'and you,' she said to me, 'were away at the European school.' Not European, I told her. Venezuelan. Why did I speak thus to her? She was dying. It was the smell in the tent, the heat radiating from the canvas absorbing the sun. Heat and foul odors made me dizzy and faint and stirred my brain into mush."

"You didn't kill your grandmother," Tom said.

"Yes," Mata-Mata said. "You killed them. I see the tree growing on your shoulder."

"Be quiet, Mata-Mata," Tom said. "Catrina has nothing to do with Rosa. You told your story, now go away."

"No. He must hear me. Look, he isn't Maybre anymore. He's put on the face of my father."

"You killed me, Rosita," my father said. "You did it with abandonment."

"I did, I did, I did." The truth of his accusation cut deep, and I knew I had to finish the story of the cholera tent. "Abuelita said no Venezuelan would steal away a daughter and granddaughter who was needed at home. She said it was a European school with European nuns who took me away and that I went as a wicked child might go. 'If you had been here to go to the river for me, we could have saved your mother, my own daughter, and her husband, your father. We could have saved them, you and I. But you were studying foreign and wrong ways in Cantaura, far up in the costal mountains. You allowed them to die.' She became quiet with exhaustion, and I knew her to be right."

"Stop it," Tom said to Mata-Mata. "Your job is to talk about your own murderous heart, not about how I left Catrina. She seduced Todd. My own brother. I know the story better than you."

"You deserve your thorn tree," Mata-Mata told me.

I began to sob. "Yes. Give me your tree. Plant it on my shoulder. I deserve the load much more than you."

Tom got out of the chinchorro, took the machete, and approached Mata-Mata. "I've had enough talk about the thorn tree. Hold still, goddammit. Hold still."

The machete flashed in the moonlight and the thwack of it striking the thorn tree on Mata-Mata's back filled the jungle night. Crickets fell silent and frogs ceased their whistling. Birds became quiet, and soon the entire jungle listened to Tom's chopping. Mata-Mata bent down, touching his forehead to the ground in front of Tom's feet, and when the tree fell, he sighed with relief, stood, and began dancing.

"A spirit dance," I said and got out of the hammock to join his celebration, but he faded into the darkness, into the sounds of frogs and crickets and birds beginning anew their song of the jungle night.

"I did it," Tom said. "I did it."

"Yes. Thank you, my beloved Don."

"Tom."

"Tom. Thank you." When I took his hand he dropped the machete beside the wood chips and the fallen thorn. I led him back to the chinchorro. "Now we can both sleep. The ritual of the tree is finished."

"Was that a ritual?" Tom asked, his tone revealing that he knew the answer even as he asked the question. We climbed into the chinchorro and Tom sang an English song about a magic dragon named Puff, and I drifted off to sleep.

We awoke to the wing beats of returning bats. "They're back," Tom said, stirring in the hammock, moving against me. "I want to watch them fly back into the cave."

"Shake out your boots," I warned as he stood. "Make sure nobody is inside."

"Scorpions, you mean." He knocked his boots together.

After giving my alpargatas a quick shake, I slipped them on and joined him at the edge of the cliff. Bats flowed together to form a funnel in front of us, thousands and thousands of them. They smelled like wet rats. "The cave must be much bigger than we realized as children," I said.

"They've vacuumed hundreds of kilograms of insects from the night sky and will go inside the hollow hill to turn their meals into guano." Tom put an arm around me. "I had such a strange dream. Mata-Mata came and talked to us."

"It was no dream. We both talked with him. This time he didn't look like my father, not at first. He had Maybre's face."

"No. He was a dark, sunburnt little gnome of a man, almost black from the sun."

"His skin shimmered a ghostly white, and he stood more than two meters tall."

"So it was a dream, after all," Tom said. "We both dreamed about him. He talked about Catrina."

"Did he tell you that Olivia was Catrina's mother?"

Tom stiffened, his hand gripping my shoulder. "How could you know that?"

"You talked about it. I didn't hear him mention Olivia or Catrina, but you apparently did. To me he said other things."

"And you talked about your abuelita? About feeling guilty over the death of your parents?"

"Yes. I told you about the cholera tent. Then you chopped the thorn tree off of Mata-Mata's shoulder, and he danced a spirit dance of joy. I tried to join him."

"This is so weird. How did we manage to share the same dream and yet not share it? Mata-Mata was a black gnome, not Brother Maybre. I guess I talked in my sleep and you heard."

We stood in silence watching the bats until the first streaks of genuine morning slid across the twilight and the last of the bats funneled downward into the cave beneath us. Tom kept his arm around me, kept his grip on my shoulder, remained taut and stiff as we turned around. "The thorn," he yelped.

Beside the overhang of rock, to the left of the bamboo legs that held our chinchorro, the thorn tree lay on the ground. A pile of white chips lay beside the stump with its roots snaking into a crack in the rock. The machete lay where Tom dropped it in the night. "It was no dream," I said. "You chopped the thorn tree from Mata-Mata's shoulder in a ritual to relieve him and me of suffering."

"But no. I cut down the sapling thorn growing out of the rock, even if I thought I was chopping it from the shoulder of a black gnome."

"The ritual helped me, Tom. I feel lighter—so light I could almost lift off the ground and fly down to the breadfruit tree. You cut the tree from the shoulder of Mata-Mata. You cut it from my shoulder."

"I cut it from the rock."

"Yes. Yes."

"I don't understand any of this."

"Is that important, that you understand the facts of the matter? The truth is more important, and I think we both understand the truth of what happened last night when Mata-Mata came to us and I talked, finally, about Abuelita and the cholera tent."

"Truth and facts are the same thing."

"No, Tom. They are not."

"I don't understand."

"Understanding is nice but is not so terribly important." I kissed Tom's cheek. "Today we will have some exciting adventures. Remember the tree with ants that caused me to jump into the river? Remember the caimán who came after me?"

"That was when I threw what remained of our roasted rabbit into the water to distract the beast, and you got back into the canoe."

"And we went over a waterfall. Do you remember the jungle below the falls? How we slept in a tree, then on the ground near the swamp. That part of our long-ago adventure is my favorite time of childhood."

"And mine. We found minnows in the heart water of a jungle plant and a Jesus frog that could walk on water."

"Hop on it, anyway. Yes. We're close to that magic place, Tom. Today we'll go there. We'll avoid the ant tree and the caimán, if they're still around, and we'll slide our canoe down the hill on land so the waterfall won't take it from us. Then we'll be in paradise again."

31

C*atrina wanted* to talk to me, but I shrugged her away with a heart too happy to be bothered even by beads clicking together over a strawberry. Go away, I said, and Catrina faded beyond the breadfruit tree, among ferns along the bank near where we shoved the canoe out into the river, and we left her on the bank somewhere close to the hollow hill that Kaita thought housed the women of thunder but in fact held only bats and centuries of guano and bones, ancient ones as well as those of Olivia Radcliffe whose oversized locket contained some words I needed to ponder; and I was amazed at how easy it was to leave Catrina behind, easy because of our excitement, Rosa's and mine, over being so close to the Eden of our childhood. I plunged the paddle into the water, keeping an eye out for the caimán that had attacked Rosita, and Rosa paddled at the front of the canoe. She scanned the banks, no doubt looking for trees from which ants would leap upon us if we brushed the branches. Acacia trees. The name came to me unbidden just as we heard the faint growl of white water.

"The falls," Rosa said, her voice pure with pure energy, her eyes dancing about as she glanced back at me, and I knew that with Rosa I was no foreigner, no foreigner's son; there were no flies on me, no maggots in my head, and I was not on the run; perhaps there were no flies or maggots at all in the paradise jungle just down the river, below the falls, in the region where Rosita and I once constructed a green igloo, a round shelter thatched with palm fronds over a bush, a region where we found bananas growing wild and caught catfish with bark string and wooden hooks, where minnows appeared as from the sky in the heart water of gigantic bromeliads and frogs hopped across the surface of water.

The river narrowed into a swift channel, and Rosa pointed to our right where the bank didn't seem so steep. I dragged the paddle to turn us toward the bank where Rosa stepped into the shallows to pull the bow out of the water. Lifting even one end of the canoe wasn't easy, but we managed to hold the bow high enough to pivot the boat over rocks, then drag it through ferns and grass and to slide it down the hill beside the roar of the waterfall, the one we went over as children, a smaller waterfall than I remembered because the river was down from less rain or because perspectives were different back when we moved about in smaller bodies.

Below the falls where the river spread to run shallow except in a few channels of crystal water, alive with fish, we floated the canoe, its bottom touching sand and gravel, and we walked beside it, nudging it on, all the while taking in the beauty of the wide shallows and jungle along the banks, the flocks of parakeets and a deer drinking farther down and tiny insects like dust motes floating over the water to catch shafts of morning light angling through the trees and making spots on the water. "We're here," I said.

"Nearly. I found you over there." She pointed. "You sat weeping because you thought I had drowned, and I came up behind you to touch your shoulder. You took my hand and we danced."

"We fell into the water because I couldn't dance properly."

"No. We fell into the water to celebrate finding each other alive. Our canoe and our clothes had washed down the river."

"Yes." I took off my shirt. "We were naked because of falling into bat shit and taking off our clothes before the falls got us." I threw my shirt into the canoe and lifted a foot out of the water to untie my boot strings. Rosa dropped her alpargatas into the boat, pulled at her blouse, and in seconds we stood nude on opposite sides of the canoe, in water only inches deep, and looked at each other.

"You're beautiful," she said.

"And you. Beautiful. You're Rosita and more, so much more. Rosa."

"Donald Thomas Seal," she said, trying with some success for the English pronunciation of my name. "But of course we will sunburn, and we could cut our feet on sharp stones."

"We could, but we won't."

"Shall we float down the river until we come to the place where we made a shelter from a bush and ground palms?"

"We could do so again." I glanced at her, brows raised, and she smirked, knowing I wouldn't push such a plan, for not even in our reclaimed Eden should we court trouble in a river jungle that had proven it could kill. "We'll sleep in the chinchorro then, or perhaps on a tree platform well above the ground."

"How long have we been on the river?"

"Years," I said. "We've been here for years."

"So it seems. But I mean really. How many nights?"

"One night, or part of it, in a chaparro tree," I said.

"And one in the canoe."

"Yes. And one in Poí's hut. Then one down the river from Kaita's village, and another on the bank of the inlet where we found Kaita again. Five nights. Amazing. We've been on this river only five nights, yet it seems much longer." I began wading again, bending over the canoe to push it along with Rosa splashing on the other side.

"In my El Tigrito home," Rosa said, "I lived a life of sameness. Each day was much like every other day: I got up, prepared breakfast, went to see those who needed my medical help, returned home for lunch, met with villagers who brought their cuts and hurts and illnesses to me, and retired shortly after dinner. Seldom did anything different happen, so years slipped by, years of days that seemed alike and were alike, and time passed quickly or it seems it did when I try to remember those days and years. There was nothing much to mark the time, no new experiences, just variations on the same ones. But here, on this river with you, time operates differently. Time is crowded with new events, strange and wild and sometimes unwelcomed. So it seems to me that we have been in the river jungle much longer than a mere handful of days."

"Time slows, then, when we're busy with new events?"

"No." She seemed perplexed, bent to catch the side of the canoe to stop its progress. "The channel there, ahead. We should float downriver in it. But not yet. Talk to me more first."

"About where we're going?"

"I don't know. Perhaps not. Perhaps not even about where we've been."

"Then what? Talk about what?"

"Just listen, then? Stand and look at me and listen?"

"I like looking at you and listening to you." I let my eyes rove over her body, and she seemed not at all offended, nor did she catch her breath as Kaita had done when I looked at her as we left the mat she wanted us to use.

Rosa simply nodded and said, "I like your looking and listening. I want to talk about time. It's supposed to go faster when we're busy, and perhaps it does. But in memory, it appears to have passed more slowly, for we have so much to think about. Oz and his strange house. The blue butterflies and the ceremonies in Kaita's village and the monkeys that befouled us. So much. It might take years to think about all we have already experienced. Certainly I've done a greater number of unusual things in the last few days than I did in the last ten years of being a nurse in El Tigrito."

"I envy those years." I nudged the canoe toward the channel. "Mine were full of turbulence, of betrayal and war and anger and guilt."

"I have guilt enough. You've seen that. But you're right. My life must seem peaceful to you, compared to what you have been doing in the United States and in Vietnam."

"Peaceful. Yes. You don't know how I yearn for peace. Come. Float with me to the place where you and I once lived the most peaceful and wonderful days of childhood."

We stepped into the canoe, felt it crunch against the bottom, shoved paddles against sand until we slid into the narrow channel and down river where eighteen years ago I had tried without success to spear fish and we had slept in a tree, where tiny monkeys led us to bananas, monkeys that looked at us with round eyes, where Rosita made sandals for us from woven grass. Soon we floated from wide shallows and sandbars into a place where the river became a single cut through jungle and the sky narrowed with trees, and Rosa turned so I could see her point with a pucker of lips toward the left bank. We put ashore and dragged the canoe up the bank.

"We're here." Rosa's voice sounded thick with feeling and verged upon breaking, and she blinked back tears. She took her alpargatas from the canoe and nodded toward my boots.

"I'll look silly with nothing on but boots."

"Then put on pants." She stepped into her sandals and pushed her way through tree ferns.

It took long moments to struggle into the wet boots, to tie them, and by the time I could slog past the ferns, she was out of sight, swallowed by the thicket of younger tree trunks too close together to allow for undergrowth, their shadows seeming almost tangible compared to the flood of light along the river. This is it, I thought, finally, the primordial jungle with a flutter of wings from a red-capped cardinal above me, a nest hanging from high branches, the *pee-PEE-o* calls of piha birds deeper in the woods, this is it, childhood Eden with no grunts carrying weapons, no mines to blow up mouse deer, no mouse deer and no Charlie; this is it, paradise again without blue butterflies flocking to carrion, without poisoned darts and bamboo walls and oleander poison.

Farther into the shade, trees became more sparse, trunks larger, the canopy higher, and I found myself looking at the winged buttresses of silk-cotton trees, huge, magnificent, standing among rosewoods and other giants I couldn't identify. I stopped beside a dark tree perforated with a million tiny holes similar to Brother Maybre's devil tree that he used to mark the limit of his walk from the compound. Could a snake fall on me here? I looked up and concluded that such snakes had to live up river, as did red howler, shit-slinging monkeys. The ground slanted down, and trees became smaller. Ahead I could see the beginnings of undergrowth, though not thick, and from my right I heard the sounds of a jungle animal, then the voice of Rosa calling my name. Not a jungle animal at all, I thought, unless here in this garden Rosa and I both became natives, unless by our mere presence we reverted to the naked and animal innocence of childhood. I hurried to catch up with her.

She stood beside a pool of still water, a big one with the tops of green plants spotting it here and there, a recent pool fed by wet-season rain, and I knew where we were, knew this was the swamp that bordered our jungle on one side with the river on the other, a swamp that kept us from following the river when we were children and had lost our canoe to the waterfall.

"There," Rosa pointed at a squat plant, circular from leaves like a houseplant Catrina called a mother-in-law's tongue but bigger, much bigger, a plant I remembered from years ago, a plant I had looked for in books on the jungle before returning. "Look in the middle," she said.

A bromeliad. Even as I stepped closer, I knew what would be there, knew I would see a substantial bowl of water, heart water we called it as children when we didn't know the word *bromeliad.* And in the water? Rosa took my hand and we were as children again peering with amazement at minnows in the heart water of the bromeliad. I didn't see the frog until it jumped. It was tiny, smaller than a fingernail, and it splatted on the water, jumped again for another splat, then again, and was across the water where it vanished among folds of greenery. "A Jesus frog," I whispered and drew closer to Rosa.

32

I still felt buoyant from Tom's chopping the thorn tree on Mata-Mata's shoulder. The man with the tree could not come again to me at night, that seemed certain. In the jungle garden where God put minnows into tongued plants I could at last walk free and nude beside Don. He was still in there, still inside this strong, blocky, and scarred body of my new friend Tom. I watched him leaning over the aquarium plant to look at minnows, and I liked what I saw regardless of the white scars. Scars laced across me, too, invisible ones, for the years had damaged us both. If he was no longer a boy, that had to be all right for I no longer had the small body of a girl but a curving adult body that resembled Sylvia when we first saw her.

She had lived across the swamp, and she removed her clothes to meet us because we were nude. Don was amazed by her triangle of hair and her breasts, and I was jealous. His gaping at her had been so long ago. I pushed away the memory and took Tom's hand, liking that he looked at me, liking that he was content not to grope around on me but to walk beside me through the forest. "The children are still inside us," I said.

"Little Don was better than I."

"When did you begin calling yourself Tom? It must have been when you came back from Vietnam."

"I was Don when I married, and it was Don that Catrina betrayed and Don who went to Vietnam where he killed and saw too much death, and he didn't shoot the snake as it loomed over Allen. When I signed the report, I did so with the name *D. Thomas Seal,* and I knew as I moved the pen that I could no longer be Don."

"When you killed in that terrible war, you did what seemed best at the time. All we can do is the best we know how to do at the time, then work at forgiving ourselves afterward. When we make love, may I call you Don?"

He stopped walking, dropped my hand, and blinked hard. "I'm not worthy of making love with you, Rosita."

"Rosa. And you are the most worthy man I have ever met."

"You like me after all I've confessed?"

"I like you for the confessions."

As we looked at each other, I became aware of the smell of freshly flooded plants, of tree sap and moist earth. Birds moved around in the canopy high above us, and a flock of parrots flew over, announcing their presence with the sound of trilled *Rs*, and the warm air stirred with a breeze that was moist and promised rain. I brushed his cheek with my fingertips and said, "We have much to do."

We worked without the need for many words. The canoe had to be dragged to the swamp, and we did that. If we were to make love, we needed a safe place above the forest floor, though such reasoning went unspoken. Tom chopped branches into small pieces; I pulled twine from bark, and we tied the pieces for a ladder to the trunk of a tree not much bigger around than the chaparro we slept in five nights before. Where the tree forked in many directions, we made a platform of stripped saplings harvested and trimmed beside the river. We carpeted the platform with broad leaves—traveler's palms, Tom called them while admitting he didn't know their proper name.

Banana leaves were available, and we chose to use only a few for the aroma of them. We didn't want to harm the plants by stripping too many of their leaves. Tom thought it was the same stand of banana trees we had found as children, though of course that was not possible. Banana trees don't live long, I pointed out. "Their descendants, then," Tom said.

Termites built nests on the trunks of several trees in our garden, and other trees stood hollow and dead. One of the dead trees had died in the grip of the vine-like arms of a strangler fig. We paid little attention to dead trees and termites and passed the strangler fig without comment, choosing instead to speak of the sweet odor of flowering trees and to point out to each other orchids and parrots that nibbled on orchids.

Our tree house had no roof, for we ran out of time, and we decided that the tangle of greenery overhead had to suffice. Tom thought it was not necessary, but I carried the travel bag to our tree house. "What need will we have of medicine or clothing in our magic garden?" he asked in a tone that didn't leave room for an answer. Because we had seen no biting insects of any kind, we didn't even discuss putting up the mosquito netting for the night.

By the time rain came and night fell, we had eaten one meal of breadfruit, one of roasted fish, and one of bananas. Rain began as we peeled the bananas. "The women of thunder have arrived," I said, referring to a clap of thunder. We sat on our platform, the leaves above us gathering water, shifting it to larger drops, and letting some of them fall upon us. The sky darkened and lightning crackled above the canopy. High leaves stirred into a sound like white water and falls, and we moved closer together.

Before gathering bananas we had taken soap and waded into the still waters close to the canoe and beside the bromeliad where minnows and frogs lived. We splashed little and spoke even less, and we emerged clean to dry in jungle-warm air. It cooled with the arrival of rain, and we held each other on the leafy mat of our tree platform. Our bed smelled of apples from the sweetness of banana leaves. The high green turned gray, and drops running together from leaf to leaf struck our bed with a rattling sound. We made love while rain and trees sang their wet song, and in the intensity of our touching, we both shed tears.

When peace and stillness came to us, Tom said, "I'm sorry for crying."

I rested my head on his shoulder and pressed against him with a leg over his. "Don't apologize for feelings."

"But making love is supposed to be joyful."

"It was. It also reached deep into each of us to touch old pain.

Maybe the relief of finding some love after so many wounds was more than either of us could contain without tears."

"You're good, did you know? Good."

"We're good together," I said. "But, but—Never mind."

"But what? What? Is something wrong?"

"Not right now. In this moment everything is perfect."

We listened to the night chorus of insects, frogs, and nocturnal birds singing along with the river and the stirring of high leaves and the remains of the rain dripping around us. Our shared warmth felt good in the cooling night.

"You're right," Tom said. "This is a perfect moment. But later, in the morning or tomorrow or next week, there will be problems. Is that what you were about to say? What kinds of problems?"

"Do you foresee a future that includes me?"

"I foresee nothing. I'm firmly here in the present. Do you foresee such a future?"

"I want to. But we live in different worlds. And you are married."

"I am not. I'm divorced."

"In your world, perhaps you are divorced. And maybe you are not. You're not finished with Catrina, you know. She still comes to you, and you still speak to her. She haunts you because you cannot cast her out."

"I want to. I shall."

"If you want, I can help with the casting out of the cat. But there will remain another problem. You will still be married in the eyes of my village priest."

"Because the Catholic church doesn't recognize divorce?"

"Yes."

"What about in your eyes? Do you see me as divorced?"

"I see with what I am. And I am Catholic."

"You're not. You're a weird blend of animist and other things I don't understand."

"Perhaps in many ways I am what my grandmother was, what the Indios were, even the ancient ones whose finger bones we returned to the cave. But I am more. Sometimes I don't want to be Catholic, but what I want changes nothing. To me, you're married, and for me to be comfortable with myself and with you, we must go our separate ways, regardless of how beautiful we find this night."

"I won't allow that to happen."

His words reached deep inside me. They felt good. They hurt. "You have no choice."

There seemed nothing else to say. We listened to the singing night, and I tried to draw myself closer to him. Moonlight drifted through the leaves, and I could see his profile, dim and lovely. Somehow I went to sleep.

The vampire bats didn't come until the night moved toward morning. Tom shifted in sleep, and I felt a slippery wetness as his leg moved against mine. More rain, I thought, then came awake with a cold feeling tingling in my scalp. With an effort to remain stone-still, I looked toward our feet. In the leaf-blown light I saw dim shapes on the mat beside us. One of them tickled my ankle. I heard myself cry out, and Tom came awake. He sat up and grabbed the bag, unzipped it. In seconds he had the flashlight on.

"Here," I said. "Shine the light here." I took his hand and directed the beam at my leg. Above the ankle blood oozed across my skin.

"Something bit you."

"Yes. A bat. Probably many bats. Put the bag over here where I can reach it."

He moved the bag, then kept the light on my leg as I treated the wound.

"The blood seeps out thin and constant," he said. "It looks like the places where leeches got me."

"The effect of a bat bite must be similar." I put antibiotic ointment on a gauze patch and held it to my leg. "They'll be back."

"The bats?"

"Yes. It's the way they make a living. One of them uses its razor-sharp teeth to scratch an animal. The scratch is so subtle that the animal seldom awakens, and bats gather around to lap the blood. I think something in their saliva keeps the blood from clotting." I taped the patch to my leg. "They like to return to the same animal if they get disturbed. They will be back tomorrow night, also."

"The same bats," Tom said.

"Of course."

"I meant that these are the same bats that bit me eighteen years ago. It was the bats that made us decide we had to leave this area. I had forgotten."

"I also forgot. But of course these cannot be the same bats or even the descendants of the ones that bit you. Remember what we did to those bats?"

"I had forgotten that, also," Tom said. "We burned them inside their own hollow tree. Killed them with smoke. I remember, now. But I don't like the memory. We won't do that this time."

"Back then I thought of the bats as things to be killed, like I would slap a mosquito." I shuddered. "There will be no more killing."

"No more killing," Tom agreed. "Would the mosquito netting stop them?" He began pulling the netting from my bag.

"It couldn't hurt. It would at least slow them down."

I held the light while Tom tied the netting to branches close overhead, and we crept under the net tent. After a time Tom fell asleep, but I remained awake. Bats fluttered around twice, and I frightened them away with the flashlight. It was not vampire bats, though, that kept me awake. It was the memory of making love with Tom and the memory of our conversation.

When morning came, I lay with an arm over his chest, and I wanted him again even while knowing him to be married.

33

S*he said vampire* bats came in the night again, several times; she said they fluttered around the netting, that some landed on leaves beside us and tried to creep like rats under the net. It seemed so clear to me in the gray light of morning that we were wrong to believe we could return to Eden, to believe in something that might have existed only in a memory constructed from what we wanted rather than from what we had experienced, and I voiced my thoughts, though they were painful: "Innocence must have existed only inside us when we were children."

Rosa pushed herself on top of me. "I thought you were still asleep."

"I am asleep and dreaming." But it was no dream. On a green bed redolent of banana leaves, a platform above the jungle floor and under the mosquito webbing holding drops of dew, we made love as day sounds replaced those of the night, and we added our voices to those of the morning jungle to blend ourselves in ecstasy into the Eden that wasn't Eden except when we created it, and even then I was aware of the bandage on her leg, of the bats that would come again when night fell; they would come with their razor teeth and blood-lapping tongues in search of Rosita, but they wouldn't find her because we would be gone. We would cross the swamp, climb to the place where Sylvia the witch once lived, walk to the village nearby and perhaps visit with villagers, then return to the swamp, cross it again, return our canoe to the river, then resume our trip with the high point behind us, leaving forever the Eden of our childhood. How could I have forgotten the bats?

Time drifted around us in a haze of green light and the splash of river water running toward the sea. "We didn't cry this time," she said.

But she did cry when the spider got her. We walked toward the canoe, both of us still nude, when she brushed the web, a silky presence almost invisible between two trees, something I saw too late, and as the spider dropped toward her shoulder, I let go of the bag to run to her but was too late to stop the bite. I knocked it away as she screamed, knocked it to the ground and stomped it with a bare foot, feeling the crunch of it even as I turned to Rosa.

"Araña mona," she said. "I will die."

"No, no. It was a much smaller spider. I killed it. There." I pointed.

She looked at the crumpled spider and began to cry. "I'll live, but it hurts worse than a wasp sting."

I took her arm and helped her to the canoe. "This place is too dangerous. Sit here and I'll bring the bag. Perhaps you have medicine to put on the bite?"

"None that would help. But get the bag." She settled into the canoe, her eyes almost closed from the pain.

When I returned and started to untie the boat, she stopped me. "Please. Wait a few minutes for the sting to ease. I want to enjoy our trip across the swamp. We have one breadfruit left. Prepare it for us."

As we sat in the canoe, our feet touching, I watched her face while the pain became less, then handed her some pulp from the breadfruit.

"No spider's bite can be as bad as what I must say." She rolled her shoulder, testing it, and looked at the rosy place where the spider landed on her. "In the night we made love out of pain. This morning we did so out of joy and regret. We will not make love again."

It took effort not to look at her and effort not to look behind me where Catrina had appeared on the shore to laugh at my distress, the effort focusing upon a single deep breath and slow exhalation before daring to speak in a voice I knew would crack. "Is that what you want?" And my voice did crack but not loud so I could hope she didn't hear it.

But she did. The pressure of her feet against mine told me so, as did the emotional tone of her voice. "It matters not what I want. And no. I want you every night and every morning and maybe sometimes during the day." She sighed. "More than that, I want you in quiet moments when we share more silence than passion."

"Reach for me, then." I winced at Catrina's laughter.

"She's there, isn't she?"

"Who?" I looked at Rosa, found her eyes searching my face, found in her look a penetration of my guilt, of the lie in my question. I nodded. "She's laughing. There on the shore." I turned, expecting Catrina to be standing beside the bromeliad, but she was gone and only the ringing of her laughter told me she had been there. "It's best, then."

"What's best?" Rosa said.

"That we complete our trip and go separate ways again. I have come back to you as a crazy man. Much more crazy than El Loco Merzi after Rosita and Don brought him a bottle of whiskey, and more of a lunatic than Oz painting a jungle house on a rock wall. As mad as the poet eating oleander leaves."

"But you're not crazy at all. That's not the problem. The problem is that you're married."

"I see people who are not here. I hear them. I heard Catrina laughing at me—she stood there, beside the minnow plant."

"And yet you know she's not here, that she's here because you bring her here, that she is inside you."

"Sometimes I know that. Sometimes she's really here."

Rosa's voice dropped as if she were about to reveal a secret. "Each time you hear her, each time you see and talk with her Catrina is really there. Even if she is only inside your head, she takes on external reality."

"That isn't possible."

"No, it's not possible. But it's true. Mata-Mata came to me several times on different nights. He stepped out of myth, out of the stories in my head, out of my conviction that I killed my grandmother. But he was not real."

"He was real. I saw him. I talked with him."

"Of course. You had to deal with Mata-Mata as if he were real because I knew he was. You helped give him external reality. You even chopped the thorn tree from his shoulder, so that while he was not real, there was nothing more real when he appeared."

"I don't understand this."

"Nor do I. Understanding isn't so important, remember? I knew Mata-Mata was real, so we both had to interact with him, which gave him reality out there and not just in my head. Did you know I have seen Catrina?"

"What did she look like?" I demanded.

"Does it matter?"

"It matters. I would rather be crazy than for Catrina to be really here in this jungle with us."

"What you want in the matter isn't important. I never wanted to see Mata-Mata, but I saw him."

"What did she look like?"

"She wore beads and had a strawberry on her neck."

My hands felt numb and my tongue dry. "Then we're both crazy."

"Yes. A little, perhaps. We're also not crazy. Do you want to cast Catrina out of the jungle?"

"Yes. But if she comes from inside my head, how is that possible?"

"You helped me cure Mata-Mata. I'll help you send the cat away."

I listened for Catrina, but she remained silent or perhaps I kept her silent in my need for Rosa not to be infected with my lunacy and maybe with my own need not to be crazy right then, for a more important issue somehow got pushed aside by all the talk of the woman who once was my wife, the woman who made love to my own brother.

We finished our breakfast and I kept wanting to talk again about that more important issue, about Rosa's affirmation that we must part soon, but there seemed no way to get around the wall of her Catholicism, of her absolute denial.

I looked back through the maze of trees, hoping to catch a last glimpse of the treehouse we had constructed, the green platform where we made love and where vampire bats found us in the night, but it wasn't possible to see it because the tree with the platform stood beyond too many trees, closer to the river than the swamp. Rosa gave me a raised-brow look with a tilt of her head, a silent question to find out if I were seeing Catrina again, a question that embarrassed me because it reminded me that I was crazy to believe Catrina the cat was really there even in those moments when I knew she was because of the clicking of her beads and the flutter of her fake buckskins. Fuck her, I thought, trying to dismiss her as Allen liked to do before the cobra got him and his hand came up with the pistol, came up too fast for me to bat away: fuck her, I don't want to see her ever again, especially not now that Rosa made love with me with such wild passion. "But she won't stay with you," Catrina said.

"Neither did you," I said, feeling only vaguely aware of a startled look from Rosa. "You had many lovers, even my own brother, and you want to criticize Rosa for not staying with me?"

"Catrina," Rosa said. "Catrina."

I turned to Rosa with a startled jerk, one that caused the canoe to rock. "Can you see her?"

"No."

A quick glance around told me that I couldn't see Catrina either. "I'm making us both crazy. Let's cross the swamp, climb the hill to see if the house that Sylvia the witch lived in is still there, then come back. Let's forget Catrina."

"Untie the boat." Rosa picked up a paddle and grimaced only a bit from the spider bite.

Morning sun slanted in leafy spotlights through the canopy and flooded where trees thinned, where bushes protruded from the new water brought to the low area by wet-season rain, and in that light I could see the bottom carpeted with dead leaves too far down to reach with the paddle. Turtles broke the surface to look at us, and a green snake swam close to the canoe. Rosa turned in the canoe to look at me, tears in her lashes. "It's all so beautiful." Her voice had the rich tones of a mature woman, and the tears were a woman's, but the intensity on her face was pure Rosita. "Sylvia's voice floated across these waters eighteen years ago when she sang up the morning sun and drew us into wading the swamp to her."

"We had to swim part of the way," I said. "But, of course, it wasn't the same water."

"Water is always the same water. I killed a snake with the machete."

"It's still here, or a rusted lump of that machete is still here. The swamp ate it while trying to swallow us in quicksand. You stood among spiders to pull me out with the canoe rope." I looked around for the tree stump, knowing even as I searched that it would have rotted away years ago. We slid toward the shore where Sylvia once greeted us.

"Spiders! I had forgotten the spiders in the tree stump. Small ones, too small to bite. Sylvia later told me they helped us escape the grip of the swamp mud. She gave us medicinal tea, remember?"

"It was a powerful hallucinogenic. How could I forget becoming a parrot?" I stopped paddling and let the canoe drift across the glass-like water.

"The witch's drugs helped strip away barriers within ourselves so we could remake reality."

"I took LSD once, and I hated the results. My apartment stank of purple."

A capybara swam toward us. We could see the play of its muscles, the curiosity on its face, but we didn't see the dark shape of the crocodilian until it lifted the capybara out of the waters. It squeaked in alarm only once before the jaws clamped shut, opened and closed again, and the capybara was gone. "Black caimán," I said, and fear gripped me as it did when the cobra lifted its spooned neck beside Allen. The ridged back of the caimán surfaced like a serrated snake longer than our canoe, swimming away from us to give me the hope of escape, and I dipped the paddle as silently as possible to push us toward shore. As the canoe hit bottom just meters from dry land, the caimán turned toward us. "Hurry!" I grabbed the travel bag, leaped into the water, and we both ran splashing to the shore and up the bank, pushing through ferns and grasses.

Behind us the caimán splashed into the shallows.

34

Tom put his arm around me as we stood at the top of the final climb from the swamp. "We're safe for now," he said.

I winced when he brushed the spot on my shoulder where the spider bit me.

"I'm sorry." He lifted my hair aside. "It looks better."

I touched a red line on Tom's stomach, a scratch from the sharp grasses we ran through, perhaps from a bamboo leaf. Other such lines ran across his legs and mine. "The grass cuts aren't deep," I said, "but they'll need some attention to keep out infections." I looked down the hill. "We bathed in that water." Because of ferns and other plants on the hillside, we could see little of the water below.

"The black caimán must have come from the river this morning or the capybara would have been more wary."

"Our canoe. Gone. The machete. We lost it to the swamp again. Is it in the canoe?"

"Yes. And your alpargatas." Tom nudged my foot with his.

"And your boots. We left them in the canoe. Perhaps we can sneak back later and—"

"No, Rosa."

"You're right, of course. At least you saved our clothes."

Tom laughed. "I thought I was saving your medicine. If I had remembered the clothes were in the bag, I would have flung it to the caimán."

"With luck you left Catrina down there for the beast to eat."

"You don't mean that, even if it could be true."

"No. I don't mean it." I turned to look for Sylvia's house. "We'll need the clothes you saved. The village is right through there, if I remember properly. The people are not Indios."

"I remember," Tom said. "They spoke Spanish. Why didn't we encounter any native jungle people eighteen years ago?"

"Because we were too close to civilization? We did, of course, find some of them. Their bones, anyway, in the cave."

Close to the canebrake that once marked the edge of Sylvia's yard and beneath the mango tree that once shaded the witch's house, we stopped for me to spread antibacterial ointment on our scratches. "The tube is nearly empty," I said.

"Let me put some on the spider bite?"

"Touch it with care." I handed him the tube. "And use very little."

Tom barely touched me with the ointment, then stared at the remains of Sylvia's house. "There's less left than what we found of Mamacita Moreno's cantina."

I took khaki pants and cotton tee shirts from the bag and handed clothing to Tom. "Put these on and we'll find the village. I have money for another canoe."

"So do I."

"Try not to wipe off the ointment." I heard myself sigh as I watched him dress. "So we lost paradise again. You look better with nothing on."

"So do you. When we leave the village perhaps we can take off all this cotton?"

"No. There's the tropic sun. And other dangers. Spiders. We will not again make love. Our Eden is behind us." I pursed my lips to point toward the swamp.

"Eden was there because we created it. In reality it was the most dangerous part of the jungle with its vampire bats and spiders and the caimán. We could create another Eden in a safer place."

"You're trying to distract me." I slipped the tee shirt over my head. "I must focus on the main reason we cannot make love. You're married."

"I'm not. But never mind that discussion. I hate clothes. At least we left our footwear for the monsters of the swamp."

The trails were gone, so we had to cut poles from the canebrake for poking among grasses and ferns to scare away whatever might be there, waiting for bare feet. Tom grumbled about using my hunting knife and threatened to return to the canoe for the machete, but it was just talk. When we reached the river, we found only two houses.

They stood on poles, as jungle houses should, but included in their construction was some sawn lumber, and the roofs were corrugated zinc. "Where's the village?" Tom asked.

"These houses are new." I looked downriver among the tangle of plants at water's edge but saw nothing of the former village, not even ruins.

A man sitting beneath one of the houses heard our voices and came toward us. He wore blue bathing trunks and canvas shoes. "I didn't hear the motor on your boat," he said. "Welcome to my home. I am Julio." His bare skin looked like tanned leather, and wrinkles around his eyes said he was no longer young.

"Tom." He offered his hand and Julio took it for a formal grip and pump. "This is Rosa."

"With pleasure," I said. "Where is the village?"

"There is none, yet." Julio nodded toward the two houses. "These two are the beginning. One for me and my wife, and the other for my son and his wife."

"But there was a village here twenty years ago," Tom said.

"It's true. I lived here. But we left when calamity struck."

"When the missionary killed Sylvia," I said, feeling a tingling along my neck.

"How did you know?" Julio's eyes went round.

"We were here," Tom said. "We were trying to escape from Maybre when he fired his shotgun to kill Sylvia. She stood in a canoe with us."

"Not Maybre," I said. "Tom, he was not Maybre. I think his name was Marlin."

At the mention of Marlin, Julio crossed himself. "Could it be? You were the boy with purple hair? I thought you were a demon at first. I found your jeans in the river, but Mr. Marlin wouldn't let me keep the pocket knife."

"Julio?" Tom said. "Little Julio who warned us that the missionary was coming and he meant us harm? But you're, I mean, uh, I thought you were my age."

"Not little Julio anymore," I said. "Your father brought you to Sylvia because you suffered from soul loss. We watched her restore your soul to your body."

"Yes, yes," Julio said. "A ghost touched me, and when I looked back, he made my jaw freeze." He thrust his jaw to one side. "Like this. I couldn't speak until the witch rolled my soul up like a tortilla and put it into my mouth. Sylvia saved my life. Are you really the boy with purple hair? And you the little girl who told Juanita about the death of her mother?"

"You said the other house is for your son and his wife. How could you have a son old enough to be married?"

"You should have married Rosa years ago," Julio said. "Then you could have a grown son as I do."

"You spoke of Juanita," I said, "the daughter of Sylvia. How is this possible?"

"Juanita is now the most powerful witch on the river. She lives in the big village down the river. That's where most people from here went when the missionary killed the witch. That's where I went with my family."

"Everyone left homes here because, because . . . " I faltered.

"You are not responsible," Tom told me.

"Elena. My wife," Julio nodded toward the brush behind his home. "She tends potatoes and ground nuts where we burned the jungle for a garden. I'll tell her we have guests. Please. Come to the shade beneath my home."

He led us to the larger of the two houses and made sure we had grass mats to sit upon, then vanished down a path behind the house.

"He has a spare canoe." Tom pointed toward a grove of trees down by the river. Two canoes sat, bottom-side-up, in a grassy place similar to the one where we had pushed Sylvia's canoe into the water eighteen years ago. Perhaps it was the same place where Marlin shot Sylvia.

"We were too young," I said.

Tom took my hand. We sat on Julio's grass mat in the shade of his jungle hut. Gnats hummed around us, though none offered to bite, and the river gurgled below us, down enough of a hill to keep even high waters away from the house. "Too young to witness what Maybre did to Sylvia?"

"Tom, it was not Maybre. His name was Marlin. And yes, that's what I meant. How old were we?"

"I was ten. You were twenty-five."

"Eleven. I was eleven. Why did you say twenty-five?"

"Because you had maturity that I didn't. I was a little boy."

"And I a little girl. You probably don't know how much I came to love Sylvia in that short time we had with her. She had the wisdom my mother never had. She was the expert curandera my grandmother aspired to be but was not. She was the woman I wanted to become. Had she lived, I would have gone again into the jungles to study with her instead of going to the Sisters of Mercy nursing school in Cantaura."

"Marlin killed her because he thought she was a witch," Tom said.

"That, too. He killed her because she had life and vitality, because he wanted her and she obliged by taking him to bed with her. We saw that. We watched from the loft. He killed her because he was ashamed of the passion she aroused in him. He killed her because he loved her but could never possess her. Marlin came to the wild part of Venezuela so he could change it, but something went wrong. Venezuela changed him, instead. Sylvia showed him a mirror when she gave him the tea and let him remember his childhood. He killed her for showing him the mirror and for being vital and female and wild."

"I didn't know all that." Tom looked at me with intensity. "I didn't know. Then he put the shotgun into his mouth when I yelled at him that he was a murderer."

"No, Tom. He killed himself for murdering something so beautiful as Sylvia. You're not responsible for the death of Marlin. You are not."

"I killed Phung Phuoc. With a bamboo stake. In his neck." Tom's breathing became uneven.

"That was war. You did what you had to do."

"I could have wounded him or knocked him out. I didn't have to kill him. But part of me wanted to do it. And I killed Allen."

"A snake killed him, or helped kill him. Allen took his own life. Marlin took his own life. You were there, but you are not responsible, Tom."

"I could have shot the snake. I could have started the motor faster and moved us out of range."

"Stop it, Tom. Maybre killed Rochelle, not you."

"If I had stood by and let the boa do its work, Brother Maybre would not have shot Rochelle. He wouldn't have poisoned all those people. He wouldn't have swallowed the oleander leaves."

"You saved his life. He chose to misuse what little he had left."

"No court would convict me, I suppose." Tom wiped his eyes. "But I touched the web. The spider came out because I touched the web."

"Did you intend the consequences?"

"No."

"Then why punish yourself?"

"Can I be absolved because I intended no harm? Were my intentions clean? I wanted to slam that spike into Phuoc's neck. I wanted to kill Brother Maybre with my machete."

Tom's words frightened me, and I had to argue with them. He wasn't the guilty one. I was. I gave Maybre the information about poisonous plants. I killed the poet. I killed all those other people, so I had to argue with Tom to keep myself from sliding into the trap Mata-Mata fell into. Was I not through with Mata-Mata and the shame over the death of my grandmother? Must I now shoulder another thorn tree? It seemed unfair. "It's not you, Tom. I'm the one beyond redemption. The poisonous leaves." I shook free of his hand and put my hands over my face. "No thorn this time. An oleander sprouts on my shoulder. I feel the sting of its roots reaching into me."

"What you feel is the sting of the spider."

"Yes, that also. The spider."

"Perhaps the jungle changed Maybre," Tom said. "Like you said it changed the missionary who killed Sylvia. Perhaps Brother Maybre came to the jungle with his flock to find Eden like we did and instead he found heat and the red howler monkeys with their filth and beautiful blue butterflies that eat corpses. Wasn't he burning and clearing part of the jungle for crops? Didn't he build houses? He came here to change the jungle but it changed him and before long all he could think about was death and the sign from his god that it was time for death, so he forgot the reasons that brought him to the jungle in the first place and forgot all of his wisdom or else remembered only the words that were hollow to him and needed someone like you to see the wisdom behind words about forgiveness. So don't you see it isn't your fault that he cut the oleander plants and used them to kill his people? Many people know about many kinds of poison yet they don't use those poisons to kill like Brother Maybre did, so giving information about poison isn't the same thing as being responsible for how the information gets used."

"I still should not have told him."

35

Come with me," Julio said. "We'll kill the caimán and feast upon its meat."

"Eat caimán?" The astonishment was clear in my voice.

Rosa responded in English: "Only people who are hungry could consider reptile meat to be a feast."

Julio looked at her with raised brows. "I speak no English. But never mind. The caimán is evil when left alive. But dead it's sweeter than pig. Also, its skin will bring enough Bolivars to build two more houses. Two more. You and Rosa can live in one of them. The priest down the river could marry you." His eyes bulged as he spoke.

Rosa seemed amused and watched me, and I thought that she knew how I would respond to the idea of hunting. I kept my attention on the bland-tasting *pan de mano* Elena had cooked while Julio talked about the value of the caimán's hide; the four of us sat in the shade of a letterwood tree beside Julio's house, a location Julio assured me was excellent for building because soon other people would come upriver to become his neighbors, and some of them would be crude enough to piss on the ground in the village, "But not during the day, of course," he explained, "when everyone could see. No, no, they would do it at night because they're too lazy to walk the necessary distance to drop their water. But none of them, no matter how crude and dishonorable they might be in their pissing habits, will dare make water under a letterwood tree."

"Why not?" I asked.

Julio looked at me as if I were a simpleton. "Because of the bad luck. No one urinates under a letterwood."

I expected Catrina to laugh, but she stayed away during our meal of tasteless pan de mano, served on a folding card table with metal legs and surrounded by four canvas-backed chairs that looked out of place so deep in the jungle; "Good chairs," Julio had said with pride, then went on to tell us how he brought them upriver in his longboat powered by an outboard motor, the same boat his son and daughter-in-law had taken downriver in their quest for salt.

The lack of salt had explained the flat taste of the pan de mano. "You're kind to invite me on such an exciting hunt," I said. "But I would prefer not to hunt anything."

Julio shrugged. "You should share in the wealth from the kill because you discovered the caimán. My son and I will go on the hunt, then. Tomorrow. We'll also try to find the home of the bats and kill them. But that will come later."

"Why," Rosa directed her question to Julio's wife, "is it bad luck to make water under the letterwood tree?"

Elena raised her brows and looked alarmed. She had spoken only a dozen words since Julio brought her from her work in the burned field. Her response to us had been to smile in a shy way and to nod a great deal. She looked to Julio for help with Rosa's question.

"The snake-dog spirit of the tree hates certain smells," Julio said, then told us the story of the letterwood spirit.

In an age when animals could talk, Julio said, a gigantic dog chased a rabbit from the savanna into the jungle. The rabbit ran too close to a jaguar, who caught the rabbit and ate it. The big dog sniffed the trail of the rabbit all the way to the jaguar. "You ate my rabbit," the dog said.

"No," said the jaguar. "I ate my rabbit. This is my jungle, and you live in the savanna. Grassland rabbits might be yours, but any that wander into the jungle become mine."

The dog, who was much larger than the jaguar, considered eating the cat but decided against it because the jaguar looked to be all muscle and bone. Instead of eating the cat, the dog lifted his leg and pissed on the jaguar. "That's what I think about your claim to owning the jungle." The dog laughed, then went about marking trees to claim the jungle as its own. The animals of the forest hated the smell of the dog's urine, and each one complained as the dog wet the trees.

"Go away," the armadillo said. "You'll stink us out of our home."

In answer, the dog hiked up and squirted the armadillo, then went back to marking the trees.

"Stop wetting on the trees," the anteater said. "You're making the ants go far underground so I cannot catch them."

"I'll stop long enough for this," the dog said as it watered the anteater.

The python listened to the other animals trying to stop the dog. It does no good to reason with that dog, the python thought. It slid into some bushes and waited until the dog came close, then sprang upon it, biting the dog's neck. The dog snapped its powerful jaws on the python, close to its head, and each struggled to shake the other loose. But neither could loosen the other's grip. They thrashed around on the jungle floor until both were exhausted, then they became still and tightened their grips on each other until both died.

From the corpses of the dog and the python sprang a tree that had branches resembling a python and leaves that looked like a dog's ears, and the other animals of the forest saw that the tree's spirit was both dog and snake. When any animal dropped its water under the tree, the snake-dog spirit became angry and plagued the animal. Some animals were afflicted with ticks, others with starvation, and still others with illness of many kinds. People who pissed under the letterwood also became the objects of the snake-dog's wrath.

"But why," I asked, "would the snake-dog become angry about creatures making water under the tree?"

Julio looked perplexed. "Perhaps because the snake hated what the dog had done and the dog didn't want others marking his tree? I don't know. But everyone knows it's a dangerous thing to urinate under a letterwood tree, so my house is a place safe from marauding pissers."

"Why is the tree called a *letterwood*?" I asked.

"Because that's what kind of tree it is."

Rosa seemed amused. "Seldom are there answers to questions that ask why. When people do answer them, they usually speak of beliefs.

Questions that ask how are the ones that have a better chance to get factual information."

"That sounds good," Julio said, "though I'm not sure I understand."

He did understand, though, the processes for hunting caimanes, and he had shared that understanding with his son, who turned out to be a mere boy even if he had a bride—who was herself little more than a girl. Both bride and boy had something in their faces and general demeanor that said they were older than they appeared. They arrived that afternoon on a longboat driven by a popping, sputtering engine, and they brought with them a huge bag of lumpy salt, two wooden cages of chickens, and a yellow, generic dog that sniffed me and Rosa before falling asleep under the smaller of the two jungle houses. Julio introduced us to the children who weren't children, to Raul and Mona, who shook our hands and smiled to show mineral-stained teeth, then set about unloading their canoe, Mona working with a grim, determined frown and Raul seeming perpetually amused, and both beautiful with their jet-black hair, dark skin, and angular features that bespoke of Amerindian ancestry.

That night Rosa and I shared our hammock in Julio's home and awoke to the smell of approaching rain and the sound of the outboard popping and clattering. I remembered awakening in Poí's house to foul smells and to the sound of his urinating on plants below the house, and I thought he must not have built under a letterwood tree.

Rosa sighed awake. "I wish they would leave that caimán alone," she said. "It's the business of the caimán to eat the capybara and other small creatures."

"Small creatures such as Rosita if she should jump into the water to escape the ants?"

"Yes. "

"You don't mean that."

"But I do. Julio thinks the creature is evil, but that's wrong thinking. When it eats a little girl, it's not choosing to do something bad but to do something good for itself. To it, a little girl is only a snack.

It's also the caimán's business to eat those who hunt it, though of course that seldom happens in spite of all the stories. The caimán is in more danger from us than we are from it. We choose to kill it when we could choose to let it live since we don't have the need of taking its life. Perhaps we are the ones who are evil, not the caimán."

"I chose to plunge the bamboo into Phuoc's neck."

"That's not the same." Rosa sat up in the chinchorro, causing our bodies to bump together. "You killed a soldier who himself chose to beat you and kill your friends. Forget what I said."

"Evil is weird and difficult," I said.

"Get up," she said. "We need to think about breakfast before rain comes."

We found Elena and Mona preparing corn cakes beneath Mona's house, Mona going about the task with a grim frown of concentration and Elena looking as if she feared we might speak to her. Rosa joined them with hardly an exchange of words, and I sought to do the same but met a wall of female disapproval.

"You will have other work," Rosa said. "For now, go get the chairs from beneath Julio's house and sit in one of them."

"But you resented being expected to do such work in Brother Maybre's compound," I said.

"That was different."

"How?"

"Get the chairs."

The rain came as I carried the chairs, and with it came thunder. Among the thunder was the roar of Julio's shotgun, a sound that stopped me in the rain, my eyes fixed on Mona and the way her frown line vanished as a smile transformed her into a little girl, and I heard without much understanding her words. "That is the sound of my husband killing the caimán so we will have meat for lunch," the words coming to me through the hum of rain and the rumble of thunder, and the second shotgun blast jangled me enough to want to dive to the ground, though I didn't but stood in the rain remembering how the mention of a shotgun had sent me stumbling through darkness to find cactus with my knees, remembered holding the flashlight while Rosa the nurse picked out the thorn tips.

"You're safe here," Rosa whispered, taking my arm and urging me under the house to set down the chairs with Mona and Elena glancing at me as they patted corn cakes over a griddle while Mona's words about meat registered though I heard them earlier but didn't listen to their meaning because the shotgun blast had put a tightness in my stomach, and I remembered Sylvia the witch spinning around to fall bloody into the water where caribe regarded her as meat and Rochelle trying to stand in the canoe when Brother Maybre called her name, his pistol snapping death to send her into the water like Sylvia, and my own hands moving as under someone else's power to plunge the sharpened bamboo into the place where life throbbed in the sleeping man's neck for my bamboo to turn him into something else, dead meat, Allen said: dead meat, a phrase that tightened my stomach even more as Rosa guided me into the canvas chair she took from me, guided me to sitting where two women, one a little girl, glanced at me while they patted corn cakes and rain fell thick and white.

"Juanita the witch will help you," Rosa said. "She'll help us both. She must."

36

Tom gave his Barlow to Julio.

"But this is a treasure I cannot take." Julio held the knife toward Tom. "You must keep the knife of your childhood."

I sat in our canoe, the one we bought from Oz and gave up to the caimán's swamp. Raul and Julio had brought it back when they returned from killing the caimán.

"It isn't the same knife." Tom nudged the end of the canoe from the bank and stepped into it. He turned to Julio. "It looks the same, but isn't. I want you to have it."

"Thank you. I'll treasure the knife. But you and Rosa must return when you are married. We'll build you a house and plant a letterwood tree beside it, and you can raise strong sons here in my village."

"An excellent plan, Julio, and I promise that I'll think about it." Tom sat in the canoe and picked up a paddle.

I used mine to get us into the main current, then waved at Elena, Julio, Raul, and Mona. "Are you pleased to have your boots again?"

"At least it's good not to have to worry about stepping on poisonous frogs or spiders." Tom waved at the people on shore, then turned the canoe. "We'll soon be out of the jungle and yet somehow it feels as if I'll never manage to get the jungle out of me—not this one or the other jungle in Asia." He began paddling, pushing harder than necessary to move us down river. "You're right to reject me. I had been foolish to think I was finished with Phung Phuoc and Allen and the horrors of the war jungle, but now I see that I'm not, and I'm as crazy as ever. You're right to turn from me."

"But Tom I will never turn from you, and I will never reject you. You're not crazy, or if you are, then you and I are crazy in similar ways. All I said was that we must not again make love."

"Because I'm married, you think. Your reasoning might be flawed, but your conclusions are proper." Tom thrust his paddle into the water and dragged, thrust and dragged with almost the same fury that drove him after we saw the blue butterflies. We flew in the current with Tom working like a piston, dip and drag, dip and drag, until he was soaked in sweat.

At first I thought it was a log, then it seemed to be more like the caimán, and I pointed ahead. "Be still, Tom," I whispered. "There, in the water. Is it an anaconda?"

The snake vanished, then surfaced again as a lazy movement of curves, impossibly large in diameter and much longer than the caimán, more than twice as long as our canoe. We drifted by it as it sank. "I doubt we're in much danger from that snake," Tom said.

"The tingle of my spine doesn't feel like we're safe." I leaned down in the canoe to reduce the chances of the snake seeing me. "Perhaps it's the same one we saw knock the deer into the water when we were children? It struck like lightning. It could pluck one of us from the canoe."

Tom continued paddling. "That isn't likely."

"But it is possible. Please be still and make yourself less visible."

"I should have shot the cobra. My impulse was to do so, but I missed the opportunity." He moved the paddle faster.

"Please." I gestured to indicate he should be still. "Please."

But he kept paddling, and I sat up and turned toward him. "Very well. I shall make myself a target also. Why are you pushing so hard to move us downriver?"

"There are seldom answers to questions that ask why."

"Are you making fun of me? Are you being mean to me?"

Tom dragged the paddle to straighten our course, then put it in the canoe and looked at me. His face and arms streamed with perspiration, his hair matted, and tiny bits of moisture steamed from him into the humid air. "I could never be mean to you, Rosita."

"Rosa. Look at me, Tom. I am Rosa, not Rosita, not the child you remember. We're adults and equal. We were lovers, and we're now the best of friends. Sometimes you look at me and don't see me. I cannot tolerate your not seeing me." Far behind us in the ripple of the current I saw the anaconda surface again, then vanish. It seemed to be going the other direction. "The anaconda is gone, but perhaps there are others. We need to be careful on this river."

"I see you, Rosa. I see you. But I see others from my past also. You must remember that I'm crazy."

"No, Tom. You're damaged, but you're not crazy. I'm also damaged, and we both can become better. We are becoming better." A flock of parakeets flew close, and we turned to watch them dip, then climb the air to settle in the high branches of a tree.

"Do you suppose the beauty of this place can help us?" Tom waved a hand toward the parakeets, a gesture that encompassed all of the jungle.

"Yes. But not just its beauty. We can also change from contact with the wild and dangerous sides of the jungle, with the dark and deadly parts."

"If we survive."

"Yes. If we survive. When you first asked me to return to the wild part of the country with you, I thought of many dangers. Still, I didn't believe that we might meet death here. Did you?"

He sat still, watching the parakeets. "I don't know. We met death here before, when we were children. We heard it in the gunfire of men attacking the bandits. We saw it when Maybre killed Sylvia."

"As children, we saw death as happening to others and not to us. And, Tom, it was a man named Marlin who killed Sylvia, not the nasty person who called himself Brother Maybre."

"Marlin. Yes. Marlin." Tom picked up the paddle and began a slow stroking of the river. "I don't think I came here to find death."

"What did you come seeking?"

"I don't know. This, maybe. This riding the river and feeling the sun on my body and seeing the parakeets. I don't know. The tree sloth. Orchids and fruit and butterflies."

"So you're finding what you came to find?"

"I guess."

"When you were Don and I was Rosita, and we became lost in the wild part of the country, I came to love you with the purest kind of love. After we returned and your family left for North America and I grew older, I found such purity only once. My parents and my grandmother died, perhaps with my help, and I became a nurse and had a child, a boy named Don." My voice broke.

Tom stared. "You had a child?"

"I cannot talk about it." It took several deep breaths to calm myself enough to speak. "It's too painful."

"Little Don died, then."

"Yes."

"I didn't know you had married."

"I didn't say I was married."

"You never married?"

"No."

"There's much I need to know about you, my Rosa who once was my Rosita."

"Perhaps I'll tell you one day. But not now. Now it would be better to think about the village we shall soon come to, about what we'll do in that village."

"If there are authorities there, we must report what we know of Brother Maybre and his compound."

"Likely Poí has already reported the murders and suicides."

"Perhaps he has," Tom said. "Perhaps not. He did, after all, take two of the compound's boats and motors. He might choose not to say anything about Brother Maybre's place."

"We found death again in the jungle, and this time it nearly happened to us. I don't think I came here seeking death, either. But we found it when we found Maybre."

"I nearly killed Brother Maybre. I should have done it."

"Perhaps not. I'm glad you didn't kill him—glad for you and for me. Tom, you are not responsible for Maybre's insane acts. Would we live in a just world if we killed people we thought were about to commit atrocities?"

"We don't live in a just world now."

"Seeing the unfair death of Sylvia tests my faith. Seeing Maybre kill Rochelle tests my faith."

"I have no faith."

"That's not true. You have much faith. You are a good man, Tomás Seal. You have faith in me. You're learning to have faith in yourself. Perhaps the jungle is teaching you."

"This isn't the same jungle we knew when we were children."

"No. It never was the jungle we knew as children, and we must make it into that jungle. The village we will come to soon could be important to us. It was the village of Sylvia the witch. It's her daughter's village, and if she's still there, we have more important things to do than tell the authorities about Maybre and his compound." I turned around to face the front of the canoe and picked up a paddle.

We saw the burn of civilization long before we arrived. Primary jungle vanished, and the low, impoverished trees such as grew around my El Tigrito home appeared, then blackened fields from recent burnings, then fields of corn, beans, and potatoes. Beyond these the village sprawled. Only houses lower in the river basin stood on hardwood stilts. Others, higher up, looked like the mud-and-thatch of savanna dwellers, and many of the houses had metal roofs. I glanced back at Tom.

He stared, open-mouthed. "This isn't the same village."

"No."

"Where's the jungle?"

"Used up. For many kilometers. These are now farmers who burn the jungle. There are other changes. See them, there, among the houses?"

Tom squinted in the sun. "I don't see anything but houses."

"The electric wires."

"Electricity." His voice was filled with contempt. "We're out of the jungle, then. I don't want to stop here."

"Not even to report the doings of Maybre?"

"The river. Look at the waters. These people have turned the wild jungle river into a muddy ditch. Maybre killed his people. These people are killing the river and the jungle itself."

"We'll go on, if you wish."

Boys on the bank shouted greetings to us, and Tom turned the canoe toward a low pier where dozens of canoes were docked. "We'll find the police and make a report. Then we move on. How many people do you suppose live in this parody of a jungle village?"

"Five thousand? Fewer? I don't know. The mud in the river comes from topsoil exposed to rains when people burn and cut the jungle. I suspect the clear waters are all behind us, and we'll find nothing but muddy water from here all the way to the coast."

Ten to twenty villagers gathered to greet us. Among them was a man in uniform. "The reception committee," Tom said, "includes a policeman and a one-eyed shaman."

"Poí. Yes, it's Poí." I waved to him, and he responded with a broad grin and with holding up the pouch Tom had given him for storing the Irishman's glass eye.

"Poí," Tom muttered as he moved the canoe between two others. "I hoped not to see him again. But we'll not be here long."

"We could have lunch here before we set out again on the mud river?" I looked among those gathering beside the dock, hoping to recognize the daughter of Sylvia the witch.

37

I looked with hostility at the people gathering beside the boat dock as Rosa stepped out with a rope in hand. So they planted flowers and a few scruffy-looking trees, so what? The villagers had ripped the jungle open all the way to the savanna on both sides of the river, opening the wound with saws and fires then moving on to the next part of the jungle when rains washed the soil too thin for farming, leaving the earth gaping and ugly beyond the ability of scruffy trees and flowers to do much about the wound that no doubt stripped the night of its ability to sing in a chorus of insects, frogs, and birds because the voice of the jungle had been torn out. Here the only night sounds would be the barking of dogs and drunken singing from whorehouses; here the sweet musk of jungle plants and leaves turning into soil had been replaced with the pungency of cat urine and donkey shit, with human sewage, with the stink of humanity and mortality.

Poí greeted me with exaggerated show and a voice that was too loud. "My friend Tomás, please allow me to introduce you to my good friend Señor Castañeda, the chief of police. He wants to ask some questions about the gringos upriver who murdered themselves."

I set the travel bag on the dock and shook hands with Castañeda, and we said the proper social words of greeting, then I introduced Rosa.

Castañeda glanced at her in a dismissive way and returned his attention to me. "Did you know the norte americanos before you came to Venezuela?" He produced a tiny notebook and the stub of a pencil.

"No. Neither did my friend Señorita Rosa Rojas." I glanced at her with a wink.

"Do you know any of their names?"

"The leader called himself Brother Marlin."

"Maybre," Rosa said. "Not Marlin. Maybre."

"Yes," I said. "He called himself Brother Maybre, but I don't know his other names. There was a woman there named Louise and a little girl named Rochelle. Brother Maybre shot her with a pistol and she fell into the river."

"Shot? He shot her? But I thought," Castañeda turned to Poí, "I thought you said the *gringo jefe* poisoned them."

"He did. He poisoned the rest of them, then ate the poison himself. The girl is the only one he shot."

The policeman wrote in his notebook. "You didn't tell me he shot anyone."

"I forgot. So much happened so fast."

"This gringo jefe, he shot at you, also?"

"Yes. At me and at Rosa Rojas." I nodded toward her.

"But he did not hit you?"

"No. Nor her."

"Why did the gringos kill each other and themselves?"

"I don't know. They were religious fanatics. Have you gone to the compound yourself?"

"No." Castañeda squirmed. "Others have gone, of course. I have not heard a report yet. Can you tell me anything else about the people there?"

What could I tell him? That Brother Maybre had devised an entertainment for Rosa? That she refused him, that he sent a little girl to me as a sex slave? That Brother Maybre had eyes like Uncle Ray's so I trusted him because of the way he looked? Could I tell him I went after Brother Maybre with a machete but ended up killing a jungle snake instead? Such information would cause consternation and would be of no help. "No. I know nothing else."

"Why are you traveling down the river?"

"Because I did so eighteen years ago."

"This is a reason that makes sense?" Castañeda tapped his pencil on the notebook.

"It makes no sense at all. I'm doing it for an adventure."

"Ah." He eyed Rosa, letting his eyes wander over her breasts. "I understand wanting an adventure. You are married, then?"

"I once was but no more."

"Ah. Your adventure, is it a good one?" He put pencil and note-book into a pocket.

"The best and the worst."

Castañeda clasped my hand. "That is even as a proper adventure should be, for we must know the depths in order to experience the heights. Enjoy your visit in our village. If you think of anything else to tell me, please do so before you leave."

Rosa watched with contempt as he walked up the muddy road and into the heart of the village on higher ground, then she spoke in English. "That man is a goat who hates women." The small crowd began to disperse.

Poí grinned and spoke in a low voice. "I can guess you were not happy with Castañeda, and with reason. I detest the man."

I picked up the travel bag. "But I thought you said he was your friend."

"Of course I said that. He's a man of power, and I would be a fool to treat him as he deserves to be treated. I'm new here, and even with my wealth, the people dislike me and give me no respect."

"Wealth?" Rosa asked. We began the climb up the embankment to the sorry-looking village.

"From selling the canoes with motors. Back up the river in the village of Kaita, the people would be astounded at the idea of canoes of any kind being more valuable than a house. But that is the case. I bought a house and a good one, and I have money for food until people begin to trust me as someone to treat the ill—if they ever do."

"Is there a cantina where we might have lunch?" I asked.

"Yes. But first you must come with me." Poí grinned again and rolled his good eye to indicate he had something amusing to show us.

I started to object, but Rosa took my arm and tugged me into following Poí, who led us through a maze of narrow streets among impoverished-looking houses and up an incline where the houses became larger and no doubt by local standards more expensive, though they still looked like shacks even if they had more greenery around them and had metal roofs instead of palm fronds with weeds growing from the thatching.

"There," Poí puckered his lips toward a house made of whitewashed adobe and a rusty roof. "My new home. Never have I lived in such a house, though the neighbors don't make me welcome. One does, and she wants to meet you. She lives there." He puckered his lips again, this time toward a house in better repair, one with hibiscus growing around it and a bougainvillea vine in full bloom covering a trellis over the front door. An adobe fence, whitewashed and almost new, enclosed its side and back yards, and we could see sugarcane and mango trees towering above the back fence.

As we approached, a figure emerged from the front door and stood in the shade of the bougainvillea arbor. Rosa caught her breath and moved closer to me. "My god," I whispered. "It's Sylvia the witch."

"No," Rosa said. "Hello, Juanita."

"Rosita?" The woman stepped into the sun and her features became even more those of Sylvia, her eyes black, her hair shimmering in shades of navy among the black, her skin dark, Indio in her pronounced cheek bones and the exotic slant of her eyes. She was all that Sylvia was, only this time I saw with adult eyes, noticed the curve of her breasts and waist. The traditional red Indio dress with its embroidery fit her perfectly. "Are you the one who told me of my mother's death?"

"I'm so sorry I had to do that." Rosa's hand went to her mouth.

"Please. It's not a problem. I was just a child then. And you, señor, you once were a white boy with purple hair?"

"Purple hair?" Poí laughed. "Purple. That's hard to imagine, though of course it is funny."

"It was an accident," Rosa said. "I tried to dye his hair brown, but something went wrong with the berries I used."

"Please come into my home. Poí told me you call yourself Rosa. That's fitting now that you are such a beautiful woman." She stepped aside and gestured toward the door. "And you, señor, I remember you but do not remember your name."

"I am Tom, though when I was a boy people called me Don."

Juanita took my arm and spoke as Rosa entered the door. "I welcome you most sincerely into my home." She squeezed my arm and looked at me with intense eyes. Rosa glanced back at us, her brows raised.

I expected to find the interior of the house dark, expected to step down to a cool dirt floor. But the house sat on a cement slab with an abundance of throw rugs decorating it, and light flooded in from windows opening to her backyard. "Glass windows," I said as I set the travel bag beside a chair that seemed to have the wings of a bird.

"Yes. Many of the houses now have glass windows, but always in the back so neighbors won't think the owner is trying to show off, and always fenced to discourage vandals and thieves."

We sat on wicker chairs around a low table, and Juanita served us glasses of sugarcane juice poured from a container she took from a refrigerator. Above us whirled a ceiling fan. Through the glass window I could see the garden that was her backyard, a garden containing stalks of sugarcane, a hibiscus bush large enough to qualify as a tree, and flowers in abundance, including orchids.

Juanita sat at the head of the table. "Thank you, Poí, for bringing my old friends to my home. Tell me Tom and Rosa, have you found what you sought when you returned to the river jungle?"

"How did you know we sought something?" I asked.

"It's my business to know such things."

"I found some of it," Rosa said. "Tom found some of what he needs to find. But we're both still on a quest."

"So are we all, all of us." Juanita looked at Poí. "Tell us about your quest."

"Quest?" Poí frowned. "But I'm searching for nothing."

"You came with a lovely Indio woman. She left you for the police captain."

"Bah. He is a goat. She'll leave him in a matter of days."

"And come back to you?"

"Maybe. Maybe not. She likes men."

"Poí is my neighbor, but few people trust him because he's a stranger. Trust of the kind he seeks will be slow coming."

"It will never come." Poí hung his head. "I'm of mixed blood and did not belong even in the village of my birth. When starvation came and I moved with my father to the coast, people thought I was odd because of my magic eye and because they considered me Indio. In Kaita's Indio village they considered me Venezuelan or even European, and most of them distrusted me, even the women who sought to take me into their arms when the men were gone. And now I don't fit here, either, though I'm rich and have two magic eyes for calling the spirits that cure sickness."

"It's part of the curse of your life," Juanita said, "to feel always like the outsider. People here will accept you, given enough time, but you will not ever believe it. Your quest is for acceptance."

"You have your mother's wisdom," Rosa said.

After drinking sugarcane juice, after eating corn cakes, after much conversation about the fate of Brother Maybre's compound, after Poí excused himself to go to his own house, Juanita asked us to talk about her mother. "I'm younger than you," she said. "My memory fades when I think about my mother so that I cannot remember what she looks like."

"Look in the mirror," I said.

"Tell me about her. Tell me everything you remember. Then, perhaps tonight if you're interested, I will help you in your quests."

"Tonight?" The notion dismayed me. Stay in that parody of a jungle village? Out of the question, I told myself.

"But of course. You must stay the night with me. Tomorrow be on your way, or the next day."

"How can you help us with our quests if we're uncertain about what we seek?" Rosa asked.

"I can help you become certain. Perhaps neither of you will find what you want to find, but at least you'll know what you are looking for—with my help."

"Is that possible?" I asked.

"It is. Also there are some other things about you that you don't know. I could tell you, but it would be better if we invited some of the old women to come into my home to tell you."

"Whatever are you talking about?" I asked. She had me, though, this daughter of Sylvia the witch, this village woman who once lived in a river jungle. There was no way I would leave without finding out what she and the old women of the village thought they knew about me and Rosa.

Rosa picked up the travel bag, opened it, took out the chinchorro, and glanced at me in a defiant way.

"Only one?" Juanita seemed amused. "You two are more romantic than practical."

38

W*hen the shadows* of evening cooled the village, I sat in Juanita's garden beside Tom on a log bench with Juanita nearby us in a canvas chair. Other guests were two women, sisters, Juanita told us, who were about forty years old. Lucinda and María once lived in the village where Marlin murdered Sylvia. "This norte americano and this woman from El Tigrito," Juanita said to the women, "are curious about Sylvia the witch." *Bruja,* she said and not *curandera.*

"A most powerful witch," Lucinda said. Lucinda wore a hibiscus in hair shot through with gray, and her cheeks gleamed an unhealthy white. Something on her lips made them dark blue, and she had painted a black line around them. The skin under her eyes resembled a raccoon's mask. She looked more like a witch than Sylvia ever did.

"The witch rode upriver in her canoe without using a paddle or a motor," María said. Her hair was river-stone gray, and she had lines on her face, kind lines that emphasized her beauty.

"She could call spirits out of rocks and trees," Lucinda said. "She talked to jaguars and tapirs. I have seen her hold discussions with such animals."

"Tell them one of the stories about Sylvia," Juanita said.

Lucinda sat forward, her eyes flashing, and began her story. Her hands made fluid motions through the evening air to aid in the telling. "When I was young, I was ugly."

Tom worked to stifle a laugh in an effort so subtle that I could hope no one noticed. Juanita glanced at him with a playful smile, then turned back to Lucinda.

She wanted us to know that as a young girl, she was shaped like a twelve-year-old boy. "I had no tetas at all." Lucinda sat back and glanced at her breasts. "While my beautiful sister had tetas like melons. All the boys watched her and fought each other for the privilege of walking with her. None of them paid me any attention, which made me the most unhappy girl in the world. Then I went to see the witch."

"I suggested that she go," María said.

"You did not. It was my idea. Perhaps I was the last one to seek her services, for just hours after she helped me, she was dead."

"That part is my story," María said.

"Yes. I was not there when the woman of thunder and the jaguar spirit did the dying witch's bidding."

"Lucinda," María said with a note of warning in her voice.

"In the witch's den I complained that I was ugly. She told me to paint my face to accent my natural beauty, and she asked me to show her my tetas. But I have none to show, I told her. Still, she wanted me to bare my poor flat chest to her. When I did so, she picked up two pomegranates and tossed them into the air while chanting some magic words. The pomegranates moved so fast I could not follow what they did, but somehow they became flesh and attached themselves to my chest and turned into two perfectly-shaped tetas."

"Pomegranates?" I said. "Pomegranates? There's something familiar about this story."

"It is a famous story," Lucinda said. "Many people up and down the river tell this story. It happened to me. But of course as a young girl I was not so appreciative, and I said to her that she should have used melons. That's when she showed me her own tetas, the largest I have ever seen, larger even than the melons my sister has, larger than Juanita's. She told me tetas made from melons will one day sag, but those made from pomegranates will look forever young, and of course she was right." Lucinda cut her eyes toward her sister. "Ever since the witch made me beautiful, boys and later men paid me more attention than I wanted. But I was pleased with her magic, and I like my pomegranates that do not sag."

"Men from many kilometers over the savanna and from downriver came to look at my sister's small pomegranates," María said. Her voice carried a note of mockery that her sister seemed not to notice.

"So you see," Juanita said to me and Tom, "my mother has become larger than life."

"She was larger than life when she lived," Lucinda said. "Certainly her tetas were, and the truth is that they were beginning to sag, just as she said melons will do."

"María," Juanita said, "tell my friends about how the witch died."

"A buzzard man killed her," María said. "He came unbidden one morning. I saw him first as a black spot, and he looked like any other *zamuro* circling in the sky, looking for dead things to eat. But as he came closer, I could see that he was huge, much larger than a zamuro has any business being. As he lighted in the top of a tree, his clawed feet became human, and his whole shape changed into that of a most ferocious and toothy man. He climbed down from the tree, and I then saw that he had the penis of a donkey and eyes that stared unblinking, like those of the buzzard he had been just moments before. This terrible creature came up to me, and I was too frightened to cry out or to run. He said Sylvia the witch was dangerous and needed to die, and he demanded that I tell him where she lived."

"You said nothing about his penis when he came down from the tree the last time you told this story," Lucinda said.

"But I did tell you about it. I did, and you forgot. The zamuro spirit went crashing through the woods toward Sylvia's house, and I wanted to warn her but thought it best not to become involved with such magic creatures. In minutes, Sylvia the witch appeared, and behind her in the woods came the crashing sounds of pursuit. She went to her canoe, which was on the bank, and she tried to push it into the water, but could not. So she took a stick and hammered it against a rock while speaking magic words, and from the rock came a woman of thunder. Then she hammered the stick against a tree while saying more magic words, and from the tree came the spirit of the killer jaguar. With the help of these two spirits—"

"Wait," Juanita said. "Please tell my friends what these two spirits looked like."

"They were ugly," Lucinda said. "Uglier than I ever was before I got pomegranate tetas and learned to put on proper makeup."

"You didn't see them," María said. "I did. The tapir woman, called a woman of thunder, had black skin and black hair and eyes black as a thundercloud at night. She had the body of a little girl, and yet there was something about her that frightened me. The jaguar spirit was an albino with green eyes shaped like a cat's. His body was that of a boy, and he had purple hair."

Tom jerked in surprise. "Purple?"

"Yes. He was even more hideous than the tiny woman of thunder, who had leaped out of a rock. The woman of thunder put her head against the canoe and the killer jaguar spirit put his shoulder against it, and with no effort at all they pushed the witch's canoe into the water. Then all three got into the canoe just as the zamuro man came out of the woods, his donkey penis dragging on the ground. He opened his mouth and a ball of flame leaped from it and hit the witch, knocking her into the water where cannibal fish began to eat her flesh. She leaped out of the water, her face horrible and cannibal fish hanging all over her, and she spoke some commands to her spirits before she sank back into the water where the fish ate her. The albino boy flew to the zamuro man and clawed his head from his body, and the woman of thunder jumped from the canoe to the buzzard man and stomped upon him until there was nothing left. Then the black girl and the albino boy dived into the river and vanished. By the time I became brave enough to investigate, the only thing left of the zamuro spirit was a black mushroom, which is still there today, if anyone is foolish enough to go to that part of the river for a look. Those of us living in the village moved downriver to this town. None of us wanted to have anything to do with the black woman of thunder or the purple-headed albino boy who is the spirit of the killer jaguar."

"My mother," Juanita said, "has become myth."

"No," Lucinda said. "My sister told the story exactly as it happened."

"What I said is true and not myth," María said.

"Of course it's true," I said.

"It is?" Tom sounded astonished. "But I rem—"

"Please," I patted his hand. "Please."

Later, after the sisters left, after the short twilight came and went, Tom, Juanita, and I sat in Juanita's living room. Juanita leaned into Tom's space, though he didn't seem to mind, and said, "You and Rosa have become myth. How do you like being a jaguar spirit?"

"Was I white as an albino when I was a kid?" Tom asked me.

"Were my eyes black as a thundercloud at night? Was my skin black? Myths change details even while being true."

"This is all so weird," he said.

"There is truth in the myth, judging from what you told me about my mother. The villagers instinctively knew of the sexual tensions that had to exist between the man Marlin and my mother, and María's story expressed those by giving the buzzard spirit a penis like a donkey's."

"They also knew something I have suspected for years and felt guilty about," Tom said. "After Marlin shot Sylvia with his shotgun, I yelled at him from the canoe, telling him that he was a murderer, and my words caused him to put the shotgun in his own mouth."

"No, Tom. You didn't cause Marlin to take his own life," I said.

"Even María's myth says I was the instrument of his death."

"Such stories," Juanita said, "cannot be taken literally, and they're open to many interpretations. In the story, my mother arose from the water long enough to command the death of her killer, so she killed him. I think it is true that she caused his death because when he saw what he had done to her, he killed himself. The story is full of magic, but it is also full of truth."

"I told Tom years ago that he didn't kill Marlin," I said. "But we were just children and too stunned to make much sense of what we had witnessed."

"Is this what you seek?" Juanita asked. "Did both of you return to this river so you could resolve what happened in that violent moment when the crazed missionary killed my mother?"

"I don't know," Tom said. "Maybe. Sylvia's death has troubled me for years, but there are other troubles that have become much worse."

"And for you, Rosa?"

"Sylvia's death was a defining moment in my childhood. But I think I didn't come here to relive what happened in that moment. I'm not sure why I came, though part of the reason had to do with my grandmother's death. There's more, though."

"Would you like to go on another trip where you will discover what troubles you? Tom?"

"Another river trip? No. Too much has happened on this one."

"That is not exactly what she meant," I said.

"But I didn't mean anything exactly," Juanita said. "Would you go on such a trip, Rosa?"

"Tonight? Yes."

"Tonight?" Tom looked puzzled. "Is this some sort of woman talk that I'm not supposed to understand?"

"Not at all," Juanita said. "I learned much from my mother and from my great aunt, who taught us both. Are you familiar with magical truth?"

"Does magical truth," Tom asked, "have to do with some bitter-tasting tea?"

"My mother gave you some, perhaps?"

"Yes. It did such strange things to us. I became a parrot. It wasn't possible that I became a parrot, but I did. Rosita said it was magic, though that seemed unlikely. Even as a child I didn't believe in magic. Now it all seems like a dream, a vivid dream that I still remember. Sylvia became a cricket in my dream."

"What about you, Rosa? Did my mother make some of the tea for you, also?"

"Yes. Sylvia used magic to show us the truth." My heart beat wild, and I knew I was afraid even while wanting to know what magical truth Juanita planned for us.

39

Rosa liked what Juanita said about magic truth, but it seemed like nonsense to me.

"You have within you," Juanita said, "everything you need to know. The difficulty comes in locating and understanding what you already know. The key is proper use of imagination."

She said more but I didn't listen with much sympathy, and I said no to the tea but did it without conviction so Juanita poured me a cup, and when I saw Rosa drinking hers, I took the tea, a bitter and dark concoction though the darkness of it might have been only the dim light in the room, candlelight, a flicker of flame and shadows from three directions even if she had electric lights, lamps and an overhead fixture in the living room where I lounged in a wicker chair shaped like a hummingbird and Rosa sat on the sofa still sipping her tea when Juanita asked me where I might go in order to confront that which had been bothering me for so long.

"Santa Cruz," I said.

"Go there when you're ready, and I'll go with you. Talk to me as much as you can, and I'll offer guidance. How will you go?" Juanita took the cup from me, and she sat on a knotted rug between me and Rosa, who had begun to slump.

"It's a long way off. To get there would require a jet plane. A fast one." The idea of finding a jet plane in that jungle-killing village struck me as funny, though I didn't laugh because I heard the sound of the jet landing out front.

"Rosa," Juanita said, "he spoke English. Can you translate for me?"

"Yes." Rosa spoke words that floated around me in the flickering light, Spanish words that came from her marvelous lips, lips I wanted to touch with mine or with a fingertip, words that made no sense, though that seemed fine with me in the candlelight that Juanita swam through to take Rosa's cup then sit on the knotted rug again or maybe she sat on the knotted rug and then took the cup. Events jumbled and time ran in quick spurts, sometimes stopping and sometimes going backward to make the jungle around the village alive again with whistle frogs singing in the night until I knew it was time to go to the jet that had landed hours before and waited outside the front door.

"Will you come with me, Rosa?" I asked and put a fingertip to her lips to feel the sibilance of her yes buzz against my skin as she stood and Juanita stood to follow me beneath the trellis of bougainvillea in a darkness of flickering light where we heard the whistle frogs from restored jungle and climbed into the military jet, a needle with wings that would take us to Santa Cruz.

"Where will you go, Rosa?" Juanita asked as we buckled ourselves in, and I started to answer with the obvious, to say that she was going with us to Santa Cruz, to the little house on Tree Frog Lane, a place easy to spot from the air because of Neary's Lagoon close to the house and because of the railroads like dotted lines around three sides of the lagoon, but before I could make the explanation, Rosa spoke.

"People from San Tomé go there to swim." She also said something about *el lobo.*

"To Neary's Lagoon?" There were no wolves in California anymore, and never had I seen Venezuelans swimming in the lagoon, but perhaps it was because I had paid insufficient attention during the time I lived with Catrina in the house on Tree Frog Lane; perhaps people in San Tomé often hopped aboard such zippy little winged needles to go for a dip in Neary's Lagoon, but Catrina kept me too busy with her marvelous passion even to glance out the window at the jets landing and people streaming out of them in their bathing suits, dark people with black hair with names like Romero and Gonzales, people who could well take dogs with them, large dogs that Rosa might mistake for lobos.

"There are reeds there," Rosa said, "and small wet-season streams feeding the pool. The streams run shallow, just a few centimeters of water running over sand warmed in the sun to warm the water. The pool is too shallow for swimming, more a wading pool, and across one end of it are the reeds growing out of still water. You will go with me, Juanita? I need you with me for this."

"Of course. I will be right beside you the entire time."

"Tom, please come. This trip to the place of sunning and wading frightens me."

"Yes. I might watch from the window, but I'll be with you."

"Are we there?" Juanita asked. "I see the water."

"Yes." Rosa's voice shook, and I knew if I touched her lips the sibilance would be full of fear, a contagious fear that ran through me as we disembarked from the jet and I saw Todd's car parked close to the house on Tree Frog Lane.

"I don't want them to see me," I said. "Todd has no business being there, not with me gone."

"Where are you?" Juanita asked.

"At the university, taking a class in Victorian poetry. Todd knows that."

"Go as a parrot," Rosa said. "Sit in that tree, the mango. Sit on that branch close to the water."

"It's a monkey puzzle tree. People in Santa Cruz like to plant them. I think they came from Africa."

"Speak Spanish," Juanita told me.

"I'll go as a tree frog." Did I say it in Spanish? Juanita patted my arm, and when I looked at the spot she touched, I saw it turning green, felt my face metamorphose, my legs bend in odd ways, and I was a tree frog and worried about Boots, Catrina's dog, so I hopped on the monkey puzzle tree and from there to a window ledge.

"I don't want to do this," Rosa said.

"If it becomes too intense, close your eyes," Juanita said.

But how could I close my eyes when my brother stood over the futon and my wife reached for him, pulling him to her? Eyelids like a film of milk went up to make the world look as Poí might see it through his white eye, blank and grainy like a movie screen waiting for the flicker of action, and I rolled the milk lids back down in time to see Catrina pull him beside her and hear the click of beads on her neck and the rustle of fake buckskin as Todd unbuttoned her and she him, their skin albino white in the flickering light and I said "No, no. It isn't right."

"What isn't right?" Juanita asked, though she could see for herself since she looked in the window beside me and could see what was going on.

"The stream," Rosa said. "It isn't right that I sunbathe in the stream. But look. I am doing it."

"You'll freeze," I said, knowing the waters of Neary's Lagoon to be colder than any jungle river, cold enough to ripple your skin and make you snatch in breath like Todd did when he kissed Catrina's breast and she sighed and I felt a tightness in my own groin when I shouldn't have because what he was doing on that futon with my wife was wrong, dead wrong, and yet their passion was contagious even for a tree frog.

"Where are you?" Juanita asked.

Where was I goddammit when my brother tupped my wife? Tupped, fucked, screwed, slammed, diddled, fornicated, rammed, *fuche-fuche*, did the dirty deed, balled—when the two of them rutted like animals, where was I? In a literature class reading "The Jabberwocky," though reading was unnecessary since I knew the poem by heart, *slithy toves,* the *slithy toves* that Humpty Dumpty thought were a cross between pigs and corkscrews and liked to eat cheese but at that moment as a tree frog watching through the window I knew better, I knew the slithy tove was Todd's slithy going into Catrina's tove so Humpty Dumpty was wrong in what he told Alice, Hoomté Doomté missed in his explanation because Victorians didn't write much about sex except under titles like "The Vision of Sin," which made little sense to me because I didn't believe in sin, in wrong maybe, but not sin except for moments such as the one when I was a tree frog sitting on the window sill watching sinful slithy toves, watching my brother tup my wife.

"But you weren't in class," Todd said, looking at me and at Juanita as we peered in the window, and he didn't stop slithying the tove though he spoke to me: "You weren't in class, not at the University of California at Santa Cruz because when I first tupped Catrina it was still under construction among all those redwoods at the edge of town," and he finished her off by sucking a strawberry onto her neck and she finished him off with histrionic moaning and thrashing about on the futon, riding him like a dog until they fell apart, panting and gasping for breath and rolling onto their stomachs to prop heads on elbows and fists so they could look at me in the window.

"Why are you here now?" Catrina demanded. "You never were around much even if you feigned profound love for me and great sensitivity and for a time made me believe you had the soul of a poet so I loved you beyond any reason, even if you came around only once in a while and spent the rest of the time smoking dope and dropping acid and in general fucking yourself over with wine and greenies and uppers and downers and all the nasty things you could buy on the beach to make you think you were profound when you weren't, when you were just a turned-on, dropped-out drugger hoping to dodge the draft because in your own words grooving on beach shit was better than getting your ass shot off in Vietnam, and don't look so surprised that I heard those words, and don't try to tell me again how immoral the war is and how you would go to Canada out of principle rather than submit to the draft because you went to Vietnam, didn't you?"

"I loved you with all my body and soul," I said.

"I understand such love," Rosa said, and I glanced at her lying in the cold sand of the stream running into Neary's Lagoon and thought how odd it was that she had come all the way from the wild part of Venezuela just to swim in that cold lagoon and how odd it was that I wasn't peering out the window to see the people from San Tomé taking a dip but peering from outside the window with my brother peering out at me, my brother who had just tupped my wife.

"She isn't your wife," Todd said.

"Catrina and I told everyone we were married, and by law that makes us married even if our ceremonies took place on the beach with cold wind in my hair and a flower in hers, ceremonies we wrote ourselves to include a folk song by Joan Baez and a wedding song by Ric Masten with Leroy playing the guitar and singing us into a union that is legal in this state, one that even required a divorce to break."

"That's not what the lawyer said." Todd smirked.

"The lawyer said if divorce proceedings would make me feel more divorced, then we should do them even if ours was a common-law marriage and we could get by without one, so I had him draw up the papers and I signed them, and I went to a barber and I went to the recruiter and I went to Vietnam so I would never have to see either of you again."

"Speak in Spanish, please," Juanita said, "so I can offer guidance when you need it."

So I said it in Spanish. Todd told me that my Spanish was rusty, that I had some of the verb tenses wrong, and I said, "You have some nerve to correct my grammar right after fucking my wife."

"You use such foul language," Todd told me. "Catrina and I did not fuck. We made love. The earth moved, the stars sang, and we slipped into divine union and an understanding of everything that is."

"Spare me the mystical bullshit, you fucker." Tears burned my eyes.

"Be gentle, Don," Catrina said.

"Don't talk to me you bitch. You fucked all my beach buddies and you even grubbed around with women and you had the audacity to admit it, to tell me it was not my business whom you chose to love."

"That was in anger, Don, anger born of your abandoning me and my seeing for the first time that I deluded myself into thinking you and I were made for each other. I was made for Todd, not for you. Todd was embarrassed for you and tried to comfort me, and I liked his comfort, liked him, soon came to love him while you lived on the beach in your dirty clothes and among your dirty friends and on your dirty drugs."

"But you never told me any of this."

"I thought you knew. It all seemed so obvious to me, far too obvious to need saying."

"Are you still angry?"

"No. I'm a mother. I'm a wife. I have a career and a home and a husband who adores me. My husband is your brother, so how could I be angry at you? Todd needs you to be his brother again, to speak to him. Did you know you haven't spoken to your own brother since you discovered us together? You need to forgive your brother, Don."

"Forgive my brother?" I said in amazement.

"Yes," Juanita said. "Forgive your brother. Then forgive yourself."

"So I must give up hope of ever having a better past?"

"Well said." Juanita smiled at me in the flickering light.

"Maybre said that, and he was an evil man."

"You don't believe in evil or sin," Catrina said. "But that doesn't matter. Go away now. Quit being a tree frog and go away."

"Call me," Todd said.

40

With Tom sitting across from me and Juanita close by in the warm candlelight, I felt safe for the moment, and the prospect of taking a trip to dark places seemed less frightening. Juanita tried to explain the value of stories, but Tom gave her scant attention. "The key is the proper use of imagination," she said. "You have the ability to become anything and to go anywhere, and in the becoming and the going, you gather the information that you already know. A good way to gather such information is to witness a story and perhaps be part of what you witness. Sometimes the story is enough, and sometimes you have to think about the story to understand what you have told yourself." She gave us bitter tea. "This will help you go and become."

When the tea began working its dizzying magic and Juanita asked us where we would go, Tom named a city I thought was in Venezuela, and I said I was going to a place on the El Tigre River where people from San Tomé like to swim.

"Go there when you're ready," Juanita said, "and I'll go with you. Talk to me as much as you can, and I'll offer guidance. How will you go?"

Tom spoke and I had to translate because he chose English. Then she urged me to answer. "Bicycles," I said, seeing them as I spoke. Mine had fat tires, a basket on the front for our lunch, and a seat behind me for Donito. El Lobo rode one with more narrow tires and three gears.

"Why do you call him el lobo?" Juanita asked.

"He wants me to call him that."

Tom asked if he could come with me, and I told him yes, and he reached toward me, reached to touch my face, and I felt the touch though he remained seated and I did not move from the couch until it was time to get the bicycles. "Go with me, Juanita," I said, and I told her the place where small streams entered the swimming area frightened me, and she said she would be beside me. El Lobo with his geared bicycle went on ahead while I rode with the awareness of Donito behind me, Donito at age four, named for Don, the one pure love of my life until Donito. Behind me came Tom on a rusty bicycle with low tires, and beside him Juanita on a pink bicycle, a new one with flowers painted on the fenders.

We left the blacktop for the rutted trail dipping toward secondary-growth jungle and the river. A loop of El Tigre formed the swimming area, though most of it was far too shallow for swimming, and we thought it was safe for Donito, though he already at age four swam better than I. Reeds grew across the river, and among the reeds swam water birds and minnows. Fish lived there, El Lobo claimed, and there to eat the fish lived eels, some that had the power of electricity. When Juanita, Tom, and I arrived, El Lobo was already there, as were Donito and Rosa, a younger Rosa whose hair fell long to dance over her shoulders and back, all of her back and almost to her legs.

"Such hair," I said, remembering how it felt, remembering how El Lobo loved it long and how I wanted to cut it but did not because I wanted to please him and not because he commanded me to keep it long.

"Where are we?" Juanita said. "I see water."

Tom talked of tree frogs and cold water, but the place of swimming felt warm, I knew that, and the younger Rosa knew it. She stripped to her bathing suit that left hair showing at the tops of her legs, hair that other men glanced at, the waders and swimmers and sun bathers, though the younger Rosa seemed not to notice their covert glances.

"She's beautiful," Tom said.

"She's too short," I said, "and her hair is too long. Her breasts are too big."

"Her breasts are perfect," Tom said.

"Look at the way she watches El Lobo," I said. "She's a fool for dreaming him capable of one day loving her. When she first met him, he told her Rosa had always been his favorite name for women."

"I don't like El Lobo," Tom said.

"Nor do I, now. Perhaps I didn't like him much then, either. The reeds across the river, look at them. They grow in murky water, and I hate them."

"Explore the reeds, Rosa," Juanita said.

Tom and Juanita sat in the shade of a cashew, a small bit of cool that would vanish as the sun climbed toward noon. I stood beside them, my head and shoulders in the sun, and I wondered how to explore the reeds. The young Rosa sat in a shallow stream of water, a rippling crystal washing over sand to catch the sun before it joined the wading pool. I could feel the liquid warmth of it washing over my legs as I watched her.

El Lobo and Donito splashed each other in the pool, and young Rosa's eyelids drooped in laziness from the sun and warm stream. How young? I wondered, and did some counting.

"Twenty-two," I said. "I was twenty-two because Donito was four, and I gave birth to him when I was eighteen."

"El Lobo was the father?" Juanita asked.

"Yes. An older man. I think he was thirty when he first took me, though he told me he was twenty-six. He told me I was his only love, but he had others."

"I'll become a tree frog," Tom said.

It seemed like a silly comment, but if he wanted to become a tree frog, that was fine with me. "Stay out of the water," I warned. "If you do go in the water as a frog, stay away from the reeds."

"Explore the reeds, Rosa," Juanita said.

"How?"

"I don't know. Become a water bird or a fish."

Why not a bird? I thought, and felt my feet grow thin, my toes group into bird feet too small for my alpargatas, which I had to step out of with long legs, more spindly than a chicken's. I flew on white wings to the reeds, landed on one to bend it close to the water, closer than I wanted. Minnows darted among the reeds, and larger fish surfaced like bubbles to snap at insects on the surface. Across the water,

Rosa with long hair made a sand pillow and went to sleep while the tiny stream washed warm around her legs, and El Lobo splashed with Donito. Other people wandered around, some sitting on towels, some wading close to the bank, and all staying far from the reeds where I stood.

El Lobo watched a woman wade into the water. Not a woman—a girl. Perhaps she was sixteen. "Is that pretty child your son?" the girl asked. She smiled at him, and I could tell she wanted to hear that the boy was not his son. I could tell that she wanted him to look at her as a man looks at a woman, even as the men glanced at the hair showing around the bottom of the young Rosa's swimming suit.

"The boy is my nephew," El Lobo said.

"He's lying," Tom said. He sat on a reed close to me, a tiny frog that could hop across the surface of the water if he chose, and not a tree frog at all.

"My name is Celia," the girl said.

"People call me El Lobo, but do not let the name frighten you. I am a nice lobo."

"I like the name. It fits you because you are so strong and powerful."

"I could pick you up and run away with you," El Lobo said. "Always the name Celia has been my favorite name for women."

"Pick me up and run with me in the water," Celia said. "I would like that."

"Donito," El Lobo said, "Go sit beside your mother, but do not awaken her."

"I want to play in the water," Donito said.

"We'll play later. Go to your mother. Go. Go."

"I don't like the harsh way he talks to the boy," Tom said.

"I don't like the reeds," I said.

"Explore the reeds," Juanita said. She was a fish rising like a bubble to speak to me on the surface.

Celia squealed as El Lobo picked her up and ran with her in the water. They fell, and their hands explored each other under the surface, and they laughed. Donito started toward his sleeping mother, a pout on his lips, then turned toward the reeds.

"Don't come here," I warned.

"He doesn't understand the language of birds," the Jesus frog said.

"Explore the reeds, Rosa," the fish said.

Donito waded toward the reeds. Other fish swam among them, eating minnows and ignoring the one who was Juanita. Water came up to Donito's waist and higher. Minnows splashed, some jumping out of the water in their panic to escape being eaten, and Donito clapped his hands to applaud their skipping across the water. He came closer for a better look just as the eel slid through the reeds to eye a fish.

"Go away, eel," I said, and I prepared to dive into the water to peck its eyes out.

"Stay still and watch," Juanita said. "This all happened eight years ago."

It was hard to watch. Donito moved to the edge of the reeds, leaning this way and that in looking for minnows. The eel turned toward the fish and shot its electricity. The fish turned on its side, and the eel snatched it with needle teeth. Donito jerked, his eyes bulging, and sank into the water.

I flew to the top of a palm so I wouldn't have to watch his life bubble away, and I heard El Lobo talking to the girl: "When may I come see you, Celia?"

They splashed in the water, their hands where they should not be, and the young Rosa fluttered her eyes. "Donito," she said. "Donito?" She sat up and looked around. "Donito!"

"I cannot do this," I said.

"Just a few more minutes," Juanita said. She was a golden butterfly sitting on the end of a palm frond. "Explore the reeds."

"I did," I snapped. "The eel took my baby." He was there, on the bottom among the reeds, and Rosa rushed about, looking, calling his name.

El Lobo dropped the child Celia, giving her breast one last rub as he did so. "Donito," he said, looking around in a fierce way. Others stopped wading and splashing.

"I saw a boy go toward the reeds," a man said.

In seconds El Lobo had bounded to the reeds, and he took the body from the water. Rosa screamed. El Lobo waded ashore to lay the boy on the sands. The young Rosa bent over the body and blew into its nose and mouth, pushed on its chest, blew and pushed, blew and pushed because I knew the way of it from nursing school, knew the way of it, but his lips were cold and the breathing and pushing did nothing. She could see feet standing around her and could hear the rough breathing of the wolf.

Then she sat back and El Lobo cursed her.

"Your child drowned?" Juanita asked.

I flew to the ground with Juanita fluttering beside me. "I'm done now," I said.

"Perhaps. What did El Lobo do? Watch him, Rosa. What did he do?"

He jerked the young Rosa to her feet and slapped her. "*Puta*," he said to her. "Puta." He hit her again, this time with his fists, and hit her some more until the other men, the ones who had looked at her swimsuit hair, caught his arms and dragged him away from her. "I told you to watch him." His voice came out like a growl, dangerous and low. "You killed my son."

I hopped close to him as the men let go of his arms. "It was an electric eel," I said. "In the reeds. The eel wanted only to eat the fish, but its jolt got Donito."

"Go away, stupid bird." He kicked sand at me.

I hopped to the young Rosa. "It was not your fault," I said. "El Lobo was too busy feeling the breasts of the little girl to notice Donito wandering toward the reeds. It was the electric eel that stunned him."

"No, little bird," Rosa said through bleeding lips. "I killed my son, my Donito," and when she cried, tears poured over the wounds from

El Lobo's fists, and red tears ran down her face. Rosa cried blood, and there was nothing I could do about it because I was only a bird, a white bird.

41

I *watched me from* another angle, watched me sitting in a chair shaped like a dung beetle and wondered how I ever thought it looked like a hummingbird. Rosa sat on the couch, tears on her cheeks in shining lines that glinted in the candlelight, a dimmer flicker than before because one of the candles had burned away into a puddle of wax on a plate while the other two still stood as nubs, still giving light so I could see Juanita had returned with me to sit again on the knotted rug while I watched from beside the plate of puddled wax, watched and bunched my legs to jump.

"Come back," Juanita said. "You're through with the story."

"But I like being a tree frog."

"Come back."

"I don't like being a white bird," Rosa said.

"Once I dreamed of being a parrot," I said. "It was a good dream."

"Close your eyes," Juanita said, "and think about drifting down the river in your canoe."

I sat in the canoe watching Rosa, who was a white bird standing in the bow.

"Become yourself again," Juanita said. "Breathe the thick air, the moist air full of jungle flowers, and listen to the river. Listen. Listen. You can hear the trees moving, the leaves in the wind, and you can smell rain coming, clean rain to cool and wash you and make you whole."

It fell in warm drops, not in cold needles, and it wet my pants and shirt. In the front of the canoe Rosa, no longer a bird, turned toward me and took off her blouse, and she was so magnificent I wanted to touch her, to taste the rain running across her brown skin.

"I like rain," she said. "Tom and I bathed in the rain, and we clung to each other while rain washed much from us. Much."

"Come back now," Juanita said. "Come back. Come back."

I sat in the hummingbird chair and looked at Rosa, who wore a dry blouse though her cheeks had lines of water on them. She looked beyond me, and she seemed alarmed by something she saw through the window, something in Juanita's garden. "Mata-Mata," she said "has come back, and look, he stands there with the thorn tree bigger than it ever was, and it hurts. It hurts." She rubbed her shoulder as one of the remaining candles went out.

"Avert your eyes." Juanita stood over a lamp, clicked a switch, and the room flooded with light, hard light, and Rosa put hands in front of her face. "You're back now," Juanita said. "But now is not the time to tell your stories. Now is time for sleep so all of the effects of the tea will leave you. I'll hang your chinchorro here." Somehow our hammock was in her hands, and she hung it on hooks beside a window to her garden. "Tom, you will sleep here." She hung another hammock. "And you, Rosa, will sleep there."

It was difficult to stand and even more difficult to get into the hammock, a feat that might not have been possible without Juanita's help slipping somehow into Sylvia's help with the house becoming the witch's thatched house on the river, especially when Sylvia leaned over me and pressed her lips to my forehead almost as if I were a little boy, almost but not quite because the heat of Juanita's lips did something erotic, and as she withdrew and her eyes locked on mine, I thought it wasn't just a maternal kiss for her, either, and I knew she was Juanita, beautiful Juanita and not Sylvia, though Juanita also was a witch. She had to be a witch, given that she had just taken me from the jungles of Venezuela to Santa Cruz.

No dreams came, or if they did, I didn't remember them as morning grayed through the window and Rosa stirred in the hammock beside mine and the odor of coffee filled the room. It seemed as if I had slept only a few minutes, but there it was, morning, and there stood Juanita, nudging me awake, then patting Rosa, telling us good morning and saying something about coffee and not seeming to remember anything about the maternal and erotic kiss she had pressed upon me at bedtime.

After we had taken down the hammocks, after we drank coffee, dark coffee with the power to make my fingers tremble and my heart race, we sat as we had when we drank bitter tea the night before, as I had when the chair looked like a hummingbird or maybe a dung beetle.

Juanita seemed amused by the trembling in my hands. "It's now time," she announced, "for us to talk about the trips we took last night."

Rosa looked alarmed. "Not yet." Her voice quavered. "Tom, tell yours first. Please."

"I became a tree frog." The statement struck me as stupid enough to draw mocking laughter, but none of us laughed, and I took courage from the silence, took courage from Juanita who seemed not to remember the kiss, took courage from knowing that by telling my story Rosa could relax for a while before telling hers.

It was easy at first to tell about the flying needle that was a jet plane, about landing close to Neary's Lagoon and going to the window of the house on Tree Frog Lane, but it became more difficult to tell about what I saw my brother doing to my wife.

"Was he doing something to her or were they doing something together?" Juanita asked.

"He put a strawberry on her neck." Years of anger about that strawberry washed over me then seemed to wash away, and I admitted that Catrina and Todd collaborated to make that strawberry, and I got back to telling the story as it unfolded with my standing on the windowsill and watching through the eyes of a tree frog. Rosa sat on the couch, examining her hands until some point in the story when she looked at me with such intensity that hair on my neck prickled, but I went on with the account, a part of me feeling silly and a part of me dreading the confession that Catrina was right about how I lived on beaches and drank and took drugs, many drugs. "I became the scum that lives in tide pools," I said.

"You blamed your brother and Catrina." Juanita's voice carried no blame. She sat on the knotted rug.

"The strawberry," I said, then became silent, ashamed, embarrassed, and somehow Allen's death loomed larger than before, and I knew he would be alive if I had killed the cobra. I put my hands over my face.

"There's more," Juanita said. "But you've told us enough for now. Rosa. Tell us about the swimming place on the El Tigre River. Tell us about the reeds."

"I cannot. I cannot. I cannot."

"Then tell us what happened after your child drowned."

"What?" I dropped my hands. "What was that?"

"For now," Juanita glanced at me, "you will remain silent and listen." She issued the command in a firm voice but with a soft face and soft eyes, with a look similar to the one she gave me after pressing her lips on my forehead, though Rosa didn't seem to see.

Rosa, beautiful Rosa whose face struck me as Asian back when she looked down from the palm-frond tree, Rosa who had traveled again the wild river with me among blue butterflies and beyond Brother Maybre's compound, Rosa who loved me in the Eden of our tree platform high above a jungle of spiders and swamp, Rosa who would not make love with me again shuddered and began talking.

Would Tom still like me after he learned about the darkness of my soul? I would have to chance that and stand before him more naked than I had been when we bathed together in the river, more nude than when we made love. But I couldn't look at him as I told the story of my guilt. "I named him after you, Tom. Maybe not you but for the child you were when we traveled the river together after the candyman left us close to Mamacita Moreno's cantina. I named him Donito. Little Don. El Lobo objected to that name, but he had no choice in the matter. He ruled my life in other ways, but I took command when it came to Donito. Or I did until that day at the river when—" My voice broke.

"When Donito drowned," Juanita said. "It was not your fault, Rosa."

"I tell myself that, and sometimes I believe it." Mata-Mata had troubled me in the night. He came to the window with his thorn tree and he whispered my name and he had my face, but I didn't tell Juanita and Tom about him. Instead I talked about El Lobo.

He stayed away from our home for three days after the funeral, then he stumbled in stinking of tobacco and beer. Heat oppressed the house, dry season heat clicking and popping the roof during the day and radiating from the walls at night. I sat at the table, numb, too empty to cry when he flipped on the light switch and snarled at me. In one hand he held a bottle, and in the other a machete. When he struck me with the bottle, I knew I deserved it. His second blow broke the bottle and cut my cheek and knocked me to the floor where I lay on my back and watched him raise the machete.

"Chop the neck." I tilted my head to expose the place for death, since nothing remained in that house or anywhere else for me. Blood ran across my face to gather under my head.

"You killed my son, my Donito."

"Yes. Here. The neck."

His machete flashed and I closed my eyes as the blade bit into the table. "I should kill you, but my hand refused." He tugged on the handle, gave up the effort to free the blade, kicked my thigh, and stumbled out into the night. I didn't tell Juanita and Tom about the kick, about how the pain from it made me stumble to the medical supplies. I did tell about treating the wound from El Lobo's bottle, about putting all medical supplies into my bag, and about holding a lighted match under the curtains.

Later, when the house I had shared with El Lobo lay in ashes, neighbors told me that he tried to enter the burning house to retrieve his clothes, but it was not possible because of the flames. I saw him from time to time around El Tigrito, and always he looked drunk or sick from drinking. Then he vanished. People told stories about him. He worked in Maricaibo and had a woman whom he beat. He killed a man in Cantaura and went to prison where guards beat him and he died. He became a fisherman in Puerto La Cruz where no one liked him because he was so cruel. Three years later he returned.

By then I had my home beside the river, a tiny house of adobe and thatch designed after the hut where Sylvia lived when Don and I emerged from the swamp and she found us and took us in. I built a loft where children might stay, a loft with latticework to make it possible to see into the room where I received patients. But of course no children ever climbed the loft to watch my work as a nurse. When El Lobo returned, he parked his car, leaving a woman and child in it, and he entered my home without knocking.

El Lobo wore black trousers and a white shirt. His shoes smelled of fresh polish. I made no effort to greet him. He strutted about the room, brows raised and eyelids sweeping down to look important, and he told me he had a child, a daughter. "My woman is pregnant again, and this time she will give me a son."

I said nothing. How did I ever live with this man? I asked myself.

"We have a large house and a servant." El Lobo made a show of examining my hut. "At least you have electricity here. That is something, I suppose."

"You're fortunate," I said, "and one day I might be happy for you. Did you come to brag about your family and your house?"

El Lobo seemed startled. The look of superficial superiority disappeared, and his lips twitched into a nervous smile. "No. I came to tell you that it was not your fault Donito drowned."

"Is that all?"

"Yes."

"Then you may leave now."

With a curt nod he went to the door, turned and said, "It was no one's fault. It was fate. I forgive you, Rosa." And he was gone.

As I listened to the sounds of his car door, the motor starting, the tires on the dry road, and as I smelled the dust of his departure, I began to cry. It came soft at first, not much more than a watering of the eyes, but soon my entire body heaved with the unfairness of Donito's death and guilt for allowing him to die. After the sobbing stopped and I began to wipe the water from my face, I asked if I cried for the loss of El Lobo and admitted that I missed him even if I didn't want him to return. I wanted only Donito.

Tom's face showed such concern that I fought back tears, and I resolved to speak with a priest before we left the village.

Juanita waited until she was certain I had nothing more to say. "El Lobo did something remarkable for such a man."

"Yes," I said.

"But you haven't been able to do what he did."

I saw that Tom failed to understand what Juanita meant, and I said, "Forgiving myself has been impossible."

42

*R*osa left early to find a priest, she said, though I wanted her to stay with me, to bid goodbye to Juanita the witch and go with me through the village of jungle-wreckers, get in our canoe, and explore the final part of the river before we met Manuél, before we completed our trip down the river. "No," Rosa said. "I must talk with a priest. If you want to go to the canoe, do so alone. I can find my way back to El Tigrito."

She dimpled as she talked, and I understood that she only half meant the invitation for me to leave her before the trip was over, so I nodded. "The priest. Find him, then meet me here."

Juanita said she didn't deal with priests, though she gave directions for finding the only one in the village. "People call him a puta-priest," she warned, "but of course he is still a priest."

After Rosa left, I sat in the garden where Mata-Mata had appeared again to her, where heat drove humidity into my clothes, where Juanita dragged a chair close to mine in the shade of sugarcane, dragged a chair and sat near enough for me to feel the warmth of her and to know she smelled like bougainvilleas, close enough for her to speak in little more than a whisper: "I once loved a man much like you."

The look in her eyes was familiar, a look I had seen in the eyes of other women, Catrina's back in better days for us, in Kaita's eyes when she tugged me toward her mat on the forest floor; it was similar to the look Juanita had given me the previous night when she pressed her lips to my forehead and stepped back to let me know with soft eyes that the kiss was innocent and more than innocent, so that there in the shade of sugarcane when I looked at her eyes and her lips, her full lips parted just a bit, at the way she leaned toward me, I knew she wanted me to touch her. I sat back. "Why did you leave him?"

"He left me." She moved away but not by much. "He knew many fine things, while I am only a jungle girl, the daughter of a witch, and a curandera. I told him I would love him forever."

"For this he left you?"

"Yes. 'I want you for now,' he told me. 'Speak me no forevers,' he told me. But I wanted more." She stood to pace the garden with sun striking her in patterns of mango leaves, then leaving her in the shade of sugarcane, then again sprinkling her with light. "He was a subtle man, and a passionate man. Like you."

I watched her pace. "You wanted forever with him."

"Yes."

"I wanted that with Catrina."

"And she betrayed you?"

"With my own brother. But of course it was my fault."

"This man." Juanita stopped pacing, stopped close to me. "He said we find meaning in moments only. He said passion comes and fills us and makes us feel whole and then it leaves. He said a relationship is like a light bulb. It gives heat and light and then burns out. He said there is no repairing a light bulb and forever is not a word for people or light bulbs."

"So all we can do is get a new one?"

"He said that. But I wanted more. You, Tom, you wanted more with Catrina but lacked the wisdom to find a way. You want more even today."

"Not with Catrina. I will not talk with her again."

"But she is married to your brother. You should forgive her."

"That's not what I meant. I meant I will not speak again to her if she appears to me. With luck, I'll never again allow her to appear to me. That sounds crazy, I know."

"It is always wrong to say never, and it is never right to say always."

"Do you believe that?" I asked with astonishment.

"Those words came from the man who talked of light bulbs. Do you know what I became to him?"

"A burnt light bulb?"

"Yes. But he spoke only part of the truth in saying we can find connection in moments only."

"Connection in moments only," I whispered, hating the idea, fearing it might be true, remembering how Rosa and I held each other in cold rain, the two of us standing in clean water flowing over sand into our wild river. "Rosa and I had a wonderful moment, but the moment died."

"As such moments must, as all moments must. Yet knowing they will die is part of the glory of them. If I didn't know that all moments die, perhaps I would fail to understand the importance of connection. Maybe I wouldn't even seek connection in meaningful ways and would stumble and drift and fail. You and I had a glimpse of wonder last night when I kissed you. Right now we have opportunity to see into each other." She stopped in front of me, looked at me with expectation, and I knew that this was not a mere jungle woman, that she was more than a trickster witch dealing in hallucinogenic teas, though of course she was also a witch.

"But you're being inconsistent," I said.

"All of us are inconsistent, and we must find forever in moments only. No one can be immortal for long."

"You confuse me. Time confuses me. Rosa taught me that the past runs from earliest memory to the present. The river taught me that I must try to understand what I did with even the most recent parts of that past, including thinking about what I didn't do. I didn't kill the cobra. I didn't kill Brother Maybre, and both omissions make me unworthy in this moment."

"So you refuse me because you're unworthy? I don't believe that." She began pacing again. "You're a good man, far too good for, for—never mind. Wait for Rosa. She will come to you."

"You see me as good?" But how could she, especially after standing beside me at the window to the room where Catrina and my own brother rutted over one another and learning I was the one who set them up to do so? I liked seeing me with Juanita's eyes even if I knew her vision of me was inaccurate.

"The light bulb man said we must seek our forevers in ways other than human ways, even if he never found his forever. So he goes from woman to woman, and he goes with cynicism that makes him someone I could never again want to hold. I'm not burnt out, and I would work to make new varieties of connection if he had not discarded me. Forever is more than an illusion of lovers if they're willing to take command of moments." She took my hand as if to pull me from the chair. "Are you the man to join me, even for a short forever?"

I remained seated. "To make love while Rosa is gone?"

Juanita released my hand and shrugged. "If the moment led to that, yes. If not, maybe only to hold each other in loneliness."

"But we have no past together."

"You were present when Marlin killed my mother. I once brought you *empanadas dulces* when we were children and you had purple hair and came to my village with the wild Irishman."

"I came with Rosita, not the Irishman. I traveled the river with Rosita, and I returned to travel it again with her, though she now calls herself Rosa."

As Juanita turned from me I saw a stiffening of her shoulders, and when she spoke, her voice had a coolness to it. "You have loyalty to Rosa. I admire that. Do not let her slip away from you, Tom. People are smarter than light bulbs and don't need to burn out, and no one deserves to be thrown away. You came again to Venezuela not to travel the river of your childhood but to find Rosa and to make good moments into forever with her. Of course she deserves such devotion. All of us do." Juanita rubbed her eyes with her palms. "You will go now, purple-headed demon-boy." She went into the house.

With her gone, the garden of sugarcane and mango, the garden of orchids and hibiscus seemed small, dusty, little more than an enclosed patio with a few odd plants, an inhospitable place in the middle of a village where people destroyed the jungle Rosa and I wanted to find again or at least I did because I didn't return to the wild part of the country in search of Rosa and would have traveled the river by myself had she refused to go with me, had I found her married to some idiot local with a name like El Lobo and busy pinning diapers on half a dozen kids, which is what I half suspected would be the case back when I began searching for her in El Tigrito and where I had been glad to find her and even more glad that she would come with me even if finding her wasn't the primary reason for returning to the land of childhood.

Inside the house I found Juanita setting the travel bag beside the front door. "The ripe moment for you and me came and went, and yet someday we might make another, if you ever think it worthwhile. Perhaps not. Come back to my home, if you wish, but expect nothing. Do you remember the directions I gave Rosa for finding the priest?"

"Yes."

"Go. Find her there. If you miss her somehow, she will come here, and I will send her to your canoe." Juanita opened the door and stood aside for me to leave.

"So I am dismissed?"

"Goodbye, Tomás." Her voice carried a touch of anger.

The sky growled its promise of wet-season rain as I left the witch's house through the arbor of bougainvillea and turned for a final farewell look at the witch who was no witch in that moment but a beautiful woman with eyes flashing dark anger and hurt, her chin lifting to show me disdain in contrast to Kaita who had bared her breasts to show me what I turned down, though what Juanita offered had far greater appeal for being more, so much more than a rubbing of bodies. Make a moment into forever? The idea wasn't so different from Poí saying he could become immortal for only a few days at a time: both notions sounded absurd. And yet I found Juanita's invitation into a forever moment tempting. So why did I sit back and fold my arms when she made her offer? I didn't know with any certainty the reason for refusal, didn't even understand the entire offer with its murky way of coming only when Rosa left the house as I once left the house on Tree Frog Lane back in Santa Cruz, and my brother, my own brother watching perhaps for me to leave took the opportunity to enter my home and make an offer of his own even if he did more than devise an entertainment for Catrina and was willing to stay around and marry her instead of gathering oleander leaves as Brother Maybre did to make an offering of death to his terrible god. The moment of looking through the bougainvillea arbor at Juanita's angry eyes was the present slipping into the past, and as I turned and as the door closed in a click of finality, I knew the moment would be one I had to live with, one that needed understanding and examination as did other moments of decision, though it seemed less crucial than the moment when I failed to shoot the cobra or when I turned the machete from Brother Maybre's neck to slice the snake that was trying to kill him for its meal, the snake unaware he was too big to swallow much as I was unaware how Brother Maybre's survival of that moment would lead to his calling Rochelle's name and shooting her when she tried to respond by standing in the canoe. What would come of my leaving the witch's house, of my sitting back and crossing my arms to cause Juanita's eyes to smoulder and her chin to lift with disdain as I turned for a final look? The sky crackled again its promise of rain, and I moved on to seek Rosa at the priest's house, the puta priest whom Juanita scorned.

He was easy to find for his house, an adobe and whitewashed structure with thatching, shared a wall with the village church whose walls leaned and seemed stark, penitential, unadorned and whose grounds had no garden. "Tomás," he said from the doorway that barely cleared his white hair, the door hinged with hemp to hang crooked and dig an arc in the dirt as it swung outward. "Come in. I am Father Martes."

His house smelled of mold, of rotting thatch, of rancid tortillas and grease. I stepped into a room of stained walls, of chairs made from rough lumber. "Father Tuesday," I said in English.

"A strange-sounding name, I know." He spoke English with no trace of a Spanish accent. "I didn't choose the name. My father chose the name when he arrived from Ireland on a Tuesday. Please. Sit here."

"You're not Venezuelan." I made no move to sit.

"But I am. This gray hair once was red, a gift from Irish parents. The gray was a gift of the church, from the bishop, to be specific, since he assigned me to this god-forsaken village. This," he waved his hand to indicate the house, the church, "was his notion of penitence to cure me of liberal ideas. I was born in Caracas."

"Where is Rosa?"

"You came from Juanita's house. Did she try to seduce you after your woman left?"

"My woman?"

"Juanita is the most notorious puta in the village, though she be intelligent and beautiful. I loved her once—as I'm supposed to still, of course, since she's technically a member of my flock. I once loved her as a man loves a woman."

"But you're a priest."

"And a man. Jesus was a man. Do you think he never made love with a woman?"

"Juanita called you a puta priest."

"She would, of course. But the only whore I've gone to bed with was Juanita, back before I found out her habit of going from man to man."

"You must be the light bulb man."

"She gave you that metaphor, did she? It seems to be a favorite of hers, and believe me she lives by it. She goes after any man who shows the slightest bit of sophistication, and she always succeeds in seduction."

"This is not true."

"So she worked her romantic magic on you, did she? Don't fall for it, Tomás. She'll discard you like a used light bulb. One of her basic mistakes is believing that we as human beings find meaning only in romantic relationships. Life offers much more than romance between a man and a woman, and even such romance cannot last. We must seek more than romantic love."

This priest annoyed me, and I backed out of his house into a light drizzle. "Where is Rosa?"

He shrugged. "She came to me as a believer, and I counseled her as a priest should, and she left."

She went back to Juanita's, I thought, and we missed each other by taking different routes through the village. I turned to go.

"Romance," Father Martes said, "is ephemeral, but love is forever."

"So you're not the light bulb man."

"No. Such a man exists only in the lying imagination of the village curandera."

"You and Juanita confuse me. One of you isn't telling the truth."

"What is truth, said jesting Pilot, and would not stay for an answer. Go find your woman. Go find more than your woman." Father Martes closed the door, dragging it against earth that soon would be mud from the rain.

I walked through mist to the river where Rosa and I had left the canoe we bought from Oz, and I thought of Olivia Radcliffe, trying to imagine why a woman from South England would come to the jungles of Venezuela to die and . . . and I wondered if I would give the locket to Rosa, a romantic gift of gold with words inside, words that dealt with time.

43

Down one street I saw a woman in red who looked familiar, but that wasn't possible in this strange village, so I dismissed the thought. My alpargatas stirred dust in the powdered streets and rain drifted toward the village to settle the dust. It was good to walk when the air was full of the clean odor of coming rain. Even Juanita's village had intensity to its colors and a surprising beauty, maybe because the priest had told me what I needed to hear. I wandered through some curving streets, taking time in returning to Juanita's home. Tom and I could again make love, perhaps live together: this information no doubt was the source of beauty in the dead jungle, now a village. If I made the ugly village into a lovely place with thoughts of Tom then that was all right with me.

The priest said some other things, such as how I should not look to Tom or any man as my source for being happy. But what could he know about love between a man and a woman, he being a priest? I went to him for an opinion on church law, not advice on what made life sweet. It was good to take time walking through the village, remembering nodding to sleep against Tom in the pickup, pressing against him in the chaparro tree, taking a bath together after the howler monkeys flung their filth upon us. That bath had been magic, as much so as making love in the tree shelter near the swamp.

It was such memories of touching that danced through my head when I knocked on Juanita's door. She opened it only a little, enough to make the act a hostile one. "Tom has gone," she said. "He and I talked of making love soon after you left the house." She closed the door.

The ground seemed to shift, and I had to grip the bougainvillea arbor to remain standing. With a heart beating wild and breath coming in short gulps, I knocked again, and she opened the door enough to peer at me with hostile eyes.

Words poured from me with a flood of anger: "Did you and Tom do that? Did you?"

"Ask Tom. But of course we both know how men lie. Do not knock again." She started to close the door but I shoved it hard, knocking her back, and I stood in the entry to watch her catch herself against the wall, to watch her hand go to her lip and come away with blood.

"You don't deserve to have any of Tom. You don't deserve to be the daughter of Sylvia."

We stood for a long moment as lizards do before they battle, as cats do. Then came the sound of rain, the paper rattle of bougainvilleas, the hiss on the roof, and I backed out of the entry to the witch's house and turned my back on the sound of the closing door.

Kaita, I thought, and Rochelle, who was a child, and Catrina, the females Tom wanted. Anger ripped through me. He returned to Venezuela to find Rosita only to get stuck traveling with me, Rosa, and not the child he sought. Now Juanita the witch, Juanita with breasts like her mother's and eyes to tempt any man, now at the moment when the priest's opinion had given me such hope.

And the little one gone, Donito, who drowned because I was not vigilant enough to guard him. A lack of vigilance has been my downfall: I should never have left Tom with such a woman as Juanita. I strode downhill, glancing at the sky, aware of rain but not feeling the cold of it, as if my anger were turning it to steam.

Then somehow the anger lost its fire, turned into something hard, something cold as a river stone, and drops seemed to appear above me in a rush to remind me of what I read once. Big stupid birds, turkeys, I think, sometimes died because they would watch rain falling. They stood looking at the sky until water ran into their noses and drowned them. Such stupidity deserves punishment, I thought, and looked again at the sky.

A figure in red approached me as I stood watching drops slam down upon me.

"Rosa?" she said. "Rosa?"

"Kaita?"

Someone had struck her face to make her eyes puffy, and dried blood clung to her lip and nose—someone had struck her as I would have been tempted to do had she appeared moments before.

"Why do I choose men who mistreat me?" She looked pathetic.

"Perhaps all women chose men who abuse them," I said. "Perhaps we are all stupid birds who drown in raindrops."

"I want to go home." Her voice broke, and she looked like a child, a lost child. "I want to go home."

Rain came harder, colder, and I tried to find hot anger to fling at this woman. "You took Tomás into the jungle to lie with him."

"I did?" Her voice came out as a whimper. "Then you will forgive me. Tomás said I had beautiful tetas, but he would not touch them. Señor Castañeda also liked my tetas, yet he drove me from his house." She gestured toward the sky. "In the rain. He drove me out in the rain. What am I to do?"

In that moment I found her self-pity almost humorous, perhaps because it seemed a parody of my own. "Don't ask me for advice about men, Kaita. I'm a failure with men. Go talk to Poí."

"Go to Poí? Yes, I should do that. He is my true love." She began unbuttoning her blouse. "Señor Castañeda gave me this terrible clothing. I will not go to Poí wearing it."

I stared at her brown skin, at her young breasts with water beading and running on them. Did Tom refuse to touch this woman? But she seemed in that moment more child than woman, and I felt someone should warn her not to go through the village without proper clothing.

Kaita turned, flung her red blouse into the gathering mud, and started uphill toward Poí's house. She seemed so silly to me, and yet I seemed even more stupid for wandering about in a strange village, for being more naked than Kaita in spite of my clothing, for shivering, finally, in the rain, for telling myself how miserable I was, and over what? A man? It was time to go to the canoe, to paddle to the next town where my cousin waited, and to go home.

At the docks I found Tom bailing out our canoe. Rain had soaked his clothes, his hair, his beard, and I wanted to laugh at his stupidity, for beside him in the canoe was the travel bag and inside the bag a poncho. He knew it was there, and he chose to get wet. When he saw me, he came ashore.

We stood close without touching. The rain came down harder to hiss against the river. "I killed the wrong snake," he said. "Brother Maybre was no brother. He was evil. Did you know I hadn't believed in evil since I was a child? There's plenty of wrong in the world, I knew that. But evil?"

"Talk to me, Tom. You lay with Juanita."

"Why are we standing in the rain?"

"You lay with Juanita. You lusted for the child, Rochelle."

My words seemed to stagger him. "Lusted? For Rochelle? But no. A child. She was a child, and I'm responsible for her death."

"You lay with Juanita. Don't deny it."

"Who are you?" Tom's voice was high and stressed. "Who are you?" He returned to the canoe and sat in the water it held.

I untied the rope, climbed into the canoe, and pushed us into the hissing river. Tom sat facing me and did not move. The village dimmed into the gray-white lines of rain and a smear of mud as I paddled away from it. Trees appeared again, but not tall ones, and the jungle looked more like a garden gone to weeds than a natural and wild place. Who am I? I asked and had no answer for Tom's question other than knowing my own stupidity and my lack of vigilance and my blindness to Tom's interest in girls. "You lied when you told me Catrina is a tall woman, that she does not look like a child."

Clouds drifted away and the rain stopped. Tom picked up the coffee can to bail water from the canoe. "Don't ask me about Catrina again."

The cold anger within me flashed red. "How can we talk if we don't talk?"

"What?" Tom paused in his dipping, looked at me with raised brows, with rounded eyes. "What did you say?"

The comical look on his face and the silliness of what I had said made me laugh, startled me with laughter that had pain in it, laughter that changed into crying.

Tom stared. Clouds moved and sun struck the canoe, the water.

Annoyed with myself for the outburst, I thrust the paddle into the gleaming water. "We are done with our trip," I said.

"We should not have come."

"Did we have a choice?" Anger settled back into the cold river stone under my ribs.

Tom picked up a paddle. "I don't understand that." He started to turn to face the front of the canoe.

"No. Don't cause us to go faster, and don't turn around. I like looking at you when we talk. We have so little time, and the river rushes us too much. Talk to me, Tom."

"Talk?" He set aside the paddle. "You will accuse me again of lusting for a child and of having sex with the witch, but what does that matter? Believe it if you want."

"It matters. But there's something more important, and much I wanted to say before the witch took you. I wanted to tell you that the priest said you never were married, not in the eyes of the church, because your ceremony on the beach was not a real marriage. You were not married in the eyes of God."

"I'm guilty of far worse things than not being married or having sex with a jungle curandera, guilty before I went to Vietnam and guilty there in its terrible jungles and here on the trip we should not have taken."

"I wanted to tell you that you are a good man, Tomás. But you're also a difficult man for women. For me."

"You believe that I felt lust for a child. That I couldn't wait for you to leave so I could fuck the witch."

"Such language, Tomás. I wanted to believe in your goodness, and I wanted to tell you that in El Tigrito there is a shop run by a man we once knew as Mahadi when we were children. Do you remember him? I wanted to tell you that he has beds and other furniture in his shop."

"What?" Tom stared at me.

"I wanted to tell you that I could make us a large chinchorro, a better one than Kaita's, and more comfortable for the two of us, or that we could get a bed at Mahadi's shop. I wanted to find Donito again." It seemed so unfair that Tom sat in the canoe looking at me with his beautiful face, with drops of water catching the sun in his beard, with the sun steaming his shoulders dry, and the river flowing with mud. From looking at Tom I might think a crucial moment had arrived, but that was an illusion, and I knew the right time for inviting him into my life would never come.

"Perhaps it's best you don't tell me such things. I'm not without guilt." He picked up the paddle and turned to face the front of the canoe.

"Nor," I whispered, "am I."

We moved the canoe faster than the current, and I couldn't regret that the trip was over, for the anger flared as I paddled. The fire in my head flashed in many directions. At El Lobo for fondling little girls. At Tomás. At me for being so stupid in loving Tom, a man not unlike El Lobo.

44

G*lancing back* I saw vapor leaving Rosa like smoke, saw the sun striking her face, her eyes still set in anger, and I wanted to do something to soothe her but didn't know the trick of it and so did nothing except keep paddling in water ruined by mud from the village that should be jungle. Images from the night of loving with Rosa in our poisoned Eden came to me: the feel of her heat and the crying that broke from her, from me even, crying while making love—such a strange experience and soothing somehow, restoring.

She will not have me again, even if the priest gave her permission, would not because of my guilt—and what did it matter that she found me guilty of acts I had not committed? My being innocent of bedding the witch or lusting after Rochelle didn't make me an innocent man.

The river widened from creeks, from wet-season rain, and we rode the brown current toward the sea where it sends its spike into the Caribbean like the stem of a mushroom and grows a toadstool head of silt to change blue waters to the color of village mud. I had seen such mushroom rivers from an airplane. "Suppose," I said, setting aside the paddle, turning to face Rosa, "suppose we just kept going on the river, maybe all the way to the coast, you and I? We've traveled the old river of our childhood, and it hasn't been so good except in moments, so why not travel the new river of our adulthood? We could stop long enough to tell Manuél not to wait for us, then push off again."

Her face softened and she dragged the paddle to slow us. "Why would we do something so foolish?"

"I don't want to leave the river."

"If I choose to go with Manuél? Would you go down the river?"

"There would be no point. No. I would go with you to El Tigrito."

"And from there? Would you go home?"

I shrugged. "What is home? A place where people love you and where you feel you belong. For me there's no such place."

Rosa's eyes searched the banks. She thrust the paddle into the water, changed our direction—toward the village, I thought without turning to look, and I have my answer in her taking us ashore—she's ready to leave the river.

But she took us to the right bank, and the village is on the left. When I looked around, there was no village. "What is this?"

"A place to rest. A place to get out of the sun. A place to build a safe camp for spending the heat of the afternoon and perhaps for staying the night."

"Amazing," I said.

The canoe nosed into a creek, one that ran clear water into the mud of the river. I turned to face the front, to watch for snags, and Rosa moved us against a gentle current. Trees crowded the creek, meeting above it to give us a tunnel of air cooler than what hovered in the sun above the river. The creek widened, grew shallow, and sandbars appeared. When Rosa drove the canoe toward one, I hopped out to drag the boat from the water, skidding it on moist sand.

"Up the bank." She pointed with a pucker of lips. "Banana trees."

"Topochos," I said, using the word for plantains. These grew long as my arm, and green, greener than the jungle around them. "You will spend the night with me in this little pocket of paradise?" Caciques fluttered among the trees, and parakeets, and the air was alive with sounds of birds, their wingsbeats, their piping songs.

"We must cook the topochos, if we want to eat them. You will catch us a fish while I find a place to hang the chinchorro. This time use the twine I brought, and the hooks. We would make a wooden hook and use bark string if necessary, but we have better gear for fishing." She got out of the canoe. "Help me pull it high on the sandbar."

Her eyes darted about in excitement, and her face looked like the Rosita of childhood. I whistled a tune, "Puff, the Magic Dragon," and took Rosa's hand, moved us around in a parody of a formal dance, and she slid into my arms, her face aglow, holding me for dancing and our movements were no longer a parody. I stopped whistling, gave myself to the dance, a fast one of twirling then moving into a slow one, cheek to cheek, the music coming from birds and the ripple of leaves and from her humming low then singing: "Ku-ku-rrrru-ku-ku paloma. *Una paloma triste,*" she sang, and we danced, and when we stopped, I wanted to kiss her.

"*Una besita corta,*" she said, a short little kiss, and turned her cheek to my lips. Then, later as we hung the chinchorro high above the ground: "Anger makes me crazy and clouds how I see you."

She had found ripe papaya, large ones with rinds full of white sap that needed bleeding with the scoring of their sides to drip the bitter from them before they were worth eating. "Better than plantains," she said.

I had broken open a deadfall near the banana trees, found a grub for bait, and caught an odd-looking bass, one with a mouth large enough to thrust my fist into, and I used the machete to change it from fish into food with scaling, trimming, washing. My hands smelled of fish, and I rubbed them with sand at the edge of the creek after skewering the bass and setting it in the slow smoke of a cookfire.

We napped in the hot part of the day, our hips bumping in the chinchorro, and in the evening she announced that I would stay among the banana trees while she bathed in the creek.

"But we should bathe together," I protested.

"No." She pointed up the bank toward the plantains. "Go there. You will not watch."

After her bath and after mine, she sat on banana leaves to brush her hair. "You are a gentleman," she said. "I like that."

"Why did you bring us to this place instead of our going to the village where Manuél waits?" I sat beside her, leaning against the tree that held our hammock high in its branches. Above the hammock we had built an A-frame roof of banana leaves thatched upon a higher branch.

"Because of what you said about staying on the river all the way to the sea. Our trip is finished, and yet you wanted to make it longer. You were courting me, Tom, and I think I like that."

"Courting?"

"Perhaps not. Perhaps only searching for something. But you wanted to search with me. I'm willing, though it would be foolish to go to the sea with wet season now upon us. But one more night on our river seemed like a good idea. You offered no protest, I noticed."

"This," I waved my hand to indicate the creek, the trees, "might be what I was looking for when I returned to Venezuela."

"I think not, not entirely. You came here to look for truth."

"Are you still angry with me?"

"No. I wouldn't call it anger."

"What, then? You act like a friend instead of a lover."

"But Tom, I am your friend. That won't change. Being your lover, though, is dangerous."

"I didn't make love with the witch. I was not—"

She held her hands up to stop me words. "Don't. Please. No more. I'm so crazy, don't you see? When you could never be my husband because you were married, there were problems, but loving you was safe, in a crazy way."

"Safe?" I felt bewildered.

"Yes. It was wrong, of course, but I knew we would make love and then part. We had to because of Catrina. The sin of our loving would be a short one, and I would repent after we parted. But now, now. It is different now."

"Because the priest said that I'm not married."

"Yes. Now I'm not safe, not if we become lovers."

"I don't accept that or even understand it."

"You have no choice. You will accept that we cannot be more than friends."

In the evening when clouds and wind announced the coming of rain, we climbed the tree to our chinchorro, to hang like a double chrysalis under the A-frame of thatching. Wind peeled away some of it, and water splashed us during a shower that thrummed the trees and made the creek talk in louder notes of running water. When the rain moved on, night creatures lifted their voices to a soprano frenzy, and I thought never before had I heard such loud affirmation, and I knew that never again would the jungle sing to me in that resonant voice.

Night did not bring Catrina or Mata-Mata. Morning brought a breakfast of papaya shared with a somber Rosa who said, "I dreamed."

I remained silent, waiting for more information. We sat on wilted banana leaves on the sandbar where we had pulled the canoe. Sweet papaya juice ran down my hands.

"I dreamed of Dolora and the women of thunder." She frowned, ate her papaya in silence, then: "The tapir spirits told each other how happy they had been when they were alive, before the man with golden skin killed them. They hated coming out only at night and being condemned to retreat into the earth when morning sun chases away the night. I dreamed a myth of the women of thunder. It was a story Abuelita told me, and I had forgotten."

As we folded the hammock, Rosa said, "I was Dolora, one of the women of thunder. The dream disturbed me. It stays with me."

With the canoe loaded again, we pushed it into the shallow waters of the creek, and Rosa climbed in. I waited until she settled and had a paddle in hand, then climbed in. She pushed us toward the river. "In the myth, the women of thunder found the golden one who killed them, or they thought they did. He slept beneath a letterwood tree. The tapir spirits trampled him to death."

The current of the muddy river took us, and I made my end of the canoe the back so I did most of the work keeping us in the middle of the river. Rosa turned around to face me, sat in silence for a time watching the trees move by. "Dolora stood aside while the others killed the golden one. He had your face, did I tell you that? He had your face and your beard, and I knew he wasn't the golden one. The others didn't know, and they trampled him, then moved into a clearing nearby to dance their victory dance in the moonlight."

A broken tree floated beside us, and upon it rode a small iguana.

I took us close to hold eye contact with the creature. Rosa raised her brows at the iguana, then continued speaking. "A glimmering woman came. I think Abuelita said her name was Blanca. She cried and accused the women of thunder of murdering her mate."

There was more to her dream, I could tell, but when I asked her about it, she shrugged and turned to face the bow, picked up her paddle, and moved us faster downriver.

Before noon we reached the village where Manuél was supposed to be waiting for us, but he wasn't there, said the woman who met us at the pier.

It looked much like the pier in my memory, but smaller, much like the same structure where Rosita and I tied up our canoe when we arrived eighteen years before with the mad Irishman. Several curious children came to gawk at us, then wandered away, and a yellow dog with ribs showing barked in a half-hearted way before following the children. As we climbed out of the canoe and onto the pier, the woman hurried out to us.

She waddled in an odd pigeon-toed way, though she wasn't large, and there was something familiar about her. "You are Rosita and Don," the woman said. "I am Conchita."

The woman wore enough makeup to cause her face to look cracked, and her lips glistened a weird shade of purple. Her red satin dress shone in the sun except for where it had worn down to naked cloth and where it had been patched in shingles of orange thread.

"Conchita?" Rosa said, and I knew she was doing the same thing I was—searching old memories to make sense of the name.

"Yes, yes. Bring your bag. You will stay in my home until your cousin returns. He told me to watch for you and to take care of you if you arrived while he was gone."

"Manuél?" I asked. "Gone?"

"To visit his grandmother in El Tigrito, yes. But he'll be back tomorrow."

"Abuelita," Rosa whispered. "What has he been telling her? Abuelita."

"Yes, yes. Did you ever see the Irishman again, after you left here with him? What was that? Nine years ago? Eight?"

"Eighteen," I said. "No. The Irishman vanished."

"Yes, yes, and he went with my diamonds, the ones my husband died for, the ones he dug out of the river and the hills, and the rogue Irishman stole them, do you remember? Hah! I threw his shoes into the street when I drove him out of my home, the goat."

"Conchita." Rosa nodded and winked at me.

The memory of her came back, of her anger that the Irishman would leave her, of her throwing his suitcase into the street, then throwing his shoes. Even back then, when she was a young woman, I remembered, she wore too much makeup.

"Your cousin is a good man, Rosita, and a smart one."

"Rosa."

"He came here, and I found him sitting beside the river, and for him it was love at first sight, I could tell by the way he looked at me. Some men tell everything they feel with their eyes, and they don't even know. He spoke about the two children who rode the river seven years ago and now have come back as adults. Then I told him the story of how you had slept in my home, how I loved you because you were good children, even if you traveled with a rogue. He courted me, your cousin, and we are to be married."

"No!" Rosa said.

"But yes. He is only a few years younger than I, and not many. Did I say he fell in love with me at first sight? He has gone to his grandmother to get permission for marriage."

45

Tom took the travel bag from the canoe while I chatted with Conchita.

She still had her beauty. It was a beauty with sharp edges and depended some upon painting her face, but still she was attractive. As we walked from the pier toward the houses of the village, she insisted we stay in her home until Manuél returned.

Tom, speaking English and glancing at Conchita with disapproval and amusement both dancing in his eyes, said, "Perhaps we should rent a room in the cantina to hang our chinchorro for the night. Or return to the jungle until morning."

"If you insist, I will do either. For now, though, I would like to find out what's going on with this woman. It seems impossible that my cousin would use our dead grandmother as an excuse to leave. He is married, after all, and this woman doesn't seem to know."

"What are you chattering about?" Conchita demanded.

"We were saying how nice you are to invite us to you home," Tom said.

"Of course. I'm generous to a fault. Have you eaten? I'll cook you a meal. Everyone knows I'm the best cook in the village."

Conchita's home was smaller than I remembered. The walls, river mud and grass, showed signs of being patched many times, and the palm thatching of her roof had grayed and shifted in its need for repair. Other villagers stared openly as we went into her home, now wired for electricity. She had hung light bulbs over doorways so one bulb could light two rooms. We had to duck more than usual in going from room to room. "Here," Conchita said, stopping us in a room not much larger than a closet, "put your suitcase here, where you slept when you were children six years ago."

"Eighteen," Tom said.

"This room will be comfortable for us." I tried to sound certain, but the room looked less adequate than the nest in the tree where we had slept the previous night. The dirt floor gleamed from moisture, and I could smell the damp and rotting roof.

Tom looked as if he has swallowed something slimy. He dragged his feet and kept glancing at the thatching, and he seemed relieved when Conchita led us out the back door to her patio.

It was a small area enclosed by a sugarcane fence, and it was where she cooked. Her furniture consisted of four stools, a crude wooden table, and a gas stove with hoses running to a rusting bottle of cooking gas. A sprinkling of gravel covered the ground. Tom and I sat on stools while Conchita prepared a meal of pan de mano, corn cakes cooked on a griddle.

"Too much is going on," Tom said.

"Nothing much is going on, not here and not in this village," Conchita said. She slapped the raw cakes with wet hands. "Manuél will return tomorrow."

"What did you mean?" I asked Tom.

"Last night was a reprieve, a time out in a wild garden. But now I need to think about the many things that happened. Poí. Brother Maybre who was nobody's brother. The bones of Olivia Radcliffe. The drug dreams we had at the witch's house. It's all too much, and yet we remain in motion so we cannot think."

"Yes," I said.

"I drove Catrina from me and didn't understand how at the time. I used bad judgment in killing."

"Are you still hoping for a better past?"

"I don't know."

"Killing?" Conchita looked at Tom. "Killing?"

"A snake," I told her. "Tom killed a snake."

"This was bad judgment?" Conchita set a cake on the griddle and waved her hand, dismissing Tom's notion of bad judgment and flinging bits of wet cornmeal on the table. "Manuél has good judgment. He said he was too young for me, but he could see the falsehood in that because I am as beautiful as any young girl in the village. It was love at first sight for us both. That Irishman five years ago? The one who brought you to our village? He fell in love with me the first time he saw me. But he had no character, and when he found my diamonds, he lost all judgment, and he stole my wealth, the dirty goat. But before avarice took him, he fell in love with me. Men tend to do that. My uncle told me that it is my cheekbones, that men go mad for such cheekbones." She put a finger to her cheek, smearing wet cornmeal on her face.

"Manuél has a family," I said.

"So? Everyone has a family."

"He has a beautiful daughter," Tom said.

"I had a son once, but he ran away." Conchita blinked back tears.

"I wonder why?" Tom's voice had a tiny pitch of sarcasm in it, though Conchita seemed not to notice.

That night, after too much listening to Conchita tell us how beautiful and loving and good she was, Tom and I hung the chinchorro in Conchita's closet of a room just as rains came. Water soaked the thatching and ran down on the inside of the room, some of it dropping on us, though not much. In the early morning hours the dream of the women of thunder came to me again, and I made myself awaken.

Tom breathed loud and heavy in his half of the chinchorro, and I could hear Conchita snoring in another part of the house. "Tom," I whispered, nudging him through the netting. "I'm going for a walk. Please come with me."

We dressed while Conchita snored, while roosters sensed the coming of dawn and made announcements from all around the village. We slipped out of the house, picked our way around puddles glimmering in starlight, and went to the pier. As we sat on the wet timbers above the river, Tom said, "We came here that last morning of our trip eighteen years ago."

"Yes."

"You brought me here because of that?"

"No. Maybe. I had the dream again."

"The one about Mata-Mata?"

"No. About the women of thunder. I was Dolora again. In the story my grandmother told me, a shimmering woman found what the tapir spirits had done to her husband, who wasn't at all the man who had killed the tapirs. Her name was Blanca because she turned herself into a white parrot and flew into the mountains. That was after she talked with Dolora."

"Was she in your dream?"

"Yes. And I was Blanca in the strange ways of dreams. Blanca pulled her hair and wailed and accused Dolora of murder. Dolora said she was sorry but the man had no business looking like the one who had killed the tapirs, and Blanca said it was wrong to blame the victim for what the women of thunder did to him."

"You dreamed all that?" Tom sounded astonished. Behind us the rolling cry of roosters punctuated the night.

"I think so. Then I turned into a white parrot and flew far into the jungle where I hoped to lose my grief over losing Donito."

"Donito? I thought you dreamed about tapirs. I thought it was just a weird dream."

"The dream taught me something important, Tom. It wasn't merely a strange dream."

"Taught you? Taught?"

"Yes." I had more to say, but the sun splattered its red across the sky, then erased it in white light. We sat on the pier, watching the transition from night to day, a sudden one and almost violent.

"So what did you learn?"

Tom's voice startled me. I wasn't wholly present in that moment but was somewhere deep in the jungle, being a white parrot.

"I learned that you are not El Lobo."

Tom gave me a wild look, an alarmed look. "I don't understand."

"I know."

"Is there more that you can tell me about the dream? To help me understand."

"No."

We sat in silence again, and the village began coming awake, responding perhaps to the roosters, and in the wet stillness of morning air a dog barked.

"Then, then I have a gift for you." Tom pulled something from his pocket. He seemed nervous.

"A gift?" I took the gold chain and locket he held out to me. Inside the locket were four lines of tiny writing carved into the gold.

"It was in the cave."

"Something that belonged to the English woman?" I looked at the words on the inside surfaces of the locket. "There's something here—a poem, I think."

"Yes. Good words about time."

It took some turning in the slanting light of morning to make out the words, but I managed to read them aloud:

> "Taste the fife-bird's orchid song
> breathe the jungle's perfumed light
> touch the mango's sugared fruit
> before the kiss of leafmold night."

I put the chain over my head and held the locket to my chest.

"It took me a while to understand those words." Tom gave me a quick, nervous smile.

Something splashed in the water, something large enough to leave a wake in spite of the current. A mist of tiny insects swam in the sunlight above the river, and the morning's first flock of parrots flew overhead. In the village a woman raised her voice in song. The arrival of the new day, the beauty and sadness of it stung my eyes. "Today," I said, "if we are to believe Conchita, my cousin Manuél will arrive, and we will go back to El Tigrito. Our second trip down the wild river is over."

"Conchita will not be pleased," Tom said. "She'll rail at Manuél for leaving as she once railed at the Irishman. She'll call him a goat."

"Of course. Don't change the subject."

"How old do you think she is? Forty? Older? Manuél must have found her attractive."

"Apparently men have always found Conchita attractive. Stop changing the subject."

"I didn't know I was. You brought up Conchita. So what is the subject?"

"I don't know. The river, maybe? Did this river trip do what you hoped it would do for you? I mean when you found me high in the palm tree, cutting thatch? When you asked me to join you again on the wild river."

"I don't know. Maybe I didn't know what I wanted from the trip."

"You haven't talked with Catrina for a while. Has the river banished her?"

"Yes. I think she's gone."

"What about the soldiers from Vietnam? Are they gone, also?"

"I think so. I hope so."

"Then the river was good to you."

"Yes. And bad. Now I need a way to learn to deal with the death of Rochelle and the others at the compound. They would be alive if it weren't for me."

"No, Tom. I'm the one who told that terrible Maybre about oleander poison, remember?"

Tom hung his head. "I should never have pressed you to come with me. Now you feel guilty over something that isn't your fault."

Two dogs wandered toward the pier, sniffed in our direction, and one of them bared his fangs at us, then they wandered back into the village. "I think Mata-Mata will not come to me again," I offered.

"Then the trip is not a total loss for you?"

"Loss? Loss? Tom, you stop that. Look," I held up the locket, "I got a piece of rare jewelry from the river."

"You're making fun of me."

"No. When we traveled the river eighteen years ago we were children, and we fell in love with the river and with each other in all the wild intensity of childhood. We must still love the river, else why sit on this pier to watch it slide beneath our feet?"

"Love the river? I guess, maybe. But it didn't bring us unqualified blessings this time."

I took Tom's hand. "Nor did it the last time, even if we came to believe it did. The river wounded us, perhaps worse this time. But it also washed away much that needed washing, and it had its gifts. Remember the howler monkeys and our bath after their attack?"

"Yes. A high point on the trip."

"So you're now glad for the attack from the howlers?"

"Yes."

The moment had arrived, and I knew it from the tingling starting on my scalp and running down my back. The brown river flowed beneath our feet, a dog barked thin and far away, the village woman continued her morning song, and Tom's gift hung its golden weight cool against my breast. "Mahadi's shop," I said, struggling to keep control of my voice, "has furniture that you would find comfortable. It would fit into my home beside El Tigre River."

Tom looked at me, startled, and I heard his breathing change. "What are you saying?"

"Tom, Don, my little Don and now my new Tom, what do you think I'm saying?"

Photo by Sally Brown

About the Author

An experienced traveler, Jerry Craven has lived for extended periods in South America, Southeast Asia, the Middle East, and Europe. He now resides in East Texas, where he serves as director of Lamar University Press and Ink Brush Press and is editor in chief of the online literary magazine, *Amarillo Bay*. A member of the Texas Institute of Letters, he has published twenty-four books, including fiction, poetry, creative nonfiction, and children's literature. In 2000, TCU Press published his novel *Snake Mountain*.